THE DARK LORD'S DAUGHTER

THE DARK LORD'S DAUGHTER

PATRICIA C. WREDE

Random House 🏠 New York

Text copyright © 2023 by Patricia C. Wrede
Jacket art copyright © 2023 by James Firnhaber
Interior chapter opener art used under license from Shutterstock.com

Visit us on the Web! rhcbooks.com

Educators and librarians, for a variety of teaching tools, visit us at RHTeachersLibrarians.com

Library of Congress Cataloging-in-Publication Data
Name: Wrede, Patricia C., author.
Title: The Dark Lord's daughter / Patricia C. Wrede.
Description: First edition. | New York: Random House Children's Books, 2023. |
Summary: When ordinary fourteen-year-old Kayla discovers she is the heir to a dark throne, she must find her place between her life on Earth and her magical inheritance.
Identifiers: LCCN 2022037706 (print) | LCCN 2022037707 (ebook) |
ISBN 978-0-553-53620-1 (trade) | ISBN 978-0-553-53621-8 (lib. bdg.) |
ISBN 978-0-593-71022-7 (int'l) | ISBN 978-0-553-53622-5 (ebook)
Subjects: CYAC: Magic—Fiction. | Inheritance and succession—Fiction. |
Good and evil—Fiction. | Fantasy. | LCGFT: Fantasy fiction. | Novels.
Classification: LCC PZ7.W915 Dar 2023 (print) |
LCC PZ7.W915 (ebook) | DDC [Fic]—dc23

Printed in the United States of America
10 9 8 7 6 5 4 3 2 1
First Edition

CHAPTER 1

So You Are a Potential Dark Lord

According to popular belief, the ability to utilize Dark magic can erupt anywhere, at any time, in anyone. In practice, Dark power is nearly always inherited, though sometimes from a remote ancestor.

—Introduction to *The Dark Traditions*

The long line moved slowly across the bus parking lot toward the entrance gates of the State Fair. Halfway up the line, fourteen-year-old Kayla Jones scowled absently at a spot where the green glitter nail polish had slopped over the side of her fingernail. She'd been hoping to come to the State Fair with someone besides family this year, but Madison and her other friends had lost touch when Kayla's family moved to the apartment, and she hadn't made new ones yet.

Besides, the fair had been a Jones family tradition as far back as Kayla could remember, and family traditions had kept them going for the last four years. Mostly small ones, like Saturday-morning pancakes and the weekly visit to the park by Lake Nokomis, but Rikita Jones managed at least one big event every three or four months, no matter how dire their other circumstances. So here they were: Kayla, with her adoptive mother and brother, standing in line at nine in the morning.

"You could at least have let us sleep late," she muttered at Riki's back.

"What?" Riki started to turn, then paused. "No, Del, we're not stopping at the cookie barn first thing. It's too early, and you're wired enough without adding sugar."

"Can I get a turkey leg, then?" Del begged. "Or the roast corn? Those are healthy. Or no, I want the deep-fried alligator on a stick!"

"You just had breakfast!" Riki said in tones of despair. "How can you want more food already?"

"You only want the alligator because you think it sounds neat," Kayla told her younger brother.

Del gave her a wide-eyed look and bounced on the heels of his running shoes with ten-year-old energy. "So? That's why they bring it up here to sell, isn't it? There aren't any alligators in Minnesota. Can I have some, Mom?"

"Maybe later." Riki adjusted her sunglasses and tipped her maroon-and-gold baseball cap a little higher on her thick black curls. "Kayla honey, are you sure you don't want a hat? I brought extras." She raised her bulging canvas tote bag.

Kayla squinted at the sky. The hazy, cloudless blue of late August promised the fair's traditional hot and humid weather, but in a moment of insanity two weeks before, she'd had Riki cut her dark hair mercilessly short, and wearing a baseball cap over it made her look like a boy. More like a boy. "Maybe later," she echoed.

The line inched forward; Kayla shifted her backpack and closed the gap. Delmar bounced on his heels again and asked, "Can we start on the Midway? I want to do the frog toss."

"No!" Kayla said before their mother could answer. Standing around watching Del toss frog-shaped beanbags at plastic lily pads in an attempt to win one of the stuffed animals had been boring enough last year, when it was a new game.

Riki frowned. "Kayla!"

"Fine, but if he wins another giant stuffed penguin, I'm not carrying it around all day!"

Riki's expression went thoughtful. "Good point. Maybe on our way out, Del."

"Awww."

"Quit whining. What are you, five?" Kayla said.

Del subsided—for the moment—and they moved forward again. They had almost reached the security screening, and Riki was fishing in her canvas tote for the advance tickets.

"Do you think Dad would have come with us?" Del asked. "To the fair, I mean."

"Del!" Kayla shot a quick glance at their mother's back, but Del had kept his voice down and Riki was absorbed in her ticket hunt. Del had only been six when cancer killed Michael Jones, and Kayla often thought that it was highly unfair that she, the adopted child, should be the one with many clear memories of their father, while Del, the unlooked-for biological offspring, had only a few blurry mental images and whatever he could piece together from photos and the things Kayla and Riki told him.

"Dad would have made us come three or four times," she told Del quietly. "Maybe every day." She hesitated. "And he'd have been really excited about that penguin you won last year."

Del grinned. "Thanks, Kayla." He opened his mouth as if he wanted to ask something else, but Riki turned and he snapped his lips closed. Kayla suppressed a relieved sigh. Even after four years, mentioning their father was still as likely as not to put Riki in a gloomy mood, but Del didn't always remember to avoid the subject.

Riki hadn't noticed; she was still digging through her tote bag and muttering. "Discount coupon book, ibuprofen, tissues, cell phone, water . . . Kayla, your backpack is nearly empty. Would you take one of these bottles?"

"I left it empty on purpose, Mom!" Kayla grumbled, but she accepted two of the plastic containers and stowed them away. At least they were only a temporary load.

They reached the screener, who checked the tote and backpack with brisk efficiency, scanned their tickets, and passed them through the gate without comment. The red brick of the grandstand loomed on their left, a tall, dark contrast to the one-story display buildings, small stages, and food booths that lined the street beside it. To the right stretched the rides and games of the Midway. Even this early in the day, it was all bright colors and motion, shrieking riders and rumbling machinery. The smell of machine oil mingled with the scents of dust, people, strange foods being deep-fried, beer, and animals—a little of everything, like the fair itself.

Straight ahead, over the sea of baseball caps and sun hats, Kayla could see the Warner Coliseum and the animal barns. She had always liked those, but she knew better than to suggest starting there. They'd been Michael's favorite, too, and Riki hadn't taken them back even once since his death.

The bungee ball ride flew into sight above the treetops, the round cage with its two screaming occupants trailing the four elastic ropes that flung it up and then slowed its fall. Delmar's eyes widened. "Mom! Can we do that?"

"I don't think it's safe," Riki said. "Or in the budget. And anyway, you aren't tall enough."

"You just don't want me to have any fun!"

"Of course not," Riki told him. "That's part of my job, to keep you from having fun. It's in the parenting handbook."

"I thought we were going to do the Midway stuff last," Kayla said, hoping to sidetrack the discussion before it turned into an argument. She looked around for a distraction that didn't involve food, memories of better times, or anything that would have to be carried around for the rest of the day. "Hey, what about the Skyride? We could take it down to the far end of the fair and walk back."

After a quick check of the coupon book, Riki approved this program, though Del complained that the Skyride was just a fancy chair lift and didn't compare to the bungee ball. The line was short; they paid for the discounted tickets and were soon soaring over

5

the fair in a glass-and-steel box barely large enough for the three of them. Kayla's bad mood began to fade. Del pressed his nose to the glass, commenting on the booths and rides and people below. By the time they reached the ground at the other end, he had a dozen places he wanted to visit, including at least six food vendors, the parade lineup, the giant slide, and a couple of open stages.

They ducked into the Horticulture Building to see the crop art. For several years, Kayla had publicly maintained that gluing seeds to boards to make pictures was more of a kindergarten activity than something for adults; privately, she was amazed by the detail people achieved. This year, there was a three-foot picture of a Lakota Indian in full traditional garb that was especially impressive—and she was secretly glad that Riki insisted on keeping the exhibit on her list of fair "must do" activities.

They skipped the rest of the horticulture exhibits (who wanted to look at row after row of apples and corn and dried beans?) and crossed the street to the International Bazaar. The first booth had a row of leather backpacks on display. Kayla eyed them wistfully, but she knew better than to ask. Even at discounted State Fair prices, they couldn't afford one.

They browsed the booths, which sold everything from dashikis to Russian nesting dolls. When Del started to get bored, they made a quick stop to cash in the coupon for a bag of cinnamon-sugared almonds at the spiced-nut booth. The bag went into Riki's tote for later, and they headed back toward the exit from the bazaar.

On the way out, a man in a black-and-white cow costume

was handing out sample packets of beef jerky and brochures advertising some event by the animal barns. Del collected three of the packets, one for each of them, though he was clearly only interested in the food. Riki pursed her lips but stowed two of the packets in her tote without comment, and they made it to the main street without further incident.

In the brief time they'd spent at the bazaar, the crowd outside had doubled. "Stay close," Riki told them. "I don't want to lose either of you."

"Hey, mini donuts!" Del said around a bite of beef jerky. He looked at his mother hopefully. "We can't come to the fair and not have mini donuts!"

"You already have something," Riki pointed out with a grin. "Pace yourself." She looked around and headed for an information booth just up the block. Kayla trailed along behind with a sinking feeling. Sure enough, Riki was asking about the Home Improvement building.

"Mom!" she objected. "Could you find anywhere more boring in the whole fair?"

"They always have special State Fair deals," Riki replied. "And they might have something we can use in the new apartment. Besides, going through one of the boring grown-up buildings is an essential part of the fair experience."

"Like the Midway?" Del said.

"All right, Del, we'll head back that way after I'm done," Riki promised.

"Can I just wait here?" Kayla asked. "There's a bench."

Without waiting for a response, she sat down and reached into her backpack.

"No," Riki said. "It's a couple of blocks each way; I don't want you sitting here alone for that long. Besides, you'll get bored."

"I'll be fine." Kayla pulled out her new school-issued tablet computer. She'd only had it for a couple of days, so she hadn't gotten it fully customized yet, but she'd installed all the operating-system upgrades, the encyclopedia app, and most of her music.

"Oh, honey, you didn't bring that thing with you to the fair!" Riki sounded as if she couldn't decide whether she was amused or horrified.

Kayla looked at the tablet, then waved it up and down a couple of times. "Looks real to me," she said. "Wake up, Macavinchy."

The tablet's screen lit, and a deep male voice with a British accent said, "Good morning, madam. What can I do for you?"

Kayla grinned at her mother's startled expression. She'd spent two hours last night listening to different voice files before she found one she liked enough to download. The Wi-Fi connection lit up, so before her mother could object, she asked, "Macavinchy, where are the best household deals at the Minnesota State Fair?"

"Kayla, really, that's—"

The screen cleared and a list appeared of booths demonstrating everything from siding and windows to hot tubs and plastic furniture. "There, Mom," Kayla said, holding up the tablet so she could see.

"Would you like to view these locations on a map?" Macavinchy asked after a moment.

"Uh, that one," Riki said, pointing.

"Macavinchy, show me where the George's Sturdy Modern Antiques booth is at the Minnesota State Fair," Kayla told the computer.

"Why did you give your computer a stupid name?" Del asked, peering over the back of the bench.

"I like it," Kayla said. "And if you think it's stupid, it's probably the best idea ever."

"No arguing," Riki said absently. She was peering at the map on the computer screen, then at the buildings around them.

"Macavinchy, add current location," Kayla said.

"Of course, madam." A bright red dot appeared a little south of the blue arrow that marked George's Sturdy Modern Antiques.

"If you got a smartphone, it would do that," Del pointed out to their mother.

"Smartphones are expensive," Riki said absently, "and the flip phone works fine."

"Your flip phone is purple," Del said in disgust.

"It's lavender, and a new one is still expensive." Riki studied the map for another minute, then smiled. "It's two blocks north and one over. Come on, you two. I get to look at furniture, and then each of you can pick something to do next."

"Fine. Good night, Macavinchy," Kayla said, and stuffed the tablet back into her backpack. She'd really been hoping to play with it, but avoiding the Home Improvement building was worth a lot. Even if they had to watch while Riki grilled the furniture people, it was only one booth, not a whole building's worth of displays.

9

They headed up the street, which was already crowded. As they approached the first corner, they heard the loud, buzzing crackle that accompanied someone talking into a microphone that had been turned up too high. "It's a TV spot!" Del said, and surged forward.

Kayla and Riki followed. They caught up with him on the far side of the street near a small stage. At the back of the stage, a large screen was running previews of the new fall season; in front of it, three rows of wooden benches filled the boulevard. The benches were half-full of unusually attentive fairgoers. The announcer with the too-loud microphone stood at the near corner of the stage, next to a row of people who apparently represented characters from the various shows on the screen. The first was a man in a purple face mask and spangled tights; next to him stood a woman in a white lab coat, a teenage girl with blue hair, and a man in an old-fashioned frock coat carrying a riding crop. The last one was a muscular blond man wearing chain mail, with a large sword strapped to his back. The preview that was playing showed someone similar battling hordes of people in black armor.

Del squinted at the stage, then at the screen. "They aren't the real actors," he said in disappointment.

"Come on," Riki said. "We can see this at home."

"We can't see live people," Del objected.

The preview screen flashed through a string of images and ended with "Coming to New Adventure Television next week!" as the actors onstage started waving. The overamplified announcer said something garbled, and the people in the front rows stood up and started collecting their belongings. "There," Riki said. "It's over. Where's that furniture place again?"

Kayla consulted her tablet. "Up that way, just around the corner." She pointed past the far corner of the stage, where the Creative Activities building was just visible beyond a display of water purifiers. Riki nodded and stood. Kayla stowed the tablet, shouldered her backpack, and followed.

Or rather, tried to follow. The little seating area was gridlocked, as half the people who'd been watching the TV display turned to leave while the other half tried to move toward the stage. It took Kayla and her family several minutes to work their way to the outer edge of the crowd. Delmar spent the time craning his neck in an attempt to see what was going on up front. "They're taking pictures!" Del said as they fought free of the crowd at last. "Can I get one?"

"No, Del," Riki said. "We stopped to watch; that's enough."

"But it was almost over! We hardly got to see anything."

"What do you want a picture for?" Kayla said. "They're not the actors from the shows. You said so yourself."

"Yeah, but that guy with the sword is awesome. And the one on the end has a mask; nobody will know it's not the real actor. Come on, Mom!"

They had reached the end of the row of benches; just ahead, they could clearly see the crowd around each of the actors. "Well, I don't know," Riki said in the tone that meant she was about to give in. "I think—"

"My lady!" boomed a deep voice, and a tall figure appeared

from behind the stage. He wore a flowing black cloak that reached the backs of his knees. His face was hidden beneath a full black helmet painted with a crudely drawn red skull, and one black-gloved hand rested on the hilt of a curved sword hanging from his belt. He looked like an extra from one of Delmar's favorite fantasy movies; the only false note was the body armor under the cloak, which strongly resembled a police riot vest painted with overlapping green and black half circles.

"My lady, I have found you!"

People turned to watch as the costumed man moved swiftly forward and went to one knee in front of Kayla. Startled, Kayla recoiled half a step and bumped into her mother. "It's just part of the show," Riki said in her ear. She patted Kayla's shoulder reassuringly. "Be a sport and play along."

"Uh, who are you?" Kayla asked.

"I am Waylan, second commander of the Dark Hordes of Zaradwin, my lady," the man said. "For ten years, ever since your father fell in battle at the hands of the Legions of Light, I have labored to find you. Now you will return, to take your father's throne and rebuild the armies of Darkness!" He stretched one hand out toward Kayla, and she saw something glowing red in the palm of his glove. It was making a high-pitched noise, just at the edge of her hearing, like a malfunctioning radio. She tried to back up and bumped into her mother again; Riki put a hand on her shoulder to steady her.

"This sounds like the best show ever!" Del announced. "Are you the villain? Can I look at your sword?" Without waiting for an answer, he started for the kneeling man. Riki put her other hand out and caught his shoulder just as Waylan's reaching hand touched Kayla's.

The noise rose to a high whine and the red light expanded, turning the stage and the fairgoers into a black-and-red still life and shutting off all sound. *Real life isn't supposed to have a pause button,* Kayla thought, and then the light faded, taking the fair with it. Kayla tried to jerk away but found that she could not move. For a long, panic-stricken moment, she stood frozen with only her mother, Delmar, and the kneeling man.

Slowly, gray light began to filter through the darkness, like the light at the height of a thunderstorm. Dim, blurry shapes moved in the shadows, circling the way sharks on the nature programs circled the divers' cages. The high-pitched whine lowered a tone. Underneath the whine, Kayla heard snatches of voices, too indistinct for her to make out words.

One of the shapes pushed forward out of the group and paused. Now that it was holding still, Kayla could see that it was part darkness and part light, like the shadow of a tall, thin person cast on a floor that was covered in golden glitter. It reached out and brushed Kayla's wrist briefly. Its touch was cold and hot at the same time, and made her hands tingle. She tried to flinch, but the force that held her motionless would not allow it. The shape paused and seemed to nod, then moved back toward the shifting circle around them.

The light grew stronger. The circling shapes faded into fog, and the fog slowly cleared. The voices became fainter, then vanished. The high-pitched whine died, leaving behind an absolute silence, and Kayla found that she could move again.

Before she could do more than take a deep breath, her mother dragged her backward, away from the kneeling man, hard enough and fast enough to make Kayla stumble. "What—" She looked up and froze.

They stood in the exact center of a circle of bare dirt at least twenty feet across. A double ring of massive gray stones, set about four feet apart, marked the outer edge of the circle. Each stone was at least three times Kayla's height, and each was a slightly different shape, as if the circle builders had used whatever giant rocks they could find. But every stone was the same dark, shadowy gray, flecked with sparkles and marked with thin black lines running top to bottom. They reminded Kayla of the shadowy shapes in the between-place.

Through the gaps between the stones, Kayla could see sparse grass and empty fields stretching in all directions. The cool air smelled sour and musty, like a basement that hadn't been cleaned in a long time. Gray clouds blanketed the sky, except for a thin strip of light on the horizon to her right.

She saw no sign of the fair buildings or the crowd, but in the distance off to the left was a line of black, leafless trees that might once have been the edge of a forest. Beyond, a steep-sided mountain loomed, crowned by a black tower with a pointed circular roof. "Oh no," Kayla muttered.

"Welcome, my lady!" Waylan rose to his feet and bowed deeply. "Welcome to Zaradwin!"

CHAPTER 2

Discovering Your Dark Heritage

Learning that one is among the proud few who possess the ability to utilize Dark magic seldom comes as a complete surprise.

—From *The Dark Traditions*

The stunned silence that followed Waylan's declaration lasted only a few seconds. "What—" Riki's eyes widened and began to look frantic as their surroundings registered. "How— Where is this? What did you do?"

"We are in Zaradwin," Waylan repeated in a patient tone. "This is—" He paused, and the skull-painted mask turned from side to side. "This is the Stone Circle of Zaradwin." His hand went to the hilt of his sword, though he did not draw it.

"Fine. Take us back to the fair," Riki said, pulling Del closer. "Take us back right now!"

Waylan ignored her. "My lady, we should make our way to the castle immediately," he said to Kayla.

Let's see if this "my lady" stuff is good for anything, Kayla thought. "It'd be easier to talk if we could see you," she told Waylan.

Waylan spread his arms out in front of him, and the skull mask tilted to look at them. "See me?" he said in a confused tone.

"Take off the mask," Kayla explained.

"Of course, my lady." Waylan pushed back the hood of his cape, then shoved the skull mask to the top of his head. He had curly dark brown hair and a pleasant, round face that currently wore a slightly worried expression. He looked about the same age as Riki, as near as Kayla could tell. "Could we begin walking now, my lady?"

"We're not going anywhere with you!" Riki told him. Her grip on Kayla tightened uncomfortably.

"I bet we have to," Del said in a slightly shaky voice. He peered around cautiously, his eyes wide and his expression wobbling between fright, uncertainty, and curiosity. Curiosity seemed to be winning. "That's how it works in the books and movies, when people get dumped in another world."

"I thought you wanted Waylan to take us back to the State Fair," Kayla put in.

Waylan's eyes narrowed. He kept them fixed on Riki as he asked Kayla, "My lady, if I may be so bold as to ask, which sort are your adoptive parents?"

"What do you mean, which sort?" Kayla let her mother pull her back another few inches before she planted her feet and resisted.

"Should they be rewarded and revered for their protection and care in raising you to this age, or should they be imprisoned and tortured for abusing and neglecting you?" Waylan's tone was matter-of-fact, but his right hand had gone back to fingering the hilt of his sword.

Kayla's jaw dropped. "What?"

"That does it!" Riki said. "I'm calling 911!" She let go of Kayla to rummage in her tote bag.

"I don't think you can, Mom," Del told her.

"Watch me," Riki said without looking up. Suddenly, she dropped the bag. "A mouse! There's a m-mouse—" Her voice rose as she backed away, eyes wide.

"Mom?" Del sounded puzzled. Kayla wasn't as surprised by Riki's reaction. Normally, their mother would take an unexpected mouse in stride, but nothing about this situation was normal.

Waylan leaned forward and plucked the tote from the ground. He glanced inside, then reached in. "Were you looking for this?" he asked. In the palm of his hand sat a creature about the size and shape of a gerbil. Its fur was the same lavender color as Riki's ancient flip phone had been. Riki stared at it, her mouth opening and closing without sound.

"What is that, and where did it come from?" Part of Kayla wanted to come unglued, but somebody had to stay calm and ask the right questions. She'd learned that—and done it—during Michael's long illness; she could do it again now.

"It is a messenger mouse, my lady," Waylan replied. "It is a result of our travel between worlds. There are always things from one place that do not exist in the other. Those things cannot cease to exist, so they change to the closest equivalent. It is part of what makes such travel difficult—the spells require enough power to accommodate the changes in the equipment. I would hazard a guess that this"—he lifted the lavender gerbil—"is, in your world, some way of sending messages from one person to another."

"It must have been Mom's cell phone," Kayla said numbly. "It's the right color."

Del stared at the lavender mouse. "Mom's phone turned into that gerbil thing?"

"Messenger mouse," Waylan corrected him. "Yes." He held it out toward Riki, who backed away. With a shrug, Waylan tucked the mouse into a pouch hanging from his belt. He offered the tote bag back to Riki; after a long moment, she reached forward and snatched it out of his hand.

"Are all messenger mice that color?" Del persisted.

"What about—" Kayla paused. She was sure that when she'd first seen Waylan at the fair, he'd been wearing body armor. The vest underneath his cape was still there, but the green-and-black pattern looked natural, like overlapping scales. It definitely wasn't police armor. "Uh, what about—*that?*" she finished on a mortifying squeak.

Waylan looked down. "What? Oh, my dragonskin vest? It changed several times during my search. Evidently, very few worlds have dragons." He sounded disapproving and faintly disappointed.

"But—" Kayla stopped and took a quick inventory. Her T-shirt and cotton shorts were unchanged, but her running shoes had morphed into soft leather ankle boots. Del and Riki were wearing similar footgear. Riki's canvas tote seemed the same, but her baseball cap had become a high-crowned cloth hat with a folded brim that looked like something from a Robin Hood movie.

"Kayla!" Riki was staring at her outstretched hand with a reproachful expression. "*What* have you done to your nails?"

Kayla looked down and barely suppressed another squeak. Instead of being painted with green glitter, her fingernails were encrusted with neat rows of tiny emeralds. "It's just the glitter polish you let me buy last week at the dollar store."

"That's not glitter."

"It is the mark of magic," said a soft and airy voice. Before it had quite finished, Waylan's sword was out of its sheath. In a smooth motion, he stepped sideways, putting himself between Kayla's family and the speaker.

"Show yourself!" he commanded.

A girl stepped out from behind one of the standing stones. She looked smaller and younger than Del, though some of that might have been because she was so thin. Her hair hung in limp tangles to well below her shoulders; its exact color was impossible to determine because of the gray dust that coated it. Her dress looked as if it had been made by cutting holes in a sack for her head and arms, and her feet were bare. She looked pathetic, until her eyes met Kayla's. They were the same deep gray as the stones of the circle, flecked with sparks of light and darkness. "If it bothers you, I can remove it, or at least the appearance of it," she offered, nodding toward Kayla's hands.

"Is taking it off going to cause problems?"

The girl tipped her head from side to side. "Those who know its meaning will treat you differently, for good or ill, if they can see these outward accidents."

"Accidents?"

"Those outward parts of your life that are not of your choosing," the girl replied. "Accidents such as the place and circumstances of your birth, your family, your health, the wealth you inherit or do not, and so on. Some you may change, with great effort; others are immutable." She gestured at Kayla's fingers. "The mark is an outward accident that reveals the inward substance of your magic."

My magic? Kayla didn't feel any different than she had at the State Fair—well, apart from being cold—but how would she know what magic felt like? She considered for a moment. Would it be better to have proof of being "marked" or not? Her father had always said he'd rather be underestimated than overestimated. She nodded questioningly at Riki, who hesitated, then nodded back. "Okay," Kayla said, and started forward.

"My lady!" Waylan objected.

"What? She at least asked what I wanted before she did anything!"

Reluctantly, Waylan lowered his sword. Kayla held her hands out toward the girl, who bowed her head over them. Kayla felt a sensation like a freezing wind and a sharp electric jolt at once. The emeralds disappeared, leaving her nails bare. "There," the girl said, sounding satisfied.

"Can you send us home?" Riki asked over Waylan's discontented muttering.

The girl's eyes flickered, and for a moment she looked afraid. Then she shook her head. "Not now."

"Who or what are you?" Waylan demanded.

The girl's eyes unfocused. "An echo. A memory. A shadow of the past and the future."

"What does that even mean?" Kayla growled. Between weird fantasy villains who could yank them off to a different world and mysterious children who couldn't give a straight answer, she was getting more than a little cross.

The girl shrugged. "The others call me the spirit of the stones. It's as good a label as any."

"What others?" Kayla asked.

"The other ones who seek to become lords or ladies. Sometimes they ensnare this me for a while." She tilted her head like a small bird looking for a bug. "Will you seize this me?"

"I'm not setting out to be a lady." Kayla's head was starting to hurt.

Behind her, Del snorted. "Good thing, too."

The girl smiled at Del, then focused on Kayla once more. "You're different from the others. That and—" She glanced at Del and Riki. Her smile vanished, and her eyebrows drew together. "You came together. Who are you?"

"That's my mom and my little brother," Kayla said.

The girl nodded slowly. "*Choice* can mean more than blood." She raised her chin, staring at Del. As she moved, Kayla caught a glimpse of red on the underside of her hair. "Theirs and yours. An impossibility is still impossible when it stands before you, and yet is there. Until it isn't."

Riki stepped forward and shoved Del behind her. "What are you talking about?"

"Magic," the girl said, as if it should have been obvious.

Kayla felt like she'd missed half the conversation; her only consolation was that Waylan and Riki looked just as confused as she felt.

"Change happens. People learn, some of them," the girl went on. Her eyes went out of focus once more. "Some refuse, though that never stops the changes."

"Could you please stop talking in riddles?" Kayla said as politely as she could manage.

"Riddles are fun. And they're traditional on both sides of the border, which is more than you can say about almost anything else." The girl focused on Kayla once more, and her expression relaxed. "I'm glad you came this way; it's been so very nice to meet you, and I don't think I would have otherwise. Not all of you, anyway. Good luck." She made a small curtsy and stepped back behind the nearest standing stone.

"Stay here," Waylan growled at Kayla. He surged forward and disappeared around the back of the standing stone. Riki hesitated, then grabbed Del as he tried to follow.

Waylan appeared on the other side of the stone, his eyebrows drawn down and his lips pressed together in frustration. "She's gone," he told them as he returned his sword to its sheath.

"Who or what was that?" Kayla asked.

"The spirit of the stones," Waylan said heavily. He glared at Riki. "We were not meant to arrive here. It is too dangerous."

Riki glared right back. "Dangerous? More than you?"

"I am a danger only to those who threaten my lady," Waylan said. "The stone circles, on the other hand, are places of unpredictable magic. Only the strongest mages dare to use them, and even they cannot completely control their results." He frowned at Kayla. "You took a great risk in treating with her."

"Is that why Mom's cell phone turned into that mouse-thing?" Del asked. "Because we're in a stone circle?"

"No," Waylan replied. "It is the travel between worlds that changes one thing into another. Though arriving inside the circle may have . . . enhanced the effect somewhat."

"So everything we brought that you don't have here has changed—" Kayla broke off, feeling suddenly horrified. "Macavinchy!"

"Good morning, madam," the deep British voice said from the backpack slung over her shoulder, and Kayla breathed a sigh of relief. Then she felt something move, and she slid the nylon pack off to look inside.

At least, it had been a nylon backpack when they left home. Now it was made of green leather and looked classier than the ones Kayla had been yearning for at the International Bazaar. The shoulder straps curled through two ornate silver buckles instead of cheap plastic slides, and the zippers had been replaced with silver buttons.

I guess they don't have nylon or plastic here, Kayla thought numbly.

The backpack moved again. Cautiously, Kayla lifted the flap that had replaced the zipper, fumbling a little when the backpack shifted in her hands.

A small monkey-like face peered out at her. It was covered in rust-red fur and had eyes so black that she couldn't tell whether they had pupils.

"Kayla, get back!" Riki cried.

Kayla ignored her. "Macavinchy?"

"Yes, madam," the thing in the backpack said in the British accent she'd spent so long choosing the night before. A tiny pair of hands with long black fingers gripped the edges of the opening. An instant later, the creature pulled and wriggled its way out into the open. It crawled onto Kayla's arm, wrapping its tail twice around her wrist, and she finally got a good look at it.

The thing that had been her tablet computer now resembled a spider monkey with cat ears. Its face was a little flatter than the faces of the monkeys at the zoo, and its fur was longer and redder, but it had the same flexible tail. It shook itself, and a pair of red wings like a bat's unfolded from its back. "This is a vast improvement," it announced, and proceeded to climb onto Kayla's shoulder, where it settled in and wrapped its tail around her neck.

"Get off my daughter!" Riki shouted, and made a grab for the creature.

There was a flash and a crackle, and Riki was flung backward. She landed in the dust several feet away, barely missing one of the standing stones.

"Mom!" Kayla cried. She took a step forward, then realized that it might not be a good idea to bring the monkey-thing close to her mother. "Macavinchy, what did you just do?"

"I performed no direct action," the creature on Kayla's shoulder said. It sounded embarrassed.

Del was at Riki's side, staring at the winged monkey. Riki shook herself and climbed to her feet, brushing dust from her shorts. She didn't seem hurt, only shocked, so Kayla turned back to the thing on her shoulder. "Then what happened?"

"Your adoptive parent's sudden proximity activated my security system, madam." The creature definitely sounded embarrassed. "It was quite involuntary, I assure you."

"Security system?" Waylan said, plainly puzzled. No one explained.

"What the hell are you?" Riki snapped. The embarrassed tone, combined with the deep-voiced British accent and formal phrasing, appeared to have reassured her slightly, but she was still watching the winged creature warily.

Macavinchy did not reply.

"It is a familiar," Waylan said, though he sounded a little doubtful. "It is probably like the messenger mouse, something that could not translate unaltered to this world."

"Is he right?" Kayla asked.

"The second commander's explanation is correct," the thing replied promptly. "To be more specific, I am Macavinchy, a premier semi-autonomous construct usually referred to as a magical familiar, currently bonded to Kayla Jones. In addition to the standard features common to familiars, I possess a maximum memory upgrade and expanded power capability, as well as the latest top-notch security features."

"Were you really Kayla's tablet?" Del asked, wide-eyed.

Once again, Macavinchy did not answer.

Kayla sighed. She was definitely getting a headache. "Macavinchy, were you my computer?"

"Yes, madam."

Riki opened her mouth, then closed it. She took a deep breath, then another, and said, "Kayla, ask it to take us home."

"Okay." Kayla didn't think it would do much good, but it was easier to ask than to argue, especially with the mood Riki was in. "Macavinchy—"

"I am not capable of transporting persons across dimensional boundaries," Macavinchy said before she finished asking the question. He snapped his wings open, tucked his chin, and added in a pointed tone, "Neither familiars nor computers are vehicles. If you wanted transportation, you should have brought a bicycle or an automobile."

"My lady," Waylan put in, "can we please continue this discussion as we walk? I am not certain why we arrived here instead of in the castle courtyard, nor can I guarantee that our passage was not detected by those who wish you ill. Also—" He hesitated. "We will all be much safer at the castle."

Kayla had the distinct impression that he had intended to say something else. She started to ask what, but just then Del nudged up against her. "This place is creepy," he said. "Even if the monkey is kind of cool."

"The monkey is not cool," Riki objected just as Macavinchy said indignantly, "I am not a monkey!"

"Yeah, it's creepy," Kayla said to Del, "but the castle looks even creepier." She nodded toward the distant tower silhouetted against the gray sky, and suppressed a shiver. She hadn't realized until Del's comment just how quiet everything was. The empty space and the absence of people were only part of it; there was no traffic noise, no whir of fans or hum of air conditioners, no distant jackhammers doing road construction. It made everyone's voice seem unnaturally loud. Even the whisper of a breeze, too gentle to stir the dust that covered everything, was startling.

"We should leave immediately," Waylan repeated. "There are things more threatening than that . . . spirit . . . which may be attracted to the magic of the circle." Kayla noticed that he did not say that the other things were more dangerous. "My lady—"

"Why should we trust you?" Kayla cut off Waylan's plea.

"Under the current circumstances, you have no reason to," Macavinchy said from her shoulder.

Riki looked at the winged monkey with guarded approval. Waylan looked hurt. "I assure you, my lady, that I mean you no ill."

"Yes, well, you would say that, wouldn't you?" Kayla said distractedly. "Macavinchy—" She thought for a moment and then asked carefully, "What's the quickest way of making sure we can trust Waylan?"

Macavinchy made a purring sound, then said, "A formal oath of allegiance with additional conditions, taken by Commander Waylan and magically certified, would fulfill those conditions."

Riki frowned. "We're supposed to trust him because he swears he's trustworthy?"

"I am already sworn to the Dark Lady of Zaradwin!" Waylan said indignantly.

"Please don't shout." Kayla turned her head to look at Macavinchy, ignoring the two adults. "Why do you think an oath will work?"

"A formal oath of allegiance," Macavinchy corrected her. "Oaths are far more serious in this world than in your homeland, and as the prospective Dark Lady of Zaradwin, you may add magically enforceable conditions to the standard oath. This would provide you with the assurance you asked for, in the shortest possible time."

Waylan looked as if he were about to explode. Kayla took a step backward, unsure whether she should ask about the magic first, or— "Prospective Dark Lady?"

"You have license to claim the title, but you have not yet done so," Macavinchy explained. "Once you have made your claim, you must be formally invested and recognized before you officially become the Dark Lady. Also, your claim may be contested."

"She is Xavrielina, daughter of the Dark Lord Xavriel of Zaradwin!" Waylan burst out. "No one would contest her right to become the next Dark Lady."

"Xavrielina?" Delmar said, revolted. "That's a dumb name!"

"For once, I actually agree with— Wait a minute. *Dark* Lord? You mean this guy you say was my father was one of the *bad guys?*"

"Bad guys?" Waylan's forehead wrinkled. "He was a Dark Lord, the greatest Zaradwin has seen in centuries."

Riki was staring at Waylan through narrowed eyes. "Kayla, ask that . . . ex-computer-thing if it can tell whether this guy is telling the truth," she said.

"Macavinchy—" Kayla paused. "Can you just answer Mom's questions without me repeating them all the time?"

"Not at present, madam." The furry tail around Kayla's neck twitched. "Your mother has not been authorized for information access."

"Just ask him if Waylan is telling the truth," Riki said.

"I cannot lie to my liege lady," Waylan said, staring at Macavinchy with a puzzled expression. "That is the oddest familiar I have ever seen."

"He's odd for a computer, too, but I like him," Kayla said. Macavinchy purred in her ear and patted the top of her head.

Waylan shook himself and looked around the empty fields that surrounded them. His right hand twitched toward the hilt of his sword. Then he took a deep breath and looked at Kayla. "My lady, if it will persuade you to move to safer ground, I will swear whatever oath may please you. But I beg you, do not delay any further."

"The only place we're going with you is back to the fair." Riki's pronouncement would have been more convincing if her voice hadn't been shaking. The eerie quiet was getting to her, too.

"Can you take us back?" Kayla asked Waylan.

"No, my lady," Waylan said. He reached into his belt pouch and pulled something out, then held it toward Kayla. It was the same gesture he had used just before the four of them had disappeared from the fairgrounds, but instead of something red and glowing, his hand held a smooth rock the color of cold ashes. "I am no mage. Only the power of the Dark Lord's token allowed me to cross from world to world to seek you, and bringing us here exhausted the last of its power." He gave Riki and Del a dark look. "It was never meant to transport so many."

Kayla bent forward. The top of the rock bore the faint outline of a skull with something wrapped around its forehead. "Can it be recharged?"

"I do not know," Waylan said. "But the Dark Lord himself created it in the seat of his power. If it can be renewed, or if another can be forged, it will be there." His eyes flicked up toward the tower that loomed above the dead forest.

Kayla looked from Waylan's worried expression to the ominous silhouette of the tower on the distant mountaintop, the empty fields around the standing stones, and the dead forest between them. A puff of wind rustled the dry grass and sent a tiny dust devil whirling around the base of the stones, and Kayla shivered. Nothing else moved or made a sound; whatever had rattled had stopped. She tried to think. Out in the open, there was little chance of anything sneaking up on them, but there was also nowhere to hide. And if there were dragons in this world . . .

"I don't think we have much choice, Mom," she said.

"I don't—" Riki broke off, looking around the dreary landscape as if she had only just noticed it. "This place . . ." Her voice trailed off and she shivered.

"It's creepy," Del said matter-of-factly. "I said that before."

Riki took a deep breath and looked at Macavinchy. "You really think the oath would be a good idea?"

Macavinchy remained silent. Kayla sighed and repeated the question. "No," Macavinchy said. "It would be a very bad idea."

"Macavinchy!" Kayla said in utter exasperation. "Why didn't you say that before?"

"You didn't ask about potential consequences, madam," Macavinchy replied apologetically.

"Fine. From now on, if you think something would be a bad idea, say so right away, whether I ask about it or not." Kayla looked from Macavinchy to Waylan. "Why would having him swear an oath be a bad idea?"

"A *very* bad idea, madam," Macavinchy corrected her. "It would be a bad idea because combining oaths and magic rarely works out well even when attempted by an experienced mage. It would be a *very* bad idea because such an attempt by an inexperienced and completely untrained mage, particularly a potentially powerful one like yourself, has a high probability of immediate disaster and a near certainty of a tragic outcome in the long run."

Kayla stared. *I'm a powerful mage?* Maybe it was that mark of magic thing, or maybe Waylan and Macavinchy were just guessing because they thought she was the daughter of the Dark Lord. She still didn't feel any different. But Macavinchy was absolutely right about the "completely untrained" and "inexperienced" parts. "Right," she said, and several of the worry lines in Waylan's forehead smoothed out. "No oaths." She looked at Riki. "Mom—"

"Can it tell whether it's better to go with this kidnapper or stay on our own?"

"I am not a seer, madam," Macavinchy said when Kayla relayed the question. "However, following the second commander has a significantly higher probability of a favorable outcome than any other available course of action, at least in the short term."

31

Riki bit her lip, then nodded. "I still don't like it, but Kayla's right; we don't have much choice. And the sooner we get there, the sooner we can go home."

"This way, my lady," Waylan said. Pulling his skull mask down over his face once more, he started briskly out of the stone circle, and Kayla and her family followed.

CHAPTER 3

Your First Steps on the Road to Power

The simplest way to increase your newly awakened abilities is to make your way to one of the known centers of Dark power. You will derive the most benefit from the greatest concentrations of power (see map, Appendix III), so prepare for a long hike. A few days or weeks spent on the road is a small price to pay for the advantages conferred by laying claim to one of the major places of power.

—From *The Dark Traditions*

Waylan led them at an angle across the short, dry grass, his head turning constantly to scan the plain and, occasionally, the sky. His wariness affected all of them, and they walked the first few minutes in uneasy silence. At least Kayla's headache was fading. She sighed in relief, and Riki gave her a sharp look. "What is it?"

"My head was hurting," Kayla admitted.

"It's probably from too much sun." Riki opened her tote and poked cautiously at the contents. Nothing moved, squeaked, or exploded. "I told you to wear a hat."

"It's overcast," Kayla pointed out. "Besides, my head's fine now."

"Here we go." Riki pulled out the small metal pillbox she'd been using for as long as Kayla remembered. "I refilled it before we left for the fair."

"I don't need— What the heck is that?" The open pillbox was crammed full of something that looked like bright blue chewing tobacco.

Riki scowled. "No ibuprofen in this world. I should have thought of that. But the pillbox didn't change!"

"Apparently, they do have cheap metal boxes," Kayla said.

Waylan peered over her shoulder. Even through the mask she could see his eyes widen. "May I inspect it more closely, madam?" His tone was far more respectful than the one he'd used before to talk to Riki.

In reply, Riki held out the pillbox. Waylan bent over to study it, then nodded. "Heal-all," he said reverently. "This is the rarest and most effective of healing herbs." He extended one finger as if to stroke the little electric-blue shreds. "It is a sovereign remedy for many ills; this much would cure an entire city of plague or see an army through many battles."

"I wonder what antibiotics would turn into," Kayla said.

"If such remedies are commonplace in your world, I regret I did not stay long enough to collect some to bring with me." Waylan closed the pillbox carefully and handed it back to Riki with a bow. "This is a treasure; guard it well."

"What else do you have, Mom?" Del asked.

"Not a lot. I didn't bring anything but essentials."

"Essentials." Kayla looked at the bulging tote and didn't even try to suppress a snort. "Right."

Riki ignored her and peered warily into the tote. "I think that stack of handkerchiefs used to be the tissues, but I'm not sure about these sack things." She poked at something, and Kayla heard a sloshing noise. "Oh, the water bottles. At least the house keys still look like keys."

"There is no immediate need to examine everything now," Waylan said. "It will be easier when we reach the castle, and there will be more room."

Kayla looked around the empty plain. If it weren't for Waylan's twitchiness and constant scanning, she might have found his insistence on getting to the castle more suspicious; as it was, she was starting to feel almost as jumpy as he was.

They started walking again. Waylan's jitters subsided as the distance between them and the stone circle grew. After about five minutes, Macavinchy leaned against Kayla's head and relaxed, making small, high-pitched noises as he breathed. Kayla wondered whether his ability to fall asleep quickly was a remnant of the tablet's automatic shutoff, or whether he was just taking advantage of the opportunity. She suspected the latter. Computers didn't snore.

The walk gave Kayla time to think. Their situation was beyond weird, but she had learned, during the long months of her father's illness, to set aside things she couldn't do anything about and focus on the things she could affect. Being transported to a different world, where magic worked and computers and cell phones turned into animals, definitely fell into the category of things she couldn't do anything about, at least for now.

So did being the daughter of a Dark Lord. Kayla had always known that Michael and Riki had adopted her, and she'd wondered what led her birth mother to leave her at the Children's Hospital safe-haven drop-off. Riki had promised her that she could search for her biological parents when she was older, but she'd been clear that there wasn't much chance of finding them. The anonymous drop-off program didn't keep records. That was the whole point.

Still, much as she loved her adoptive family, Kayla had wondered about her birth parents from time to time, especially after Michael's death. Now she had a chance to find out about her biological father, and perhaps her mother as well. She frowned and kicked at a clump of grass as she passed it. She probably wouldn't like what she learned, not if he was the kind of villainous Dark Lord that showed up in books and movies back home. But at least she would *know,* and that was something.

Well, if Waylan was right, she'd know. Kayla couldn't help doubting. Really, how would the infant daughter of a Dark Lord have ended up in the waiting room of a hospital in St. Paul? It didn't sound likely . . . but neither did computers turning into winged monkey-creatures. Maybe she should start a list of questions for when they got somewhere that she could ask them.

They had been walking for about an hour when they topped a small rise and found themselves staring in surprise at a road. If Kayla had thought about it, she would have expected any roadways to be narrow and uneven, and either unpaved or at most covered with rough flagstones. This road was as wide as a four-lane highway, flat as a tabletop, and made of glossy, unbroken black glass.

"Whoa!" Del said. "What is this?"

"The Dark Lord's Highway," Waylan said. "Though most call it simply the Black Road. The first Dark Lord burned it into the ground a thousand years ago. So the Traditions say." He turned to Riki. "Might I have the loan of your messenger mouse?"

Riki gave a wary nod. Waylan fished the lavender gerbil-thing out of his pocket and held it in front of his face. "Take a message to First Commander Jezzazar of the Dark Hordes of Zaradwin at Zaradwin Castle," he told it. "Second Commander Waylan is returning with Lady Xavrielina and companions, and requests an escort and supplies. We are a day and a half from the castle, coming east along the Black Road."

The messenger mouse looked suddenly far more alert. Waylan bent, lowering his hand, and the mouse jumped off and scurried down the black glass road toward the castle, moving more quickly with every step. When it ran out of sight a moment later, it was going faster than a car on the Interstate and still picking up speed. Riki stared after it, her mouth hanging open.

"That is way cooler than a flip phone," Del announced.

"There," Waylan said. "With luck, they will reach us tomorrow morning, at the near edge of the forest."

Riki's mouth shut with a snap. "Tomorrow morning! I have to be at work tomorrow morning!"

Waylan shrugged. "The castle is there, and we are here, and

none of us has the speed of a messenger mouse. We may reach the edge of the forest by nightfall, but I doubt we can get farther. And in any case, it is not safe to travel through the forest at night."

"Why?" Del broke in. "Are there giant spiders?"

"Giant spiders?" Waylan sounded startled. "I do not think so."

"I thought all Dark Lords had giant spiders." Del sounded as if he disapproved, though Kayla had the feeling that it was the idea of a Dark Lord without spiders that he disapproved of, not the idea of giant spiders themselves.

"Del," Riki said, and he settled for grumbling under his breath. Riki looked at Waylan. "If the forest is that dangerous and the castle is that far away, recharge that transportation-token-thing right here," she demanded. "It may be harder than doing it at the castle, but you owe us."

"I do not owe you," Waylan replied calmly. "And it matters not, even if I did. I cannot do as you ask, madam."

"What do you mean, you can't?" Riki's voice rose. "That's why we agreed to go to this castle of yours—to fix that token so we can get home! You lied?"

"The Dark Lord himself crafted the token," Waylan said patiently. "Only a mage of similar power can renew it. And as I said before, I am no mage."

Riki's eyes narrowed. "All right, if you can't do it, who can?"

"The Dark Lady," Waylan replied, as if it should have been obvious.

Kayla frowned. "You expect *me* to fix that thing?" It was one thing for him to be positive that she had enormous, unspecified magical powers. It was another thing entirely for him to expect her to just up and use them a couple of hours after arriving here.

"Not immediately," Waylan said reassuringly. "Since your world has no magic, it will take some time before you can learn anything so advanced."

"How much time?" Riki's voice was wobbling again.

"I do not know," Waylan replied. "I am not familiar with the training of mages. Some months, at least, probably longer."

"Months! We can't stay here for months! School starts next week." Riki waved her hands in agitation. "I'll lose my job. We'll get kicked out of the apartment and lose our deposit! There'll be investigations and—"

The note of rising panic in Riki's voice made Kayla feel slightly sick to her stomach. "Mom," she interrupted, "if we can use magic to get from one world to another, we can use it to get around everything back home. And Waylan already said he isn't a mage, so he doesn't really know how long it will take." Waylan opened his mouth, but Kayla shot him a warning look. "Maybe somebody else at the castle will have a better idea."

"The castle librarian might have some suggestions," Waylan offered after a moment. He paused, then with evident reluctance added, "Or perhaps the steward. My lady is correct; I know little about the secrets of magecraft."

Riki took a deep breath and then another. "Does that flying monkey of yours still think following this guy is a good idea?" she asked Kayla.

"Macavinchy?"

"I repeat, I am a familiar, not a flying monkey," Macavinchy said crossly. "And the situation has not changed in any material way. Following the second commander still has the highest probability of a favorable outcome, compared to your other available courses of action."

"All right." Riki took another deep breath. "All right. But if this goes wrong, I swear that when we get home, I am going to plug you into an ungrounded outlet and let your circuits fry."

Macavinchy shook his wings and pointedly turned his back. Kayla reached up to steady him on her shoulder and said, "Fine. Can we keep going, then? The sooner we get there, the sooner we can get this straightened out."

Riki allowed herself to be persuaded, though not without more dark looks in Waylan's direction, and they started off once more. The shiny black road looked slippery, but it felt firm and rubbery underfoot. They made better time than they had crossing the open fields.

The silence still bothered Kayla. They'd been walking for another half hour when a thought struck her. "Macavinchy."

The familiar came awake on her shoulder. "Yes, madam?"

"Can you still play back the music I uploaded to the tablet?"

"I do not believe that I can provide an exact reproduction of every piece, madam," Macavinchy said. "Some of the instrumentals, in particular, are incompatible with my current vocal abilities. I do, however, have every confidence in my ability to provide a reasonable approximation of most tracks."

"Pick something. Not too loud, though."

"Very good, madam." Macavinchy purred briefly and opened

his mouth. He didn't seem to be doing anything recognizable as singing, but a moment later the first song on her favorite playlist started with a quick run of electronic drumbeats.

At the first sound, Waylan leaped and spun around, sword raised. Kayla skipped backward. "Watch it!" Riki said.

"What is— I beg your pardon, my lady, but . . ." Waylan paused, lowering his sword and eyeing Macavinchy doubtfully. The drums had settled into a steady backbeat under rapid, rhythmic vocals. "Your familiar is making very peculiar noises," Waylan ventured at last.

"It's not peculiar!" Kayla objected. "It's music." Kayla wondered how Macavinchy was producing it, but she wasn't about to interrupt him to ask. It was a relief to know that she would still have something to listen to for however long they stayed in Zaradwin.

"Music?" Waylan sounded even more doubtful than before. "That . . . music . . . will attract attention, my lady. Possibly dangerous attention."

"From what?" Kayla asked, looking pointedly at the vast, empty expanse around them. "Are there invisible creatures out there?"

"Not to my knowledge, my lady. But sound carries a long way in these wastes, and while the unfamiliar noise may repel some creatures, there are undoubtedly others who will be drawn to it."

He has a point. Grudgingly, Kayla nodded. Macavinchy subsided against her neck once more, and they started off again.

By early afternoon, they had nearly reached the forest. Waylan was in the lead, as he had been since they left the stone circle, so when he stopped, they all did.

"What is it?" Riki asked after a moment.

"Owlhead vultures." Waylan nodded toward some fat black blotches among the branches ahead.

Riki ran her free hand through her hair and asked, "Are they dangerous?"

"Normally, they would not attack a group such as ours," Waylan admitted. "But they appear to be waiting for something. If they have chosen a victim, they will see any approach as an attempt to rob them of their prey, and they will fight fiercely to keep it."

"So what do we do?" Kayla asked. "Wait here until they kill whatever it is?"

"Maybe we should go back," Riki said, frowning.

Waylan did not respond for a moment. Then he shook his head and squared his shoulders. "Under the circumstances, it would be unwise to stop here without knowing what awaits us." He took a deep breath. "It is therefore clear that I must leave you to scout ahead while it is still light."

Riki's eyes narrowed. "So you're going to just run off and leave us? I don't think so. What happens if you don't come back?"

"Should I not return by sunset, you must retreat along the road before you stop for the night. First Commander Jezzazar should arrive tomorrow with enough men to deal with whatever lurks in the forest." Even muffled by the mask, Waylan's voice sounded as if he did not expect to come back.

"Mom's right. Splitting up is a bad idea," Del said. Riki looked at him and he scrunched his shoulder. "What? In stories, somebody always gets killed or captured when the group splits. And it isn't always the one who goes off to check stuff out." He paused, considering. "Unless it's a haunted house. If it's a haunted house, the one who gets killed is always the one who hears the weird noise in the basement and goes down to see what it is."

"Just so," Waylan said heavily. "I had hoped that the talisman would bring my lady and me directly to the castle courtyard and thus avoid these first tests, but the Dark Traditions are not so easy to evade. It is my duty to accept this role and its consequences."

"Why don't we all just retreat up the road right now?" Riki asked. "It makes a lot more sense to me than sending you off to get killed."

"But—but it's Traditional." Waylan sounded confused and bewildered.

"So?" Kayla said. "Macavinchy told us to stick with you." She grinned suddenly. "Actually . . . Macavinchy! Can you tell us what's going on at the edge of the forest?"

"I regret that I do not possess long-range scanning capabilities, madam," the familiar replied. "In general, I concur with the second commander's analysis. Some animal or person has been, or is about to be, injured by one of the creatures in the forest. It would be unwise to proceed without more information."

"It could be a person?" Riki looked suddenly uncertain.

"Can you fly closer and find out what's going on?" Kayla asked.

"That is well within my abilities," Macavinchy replied.

"Good. Go do it." Kayla staggered a little as Macavinchy pushed off from her shoulder. She had barely regained her balance when Waylan dropped to his knees in front of her and bowed his head.

"My lady," he said. "I thank you for my life. In return, I do hereby vow and swear—"

"No!" Kayla interrupted him frantically. She felt as if something cold were hovering over her, ready to fall. "No oaths! Macavinchy said they were a bad idea."

"A *very* bad idea," Del corrected her.

"A very bad idea," Kayla repeated. "So no oaths or vows or anything until Macavinchy gets back and okays it."

Waylan sat back on his heels, and the cold feeling receded slightly. "But—"

A harsh shriek from the forest ahead interrupted him. Kayla's head snapped around just as something exploded in the forest, knocking over two of the trees. A black cloud of owlhead vultures rose into the sky with more harsh cries. There were a lot more of them than she'd expected.

"Macavinchy! Come back!"

Automatically, she started forward, but Riki's hand grabbed her shoulder. "Stay here!"

The owlhead vultures swooped down. Most of them headed for Macavinchy; half a dozen flew on toward the little group on the road. Waylan leaped to his feet and drew his sword. "Get down!" he shouted.

Riki yanked at Kayla's shoulder. Kayla staggered but kept her feet. She couldn't tear her eyes from the owlhead vultures closing in around Macavinchy. It would be her fault if something happened to him, and he was so small compared to even one of the vultures. . . . If she could use the magic that Waylan and the spirit said she had, she could protect her familiar, but she had no idea how to trigger it.

She stared at the vultures, feeling slightly sick, and wished as hard as she could for something to destroy them. Nothing happened. She wouldn't have felt this bad if she'd dropped the computer and broken it, but Macavinchy behaved like a person, even if he used to be— "Macavinchy, activate security system!" she shouted with all her strength. "Full power!"

An instant later, lightning crackled from the center of the cloud of owlhead vultures. A handful of them fell from the sky, landing with an unpleasant *squish*. The rest of the vultures wheeled uncertainly. One dove toward them; Kayla got a too-close look at large eyes, a hooked beak, and wickedly outstretched talons before Waylan's sword disposed of it.

Lightning crackled again, and more vultures dropped onto the road. The remainder of the flock flapped upward and swirled away, leaving a monkey with red bat wings hovering just above the forest.

"Macavinchy!" Kayla called. The familiar swooped toward her, backwinging at the last moment to land gently on her shoulder. "Are you all right?" she asked urgently.

"I am uninjured, madam," Macavinchy replied. "However, there is a young gentleman just inside the forest who appears to have been badly injured in the explosion." He paused. "I do not believe the owlhead vultures will be returning."

"Good," Kayla said, and started forward.

"Where do you think you're going?" Riki said.

"Mom! We can't leave somebody hurt lying around the forest!"

"We won't, but we aren't running toward an explosion, either," Riki said. "Waylan knows more about this territory than we do. He goes first, and if he says run away, we run away."

"A very reasonable strategy," Waylan said, sounding relieved.

"Let's go, then," Kayla said impatiently, and they started down the road once more.

CHAPTER 4

Obliterating Your First Competitors

Killing any hopeful Dark Lords you may meet is excellent practice for your future reign of terror. Not only will you establish a reputation for cruelty and ruthlessness, but you will also significantly reduce your future competition.

—From *The Dark Traditions*

The edge of the forest was barely three minutes' walk away, but to Kayla, getting there seemed to take hours. As they reached the place where the trees began, Kayla peered into the gloom ahead. "There!" she said, pointing toward the crumpled form lying in the middle of the black glass road.

"Wait here," Waylan commanded, and strode forward. When he reached the figure, he crouched to examine it, then called back, "Madam Jones, we have need of your heal-all, if you would be so kind. My lady, you and your brother keep back."

"Why?" Del asked. "He doesn't look like he could hurt us."

Waylan hesitated. "Appearances can deceive."

Riki had reached his side; she glanced down and her shoulders went stiff. "Stay put!" she commanded Kayla and Del, and practically dove into her tote bag.

Kayla squinted at the figure lying in the road. His clothes were dark, which made it hard to pick out details against the black road, but she caught a glimpse of something red that didn't look like cloth. And Macavinchy had said he was badly injured. Feeling slightly ill, she caught Del's shoulder as he started forward. "Mom said stay put."

"But—"

"We can't do anything to help; we'd just get in the way." Which was true, but Kayla was sure that Riki's orders had less to do with keeping them out of the way than with a desire to keep Del from having nightmares if he saw the man's injuries. Well, Riki probably didn't think it was a suitable sight for Kayla, either, but if she was going to be the Dark Lady . . .

Kayla froze. Had she really just thought that? All those times Waylan had called her "my lady" must be getting to her. She shook her head and looked back at Riki, who was conversing with Waylan in tones too low for her to make out. Riki reached down to touch the man; a moment later, she pulled out a smallish leather sack that sloshed and a handkerchief. She fiddled with the water sack for a moment, then wet the handkerchief and wiped at his head.

The handkerchief turned red. Kayla turned her head away and didn't look back until Riki called to them in a voice that shook slightly. "It's all right now."

When Kayla turned back, Riki was scrubbing at her hands

with another handkerchief. She saw Kayla's hesitation and said reassuringly, "His clothes are still a mess, but the heal-all worked like . . . like . . ." She shrugged and waved a hand, unable to find a comparison.

"Of course it worked," Waylan said as Kayla and Del came to join them. "Help him off to the side, there. We'll camp for the night; even with the heal-all, he's in no shape to travel farther today."

"I owe you my life," a hoarse voice said. "In token of which, I vow and pledge—"

"No!" Kayla and Riki said together. Kayla snickered and added, "No vows, no pledges, no oaths! Not now. If there are going to be any, we'll handle them later, when we're sure it won't cause problems."

"I thought—" The voice broke off in a coughing fit.

"Easy there," Waylan said. "You may look fine, but even heal-all takes a while to repair deep wounds and blood loss. Can you sit up yet?"

The rescuee pulled himself up to a sitting position, and Kayla finally got a proper look at him. *He's not much older than I am!* she thought, though his face was so thin and tired that it was hard to judge exactly. His hair hung to just below his ears. The ends were a dull brown, but the two inches at the roots were black and wavy, as if he was growing out a bad dye job. His beard—if you could call the patchy stubble across his chin a beard—was the same black as the roots.

She swept her eyes quickly over him, hoping to avoid actually seeing any obvious wounds, and shivered suddenly in a cool breeze. Only there was no wind. Neither the dry grass nor Waylan's cloak had so much as stirred. "You're magic!" she blurted.

Waylan stiffened immediately, and his hand settled on the hilt of his sword, though he did not draw it. "Who are you and how did you come to such a pass?"

The boy straightened and tried to look down his nose. "Who are you to demand such knowledge?"

"The people who just saved your life," Riki said.

The boy hesitated. Then he put his chin up and answered. "Very well. You speak to . . . to the Dark Lord Karnroth the Great."

Waylan's eyes narrowed and his hand clenched around his sword hilt. Before he could draw, Del snorted. "Yeah, right. And I'm the king of America."

"If you're a Dark Lord, why are you running around the forest alone, getting yourself killed?" Kayla asked.

"I didn't get myself killed!"

"You came close," Riki said. "If I hadn't had that heal-all, I don't think we could have saved you." She sighed. "I really, really wish I'd brought some antibiotics. Or even cough syrup."

The boy stared, and his forehead wrinkled as he tried to comprehend Riki's last comment. Finally, he gave up and said, "I do thank you. But if I'm going to be a Dark Lord, I have to act like one, and—"

"Going to be?" Kayla said. "So you aren't really a Dark Lord?"

"Not yet," he said reluctantly. "I was hoping to wait a few more years, but . . . well, it didn't work out."

"You should not make claims you cannot support," Waylan said in a dangerous voice.

"Isn't that how Dark Lords are supposed to act? It's the way they behave in all the—" The boy broke off, eyeing them warily.

"I think you had better tell us your story," Riki said in her I-am-the-mom-so-don't-even-think-about-lying voice. "Your *whole* story."

"I— All right. You did save my life," he said, as if trying to persuade himself. "My name is Archibald. I—"

"I thought you said you were Karnroth."

"Everybody calls me Archie!" Archibald said. "How can I be the Dark Lord Archie? Nobody would take me seriously!"

"Point." Kayla nodded.

"The Dark Lord Baldy would be worse," Del said, and snickered.

"Don't I know it." Archie sighed. "I've been trying to come up with something better, but—" He shrugged.

"Don't interrupt, Del," Riki said. "Now, Archie, you were saying?"

"I'm from Skywind," he went on. "You won't have heard of it; it's a tiny village about two months' journey from the border." He waved back in the direction from which they had come.

"You're Light-side born, then," Waylan said.

Archibald nodded. "And my parents were pleased when the signs said I would have magic. They got me as much training as they could manage, in anticipation of the time I'd come into my power, and they got more and more excited the longer it took. And then my hair started to go black," he said bitterly.

51

"Ah." Waylan nodded as if this explained everything. Seeing the confused looks Riki and Kayla were exchanging, he said, "At every child's birth, there are signs that indicate whether that child will grow into magic as they age, but they do not tell what kind of magic the child will wield. That comes later, when the child's power rises and their hair changes color—black for Dark magic and white for Light. The later in life a child comes into power, and the darker or lighter the hair, the greater the child's potential."

"What about redheads?" Del asked.

"Redheads?" Waylan looked puzzled. "Their hair changes like everyone else's, dark or light."

"It doesn't matter, Del," Riki said. She looked at Archibald with a skeptical expression. "So you left home when your hair changed color?"

"Of course not!" Archie said. "I was only ten!"

"Ten?" Waylan sounded both impressed and wary.

"Is that good or bad?" Kayla asked.

"It depends on whether he is on your side or not," Waylan said dryly. "Kitchen magicians come into their power before the age of two; after that, a mage's potential power increases steadily. Those with power enough to become Dark Lords change hair color at eight or nine, or even later. If he speaks truly, he has great potential."

Kayla frowned suddenly. "My hair has always been black." She looked at Riki for confirmation.

Riki nodded. "It was black as a coal cellar at midnight when we first saw you, and you weren't old enough to have had a haircut yet."

"Does that mean I'm a kitchen magician?" And why did that thought bother her? It wasn't like she'd grown up expecting to be a powerful magician.

"Your hair color was probably affected by your passage to the world of your rearing," Waylan replied, but he did not sound as sure of himself as he usually did. "It should not have had any impact on the degree of your power. Once you have training . . ." His voice trailed off.

But Waylan wasn't a mage. *How much does he really know about spellcasting? What if training isn't enough?* Kayla's mouth felt suddenly dry.

Riki seemed to be thinking much the same thing. "So you don't actually know whether Kayla can fix that gadget, let alone how long it will take," she snapped at Waylan. She turned to Archie. "What about you? You have magic. Do you have training?"

"Some," Archie said. "But if it's a Dark spell, I won't know it. I was taught Light spells, as the Great Concordat requires." He wrinkled his nose. "They don't work very well, because they're the wrong kind of magic for me."

Riki frowned. "Didn't your teachers know that? Why would they teach you the wrong sort of spells?"

"Because I wasn't stupid enough to tell them I'm a Dark magician!" Archibald said. "I knew what would happen if anyone realized my power was Dark. I've been bleaching my hair since I was ten."

"That's why it looks so weird!" Del said in tones of great satisfaction.

Archibald nodded sadly. "I knew I'd be found out eventually, but I didn't want to be imprisoned as a Dark magician. I got away with it for five years, too, and if I hadn't caught a fever and been stuck in bed at just the wrong time, I'd have gotten away with it even longer." At their puzzled looks, he explained. "My hair grew out far enough for my family to notice the black at the roots."

"And then?" Kayla asked after a minute.

"They threw me out." He lifted his chin, as if daring any of them to comment.

"They were frightened," Waylan said softly. "They didn't realize you'd tricked them, did they? They thought your hair was only just changing—at fifteen. Had they been right, you'd be the most powerful Dark mage in history. Light-siders or not, I am surprised they let you live."

Archie nodded again. "I told them I'd been hiding it for years, but they didn't believe me."

"Well, you *had* been lying to them," Kayla pointed out.

"I suppose." Archie shrugged. "That was a couple of months ago. I've been dodging the Crown Guards and trying to get to the border ever since. I thought I'd be fine once I crossed. This is where I belong, isn't it?" His mouth twisted in a grimace.

"And you let down your guard," Waylan said, gesturing at the rents in his shirt.

"Sort of. I'd found the road, and I was just starting into the Dark Forest, when I saw a girl."

Del made a face, and Archie went on quickly, "A little girl, maybe six or seven years old. I didn't see her up close."

"Sounds like the spirit of the stones," Del said. "Was she all gray?"

"I didn't get a good look at her. She was off among the trees, and, well, I may have been raised Light, but even I know that if you wander around in the Dark Forest, you're liable to get killed. I yelled at her to get back on the road, but she just waved and skipped off. So I ran after her."

"That was foolish," Waylan told him.

"I know, but she was only a little kid. I had to try to keep her from getting hurt." He sighed. "I suppose the . . . thing got her; it came at me from that direction."

Waylan tensed. "What thing?"

"I don't know what it's called," Archie said. "It came out of the ground, like a giant mole. And when I say giant, I mean it; the head was as tall as two men. It had black claws this long"—he measured his left arm from his fingertips halfway to his elbow—"and it was fast."

"Claws?" Waylan said.

"What do you think cut me up like this?" Archie said. "I certainly didn't do it myself! Do you know what it was?"

Waylan shifted so that he faced more of the forest. "I have never heard of anything like it," he admitted. "But new creatures often appear in the Dark Forest when there is no Dark Lord. How did you defeat it?"

"I didn't. The thing blew up just as it was about to eat me."

"That must have been the explosion we heard," Riki said.

Archie wrinkled his nose. "It smelled awful. Like a barn full of

55

rotten eggs. I'm not sure what happened next. I remember stumbling toward the road and tripping over the edge. I couldn't get up because I was so lightheaded from the cuts and the smell. And then you came."

Kayla couldn't help feeling that Archie had left out quite a lot of details, but she didn't want to push him for more information while he looked so exhausted and hungry. *I bet a proper Dark Lady would ask anyway,* she thought sourly. *I don't think I'm going to be very good at this.*

"My lady, what do you wish done with him?" Waylan's quiet question brought Kayla out of her thoughts.

"I think we're stuck with him," she said after a moment.

" 'My lady'?" Archie sounded horrified. "You're a noblewoman?"

"No," Riki said at the same time Waylan said, "Yes, of course. She is the Dark Lady of Zaradwin."

"I didn't know anyone had claimed— Wait, you're a Dark Lady?"

"She is the daughter of the Dark Lord Xavriel, returned at last to take up her heritage," Waylan replied solemnly.

"But—but if you're a Dark Lady, then I have to challenge you!" Archie said. He looked horrified, but Kayla couldn't tell whether what bothered him was the thought of fighting someone when he was still badly hurt, or whether it was the idea of fighting someone who'd just helped save his life.

"You are in no shape to be challenging anybody," Riki told Archie sternly. "Even if I would allow such a thing, which I won't."

Waylan looked as if he wanted to object, but he didn't actually say anything. Archibald glanced at Riki, then at Kayla. "Who is it that can allow a Dark Lady to do or not do anything?"

"My mom," Kayla told him. "What's this challenge business, anyway?"

"It is Traditional for those who would earn the title of Dark Lord or Dark Lady to battle among themselves until one emerges victorious," Waylan said.

"Traditional? Like going off into the forest by yourself to get killed was Traditional?"

"Just so, my lady." Waylan did not seem to have noticed Kayla's attempt at sarcasm. "As the daughter of the previous Dark Lord, you may lay claim to his title directly, without need for other validation."

"So no challenges," Riki said, as if she wanted to make very sure.

"Not at this time," Waylan replied. "Eventually, there may be—"

"I have to challenge her!" Archibald broke in. He sounded upset. "This is terrible. Nothing has gone right since I was ten. You save my life, and you won't let me pledge my loyalty in return, and now I have to fight you."

"Why?" Kayla asked skeptically.

"Because that's how it's *done*!" Archibald said. He paused. "Isn't it?"

Kayla frowned at him. "Don't you know?"

"I was raised Light-side! I read all the stories about Dark

Lords, but who's to say they're right about what the rules are in the Dark kingdoms? It's not like Dark-siders go around to Light-side villages explaining how everything works here!"

There was a tiny cough in Kayla's left ear. "Macavinchy," she said, "what can you tell me about the rules for becoming a Dark Lord?"

"Quite a bit, madam," Macavinchy said, prompting a wide-eyed stare from Archie. "I have access to almost all of the basic manuals and etiquette books from this world, as well as several useful items from among the things you downloaded last night. What do you wish to know?"

This prompted a brief silence. Finally, Kayla said, "Etiquette books? There are etiquette books about being a Dark Lord?"

"I do not think I would term them so," Waylan said carefully. "But there are certainly several useful works in the castle library. And there are rumors . . ."

"What rumors?" Kayla asked.

"Rumors of a book that contains everything a Dark Lord needs to know," Waylan replied reluctantly. "Dark Lords have spoken of it in the past, but no one who is not a Dark Lord or Lady has ever read it. It is called *The Dark Traditions*."

"Macavinchy—"

"I do not have access to any copies of that title." The familiar snapped his wings twice, and his tail uncurled from Kayla's neck to lash angrily. "However, many other books refer to it, and three of them include brief citations of the text. It is therefore highly likely that it is a real book, possibly magically limited in its readership."

Kayla shook her head. "How do you know all this stuff, anyway?"

"I believe it is a side effect of our translation into this universe," Macavinchy replied. "At the time the dimensional transport took effect, I—or rather, the computer you were using—was connected to the internet, and whatever mechanism alters incompatible objects when they are moved from one world to another has attempted to reproduce the effect. I fear the result must be classified as a mixed success, as I can access very little information without the correct prompt."

The familiar sounded more than a little put out by this, and it took Kayla a minute to figure out why. "So you can answer questions, but I still have to figure out what to ask."

"That is correct, madam."

Archibald was still staring at Macavinchy. "What is that thing?" he said at last.

"He used to be a computer," Kayla said, frowning at Archibald's tone. "Now he's a . . . What did you tell Mom you were, Macavinchy?"

"A premier semi-autonomous construct," Macavinchy replied promptly. "Commonly called a familiar, in this world."

"Familiars can't talk, not more than a few words, anyway," Archie objected.

"This one can." Before Archie or anyone else could come up with more irrelevant questions, Kayla went on, "Macavinchy, this is Archibald. He wants to be a Dark Lord, and he thinks he has to fight me to do it. Is he right?"

"In a very broad sense, Mr. Archibald is correct," Macavinchy said. "You are the heir presumptive to the title; if he wishes to pursue the Traditional path to becoming a Dark Lord, he will at some point have to challenge and defeat you in order to take your place. However, he need not do so immediately, and it would be much better strategy for him to join your forces and usurp your throne later on."

"That is also one of the Traditional routes to power," Waylan confirmed, nodding.

Archie's shoulders slumped in relief. "Oh, good. At least we can put it off for a while."

"Forever, if I have anything to say about it," Riki muttered.

"Don't you want to be a Dark Lord?" Del asked. "I thought that's why you came here."

"I came here because there isn't anywhere else for me to go," Archie snapped. "I'm a Dark magician! What will I do if I don't become a Dark Lord?"

"You could become an evil minion," Del suggested.

"Del!" Riki sounded appalled. "What an awful thing to say."

"It is not the most usual choice for a magician of such power," Waylan said thoughtfully, "but power alone is not enough to make a Dark Lord. One must have the desire to rule as well." He shook his head. "Nevertheless, young Archibald is correct about one thing: this decision need not be made immediately. And if we are to make camp so close to the Dark Forest, it would be well to have a mage of such power with us, even if he is injured and unpracticed."

The safety argument stopped any chance of Riki disagreeing, not that she would have left Archie by the roadside in the state he was in. Under Waylan's direction, they gathered wood for a fire while he stood guard against the appearance of any new threat. Riki got the water sacks and the last sample packet of jerky out of her tote, and was about to share out this meager ration when Macavinchy coughed again and reminded them of the owlhead vultures that had been felled by his security system. Apparently, they would be good to eat.

Waylan had no trouble locating two of the creatures, despite his reluctance to go very far from the group. The owlhead vultures were about the size of a turkey, with broad black-feathered wings, a head like an owl's, and a mouth full of pointed teeth instead of a beak. They took some time to clean and cook over the open fire, but by shortly after sundown, they had all eaten their fill.

They spent a restless and uncomfortable night. The air cooled rapidly after dark, and the fire heated only whichever side of a person faced it. No matter what position she took, half of Kayla froze while the other half roasted. Waylan alone seemed impervious to the unpleasantness of his surroundings, though he did not seem to sleep much. Every time Kayla turned over, she saw him watching the forest or feeding more wood to the fire.

Dawn came much too soon. They breakfasted on cold owlhead vulture (after Waylan assured Riki several times that food poisoning would not be a problem even though the meat had not been refrigerated), and watched the road for signs of the help from the castle that Waylan assured them would be coming.

"What do we do if they don't show up?" Riki asked.

"They will come."

"You can't know that. You've been gone for a long time."

"Ten years." Waylan rubbed a hand across his forehead. "But they will come, regardless. It is Tradition to escort a returning Dark heir to be formally presented at the seat of their power."

"Formally presented?" Kayla said uneasily.

"You need not be concerned," Waylan told her, misunderstanding the source of her worry. "As your guide and defender, it is my duty to make the presentation. You need only let the castle folk see you."

So everyone was going to be looking at her. Weren't Dark Lords supposed to be impressive? Kayla looked down at her dusty cotton shorts and wrinkled T-shirt. No way were they impressive. "Can't I get out of that part?"

Waylan frowned. "It is Traditional."

"Hey!" Del put in. "Somebody's coming."

They all turned toward the forest. Kayla saw movement between the black tree trunks; a moment later five people emerged and marched up the road toward them.

CHAPTER 5

Your First Tests

The preliminary tests faced by would-be Dark Lords usually require little more than common sense to solve. Betray your companions; torture and kill your enemies; sacrifice family and friends to increase your power or preserve your own life—in short, behave like a Dark Lord, whether you have officially assumed the title or not.

—From *The Dark Traditions*

Waylan pulled his mask into place and stood stiffly to attention as the five people drew near. At least, Kayla assumed they were people; they all wore dusty, faded black cloaks and armor that concealed everything but their general shape. Four of them wore plain black helmets painted with the same crude skull icon as Waylan's, except theirs were done in white paint instead of red. The fifth man wore the same black cloak as all the rest, but his helmet had four horns around its top, and the painted skull on his mask was a brilliant, glittering orange.

The group came to a halt ten feet in front of Waylan, and the man with the orange skull mask stepped forward.

"Who have we here?" he said, and his deep voice boomed out in spite of the mask.

Waylan bowed. "Second Commander Waylan, sir, reporting the successful completion of the Dark Lord's final instructions," he said.

"Success? Ah, you may think yourself successful, but even if you speak true, what good will it do in the end? We are doomed to failure; 'tis the price we pay for serving the Dark Lord." The four minions behind him nodded in unison. The man in the four-horned helmet went on, "Even so, we must do our duty, and our duty is to guard the cursed castle of Zaradwin and the family of the old Dark Lord according to Tradition, until a new lord rises to set our work at naught."

The minions nodded again. The man went on without appearing to notice. "Second Commander Waylan, I received your message." He held out the lavender mouselike creature that had been Riki's cell phone. Waylan accepted it, glanced at Riki, and then tucked the creature into a pouch at his belt.

"We have come . . ." The leader of the new arrivals paused, and Kayla saw hard brown eyes glittering through the eyeholes of the mask, evaluating their little group skeptically. "We come to escort you and your companions to Zaradwin Castle, that you may present this woman you say is the true blood heir to the Dark Lord Xavriel." He paused again, then added in a low, deadly voice, "And if your claim fails and the true heir is not among you, your fates will be most terrible!"

Riki put a protective arm around Del's shoulders. "We don't want to claim anything," she said. "We just want to go home."

"Madam Jones!" Waylan ground out between his teeth. "Do not interfere!"

The newcomer ignored him. He stalked forward and thrust his masked face threateningly at Riki. "And why did you leave your home, then, if not to demand the power and pride of Dark Lordship and Zaradwin Castle, first and last home of the Dark Lord Xavriel?"

"We were kidnapped," Riki shot back, unintimidated. "So don't blame us for being here. On the other hand, if you want to arrest this guy, be my guest." She gestured at Waylan.

"Mom!" Kayla and Del said together.

The orange-painted skull mask turned toward Waylan, who still stood at attention. "Kidnapped?" The man in the mask sounded grudgingly impressed.

Waylan took a deep breath. "Ten years past, I was charged by Xavriel, last Dark Lord of Zaradwin, as he lay dying, to find and—"

"Cease! The Black Road is no place to speak of such things. By Tradition, your tale must be first told at the cursed castle of Zaradwin, in the presence of the remnant of the Dark Hordes." He gestured with one black-gloved hand, and the four silent minions marched forward, taking up positions along the edges of the road. "Let us depart."

"First Commander Jezzazar," Waylan said, "I must report that a monster was destroyed in the Dark Forest near here just yesterday. There may be another in the area."

"What sort of monster?" the orange-masked first commander asked skeptically.

"Large and burrowing," Waylan answered. "It exploded after emerging, but not before half killing this one." He indicated Archie, who bowed uncertainly. "We had the tale from him, after we tended his wounds."

"You tended his wounds? Why?"

"At my lady's order," Waylan admitted.

"Ah." The first commander lowered his head. "So you neglected to scout ahead when you came in sight of the forest?"

Kayla stiffened at his tone. She had the feeling that there was more going on in the conversation than she was getting . . . and that if she were getting it, she wouldn't like it.

"My lady chose to send her familiar ahead of us."

Macavinchy shifted on Kayla's shoulder, and his tail tightened around her neck. She put up a hand to steady him as the first commander's head whipped around. His eyes glittered at her through the eyeholes of the helmet, and she scowled back. She was getting really tired of not being able to see the faces of the people she was looking at or talking to.

After a long moment, the first commander turned back toward Waylan and nodded heavily. "And so I must send men to search the Dark Forest and perhaps die, though I can ill afford to do so. Yet 'tis Tradition to hunt whatever new creature appears, so that the Dark Lord may judge whether it may be captured and harnessed among the fearsome beasts who accompany the Dark Hordes when they go forth to ravage the land and strike terror into the hearts of the foe. So shall I do what I must." He straightened. "Let us depart without further delay."

They gathered their few belongings, put out the fire, and

started down the road, toward the forest. The black skeleton trees seemed larger and more threatening the closer they got; Kayla half expected to pass a sign reading "Dark Forest: Do Not Enter" or "I'd Turn Back If I Were You."

The temperature dropped noticeably as they passed under the first branches, and Kayla's skin prickled into goose bumps. The forest was more intensely quiet than the open plain had been; the only sounds were the slap of their leather boots against the road and the occasional creaking of the minions' armor. Although there were no leaves on the trees, the ground beneath them was thick with shadows. Even the black glass of the roadway seemed less shiny.

As they went on, wisps of mist appeared, hanging motionless among the black trees. Kayla rubbed her bare arms, trying to generate some warmth, and scowled resentfully at their cloaked and armored escort. At least she didn't have to worry about wind chill.

They had been walking for at least an hour and were deep inside the forest when the first commander stopped and raised his arm. The minions halted immediately; Del almost ran into the one he had been following. "Listen," the commander said.

Kayla listened. Hearing nothing, she peered into the forest, but between the gloom and the wisps of mist, she could not see far. Macavinchy came alert on her shoulder, and his tail tightened around her throat. And then she caught it—a faint, irregular whisper.

"Something's coming," Riki whispered. "Shouldn't we get out of here?"

"'Tis a test," the commander declared. "There is no escaping it; we must meet our fate with fortitude."

"But if it is dangerous—"

"Of course 'tis dangerous," the first commander said impatiently. "'Tis a test. But we shall stand before it as long as we may, until we go down into inevitable defeat and our bodies are trampled into the dust beneath it."

"That's not very reassuring," Archie muttered, barely loudly enough for Kayla to hear.

The four minions moved toward the far side of the road and drew their swords. The whispering grew louder and resolved into a sound like a flock of geese taking off from a lake, interspersed with hissing. A moment later, part of the mist stirred and separated, and out of it came a shifting cloud of perhaps two dozen flying snakes.

The snakes ranged from about a foot to over three feet in length. Each had scales of a different color, vibrant jewel tones of amber and ruby, emerald and sapphire, that seemed to glow against the pale mist and the dark tree trunks. They had four wings, two at each end of their bodies, covered in long white feathers tipped in the same color as their scales. They danced up and down and around each other, twisting through the air in patterns that Kayla felt she almost understood.

"Sninks," Waylan said in a low voice. "They rarely show themselves; only the greatest of mages have ever seen or spoken with them."

"What the heck are sninks?" Kayla muttered.

"Sninks are a seldom-encountered magical creature believed

by some to be a manifestation of Dark magic itself," Macavinchy said. "They are known to have appeared to at least seven of the ten most powerful Dark Lords and Ladies of all time, generally early in their rise to power. There are unverified speculations that these encounters with sninks contributed substantially to the success of these Dark Rulers, though there are no plausible theories as to how or why. In appearance—"

"Thanks, Macavinchy," Kayla said. "We can see them."

"Very good, madam." Her familiar did not settle back against her neck, but stayed crouched with his wings partly extended as if he expected to have to take to the air at any moment.

"Their presence is an honor," the first commander said after a moment, "even as it is a test." He signaled to his men.

The minions sheathed their swords and stepped aside, leaving the sninks a clear path to Kayla and her family. Waylan hesitated, then bowed to the sninks and also stepped back. The cloud of sninks moved forward until they were about ten feet from the edge of the road, where they stopped and hovered.

For a moment, all Kayla could hear was the flutter of their wings and the tense breathing of the people around her. She shifted uneasily. She didn't like all this talk about tests. On the other hand, if the sninks only showed up for extra-powerful Dark Lords, maybe meeting them would persuade the first commander to loosen up a little.

The sninks whirled and dove and rose in a hissing waterfall of color, and suddenly Kayla could distinguish voices whispering softly underneath the rise and fall of the hisses.

"We come up from the earth."

"We come down from the high places."

"Through air."

"Over water."

"In Darkness."

"In Light."

"Bringing wisdom."

"Bringing power."

"Great power."

"Great magic."

"Come."

"Come and claim power."

"Come and claim magic."

"Come and learn secrets."

Kayla shivered. The air around her stung like the wind on a bitterly cold January morning. The hissing voices began repeating themselves. "I heard you the first time," Kayla mumbled.

"I didn't say anything," said Riki from beside her.

"I meant the sninks." Kayla rubbed her arms. Maybe one of the minions would give her his cloak if she ordered them. "Don't you hear them?"

"The hissing?" Riki sounded puzzled.

"You will be great," the sninks hissed.

"Says who?" Kayla said crossly. She was tired and cold and not in the mood for more mysteries. "And what do you mean by 'great'?"

"Kayla, what— Are you talking to those snakes?"

"They started it."

"If you don't want it, can I have it?" Del put in. "It'd be cool to have magic!"

"Maybe," Kayla said. So far, just having Waylan *think* she had magic had caused them a lot of trouble. She wondered suddenly if the sninks could give her enough power to send them back to St. Paul right away. Maybe she should take them up on their offer. She opened her mouth, then hesitated. She'd still have to figure out how to use what they gave her, so it might not save much time after all. Unless she didn't have as much magic as Waylan and the spirit of the stones thought.

"You're both talking to snakes?" Riki's voice shook slightly.

"You do not understand the sninks?" Archie said to Riki in a tone even more puzzled than hers had been.

"We will give you power," hissed the snakes insistently. "We will give you magic. Great power. Great magic. Great secrets."

The hissing was getting on Kayla's nerves. "Nobody just gives away power and magic," she said crossly. That was what she'd been trying to remember. "There's always a price." At least there always was in computer games and Del's favorite movies.

"You are clever."

"You are wise."

"You are right."

"So what's the price?" Kayla asked. If it wasn't too bad . . .

"One."

"Any one."

"One what? Quit the guessing games!" Kayla snapped.

"One of the others."

"For practice."

"As a beginning."

"As a test."

Kayla stared at the shifting ball of sninks while their request sank in. Did they really think she'd give them a *person* in exchange for power and magic? But then, that was just the sort of thing a Dark Lord would do. She glanced at the minions. The masks hid their expressions, but they all stood stiff and wary, as if they expected her to hand one of them over and were waiting to see which of them it would be. "No," she said firmly.

The sninks whirled around each other in agitation. "You want power," they hissed. "You want magic. The price is small. The power will be great."

"Even greater than the power you already possess."

"No," Kayla repeated, feeling more sure of herself. Even the sninks thought she had some magic; surely she'd figure out how to use it eventually. "Mom would kill me."

Del had opened his mouth, probably to ask what the sninks would charge him, but as soon as Kayla mentioned their mother, he closed it again, nodding.

"Why?" Riki said, frustrated. "What are they saying?"

"You are sure?" the sninks said.

"You are certain?"

"Once made, the choice cannot be taken back."

"For the third time, no!" Kayla snapped.

The cloud of sninks pulled together in a mass of boiling color, shrinking in on itself until suddenly it vanished with a *pop*. The air around Kayla warmed to merely cold, and she sighed in relief.

A single feather, tipped with blue, floated down in front of her. Automatically, she caught it.

"'Tis finished," First Commander Jezzazar said in a flat voice. "Move out."

The minions took up their positions as if nothing had happened, though Kayla noticed their heads turning to look at her. She stuffed the feather into her backpack, and they all began walking once more. Questions chased each other through Kayla's mind, but she kept them to herself.

By midafternoon, they had come out of the forest into a wasteland of rocky soil and scrubby trees. The air was warm and dry, though the sky remained overcast. The black road ran arrow-straight toward the mountain, or rather, toward the walled city Kayla could see at its foot.

Slowly, the wasteland beside the road gave way to dry grass and then to fields of sparse, stunted grain. There were no people in evidence besides themselves, though someone must have planted the crops. Kayla saw no animals, either, except for a single black bird that took off as the little group approached.

As they drew nearer, Kayla could make out a large gap in the wall where the road went through. At first, she thought it must be the city gates, but when they came up to it she saw that the gates were missing, along with a large section of the wall on either side. Broken blocks of stone, half-burned logs, and piles of smaller rocks lined the edges of the road, plainly cleared away to make the road passable.

"What happened here?" Riki asked in a hushed voice as they detoured around a heap of fist-sized chunks of stone.

"The Final Battle," Waylan said almost reverently. "Or at least, the preliminary skirmishes; technically, the battle itself was fought along the road up the mountain."

"This was preliminary?" Riki sounded horrified.

Waylan nodded. "There is only one road up to the castle, and the only way to reach it is through the city of Ashwend. That is why Zaradwin Mountain has been the first and last refuge of every truly successful Dark Lord for the past thousand years. To reach the castle, an army must first take the city, then hold it while they take the gatehouses along the road up the mountain. Few have ever managed such a feat, and the castle itself has never fallen."

They had reached the opening in the wall. The city on the other side looked like an abandoned ruin. Burned-out shells of buildings lined streets half-covered by rubble. "This looks pretty fallen to me," Kayla muttered, but maybe Dark Lords didn't count anything but castles as important.

"What happened to the people?" Del sounded quieter than usual.

"Some fled," the first commander responded. "Some took up arms and were crushed by the forces of the Light. And some vanished, ne'er to be seen again."

"That's terrible!" Riki said.

"'Twas terrible indeed," the first commander replied with evident satisfaction. "The final clash of Dark and Light is always so." He stepped over a cracked block of masonry and waved them forward. "'Tis Tradition."

"I thought you said this happened during the Final Battle," Kayla said to Waylan.

Waylan nodded. "Yes, in the one hundred thirty-eighth Final Battle between the forces of the Threefold Alliance of the Light and the Dark Hordes of Zaradwin or Uxmaril."

"How do you have one hundred thirty-eight 'Final' Battles?" Kayla objected.

"One for each Dark Lord, I bet," Del said.

"It's actually one hundred forty-three Final Battles," Archie put in earnestly. "The Dark Lords Ashinibal and—"

"Those were not proper Final Battles," the first commander growled. "Those lords met their fate elsewhere. 'Tis a true Final Battle only when the Legions of the Light sweep across the plains and break twice against the walls of Zaradwin or Uxmaril before they tear down the city gates at last and surge up the mountain road."

"The Remembrance Day ballad has one hundred forty-three verses, one for each Final Battle," Archie said stubbornly. "They added the last one ten years ago, right after the defeat of the Dark Lord Xavriel."

"And well they should have," the first commander said. "The Dark Lord Xavriel was the greatest Dark Lord in centuries, and his Final Battle—the hundred and *thirty-eighth* Final Battle—was a true example of the Traditions. Those others—" He waved a hand dismissively. "Light-side exaggeration, meant to puff up their achievements."

"You're just trying to minimize the evil that Dark Lords do," Archie shot back.

"Isn't it a little hypocritical to be objecting to Dark Lords being evil?" Kayla asked pointedly. "After all, you were planning on becoming a Dark Lord yourself." All this talk of battles and evil made her uncomfortable. She wasn't sure what First Commander Jezzazar wanted, but Waylan had made it pretty clear that he, at least, expected her to become the next Dark Lady. And if that meant starting a war and getting a lot of people killed, Kayla didn't want any part of it. Besides, they weren't going to hang around long enough for battles. Probably.

Archie deflated. "I—I suppose. I keep forgetting."

The first commander sniffed. "Think you that Dark magic is all there is to being a Dark Lord? 'Tis more Light foolishness. Without the will and desire, 'tis impossible."

"It's impossible without Dark magic, too," Archie pointed out. "There hasn't been even one Light mage who became a Dark Lord."

"No?" The first commander's voice dripped scorn. "Then you do not call Iglorian a Dark Lord?"

"Iglorian was never a Light mage," Archie said, and launched into a passionate but complicated explanation that Kayla gave up on following after the first few sentences.

The argument lasted through the ruined city and halfway up the mountain. They passed two gatehouses along the way. The first had been reduced to two piles of crumbled stone, but the second still had one tower. *Probably because the invading army was too tired to blow it apart after they'd climbed this far,* Kayla thought.

The air grew colder as they neared the top of the mountain, and Kayla shivered in spite of the unaccustomed exercise. Her T-shirt and shorts weren't enough for comfort. The road curved and tightened into a counterclockwise corkscrew; shortly thereafter they reached the castle gate. Like the gatehouses they had passed on the way up, it had been a portcullis flanked by two black towers, and like them it had plainly suffered considerable damage. Unlike the earlier fortifications, these showed some attempts at repair. The walls had been patched with red bricks or chunks of creamy sandstone, giving them a mottled, moldy appearance, and the missing portcullis had been replaced with a rickety grid of branches lashed together with ropes.

Kayla frowned. The repairs didn't look solid, and nobody had done any work at all on the city wall or the two gatehouses on the road. Waylan had said he'd been away for ten years; surely someone should have fixed things in all that time. Every city-building computer game she'd played started with saving up resources so you could build a wall. Okay, this was real, not a game, but medieval castles were supposed to be fortresses. Fallen-down gates and walls full of holes weren't much of a fortress.

A head appeared at the top of the left-hand tower. "Who seeks entry to Zaradwin Castle, citadel of the Dark Lord?"

"First Commander Jezzazar and escort," the first commander snapped. Stepping aside, he gestured Waylan forward.

"Second Commander Waylan, escorting the Dark Lady Xavrielina and her family," Waylan called back.

"My name is Kayla," Kayla grumbled.

Waylan stepped aside in turn and looked at Archie, who cleared his throat nervously. "The Dark Mage . . . Zargratiforian," he said.

The head disappeared, and a moment later the rickety portcullis shivered and began to rise in a series of jerks. Kayla looked at Archie. "Zargratiforian?"

"It's better than Karnroth, isn't it?" Archie said anxiously.

"No," Del said positively. "It's too long."

Archie sighed. With a grinding noise, the portcullis stopped moving. First Commander Jezzazar signaled, and his men marched forward. Kayla frowned, feeling tension building in her forehead. She shook herself and looked at her mother. Riki gave the gate a skeptical once-over, then shrugged and followed Waylan and the minions.

As they passed under the gate, Kayla felt something like an invisible spiderweb tear loose and wrap around her. "Ow!" Del said at the same time, and slapped at the side of his head. "Something bit me!"

"Let me see," Riki said as they reached the far side of the gate. She started combing her fingers through Del's hair as he squirmed and objected. The portcullis thudded to the ground behind them, and the damp-spiderweb sensation faded away. Kayla looked around.

They stood in a wide courtyard, surrounded by a wall made of black stone. Mostly made of black stone, Kayla corrected herself; like the gate tower, the walls had large sections that had been patched with sandstone, and there were several gaps that had not yet been repaired. A thin gray-green line of low-growing weeds outlined the irregular, uneven flagstones. On her left, against the wall, lay a jumble of wooden beams, some of them charred and broken—the remains of the original portcullis, she guessed. Well, except for the part that looked like half a wagon wheel, and the bucket with the broken handle, and the broken stick with some twigs on the end that might have been a broom once. Apparently, the people living here had decided to pile their trash in the courtyard.

To Kayla's right, a long wooden building with half a dozen doors ran along the outer wall, its roof pushed tight against the sentry walk. Directly in front of her, in the exact center of the courtyard, a slender spire of smooth black stone rose three or four stories into the air. It looked barely wide enough to have one room per floor, and not a large room, either. A narrow wooden staircase zigzagged up to a door on the second level.

"This place is a pit!" Del declared.

"Delmar, be polite," Riki said.

"Well, it is," Del muttered.

"I thought you said the castle had never been taken," Kayla said to Waylan. She was still freezing, and she felt as if she was getting another headache. She had never thought a castle could be shabby and run-down.

"It has not," Waylan assured her, but he, too, frowned at the pockmarked walls and destroyed portcullis. "This damage was done during the Final Battle. Had the castle fallen, then or since, First Commander Jezzazar would not be—"

"Summon the guard!" the first commander bellowed before Waylan could finish. A horn sounded three notes, all of them decidedly flat. A moment later, six people in faded black cloaks and scratched black armor came running, one from the guard tower and five from the wooden building with all the doors. All of them carried drawn swords, and before she could stop herself, Kayla blurted, "Isn't that dangerous, running with swords drawn like that? Even if they do have armor."

"Serving the Dark Lord is dangerous," a muffled voice said from behind the nearest mask, sounding a bit taken aback.

"Sure, but you don't have to be stupid about it," Kayla said. "They teach kindergarten kids not to run if they're carrying sharp objects. Aren't the Dark Lord's minions supposed to be smarter than a bunch of five-year-olds?"

"Kayla!" her mother scolded under her breath. "Don't irritate them."

The first commander and his men strode forward. The four minions who had accompanied them on the road took up positions beside the ones who had appeared from various parts of the castle. First Commander Jezzazar straightened his helmet and stood in front of them, hands clasped behind his back. "You have entered Zaradwin Castle," he said, his voice booming out to fill the courtyard as if he spoke to a vast multitude instead of fifteen people standing close by. "Whether you leave again, and in what condition, is yet to be decided. Therefore, state your names and business, according to custom and Tradition."

Waylan snapped to attention. "Second Commander Waylan, sir, reporting the successful completion of the Dark Lord Xavriel's final instructions," he said.

"And so it ends," Jezzazar said heavily. "Yet will I do my duty according to Tradition, though it be my last. Therefore, Second Commander, I charge you to relate the particulars of your quest and its result, that all may hear and accept their fates." The minions all nodded like puppets on strings. Jezzazar gave Kayla and her family a hard stare, as if he expected them to object. Kayla and her mother exchanged uneasy looks, and Kayla was just about to ask Macavinchy whether there was something they ought to object to, when Waylan began to speak.

CHAPTER 6

Claiming a Castle

During your presentation, remain calm and collected. Your power has been amply demonstrated during your journey to your castle; further display is beneath you. Allow your current chief minion to recite a suitably embellished version of your conquests and accomplishments, decapitate the previous lord, and take possession.

—From *The Dark Traditions*

"To explain in full, I must go back some sixteen years, to the time when Xavriel, the last Dark Lord of Zaradwin Castle, was at the height of his power." As he spoke, Waylan's voice took on a formal cadence, as if he was performing a ritual he'd rehearsed in his head for years. "The lands around Zaradwin Castle, for a thousand miles in each direction, pledged their allegiance to Lord Xavriel, and the Light Lords cowered at his name."

"They did not!" Archie said indignantly.

"Yet the Dark Lord had no heir of his body to follow in his footsteps," Waylan continued as if Archie had not spoken, "nor was either of his sisters a satisfactory choice, for one carried the taint of Light magic, and though the other was Dark, her power was weak and she was easily led."

"The Dark Lord had sisters?" Delmar broke in.

"I have aunts?" Kayla said at the same time. It had never occurred to her that a Dark Lord might have family. Well, logically there had to have been parents around at some point, but if she had considered it at all, she'd have guessed that anyone who had a future Dark Lord as a kid would never have had any more. Maybe her biological father hadn't been horrible when he was young, she thought hopefully.

Again, Waylan went on as if he had not heard a thing. "So the Dark Lord sought out a woman to give him the heir he desired. He found her in the widow of a minor sorcerer whose infant daughter had shown the marks of magic. He promised her protection and the honor of sharing his throne. They were married, and fourteen years ago, the Dark Lord's lady bore him a daughter and heir."

The row of masked minions all nodded again, even the first commander. They all seemed perfectly willing to listen to Waylan's tale for as long as he wanted to tell it, though nothing he'd said so far could possibly have been news to any of them. Kayla shifted and rubbed her temples, wishing he could just get on with it so they could go inside, where it would be warmer and she could get some of Riki's heal-all.

"At her birth, the stones of Zaradwin Castle danced in glee, for she was strong in power, with the potential to one day surpass the Dark Lord himself, and she was marked for Dark magic."

Kayla shivered. "Marked for Dark magic" sounded creepy and

unpleasant, like something that would end with being burned at the stake. On the other hand, being strong would be nice, if she could use her magic for what *she* wanted.

Beside her, Riki shifted. Kayla shot her a glance and saw that she was frowning. Archie looked uncomfortable; maybe it reminded him of his own story.

Waylan, oblivious, went on. "The Dark Lord named his daughter Xavrielina, and all—"

"I still think Xavrielina is a dumb name," Del said a little too loudly. All the masks turned in his direction.

"Hush," Kayla and Riki said at the same time, though Kayla couldn't help agreeing with him. After a moment, the masks turned back toward Waylan, and he continued.

"All the empire rejoiced at the birth of the Dark Lord's daughter, but beyond the empire's borders, the realms of Light were shaken by the prospect of a new Dark dynasty. They put their differences aside and formed an alliance—"

"The Great Concordat is over a thousand years old, and nothing *shakes* it," Archie grumbled, but softly.

"—and marched against Lord Xavriel. The Dark Lord therefore left his castle and his daughter and his wife to battle the invaders. While he was away, treachery struck.

"The Dark Lord's sisters were jealous of the infant's power and position. They could not murder the child because of the protections the Dark Lord had placed upon his daughter, so they found another way. They performed a ritual to cast the child out of this world entirely, to a place and time unknown, where even if the child survived, she would grow up without knowledge of her power and her birthright."

Why didn't my mother stop them? Kayla wondered. *Or did she try and fail? There were two of them, and only one of her.*

"When the Dark Lord returned and discovered what his sisters had done, he bent all his power to discover a way to find and return his daughter to Zaradwin. After much work, he created a stone, charged with his own Darkness and with great power, that would take its bearer through the veil between worlds, drawing him closer and closer to his daughter and heir and identifying her beyond doubt once she was found.

"But the creation of the talisman had taken three years, during which he had paid scant attention to his empire. The Legions of Light had made great inroads, even to the gates of Zaradwin Castle itself. On the slopes of the mountain, the Final Battle was fought, and the Dark Lord fell, as Dark Lords have always done. With his last breath, Lord Xavriel gave me his talisman and charged me to find his daughter, to bring her home to take her place as the Dark Lady and restore the Dark Empire to glory.

"For ten years, I have traveled from world to world, searching for my lady Xavrielina, daughter and heir to the Dark Lord Xavriel. I have found her, and today I have brought her home."

There was a moment of silence; then the line of minions shifted and murmured. First Commander Jezzazar raised a black-gloved fist, and they fell silent. "'Tis a pretty tale, well told and worthy of the Dark Lord's daughter. Now comes—"

The loud screech of metal grinding on metal interrupted

Jezzazar. Everyone's head snapped toward the central tower. The door at the top of the stairs clanged open. Silence fell. A moment later, a tall, thin woman in a gray sack of a dress emerged and stepped to the railing to overlook the courtyard. Her face was deeply lined. Her hair, a faded black liberally streaked with gray, covered her shoulders in a wild frizz.

"There have always been Dark Lords at Zaradwin Castle," she proclaimed in a rough alto voice. Her eyes met Kayla's, and she bowed her head slightly and added in an apologetic tone, "Or Dark Ladies."

"Yazmina," the first commander said with a sigh.

"Jezzazar," the woman replied. She descended the wooden stairs, pausing near the bottom, where she was closer to the crowd but still high enough to see over all of them. "What means this grand commotion?"

"Naught to do with you," Jezzazar retorted. "Go back to your needlework, woman, and leave this business to those whose duty is to tend to it."

Kayla winced as Jezzazar's voice boomed out of the mask. Her headache had blossomed fully, and every word made her head throb.

"The Heiress of Zaradwin is everyone's business." Yazmina's eyes flicked back to Kayla. "Child, we have done you wrong. Great wrong, and we have paid for it, but not to you. Alas, that you have returned to this cursed castle! Yet even when I helped to perform the ritual, I knew this day would come, as a reckoning must always come to those who would spite the Dark Lord. It is"—she shot a look at Jezzazar at last—"Tradition."

"Then let it come, as Tradition requires," Jezzazar said. "'Twill end in death and destruction, either way."

"Get on with it," muttered someone from among the minions.

Jezzazar shot the group a dark look, but with their faces hidden behind their masks, it was impossible to tell who had spoken. He turned back toward Waylan. "As guide, guardian, and defender, you have brought the candidate here, to Zaradwin. Bring her forward, and let all see and judge whether she is worthy to aspire to the throne of Zaradwin."

Worthy? Kayla didn't like the sound of that. Riki put her hand on Kayla's shoulder and leaned forward to whisper at Waylan, "Is this a good idea?"

"It must be done, and best done quickly," Waylan replied, and gestured Kayla forward. She took a step, then another, feeling all too conscious of her grubby T-shirt and shorts. She stopped well out of reach of the first commander and his masked subordinates.

"*That's* the new Dark Lady?" someone muttered from the center of the Dark Horde. Kayla didn't think it sounded like the same person who'd spoken earlier.

"She ain't the Dark Lady yet," another voice snarled.

"At least she's got a familiar," a third commented in a doubtful tone.

"Silence!" Jezzazar commanded. He turned back to Kayla. "Now we shall see." He drew his sword and held it in front of his nose, pointing upward so that one eye showed on either side of the blade. It looked even creepier than his mask.

No one moved; the faint hiss of the wind was the only sound. Kayla's skin prickled. The silence stretched ominously on, and she wondered uneasily what would come next. Finally, from behind her, she heard Del ask the question she was thinking: "What are we waiting for?"

As if that had been the signal, the Dark Horde drew their swords and surged forward. Kayla took one step back, and then the pressure that had been building inside her head since their arrival at the castle exploded outward. Her vision went white. On her shoulder, Macavinchy hissed like an angry cat, and his tail tightened painfully around her neck. Kayla backed up another step and blinked, trying to clear her eyes. Slowly, the courtyard came back into view.

The front of the courtyard, where she and her family stood, was empty except for themselves and Waylan. All ten of the minions were stuck to the far wall on either side of the central tower, with their boots dangling two feet above the ground. Their weapons lay in a twisted, half-melted tangle against the ruined gate on Kayla's left. Yazmina hadn't been thrown anywhere—she still stood motionless near the bottom of the castle stairs—but her eyes were a little wild, and her hair stood out around her head like a giant gray-black dandelion puff.

Jezzazar's four-horned helmet lay rocking on the flagstones at Kayla's feet; his bright orange skull mask lay in two pieces next to it. Jezzazar himself was stuck to the wooden wall on Kayla's right, just above the door through which he had entered the courtyard. His salt-and-pepper hair and beard were attempting the same dandelion-puff effect as Yazmina's, but they were too short and only managed to look fuzzy. When he saw Kayla looking at him, his mouth moved as if he was trying to speak, but no sound came out.

Waylan had drawn his sword, and he stood in front of Del and Riki, poised as if to defend them. He looked stunned, but at least his hair was behaving normally. On Kayla's right, Riki was hugging Del, who squirmed in her hold. Neither of them seemed hurt. Archie half knelt a little to one side, staring up at Kayla with his mouth hanging open. Kayla shook herself and started toward them. Riki looked up from fussing over Del and asked, "Kayla, are you all right?"

"I'm fine." Kayla did her best to sound convincing, but Riki's expression told her she hadn't succeeded. "What *was* that?" Kayla asked, hoping to distract her.

"That was your magic manifesting." Macavinchy's matter-of-fact voice in her ear made Kayla jump.

"My *what*?" Kayla half shrieked.

"Your magic," Macavinchy repeated. "Second Commander Waylan covered it quite clearly. Even allowing for the exaggeration common during a storyteller's performance, it should be plain that the Dark Lord's daughter—that would be you—has enormous magical potential."

"Am I going to blow things up every time I have a headache?"

"You did not, in fact, blow anything up, madam. Furthermore, it is highly unlikely that every headache you will ever have will be caused by the pressure of unused magic, as this one was. Finally, the involuntary release of built-up magic rarely manifests in the same way twice. So, no, you will not blow things up every time you have a headache."

Which isn't the same as saying nothing weird will ever happen, Kayla thought. She considered what Macavinchy had said and started to smile. If not using her magic had caused the headache, then using magic for . . . whatever . . . should keep it from happening again. That was another reason to start learning spells as soon as she could.

"You still have a headache?" Riki started digging through her tote without waiting for an answer.

"Not anymore," Kayla told her.

Waylan shook himself and sheathed his sword. "My lady," he said apologetically, "I think you should release your spell now."

"Are you sure it's safe?" Riki asked. "I think we should leave."

"Sounds like a good idea to me." Archie nodded, eyeing the stuck minions warily.

"Leaving now would be far more dangerous than staying," Waylan said. "The guard should follow my lady's orders now."

Kayla took another look around. Jezzazar had stopped trying to talk or kick the wall, but Kayla still wasn't sure she wanted to let him down anytime soon. The minions weren't doing anything that she could see, but they outnumbered her side by two to one. If she let them down and they decided to attack, Waylan would be overwhelmed in seconds. The only backup weapon the rest of them had was Riki's tote bag, which wasn't much. And besides, how was she supposed to reverse something she hadn't known she was doing in the first place? "They *should* follow orders, but will they?" she asked Waylan.

Waylan frowned uncertainly but did not answer. Riki looked from the gate to the dangling minions with an equally doubtful expression.

"Great," Kayla said crossly. "Doesn't anyone have any suggestions?"

Macavinchy shifted, then spread his wings behind Kayla's head and said, "Madam, you are the daughter and heir of the last Dark Lord. Make formal claim of your birthright."

Kayla turned her head. "Claim my birthright? What does that do for us, and how do I do it?"

"A formal claim, duly recognized, will endow you with the position of Provisional Dark Lady of Zaradwin, with all the rights and privileges that entails." Macavinchy's tail swished.

"Rights and privileges?" It sounded pretty good, but . . . "Why *Provisional* Dark Lady?"

"As the Dark Lord's daughter, you inherit his position," Waylan declared. "It is your right and your responsibility."

Macavinchy coughed. "The previous Dark Lord has been dead for ten years, madam. Technically, there are three steps required to replace him under such circumstances. First, the candidate must be presented; second, the candidate must make a formal claim; third, the candidate must be recognized as the new Dark Ruler at an official ceremony of investiture, during which the candidate is installed as the new ruler. Alternatively, you could kill everyone in the castle, at which point it would be yours by default."

"No killing," Riki said.

"Right. That leaves the formal claim." Kayla took a deep breath. "How do I do this, Macavinchy?"

"Say 'Here in the citadel of the Dark, I, Kayla Jones, formerly known as Xavrielina, lay claim to the position of Dark Lady of Zaradwin, which was bequeathed to me by my father, the Dark Lord Xavriel, in accordance with Tradition and by virtue of my own power here demonstrated this day.' "

"Kayla, I don't think—" Riki started.

"Well, nobody else has any ideas!" Kayla said, exasperated. "And maybe it will keep people from calling me that dumb name. Say it again, Macavinchy."

Macavinchy repeated the sentence, pausing every few words to let Kayla echo them. As she finished the last phrase, the mountain rumbled. The courtyard hushed, and Kayla felt a tingle run up and down her spine. She realized that for the first time since their arrival in Zaradwin, she was comfortably warm. *Even if nothing else happens, that's a win,* she thought. "See?" she said after a long moment. "That wasn't so—"

Before she could finish the sentence, the courtyard shook violently. Kayla stumbled, trying to keep her feet, and Macavinchy flapped his wings to hold his balance. The flagstones moved and shifted underfoot, sliding back into place and flattening out. Just in front of her toes, a crack as wide as her little finger filled itself in as she watched, seamlessly joining two jagged pieces into a smooth, perfect stone rectangle.

Loud crashing noises replaced the shaking. Kayla heard shouts and looked up. The minions who had been stuck to the far wall had dropped in unceremonious heaps. They were surrounded by chunks of tan rock, and she realized that the mottled sandstone patches in the wall had fallen out and broken. The empty pits they had left behind were growing new stone of the same sparkling darkness as the rest of the wall.

Eyes wide, Kayla turned to look at the half-ruined castle gate. There, too, the pitted stone was smoothing out, though the left-hand tower showed no sign of regrowing its missing floors, and neither the rickety bridge nor the makeshift portcullis had changed at all. *Magic can't do everything,* Kayla thought, and found the thought oddly reassuring. Perhaps she could fit here, if they didn't expect her to fix everything with the Dark magic she didn't know how to use.

After what seemed a long while, the grinding noises stopped. Kayla looked around cautiously. The minions didn't seem inclined to move. Yazmina hadn't moved, either, except to clutch the wooden stair rail so hard that her knuckles were white, but her hair had collapsed to hang limply around her face. Jezzazar was still stuck to the wall, staring at Kayla as if his world had just turned upside down.

She waited another few seconds, then said, "Macavinchy, is that all I have to do?"

"Yes, madam," Macavinchy replied, folding his wings neatly along his back. "You are now indisputably the Provisional Dark Lady of Zaradwin."

"Indisputably, huh." Kayla eyed her mother, who was clutching Del and looking almost as wild as Jezzazar.

Waylan and Archie nodded like puppets on the same string. Del pulled away from Riki and said, "My sister is a Dark Lady? Awesome! Can I be your head evil lieutenant?"

"I don't think Mom will go for that," Kayla said as Riki frowned. "You can be on my council, if you want."

"We are going to have a talk about this later," Riki said in her you-are-in-big-trouble voice.

Beside her, Waylan shook himself and dropped to one knee. "My lady."

"Yes, fine." Kayla looked at the minions huddled at the foot of the far wall. "Does that go for all of you as well?"

The heaps of minions rippled as they knocked one another over in an attempt to find a spot to kneel. "My lady," they said in a ragged chorus. Kayla thought the one on the end was a little slower than the others, but he'd been on the bottom of a heap and probably didn't have his breath back yet.

"My lady," Yazmina echoed from the stairs, and bobbed a curtsy.

Kayla looked over at Jezzazar. "What about him?" she asked Macavinchy. "Is he safe?"

"Not in a general sense," Macavinchy replied. "But you have formally claimed your birthright in front of three witnesses, one friendly, one hostile, and one familial. He cannot dispute your authority unless he wishes to rebel."

One friendly . . . That must be Waylan, Kayla thought. *Or maybe Archie. Jezzazar has to be the hostile one. Does the magic count Mom and Del as family? Or maybe that's Yazmina—didn't Waylan say she's my aunt?* She tucked that idea away to examine later and said, "Okay. How do I—"

Abruptly, Jezzazar came unstuck from the wall. He landed heavily and went to his knees. "My lady," he croaked.

Now what? She looked down at Waylan, then around at all the other kneeling men. "You can get up now. And . . . and go back to work, I guess."

The men didn't move. Jezzazar looked up with a puzzled expression. "My lady?"

"You all have jobs to do, don't you?" Kayla frowned at the courtyard. The magical repairs had left the walls shining and the courtyard paving smoothed out, but it still looked as if nobody had taken any of the trash out for a long, long time. "What *do* you do, anyway?"

"I think that can wait until—" Riki started, but Jezzazar was already barking orders. The men scrambled to their feet and stood stiffly at attention, facing Kayla.

Jezzazar took up a position at one end of the line and made a little half bow. "Our work is rebuilding the glorious Dark Empire, for whose—"

The guard standing next to Jezzazar coughed and leaned sideways. Kayla could tell he was saying something, but his mask muffled his voice, so she couldn't tell what. Jezzazar obviously understood, for he broke off, listened for a moment, then cleared his throat. "There are some few decisions that must be made before we can set to work to rebuild the Dark Empire."

"Like what?" Kayla said.

Jezzazar gestured. A guard near the far end of the line took one step forward, bowed, and said in a nervous voice, "My lady, I am Salanor, keeper of the beasthall. Due to the long interregnum between the previous Dark Lord's death and the rising of our new and glorious Dark Lady, the beasthall is all but empty. What sort of creatures does my lady wish us to capture and train? The sooner we know, the sooner we can begin accumulating them."

"I'll have to think about it," Kayla said. Not that she had any idea what beasts were available, how hard they would be to capture, or what they would be good for. Macavinchy could tell her that much, she supposed, but . . . "Make me a list of what we have and what you recommend we get," she told Salanor. "And why."

"Your will is my command." The keeper of the beasthall bowed again and stepped back into line.

The man next to him moved forward, bowed, and said, "I am Captain Udorex of the Elite Guards, charged with anticipating threats to our glorious Dark Lady. How does my lady wish us to proceed regarding seers and oracles?"

"I'm not sure what you mean," Kayla said.

"There are forty-seven known seers, oracles, and sibyls in the Dark kingdoms," the man replied. "If we move quickly, we can kill almost all of them before they learn of your ascension to the throne of Zaradwin. This would prevent the delivery of any prophecy that would be detrimental to your glorious rule. Alternatively, we can kidnap and imprison some or all of them, so that you will have advance warning of any such prophecies and can act to circumvent them."

Kayla stared at him. "Kill them?"

"Very good, my lady," the man said, bowing. "I will send out the assassination teams as soon as—"

"No!" Kayla said. "I don't want anybody assassinated!"

"Yes, of course, my lady." The man hesitated, then said tentatively, "Kidnapping them will take longer, and there are more variables—"

"No kidnapping, either!" Kayla saw his shoulders slump and added hastily, "I need to think about this before we decide anything for sure. Can't you just keep tabs on them for a while?"

"I . . . If that is your wish, my lady." He squared his shoulders. "It is my sorrowful duty to tell you that we do not currently have the resources to monitor all forty-seven."

The tension in the courtyard increased noticeably. Kayla licked her lips, wondering what they expected her to do or say. Before she thought of anything, Jezzazar scowled fiercely at the guard and said, "Inform me of your requirements, and I will consult with the castle steward and the second commander. The treasury is seriously depleted and must be replenished in any case; if we know your needs, we can choose our targets more wisely."

"Targets?" Kayla said.

"The towns we will raid to refill the treasury," Jezzazar said. "Unfortunately, the Traditional objectives nearest Zaradwin are too strong for us to attack at present. We will have to look at more distant places. We should start at once; the farther afield we go, the less plunder we can bring back without risking a counterattack on the road."

Kayla's eyes widened as she absorbed just what Jezzazar was proposing. "You want to start a war in order to get money?"

"Of course not!" Jezzazar sounded insulted, and for an instant Kayla was reassured, until he added, "A few raids will not provoke a war, especially if we choose places farther away."

Everyone nodded, and another man spoke up. "The Dark

Lady has much to do in secret before we announce her ascension. Forgive my presumption, my lady, but have you yet begun the ritual to remove your heart, so that it may be safely hidden in some remote place?"

"Remove her heart?" Riki said faintly.

"It's a thing the villains do in books and comics and movies," said Del, of all people. "They take their heart out and hide it in a dragon's egg in a cave at the bottom of the ocean, guarded by sea monsters. Or they tear off a piece of their soul and stick it in some jewelry that they leave in an eagle's nest at the top of an unclimbable mountain, on the far side of an impassable desert at the other end of the world. Like that. It's supposed to keep them from dying."

"Just so," Jezzazar murmured, sounding as if he was impressed in spite of himself.

"It never works," Del went on. "The hero always finds it, and the villain dies anyway."

There was a horrified gasp from someone in the middle of the line, and everyone stiffened. The guard who had asked the question tried to hide behind one of his neighbors without actually moving.

"We'll leave that for later, then," Kayla said. "What's next?"

There was a pause, and the tension in the courtyard increased. Suddenly, one of the guards bent forward and dropped to his knees. "I can't take it!" he cried. "Who are you going to execute? The waiting is driving me mad! Go ahead, kill somebody and get it over with! Kill me!"

Jezzazar's face set in grim lines as the rest of the guards went completely still. Rising, he drew his sword and started toward his quivering subordinate. "You're a disgrace to the Dark Hordes," he said in a low, fierce voice, "and you'll pay the price."

As he raised his blade, Kayla shouted, "Stop!"

CHAPTER 7

Settling In to Your New Base

Your first days in your new castle are critical. Do not waste them on unimportant details; begin as you mean to go on. Be especially quick to determine the penalties you need to inflict on your new subjects. You do not wish to give the impression that you are indecisive.

—From *The Dark Traditions*

Jezzazar froze. The only sounds were the faint whimpers of the terrified man kneeling on the smooth flagstones of the courtyard. The silence thickened. Kayla felt as if she were listening from far away, or from underwater. She took a deep breath. "Nobody gets executed or—or punished—unless I say so."

Slowly, Jezzazar lowered his sword and turned to face Kayla. His eyes burned as he stared at her. "So 'tis my doom that you have intended all along," he said heavily. "I suspected it from the moment you arrived. First you undermine my authority; soon will come removing my responsibilities. Then you will take my position, and finally my life. 'Tis the final fate all servants of the Dark Lord come to in the end, choose as they may."

"Will you quit jumping to conclusions!" Kayla burst out. She took a deep breath, and then another. She felt pulled in several different directions at once, and she didn't like any of them. "I don't know yet what I'm going to do, so back off!"

The row of guards relaxed visibly; apparently losing her temper was sufficiently Dark Lady–ish to reassure them. Jezzazar bowed. "Forgive my intemperate words, my lady."

"Maybe later," Kayla told him.

"Kayla!" Riki said.

"What? He's been in charge for ten years, and look at the place." Kayla waved at the walls and gates. "It's still half-wrecked. And their whole army is, what, fifteen guys?"

"The survivors of the Final Battle scatter, but for a faithful few," Jezzazar said. "'Tis Tradition."

"Really?" Even to herself, Kayla sounded skeptical. "It's been ten years, and you haven't recruited anyone else? I'm surprised nobody else has waltzed in and taken over."

Waylan cleared his throat. "Recruits come and go until a new Dark Lord or Lady rises. They come hoping their devotion will reap rewards from a new lord, but if none appears, they move on."

"Entry-level positions," Riki murmured.

"So where are all the new Dark Lords?" Kayla asked.

"There were many attempts, in the years after the Final Battle," Jezzazar said. "None could master the castle, as you have done. Now only one or two make the attempt each year."

"Oh." Kayla thought for a minute. "How long until the next one shows up?"

Beside her, Riki froze. Jezzazar shrugged. "A few days, a few weeks, a few months. They do not come on a schedule, and when your presence becomes known it will discourage many."

"That's good." *I think.* Kayla shifted her backpack restlessly, feeling overwhelmed.

"Er, my lady, what are we supposed to do?" asked a voice from the group of masked minions.

"Clean up this mess and start fixing the defenses," Kayla shot back, waving at the broken portcullis and trash-covered courtyard. If Dark Lord wannabes were going to come and try to take her castle, her side needed to be prepared. "Oh, and lose the masks."

"Lose them?"

"Get rid of them," Kayla snapped. "I want to see who I'm talking to."

For a moment, no one moved. "What are you waiting for?" Waylan barked. He looked pointedly at the minions, who pulled off their helmets with obvious reluctance. Without them, they all looked young, bewildered, and too thin.

"Pile those helms in the corner for now," Waylan commanded. "Tomorrow, we'll see about getting something more to the Dark Lady's liking."

Something about the way Waylan said "the Dark Lady" made Kayla shiver. She took a deep breath . . . and almost jumped out of her skin at a touch on her shoulder. "Easy," her mother said, pulling her in for a hug. Kayla relaxed and leaned in with a grateful sigh. The familiar warmth felt reassuring, though part of her knew that this wasn't a situation that Riki could fix. The thought wasn't new; she'd stopped believing that her mother could fix anything and everything about halfway through her father's chemo-therapy.

"If you all are quite finished, I have two tired and hungry children here who need food and a place to sit down," Riki said over the top of Kayla's head.

Kayla pulled away, mildly indignant at being referred to as a child. "Don't forget Waylan and Archie."

"With your permission, I shall see to ordering these men for now," Waylan said, nodding at the minions. "Tomorrow will be soon enough to make more permanent arrangements." He looked pointedly at Jezzazar, who responded with a sullen nod.

Archie looked uncertainly from Waylan to Jezzazar and back to Kayla. "And I'll stick with you," he told her. "If that's all right."

"It's fine with me," Kayla told him. From the corner of her eye, she saw Yazmina descend the last few stairs and move toward them. Kayla turned to face her.

"Ah, child, I see that you are not the only one I have wronged," Yazmina said as she reached them. "Yet I will do what I can to make amends. Come." She turned and started up the stairs, then paused to look over her shoulder.

Kayla and Riki exchanged glances. "Does 'amends' mean we get something to eat?" Del asked loudly.

"Yes," Yazmina said.

Del went straight for the stairs, and after a moment, Kayla, Riki, and Archie followed.

The door at the top of the stairs let them into a narrow hall. The stone walls were smooth and cool; the only light came from thin, cross-shaped windows at intervals around the curving outer wall. *Arrow loops,* Kayla thought, and couldn't help wondering why a castle built and defended by magicians needed places for archers to shoot from. Maybe it was just the style when the castle was built.

Halfway around the tower, Yazmina stopped before a low wooden door, crisscrossed with iron bands. She pulled on a large iron ring, and the door swung open. "Welcome to my lady Xavrielina, Dark Lady of Zaradwin Castle!" she said in a much louder and firmer voice than she had used so far.

"My name is Kayla," Kayla said automatically as she stepped through into an enormous circular room. The walls and floor were smooth black marble veined with silver. On one side stood an enormous hearth, twice as tall as Kayla and at least three times as wide as it was tall. Directly opposite the hearth was a curved platform three steps higher than anything else, and in the center of the platform sat a black marble throne inlaid with gleaming silver.

There the elegance ended. Rough-hewn wooden tables and benches radiated out from the platform like spokes on a bicycle wheel. The air was thick and chilly, and smelled of smoke and something rotten. Crumbs and dust balls littered the floor; the walkways between the tables were gray with muddy footprints. The tabletops were crusted and stained by unidentifiable past spills. It looked a bit like the middle school cafeteria after a food fight.

"What on earth is this?" Riki said in a tone that managed to sound stunned and deeply disapproving at the same time.

Archie looked equally taken aback. "It's— What did you call it outside, Del? A bit?"

"A pit," Del said with extra emphasis. "It's worse than the building where our last apartment was."

"It's the great hall of Zaradwin Castle, dear," said a reproving voice from the far side of the throne.

A woman came out of the narrow gap behind the throne, wiping her hands on a faded blue apron. She looked as if she was in her mid-fifties. She seemed a little shorter than Yazmina, but that might have been because she was the first person Kayla had seen besides Waylan who looked reasonably well fed. Her dark hair had a streak of pure white at each temple, like the bride of Frankenstein, and was tied back in a neat bun; the black smock she wore was perfectly clean and fit her properly. Her black eyes were bright and wide above a generous mouth. They held a slightly puzzled look as they darted from Kayla to Delmar and Archie before fixing on Riki with a faint frown. "Welcome to your castle, my . . . lady Xavrielina?"

"Detsini," Yazmina said in a reproving tone. She gestured at Kayla. "This is Xavriel's daughter, the Dark Lady Xav—"

"My name is Kayla," Kayla cut in firmly. "This is my mother, Riki, my brother, Del, and . . ." She hesitated, unsure exactly what to call Archie.

"Dark Lord in Training Zarnak," Archie said with a bow. Then he looked at Del.

"Better," Del told him. "It's still not really you, though."

"I . . . see." Detsini's forehead creased and she pressed her lips together briefly as she studied Del and Archie. Then she shook herself and turned to Kayla with a broad smile. "How lovely for you, dear. I'm your aunt Detsini. I'm in disgrace at the moment, since it was my idea to send you off to . . . wherever you ended up. It is a pity that it didn't work out, but it was for your own good."

Yazmina made a noise like water hitting an overheated frying pan. "Vile traitor! I should never have listened to you. It is a wonder Xavriel didn't kill us both. You, at least, should have been whipped and exiled." Then, turning to Kayla, she continued. "Oh, child, I hope that one day, as you attain your full power, you can find it in your heart to forgive me. There have always been Dark Lords at Zaradwin Castle."

Detsini's smile thinned. "Now, Yazmina, don't get yourself all worked up; there's a dear. I'm sure Kayla—"

"The Dark Lady," Yazmina corrected her sister firmly.

"—will have much more important things to worry about," Detsini finished, looking a little put out by the interruption. "Especially once she claims her inheritance."

"The Dark Lady has already claimed her rights, poor child," Yazmina told her. "Did you not feel the stones of the castle dance in welcome and acknowledgment?"

Detsini's eyes widened and her eyebrows snapped together for an instant; then her expression smoothed out and she gave Kayla a sad smile. "Poor dear. I did try to protect you from all this."

Kayla was rapidly coming to the conclusion that she didn't like either of these women much. Yazmina was just strange; Detsini's condescending attitude was seriously annoying. "You're my aunts, the ones who sent me away when I was a baby?" she asked, to make sure she'd understood correctly. Detsini and Yazmina nodded. "Then can you do it again? For all three of us?"

"Alas, no," Yazmina said. "We have not the power, and in any case, the spell can be used only once."

Kayla let out a breath she hadn't realized she was holding.

"I'm afraid that's true, dear," Detsini said in a regretful tone, though she gave Yazmina an annoyed look, as if she hadn't wanted to make that particular admission. "But perhaps we can think of something else if we all put our heads together."

"Can you teach Kayla the spell?" Riki's voice was polite, but it was the kind of polite she used on people she didn't like or trust completely.

"We'll see," Detsini said. "Now, what brings you to the great hall?"

"We're hungry!" Del complained. "Can we get some dinner?"

"Of course, of course. Have a seat; it won't be a minute. Oh, not there, Kayla dear," Detsini added as Kayla started for the nearest table that looked moderately clean. "Up on the dais, that's where the Dark Lord eats. Or the Dark Lady, naturally." She nodded at the raised platform.

Why is it that the only person here who remembers my name is the one I like the least? Kayla thought. "Not tonight," she told Detsini. "It'll take too long to set up a place for all of us. We'll use one of these tables for now, I guess." She wrinkled her nose at the sticky, stained surface.

Del wasn't so tactful. "This is gross!" he announced.

"Do forgive us." Detsini did not sound at all apologetic. "It has been ten years since we have had a Dark Lord in the castle, you see."

"No, I don't see," Riki said. "What does having a Dark Lord have to do with mopping the floor and keeping the tables wiped off? Or picking up the trash?"

"Or with repairing the walls?" Kayla put in. Though her magical outburst *had* fixed the patchy holes in the courtyard walls, so maybe she could take care of the rest of the damage herself later. Castles were supposed to be defensible, after all. She shook her head. "Never mind; just get us something to eat."

"With *clean* plates and tableware," Riki added. Detsini shot her a sour look and turned to retrace her steps across the hall. Yazmina followed her, leaving Kayla, her mother, Del, and Archie alone.

Riki blew out a long sigh as she collapsed onto a bench. "Macavinchy, are you sure this is the best option we have?"

Macavinchy flicked his wings and didn't answer. Kayla sighed in turn. "Macavinchy, could you please just answer Mom's questions without making me repeat them all the time?"

"Your mother is not an authorized user," Macavinchy said. "I believe I mentioned that earlier, madam."

"How do I authorize her?"

"Tell me that she is authorized for information access and then provide your password."

"That's— Never mind. Authorize Mom for information access, Macavinchy." Kayla hesitated, then turned her head to whisper her tablet password in Macavinchy's ear. Macavinchy purred briefly, then said, "Done."

"Is this really our best option?" Riki asked immediately.

"Yes, madam," Macavinchy replied.

"Why?" Riki demanded, sounding frustrated.

"As the daughter of the previous Dark Lord, Kayla will be a target, no matter where she is," Macavinchy replied. "Every would-be new Dark Lord will want to remove a potential rival, and the Light archmage will do everything in his power to prevent the rise of the Dark Lady."

"Hey!" Archie objected. "I'm a would-be Dark Lord, and I haven't done anything terrible to her!"

"Not yet," Macavinchy said. "And if I may be so bold as to comment, sir, I must say that your heart does not appear to be fully committed to becoming a Dark Lord of any style, much less the Dark Lord of Zaradwin."

"I—" Archie started off somewhere between offended and indignant, but then his shoulders sagged. "I suppose you're right. I was raised to be a Light magician, not a Dark Lord."

"You are a credit to your upbringing, sir," Macavinchy reassured him.

"And you'll make a great evil lieutenant," Del told Archie encouragingly. "I'll give you advice, since Kayla and Mom won't let me be one."

"We're getting off track," Riki said. "Macavinchy was explaining why we're better off in this . . . dump of a castle."

"The drawbacks to which you object are largely cosmetic, and can be set right with a little effort," Macavinchy went on. "As the Dark Lady of Zaradwin, Kayla has access to resources that would be difficult and time-consuming to collect under other circumstances."

"What resources?" Riki said skeptically.

"It's a *castle,*" Del said.

"Supplies, retainers, and both physical and magical protection," Macavinchy replied as if Del hadn't spoken. "Zaradwin's magic has a formidable reputation. There is also the matter of the castle's unique assets."

"Like what?" Kayla asked.

"This place was the previous Dark Lord's seat of power," Macavinchy replied. "The talisman that Second Commander Waylan used to travel between worlds was undoubtedly created here, and it is likely that the Dark Lord left notes for his successor. It was therefore desirable to establish your ownership and control of the castle as soon as possible. Finally, as the Traditional seat of the premier Dark Lords and Ladies, this castle has the best libraries and training facilities available, which will greatly assist you in mastering your inherent power."

"You're sure that there's someone here who can teach her?" Riki asked doubtfully.

"Those aunts said they could," Kayla pointed out, but she sounded just as doubtful as Riki, even to herself.

"I confess that I share your skepticism regarding the ladies of the castle, madam. However, this remains the most likely place to find a capable tutor. If one is not currently in residence, they will be drawn here as news of the Dark Lady's arrival spreads."

Riki gave a noncommittal "Hmm." She looked torn. Usually, that meant the answer was going to be no, but Kayla realized that for once, it couldn't be. If Riki wanted to get them all home, she *had* to let Kayla learn magic, whether she liked the idea or not. No wonder she looked grouchy.

A door creaked open on the far side of the room. "Here we go, dears," Detsini said. She appeared from behind the throne, holding a black iron pot with the handle of a ladle sticking up at one side. Yazmina followed, carrying a wooden tray with four plain wooden mugs, a stack of spoons, a pitcher, and a tall, round loaf of brown bread. Behind them, two men in the dark robes worn by the castle guards brought a couple of sawhorses and a flat wooden panel about the size and shape of a door.

Detsini looked at Kayla and her family, then at the marble throne, and shook her head. "Set up over there," she commanded the guards, gesturing at a nearby stretch of empty floor space.

The first guard set the sawhorses down a few feet apart. The second put the wooden panel on top to make a new table that was only slightly dusty. They retreated a few steps and stood at attention. Detsini set the pot at the far end with an air of triumph. Yazmina set her tray beside it and poured something dark from the pitcher into each of the wooden mugs. She handed each of them a mug and a wooden spoon.

Meanwhile, Detsini picked up the loaf of bread, and Kayla realized that it was not one loaf, but four separate loaves, each about three inches thick with a hollow in the center like a very shallow bread bowl. One by one, Detsini filled each loaf from the pot and set them in front of the travelers, along with a small wooden spoon each. "There you are," she said. "It's not what it should be, but Yazmina insisted that you wouldn't want to wait for anything to be cooked new."

"What is it?" Archie was eyeing the bread bowl suspiciously. The center was filled with a thin broth that was rapidly soaking into the bread. Here and there were limp, grayish blobs, some of which had probably once been vegetables, and a couple of stringy-looking bits of unidentifiable meat.

"It looks like the mystery goop the school cafeteria serves on Wednesdays," Del told him.

Detsini shot Yazmina a triumphant look. "It's the leftover stew from the men's dinner," she said. "*Totally* unsuitable, I know, but—" She stopped as Riki took a cautious bite.

"It's hot and it's edible," Riki said after chewing for a moment. "Barely. The bread's good. You don't have to finish it if you don't like it."

Immediately, Del dug in. Kayla followed Riki's example, nibbling around the broth-soaked edges of the bowl and occasionally taking a piece of overcooked vegetable. The broth was bland and the occasional shreds of meat were tough. "We need to show these people how to make pizza," she muttered.

"And hamburgers," Del said around a mouthful of stew.

"Macavinchy, how long will Kayla's training take?" Riki asked.

"That is impossible to say, madam," Macavinchy replied. "It will depend on how much time she can spend and how hard she works at it, as well as several outside factors that—"

Riki cut him off impatiently. "Yes, of course, but you can give me a range, can't you? Are we talking days or weeks or months?"

"I would prefer not to state an opinion of anything so hypothetical," Macavinchy said. Kayla turned her head to give him a sharp look, and he flicked his wings. "I do not anticipate a short stay," he admitted at last, sounding decidedly unhappy.

"Like that's unexpected," Kayla said. To her surprise, Riki only sighed and nodded. Apparently, she'd absorbed the idea that there was no quick way back, at least enough that she wasn't freaking out about it anymore. Kayla turned her head. "Do you want any of this, Macavinchy? Or is there something else we should get you to eat?"

"My power storage is very efficient, so my needs are small," the familiar replied. "I can eat whatever you do, madam."

"Help yourself, then," Kayla said.

"Thank you, madam." Macavinchy jumped lightly from her shoulder to the tabletop and broke off an edge of the bread bowl. Kayla looked up and found both Detsini and Yazmina staring open-mouthed. "What?"

"That is— What sort of familiar is that?" Detsini spluttered. "How could it have found you so soon?"

"How should I know what kind of familiar he is?" Kayla retorted. "Honestly, why do people keep asking me that?"

"Because they are not accustomed to familiars behaving as I do," Macavinchy said.

"I'm not used to tablets that behave the way you do," Riki muttered.

"Just so, madam," Macavinchy said while Detsini and Yazmina exchanged confused looks.

"Everybody finished?" Riki waited for Del's and Archie's nods, then turned to Yazmina. "Then please show us to our rooms. It's been a long day, and I expect tomorrow will be even longer."

Detsini answered before Yazmina could react. "I'll be happy to show Lady Kayla to the master suite while Yazmina takes the rest of you to the guest quarters. The familiar can be housed in the beasthall for now, and that—"

"His name is Macavinchy," Kayla said. "And he stays with me."

"So do the rest of us," Riki said. Del looked up from the soggy crumbs that were all that was left of his bread bowl and nodded. Archie looked less certain, but he clearly wasn't planning to object.

"It may be as well," Yazmina said. "None have been able to enter the Dark Lord's rooms since his death. Who knows why, or what may linger there?"

"If you can't get in, how can I spend the night there?" Kayla asked.

"You are Xavriel's daughter, and the Dark Lady," Detsini said. "I'm sure the doors will open for you."

"I don't think this is the time for experiments," Riki told her. "We'll stay in the guest quarters. All of us."

Detsini pressed her lips together in a disapproving line. Kayla looked from her to Riki and back, then folded her arms across her chest and nodded. "If you insist," Detsini said at last. "This way."

With Yazmina trailing after, they followed Detsini out a door on the far side of the hall. They wound through halls, up stairs, and finally outside across a covered wooden bridge that brought them to a shorter tower. *Sort of like the skyways downtown,* Kayla thought, except that the skyways in St. Paul weren't decorated with carvings of bones and skulls.

Detsini led them through another dusty entry room to a long hall lined with doors. Pausing in front of the nearest, she pulled out a large iron key and unlocked the door. "Your family can stay here, dear," she told Kayla.

"What about Archie?" Kayla said, not moving.

Detsini opened her eyes very wide, as if she was surprised by the question. "Why, he'll be in the dungeon, dear. Since he's a Dark Lord in Training." Her smile had a nasty edge to it.

"Dungeon?" Archie frowned. "I don't think— That is, I'd rather not—"

"Can we go see the dungeons tomorrow?" Del broke in eagerly.

"Not unless I've inspected them first," Riki said. "Real dungeons are . . . unpleasant."

"That's the point, isn't it?" Del was in full begging mode. "Seeing a real dungeon would be awesome!"

"Are you quite sure your . . . younger brother isn't the one who's a Dark Lord in Training, dear?" Detsini murmured.

"Archie isn't staying in the dungeon," Kayla said firmly. "If he's going to be my evil lieutenant, I need him close at hand. Are all of these guest rooms?"

"Yes, my lady," Yazmina answered. "Perhaps the room across the hall?"

Detsini frowned at her. "It's not really suitable for someone of such exalted station."

"Two minutes ago, you were going to put him in the dungeon!" Kayla snapped. "It has to be better than that!"

"That's true," Detsini said, as if she was reassuring herself. "And it's only for a few days, one way or another." She unlocked the opposite door and waved Archie inside, then turned back to open the first door. "The small suite will do for your family, but we haven't had much call for the guest rooms since the Dark Lord passed, you understand, and I'm afraid they've been a bit neglected. Which is why I'm sure the Dark Lady Kayla would be far happier in the master suite."

As she spoke, she ushered them inside. The first room was small, dark, and decidedly chilly. A wooden bench and a small trunk sat next to the door; an enormous wooden cabinet, rather like a wardrobe, took up most of the far wall. On either side of the cabinet, a short archway led to a different room. Through the left-hand arch, Kayla could see part of a heavily patterned curtain and the corner of a fireplace; on the right, she could see another bench, a narrow window, and the end of a curtained bed. Like the bridge, everything was carved or painted with skulls or bones, or both.

"Can we get some light in here?" Before Kayla had quite finished her sentence, there was a small popping noise overhead, and yellow light flooded the room. Kayla looked up. An iron wheel hung from the ceiling on a short chain; seven small iron lanterns dangled from the rim, casting a flickering yellow light through a veil of cobwebs. Each lantern was shaped like a skeletal hand, with a tiny skull at the top where it was hooked to the wheel.

"You see?" Detsini said to Kayla as Riki ducked through the left-hand archway. "The master suite is—"

"—not where I'm staying tonight," Kayla snapped, "so maybe you'd better figure out how to make these rooms comfortable. Or at least clean."

A loud sneeze came from the left-hand room. A moment later, Riki poked her head around the archway. "Is there any bedding in this place that isn't full of dust and moths?"

"I'm sure we can find something," Detsini said, but she sounded far from certain.

The door behind Kayla swung open. "Here, child—Dark Lady, that is," Yazmina said, holding out a tall stack of cloth. "You and yours will be needing this tonight. Alas, that your coming finds us so unprepared!"

"Thank you," Riki said, taking the stack. "I don't suppose any of these are dustcloths? And can you bring me a broom?"

"A broom?" Detsini, who had been glaring at Yazmina, looked suddenly cautious. "I'll see to it at once, lady."

"Who's supposed to clean these rooms, anyway?" Kayla asked.

"The maids," Macavinchy said, and Yazmina and Detsini both twitched.

"You have maids and the place still looks like this?" Riki sounded horrified.

"Oh, the maids left when Xavriel was killed," Detsini said. "It's Tradition. The castle hasn't had a proper staff for the past ten years."

"It's had you," Riki pointed out.

Detsini's expression changed from patronizing to insulted in an instant. But before she could argue, Kayla said, "Weren't you going to fetch a broom?"

It took another ten minutes to get Detsini and Yazmina out of the room; neither one appeared to want to leave the other alone with the new arrivals. When they finally departed, full of promises about brooms and hiring maids and several other things, the Jones family set about doing some preliminary tidying up. The rooms at the back were both bedrooms. Each contained a twin-sized curtained bed, a padded bench, and a thing like a waist-high nightstand that Riki decided was likely a washstand. This theory proved correct when Detsini and Yazmina returned, one carrying a broom and some rags, the other a large black porcelain pitcher and washbasin, which she set on the stand.

They sent the aunts off to help Archie, on the assumption that his room was in similar condition, then made use of the broom and rags to get one of the bedchambers into a more reasonable shape. The "wardrobe" in the outer room proved to be a water closet, which was at least clean and nonsmelly, though Riki muttered about sanitation and proper flush toilets for at least half an hour. When they finished, the dust-covered bed-curtains and tapestry from one bed were piled in a corner in the right-hand room, and the futonlike mattresses from the two beds were side by side on the thoroughly swept floor of the left-hand room. The bare bed was piled with the least-dusty blankets and bedding, while the clean linens that Yazmina had brought were split three ways, giving everyone a reasonably comfortable place to sleep.

By the time they finished, all three of them were exhausted.

Del didn't even argue about which of the "beds" was the most desirable; he just curled up on the nearest one and went to sleep. Kayla and Riki looked at him, then at each other, and by unspoken agreement left any discussion of their situation for the morning. The cobwebby lamps went out when Kayla lay down. The last thing she saw before she fell asleep was Macavinchy's dark, shadowy shape perched on the top of the water closet with his wings tucked back, facing the outer door like a gargoyle guarding a cathedral.

CHAPTER 8

Early Tasks for Minions

As a Dark Lord or Lady, you must always remember that your position is on the throne. Manual labor is for your minions and your servants; more difficult and unpleasant tasks are for your evil commanders and lieutenants.

—From *The Dark Traditions*

Kayla woke from a series of vaguely threatening dreams just as the first dawn light was leaking through the narrow window of the bedchamber. She was stiff and sore, though she wasn't sure whether the long hike to the castle or the makeshift bed was more to blame. Riki and Del were both still asleep, but as soon as she stirred, Macavinchy glided down from his perch to her side. She smiled at him, then carefully untangled herself from the blanket, picked up her boots, and crept into the outer room. If she'd been home, she'd have tried for more sleep, but now she felt too restless.

Zaradwin wasn't *home.* Kayla couldn't hear the swish of cars passing on the street outside, or the faint hum of the fan, or the indistinguishable gabble of the TV in the living room that

Riki never turned down quite far enough. The air here smelled different—dust and smoke and damp inside the castle, overwhelmingly clean and fresh in the courtyard. The castle interior was colder and darker than she was used to; even when they were lit, the fireplaces barely took the edge off the chill that radiated from the stone, and though they gave off both heat and light, they did neither evenly. She'd been too busy and overwhelmed for most of yesterday to notice, but now that she had, the unfamiliar surroundings made her twitchy. Magic or not, how could she belong *here*?

But this was where she had been born, and she could already see that they weren't going to be able to head home in a few days. If she was honest with herself, she'd feel guilty if they did. So much was wrong in Zaradwin Castle that she felt overwhelmed when she tried to think about all of it. Detsini blamed everything on the lack of a Dark Lord, and Jezzazar blamed Tradition, but Kayla thought it was more likely that neither of them had any common sense.

Riki might be able to focus totally on getting back to their world before their lives there unraveled beyond anyone's ability to fix, but Kayla couldn't be that single-minded. And it didn't feel right to leave everyone in the same hole they'd been in when she arrived, not when she might be in a position to actually *do* something to fix their problems.

"Being the Provisional Dark Lady has to be good for *something*," she muttered.

Macavinchy, who had followed her from the bedroom, flexed his wings and half flew, half jumped to her shoulder. Kayla realized that she'd been pacing; if she kept this up, she'd wake Riki and Del for sure. She went over to the bench, intending to sit down, and stopped short.

In the center of the bench was a book that Kayla was quite sure hadn't been there the night before. It was about the size of a small paperback, and like practically everything else in the castle, it was black. "Macavinchy," she whispered, "where did that come from?"

"I regret to say that I do not know, madam," Macavinchy said, equally softly. "I can, however, assure you that no one and nothing entered this chamber during the night."

"That's not actually very reassuring." Kayla eyed the book doubtfully, then jumped as bright silver lettering appeared on the black cover as if someone were burning the words onto the leather as she watched. *The Dark Traditions,*" she read. "Hey, Macavinchy, is this that book you were talking about that first night? The one you didn't have access to?"

Macavinchy peered over her shoulder. "I believe so. The title is certainly the same, and its mysterious appearance in these rooms argues for its magical nature."

Before Kayla could reply, more words formed at the bottom of the cover: *Xavrielina's Copy.* Kayla frowned. "My *name* is—" The letters flickered, pooled, and rearranged themselves to read *Kayla's Copy.* "Okay, that was weird. Macavinchy, is this thing reading my mind?"

"Not exactly. It is merely responding to your desires."

"Is it safe?"

"That depends on your definition of *safe,* madam," Macavinchy replied. "If you touch it, it will not do you physical damage."

"Wonderful." Kayla eyed the book, and decided to put off dealing with it for another minute or two. "Why does everyone think you are so unusual?"

"Few familiars are as articulate, madam, if I do say so myself. I would also venture to claim that none are as well informed, though I have already confessed that not all of my data is as readily accessible as I would like." His furry expression was a combination of pride and smugness, but his wings snapped once, betraying his dissatisfaction with his final admission.

Kayla squinted at him. "Does this world have things like viruses?" she asked slowly. "Or hackers?"

"I assume you are referring to computer viruses," Macavinchy replied. "Strictly speaking, there are none, as there are no computers. However, spells can perform similar functions."

"What can we do to stop them?"

"My antivirus spells will be more than sufficient to the task, once the settings have been adjusted to allow for magic," Macavinchy said promptly.

"Your antivirus . . . spells . . . have settings for *magic*?"

"They do now." Macavinchy definitely sounded smug.

Kayla grinned. "Right, then, walk me through the adjustments."

For the next ten minutes, Kayla followed Macavinchy's directions for accessing and adjusting the antivirus spells. Some of them were a little odd—why wrap Macavinchy's tail three times around her left middle finger?—but on the plus side, nobody else was likely to think of getting Macavinchy's cooperation that way. She set all the security procedures to the highest possible level, and after some more discussion, used security questions that asked for the name of the current U.S. president and of the town where Del's favorite cartoon took place—things no one in Zaradwin could possibly know. All through the process, the mysterious black-and-silver book on the bench kept nagging at her from the corner of her eye, causing a couple of mistakes that meant starting the whole setup process over from the beginning.

Finally, she finished. She eyed the book again, then reached for it with a sigh. She couldn't put off looking at it forever. Also, she had a feeling that Riki wouldn't react well, no matter what it turned out to be.

The book felt warm and comfortable in her hands. Kayla stroked the silver lettering with her thumb, then carefully opened the book to the table of contents. The first chapter was entitled "So You Are a Potential Dark Lord," which made the book sound like one of the career-exploration books in her old school library. "Discovering Your Dark Heritage" and "Your First Steps on the Road to Power" didn't sound too bad, but as she skimmed down the page, she found "Intimidating Your Followers" and "Oppressing the Peasants."

"I don't like the sound of some of these," she told Macavinchy.

"I can see why, madam; nevertheless, the information may prove useful, at least as a guide to what we can expect."

"Maybe, but I don't know if I trust a book that shows up out of nowhere, writes its own title, and changes my name. That's just . . . creepy."

"What's creepy?" said Riki's voice from the bedroom. "Or should I say what *else* is creepy? This whole place has been one creepy thing after another, if you ask me."

Kayla looked up. Her mother stood in the archway, leaning against one side of the opening. She looked a lot less frazzled than she had the day before, despite her wrinkled shorts and T-shirt.

"This," Kayla said, holding up the book. "It looks like a how-to book for Dark Lords."

"Where did you find it? I don't remember seeing it last night."

"It was on the bench when I came out," Kayla said. "Macavinchy says nobody was here to leave it."

"It showed up magically? Cool." Del peered around Riki, blinking owlishly, and yawned. "When's breakfast?"

"In a few minutes." Riki looked down and ruffled Del's hair. "I hope. But first, I want a few things clear." She waited until Del looked up. "You are not to go off exploring, either of you. We're staying together until we find out more about this place and these people."

"Aww, Mom!" Del whined.

"You were the one who said people in stories always get in trouble when they split up," Kayla pointed out, and Del subsided.

Riki transferred her attention to Kayla. "The first thing we need to do is find out about training you so we can get home."

"The first thing should be getting breakfast," Kayla retorted. "And then arranging for some clothes and rooms and things. Macavinchy said it'd be weeks, and I don't want to wear my State Fair clothes that long."

"That, too," Riki said. "But you mustn't get too involved. Getting home—"

"Is important, I get it." Kayla barely resisted the impulse to roll her eyes. Honestly, did Riki think she was three?

"After breakfast," Del put in.

Riki laughed and gave in. "All right, after breakfast. Do you remember how to get back to that dining room?"

"Great hall," Del corrected her. "And it's easy."

"Lead the way, then," Riki said, waving him toward the door. Kayla grabbed her backpack, stuffed the mysterious book inside, and followed them out.

Much to Del's disappointment, he only got to lead them up the hall to the entryway. Detsini was already there, waiting to escort them. A moment later, Yazmina appeared with Archie, who rubbed at his eyes and grumbled something unintelligible by way of greeting. Archie was apparently not a morning person, even when he'd slept in a proper bed. Detsini sniffed at him, and they all set off. As they crossed the bridge to the central tower, Kayla noted that Waylan and the minions had been busy; most of the trash had disappeared from the courtyard below.

The great hall, on the other hand, was not much improved. Someone had swept the debris between the tables into piles against the wall, but the muddy tracks remained, and the tabletops were still unpleasantly sticky-looking. The outermost ring of seats was filled by people in guard uniforms, hunched over small wooden bowls. With their helmets pushed up and back or sitting on the table beside their breakfast, they reminded Kayla of a peculiar college football team.

Several of the places nearest the dais and central throne were also occupied. Kayla recognized Jezzazar; he and an unfamiliar older man were both glaring at Waylan. A broad-shouldered boy a few years older than Kayla sat next to Jezzazar. He looked up as Kayla and her family arrived, and his bored expression quickly changed to one of great interest.

"Here you are," Detsini said, shooing them toward the table next to Waylan. "Kayla dear, if you'll just take a seat on the dais—"

"I'm staying with my family," Kayla said. Hadn't they already had this conversation?

"We're your family, too, you know." The boy who'd been sitting beside Jezzazar swung one leg after the other over the bench and stood up. He straightened his loose green shirt as if to show it off, and made a sweeping bow. "Welcome to Zaradwin, cousin."

"Thanks," Kayla said. She knew she was staring at him, but she couldn't help it. He was the first person she'd seen since their arrival who was wearing something colorful, and the only one besides Waylan who seemed cheerful, but he made her more uncomfortable than almost anyone else she'd met so far. "Er, cousin?"

"That's enough, Rache," Jezzazar said. "You'll show respect to the new Dark Lady while I'm about, however little longer that may be. All of us in this cursed castle must dance to her tune now."

Rache's eyes took on a manic gleam. "Why, Father, I thought you disliked music. And there's no disrespect in a welcome. Is there, cousin?"

"Uh, no." Kayla felt as if she were picking her way across

a bog, where everything looked solid until you stepped in the wrong place and found yourself waist-deep in muddy water.

"Make no excuses for him, my lady," Jezzazar growled. "He is a disgrace to the family, though I sorrow to be the one to say it."

"Oh, Rache, my son, what are you doing now?" Yazmina's melancholy voice floated in from the far side of the room. A moment later, Yazmina herself appeared, carrying a tray. "You mean to break my heart, I know it."

Rache rolled his eyes, looking suddenly much more like a normal teenager. "Ah, Mother, don't take on so. It's only Father being his grumpy self in the morning."

"I'll have none of that from you," Jezzazar said. "And you'll show your mother respect, or I'll set you to work with the duty men. A few weeks of cleaning latrines will teach you to mind your tongue."

"But it's such a beautiful morning!" Rache flung his arms wide in a dramatic gesture, nearly tipping over one of the bowls. It was like watching a play. Exactly like, Kayla realized—Rache was acting. His smile didn't reach his eyes, and his gestures were too broad, too energetic, as if he was pretending to things he didn't feel. He behaved cheerfully, but he wasn't happy. No wonder he made her uncomfortable.

Del poked Kayla; she leaned toward him. "These people are weird," he said softly in her ear. Kayla nodded her agreement.

"Is that our breakfast?" Riki asked Yazmina, distracting everyone.

Yazmina nodded. She set the tray down and passed out large

wooden bowls half-full of what looked like watery oatmeal. They all looked at it doubtfully, including Macavinchy.

"What's that?" Del asked, wrinkling his nose even though it didn't look like much.

"Looks like gruel," Archie said, and his lip curled. "I hate gruel more than anything."

"'Tis Tradition," Yazmina informed him as if that settled matters.

"Tradition," Kayla repeated. "I already hate that word."

Rache snorted. Everyone's attention went back to him. "You only think you hate it now," he informed her. "Just wait a bit. You'll find plenty of Traditions you'll hate more than the food." He rose, made a theatrical bow in Kayla's direction, and strolled out of the room, leaving his half-empty bowl on the table.

During the brief silence that followed, Riki studied the gruel. "We can do better than this," she announced, "even if the only thing in the pantry is oatmeal. Where's the kitchen?"

Yazmina's eyes widened. "You can't mean to cook!"

"Why not?"

"You are our guest, and the adoptive mother of the Dark Lady," Detsini replied. "It wouldn't be seemly."

"Neither is starving," Kayla said.

"I knew it," the unfamiliar man muttered just loudly enough to be heard. Jezzazar and Waylan frowned at him; Yazmina sighed and shook her head; Detsini gave a tiny smile before her face crumpled back into mild worry.

Kayla felt her eyes narrow. "Knew what? And who are you?"

"This is my father," Waylan growled over the top of Jezzazar's "Your castle steward," and the man's resentful "Ichikar."

"Nice to meet you, Ichikar," Kayla said with pointed politeness. "I'm Kayla, your new Provisional Dark Lady." She turned and introduced her mother and Delmar, pretending not to notice Ichikar's increasingly sour expression. "Now, what was it you were saying?"

"That I knew this would end in tears." Ichikar glared at Detsini and Yazmina. "You should never have sent her off, but once you had"—he transferred his glare to Waylan—"well enough should have been left alone. We could have waited for a new Dark Lord to rise and come to us."

"I made a promise to the Dark Lord that was," Waylan said stiffly.

"Aye." Ichikar shook his head. "Would that you had never done so."

"Don't worry about it," Riki told him. "We don't plan on staying any longer than we have to."

"So." Ichikar stood and thrust his head forward threateningly. "You admit it. You're here to waste the little substance we have on frivolities, and when you've squeezed all you can from us, you'll abandon us again with an empty treasury and lands wrung dry, so that no other Dark Lord will want to attend to us."

"No," Yazmina protested. "There have always been Dark Lords . . . and Ladies . . . at Zaradwin Castle!"

"That's not what she meant," Kayla protested. "That is— How much is in the treasury now?" Maybe they could make up for whatever they spent by helping with the repairs on the castle and the town.

"It begins," Ichikar said heavily. "But you are the acknowledged Dark Lady, and I must answer you as best I may. The remnant of the Dark Hordes salvaged the few coins that were left in the ruins of the vault in Ashwend after the armies of the Light sacked it. I have done my best to preserve them against the coming of a new Dark Lord."

"But how much—" Kayla stopped, realizing suddenly that Ichikar wasn't going to give her a dollar amount, and she didn't know what anything here cost anyway.

"The village and the castle lands produce but a pittance," Ichikar went on. "'Tis barely enough to feed and clothe the few who have remained."

"That explains a lot," Riki said.

"Yeah." Kayla thought of the unrepaired gatehouses, the threadbare uniforms, and the small meals. "We need to do something about it."

"Not today," Riki, Jezzazar, and Detsini chorused. The three of them exchanged startled looks.

"'Tis your first day as Dark Lady," Jezzazar growled. "You must call a council of your advisors and allies to hear how things have been managed since the last Dark Lord, to reward those who have served well, and to torture or execute those who have not."

"She can't call a Dark Council until after her formal investiture," Detsini snapped. "And she can't possibly be invested in those clothes! Dear Kayla needs something more suitable immediately."

Kayla looked down at her T-shirt and shorts. Normally, Riki wouldn't have let her go to school in that outfit, much less to an important meeting, but—

"We don't have anything else," Riki said, echoing Kayla's thoughts. "It's not like we had time to pack." She shot Waylan a disapproving look. Waylan ducked his head.

"We could put off the investing thing for a while," Kayla suggested.

All of the castle folk stared at her in undisguised horror. "Put off your investiture?" Jezzazar rumbled. "'Twould be rank folly! Every pretender for leagues would see it as weakness and prepare to attack."

"Attack?" Riki said in alarm.

"How soon do we have to have it, then?" Kayla asked quickly.

Detsini, Yazmina, and Jezzazar exchanged looks. After a moment, Jezzazar sighed as if he had just lost an argument. "The risk will begin to grow after three days."

"If we invite lords who live several days' ride away, the delay will not appear weak," Yazmina said thoughtfully.

"We have not the funds to host so many," Ichikar objected.

"We have not the funds to supply the army we'll need, should our near neighbors decide that a weak Dark Lady makes us easy prey," Jezzazar retorted.

"I think Kayla would prefer something small," Riki put in.

Detsini's eyes narrowed. Jezzazar grimaced but gave a reluctant nod. Then he looked at Detsini and Yazmina. "Five days, and the invitations to those farthest away must go out tomorrow."

"Two formal gowns, then," Detsini said. "One for the investiture, and one for the council. And at least four everyday gowns."

Ichikar's scowl returned. "I knew how it would be," he said. "Feasts and costly gowns by the score that we can ill afford."

"I don't need—" Kayla started.

"Proper garb for a Dark Lady—" Detsini said at the same time.

Riki overrode both of them. "No. Kayla needs to learn how to recharge that talisman of Waylan's, so we can all go home." Looks ranging from disapproval to shock appeared on most of the faces around the table, and Riki raised her chin defiantly. "It'll take months, Waylan said; best get started."

"'Tis the Dark Lady's choice," Ichikar said, and they all looked at Kayla.

Summoning a council sounded as if she'd have to work with Jezzazar and maybe Ichikar, neither of whom seemed to like or approve of her. Shopping for clothes might be fun, but Kayla doubted that Zaradwin had anything resembling a shopping mall. That left Riki's suggestion. Kayla sighed quietly, then narrowed her eyes. "So, who trains new Dark Ladies?"

All of the castle folk exchanged uneasy glances. "By Tradition, one who would become a Dark Ruler seeks out esoteric wisdom and forgotten magics in the wildest and Darkest parts of the world," Ichikar answered. "Unless, of course, they are raised to inherit the throne, as you should have been." He looked at her doubtfully.

"Really?" Archie said. "They just learn on their own? No teachers or exams? How do they know when they're done?"

"When they arrive at Zaradwin, the castle judges them. If it accepts their claim, the aspirant is invested with the title and becomes the new Dark Lord—or Lady—and grows rapidly in power and knowledge. If the claim is not accepted—" He shrugged.

Riki looked alarmed. "Didn't the castle accept Kayla yesterday in the courtyard?"

"Just so," Detsini broke in briskly. "And I'm sure we don't want dear Kayla running off into the wilderness when she's only just gotten here."

"Ah, child, had you been raised in this cursed castle as you should have been, the Dark Lord your father would have taught you from your earliest age," Yazmina put in. "Alas, that I was party to the ill-advised attempt that so cruelly deprived you of your birthright!"

"There now, Yazmina, that's enough of that," Detsini said. "It's a shame Xavriel isn't here to instruct his daughter, but I'm sure that between the two of us we can teach Kayla everything she needs to know. Though I really think that she should address her appearance first."

"Peace, woman!" Ichikar growled. "You two have done enough damage."

Kayla glanced at her mother. Riki looked as if she'd just bitten into a sour pickle. So she didn't like the idea of Kayla's aunts teaching her magic any better than Kayla did. Maybe because they'd banished her away to Earth? But that meant they knew the right spell, at least . . .

"I believe, madam, that following your aunt's suggestion in regard to learning magic would be a bad idea," Macavinchy said.

Everyone jumped. Detsini frowned at the familiar. "No one asked you!"

"On the contrary," Macavinchy said blandly. "Shortly after our arrival, madam instructed me to inform her immediately should a proposed course of action be, in my opinion, a bad idea. I am merely fulfilling her request."

"Right," Kayla said, relieved. "Do you have a different suggestion, Macavinchy?"

"When the subject was first raised, Second Commander Waylan mentioned a castle librarian," Macavinchy replied. "I believe that is the logical place to begin your inquiries."

Ichikar's eyebrows rose. "Harkawn?" He shot Waylan an accusatory look. "You proposed sending her to Harkawn?"

"He's still the librarian and record keeper?" Waylan shook his head.

"No one wanted to replace him, under the circumstances." Ichikar shrugged.

Detsini's glare intensified. "Under the circumstances, it would clearly be more suitable—"

"Really?" Ichikar said. "Under *all* the circumstances, it seems to me that there's little to choose between you."

Before Detsini could respond, Yazmina broke in. "If I may offer a plan?" Kayla nodded, and Yazmina went on, "Spend the morning in the library, arranging for your learning, and the afternoon on your other duties."

"Dressmaking for the likes of a true Dark Lady will take time," Detsini pointed out.

"Even if we send a summons to the seamstress immediately,

she will not arrive until this afternoon," Yazmina countered. "In the meantime, perhaps one of Geneviev's gowns could be altered to fit Lady Kayla, so that she has proper attire until her new wardrobe arrives."

"Who's Geneviev?" Kayla asked.

"Your half sister," Detsini said in an arctic tone that forbade further questions.

Half sister? Kayla missed a few sentences in her shock. *She's here? Why hasn't anyone mentioned her?*

"—garments are not suitable for a Dark Lady." Detsini's eyes went a little out of focus. "But we do have the wardrobes of several former Dark Ladies in storage. I'm sure something among them can be altered quickly. Yes, that will do very well."

Yazmina studied Riki and Del for a moment, then smiled slightly. "As for your family—we are of a similar size," she said to Riki. "And some of my Rache's things may do for your son." Her expression turned melancholy. "I have saved all his clothes since he was a baby. He was such a good child, so dark and brooding. 'Twas for his sake that I—" She broke off, glancing at Detsini. " 'Twould have been of no use in the end; I see that now. He's changed, and it breaks my heart." She sniffed.

"Sons will do that," Ichikar said with a sidelong look at Waylan.

"What about Archie?" Kayla asked. Everyone looked at her, and she added, "He only has the one set of clothes, too, and he's been traveling in them for . . . how long?"

"Months," Archie admitted.

"If my lady wishes, I can see to providing Lord Archibald with spare garments," Waylan offered.

"Good," Riki said. "The rest of us will go to the library so Kayla can start learning."

"And what of the summons to the Dark Council?" Jezzazar's eyes narrowed. "Will you put that off as well?"

Kayla frowned. "Who is supposed to be summoned?"

"Your allies and advisors," Jezzazar said.

"What allies?" Kayla tried to keep her frustration and impatience out of her voice, but she didn't think she was particularly successful.

"Those who aided you in your long quest to build your magic and reach Zaradwin Castle to claim your throne."

"That's Mom and Del," Kayla pointed out, glancing at Riki. "And you and Waylan and the guards you brought along."

"But—" Jezzazar paused. Kayla could practically see him realizing that her "long quest to reach Zaradwin Castle" had taken all of two days, from the time Waylan transported them to the stone circle until their arrival at the castle. Unless he wanted to count the fourteen or so years she'd spent on Earth, but they couldn't even get themselves back, let alone send a summons to anyone there. Besides . . . Kayla suppressed a giggle, imagining the faces of her teachers if they got a note inviting them to come and be part of a Dark Council.

"But your advisors?" Jezzazar sounded as if he were grasping at straws.

"I haven't picked any advisors yet."

"You said I could be one of your Dark councilors," Del objected. "And Archie is going to be your head evil lieutenant. That's two."

Ichikar, Detsini, and Yazmina all wore appalled expressions, though Kayla couldn't tell whether it was the idea of Del as a councilor that horrified them or his blatant demand to be on the council. "That's two," Kayla agreed. "And you're both here in the castle." She looked around the table and grinned. "So, all of you are invited to the first Dark Council meeting on . . ." She hesitated. "Does the day after the investiture work?"

"That will be fine," Jezzazar said in a strangled voice.

"Good," Kayla said with more confidence than she felt. "That's settled, then. Now, where's the kitchen? I'm still hungry."

CHAPTER 9

Intimidating Your Followers

Never express uncertainty or doubt, even in small matters. Should you need to learn something new, do so in complete privacy, and if anyone sees you make a mistake, no matter how small, execute them immediately.

—From *The Dark Traditions*

The kitchen wasn't in any better condition than the rest of the castle, but there was a long-handled pump dripping into a stone sink and a cheerful fire in the hearth that warmed the whole room. Several large bowls of bread dough were rising on a shelf to one side of the fire; it was the only part of the kitchen that looked clean. Kayla wondered who was responsible.

While Yazmina wrung her hands and Detsini looked on with lips pursed in disapproval, Riki organized a quick cleanup and a batch of oatmeal pancakes. Kayla and Del devoured them straight from the flat stone that served as a griddle. Archie was more reluctant, at least until his first bite. Even without butter or syrup, they were much better than Yazmina's gruel. Riki made a smaller pancake for Macavinchy, who thanked her gravely.

Just as they were finishing, Waylan appeared to take them to the library. Detsini proposed guiding the group herself until Yazmina nodded and, with a glint in her eyes, offered to notify the seamstress in Detsini's place. Frowning, Detsini vetoed the suggestion and reluctantly left them in Waylan's hands until lunch. The two aunts went off to send a message to the dressmaker, and the rest of them headed for the library.

"This place is nothing like what I was expecting," Archie muttered as they left the kitchen behind.

"What were you expecting?" Waylan asked.

"I don't know," Archie admitted. "But it wasn't half a dozen people arguing about who's going to do what for hours every time something needs to happen."

Waylan shrugged and cast a sidelong look at Kayla as he replied, "It was not so bad when I left. The longer they waited for their new Dark Lady, the more they feared that some present or past misstep would result in their punishment."

Or execution, Kayla thought, remembering the guard Jezzazar had almost killed. "So they've gotten in the habit of passing the buck as far and as often as they can?"

"Exactly."

"You don't sound as if you approve," Kayla commented.

"I have spent ten years traveling through strange lands whose people observed customs that were nothing like the Traditions of the Dark or the Laws and Tenets of the Light. I have perhaps become more flexible in my outlook as a result." Waylan paused, studying Kayla. Behind him, Riki was watching him with a speculative expression.

"Is that going to be a problem?" Kayla asked.

"For you? Not if you hold firm," Waylan replied. He smiled slightly. "The oldest and greatest of the Dark Traditions is that the Dark Lady's will is paramount in all things. Turn right," he called to Del, who had gotten ahead of them.

They continued through the maze of corridors and stairs. Finally, Waylan stopped in front of a plain, pointed wooden door with no handle. "The Dark Lady of Zaradwin wishes to enter her library," he announced.

"You don't sound much like a lady to me," a hoarse voice responded from inside.

"He isn't," Kayla said. "I am. Let us in, please."

The door swung inward with a loud creak, revealing a short, stout, balding man with a cheerful expression. His bright, inquisitive eyes darted around the group, then focused on Kayla. He smiled broadly, revealing uneven teeth. "So you're the new Dark Lady, are you? Xavrielina that was, though I understand you prefer to use a different name. I'm Harkawn, librarian and record keeper for Zaradwin Castle. Come in, come in, and tell me who all these people are. Except Second Commander Waylan, of course; I've known him since he was a boy." He paused. "It is good to see you again."

Waylan introduced Del, Archie, and Riki as they entered, which gave Kayla a moment to look around. The library was much smaller than she had expected, about the size of the living room in their new apartment. A row of windows faced the door; at the near end of the room was a large fireplace, with a half circle of padded chairs and benches in front of it. Five bookcases occupied the rest of the wall space; none of them were more than three-quarters full. A desk piled with scrolls, books, and papers sat to one side of the windows, facing the door, and a long table occupied the other end of the room, well away from the fireplace.

"Sit down, sit down," Harkawn said, waving at the chairs in front of the fireplace. "I can light the fire if you're cold. Normally, I use it only in winter; too much danger of a stray spark getting in among the books, you know. It would be a shame to damage such a marvelous collection." He beamed at the bookshelves.

"It certainly would," Archie said, staring at the bookcases with eyes as wide as saucers. "Are these—can I—"

"If the Dark Lady approves," Harkawn said. "It's her collection."

"Go ahead and look," Kayla told Archie.

Archie didn't need any further encouragement to head for the closest bookcase. Del started to follow him, but Riki grabbed his shoulder. "Not you," she said. Del made a face but settled on the stone floor.

Harkawn nodded approvingly. "Now, my lady, what brings you to your library? I suspect it's more than a simple desire to know where it is."

"I need to learn how to use magic," Kayla said. "Waylan said you might have some suggestions."

"Learn magic?" Harkawn's eyebrows drew together in puzzlement. "But the castle has accepted you."

"Word gets around fast," Archie commented.

Harkawn snorted. "Word didn't need to get around. Everyone

in the castle felt what happened. So why do you think you need to learn more?"

"The world I grew up in didn't have magic," Kayla explained. "And I've only been here for a couple of days."

"I see." Harkawn's frown changed from puzzled to considering. "You'll need to improve your skills as fast as possible. I can tutor you in the basics, and perhaps a bit beyond—and I'm sure there's something in this library. It's the best collection of Dark-magic tomes outside the Scholars' Tower."

"It is?" Kayla blurted without thinking. "Why?"

"Because the forces of the Light destroy any books of magic they run across during their regular invasion, madam," Macavinchy said before Harkawn could reply. "And there are not many such books to begin with, as no one seems to have invented the printing press yet."

Riki studied the bookshelves, frowning. Kayla wasn't sure whether she was impressed, now that they knew every book was handwritten, or annoyed that the armies of the Light were in the habit of destroying them. After a moment, Riki transferred her frown to Macavinchy and said, "If the Scholars' Tower has the best magic collection, why didn't we head there to begin with?"

"The Scholars' Tower is at least a month's journey from here," Macavinchy replied. "Traveling such a distance without supplies and a protective escort would have been both dangerous and difficult. In addition, it is very likely that the trip would have been pointless."

Harkawn nodded. "The scholars are bound by ancient

magical oaths. They will give counsel to both the Light and the Dark when it is requested, but they will not teach their spells and secrets to anyone who has not sworn the same oaths, nor will they allow outsiders to study in their library on their own." He sounded rather wistful.

"We could take the oaths, if—" Riki started, but Harkawn was already shaking his head.

"The scholars' oaths bind them *to the tower*," he said. "Those who take the oath rarely leave, and then only briefly and with permission."

"So the only way to learn anything there would be to take their oaths, and then we'd be stuck in this world," Kayla said.

"Precisely, madam," Macavinchy replied.

Riki didn't look totally convinced, but she didn't raise further objections.

"I want to learn magic, too!" Del piped up.

"Kayla was born here," Riki told him gently. "You weren't. You—"

"The place of his birth makes no difference," Waylan broke in. They all looked at him. "I am no magician myself, but to my knowledge, no one else has crossed the void between the worlds so many times, or to so many places. And I tell you this: a person may have talents and abilities that have no place in their home world, but when that person passes into a world that welcomes such abilities, they spring to life, much as your computing machine became your familiar when you passed into this world." He paused, pressing his lips together, then went on in a low voice, "It is extremely disconcerting."

"You mean Del could be magical, too?" Riki sounded appalled.

"Cool!" Del grinned widely.

"As could you," Harkawn told Riki thoughtfully. "You both have the coloring for it." He nodded decisively. "I will test all of you."

He stood and crossed slowly to the desk. After a moment of rummaging and a serious coughing fit, he returned with a scroll and a solid glass ball the size and shape of a snow globe. Several objects sparkled from different levels within the glass: a bright blue ball, a tiny green rod, something that looked like a four-sided red die, a brown cube, and a small silver coin.

Harkawn set the globe carefully on the table and motioned to everyone to join him. "This is one of the oldest tests of magic that we have," he said as they took seats around the table. "If you would, my lady—"

"No," Riki broke in firmly. "No offense, but you aren't doing anything to my children until I know it's safe. So you start with me."

"But . . ." Harkawn looked at Riki's determined expression and shrugged. "Very well. It is a simple test. You place three fingertips of your main hand here, on the side of the globe." He demonstrated. "Then think of something that makes you feel a strong emotion—anger or excitement."

He paused for a moment, and his eyes narrowed. At the bottom of the globe, something stirred. A shadow rose through the glass, dimming the first few shapes, as if someone unseen were pouring dirty water into the globe.

As the shadow reached the green rod, Harkawn pulled his hand away from the glass. The shadow fell rapidly, disappearing completely when it reached the bottom of the globe.

Archie leaned forward, fascinated. "I've never seen anything like this before! May I try?"

"If my lady permits." Harkawn glanced toward Kayla.

Kayla nodded, figuring that the more times Riki watched the demonstration, the more relaxed she would be about it.

Immediately, Archie reached forward and touched the side of the glass ball, just as Harkawn had. He frowned and his lips twisted; almost immediately the shadow started rising. It seemed darker than Harkawn's had, and it rose more quickly. At the level of the brown cube it slowed and stopped. Archie held his position a few seconds more, then dropped his hand with a sigh.

Harkawn frowned but did not comment. He turned to Riki. "Madam?"

"All right." Riki set three fingertips on the side of the glass.

No shadow appeared inside the globe. Riki pressed her lips together. Still nothing . . . then Kayla thought a faint shimmer passed through the glass, like clear water washing over a windowpane. She glanced up. No one else seemed to have noticed anything.

"It seems that magic is not your gift," Harkawn said mildly.

Riki blew out a sigh of relief and dropped her hand. The shimmer came again, and again no one but Kayla seemed to notice.

"My lady?" Harkawn gestured from Kayla to the ball.

Kayla reached out. As her fingers brushed the glass, the entire globe instantly went a solid black, as if it had been dipped in black paint. Kayla jerked her hand away, and the glass cleared at once.

At least it did something, she thought. "What does it mean?"

"That . . . I have never seen anything like that," Harkawn said.

"Kayla?" Riki sounded worried.

"I'm fine," Kayla assured her. "It didn't feel like anything. I was just startled."

"My turn!" Del said, and reached for the globe before anyone could react.

For a long moment, the glass remained clear. Then it flashed once, bright orange, and collapsed into a puddle. The little objects that had been inside sat in a forlorn heap on top of it.

"Del!" Riki grabbed his hand and began checking it for damage.

Del was staring at the puddle in disgust. "Orange? Why did it turn orange?"

"I have no idea," Harkawn said, sounding shaken. "Whatever talent you brought with you must be profoundly incompatible with the magic of the globe."

"Maybe you're meant to be a nuclear engineer, and since they don't have those here, the ball melted," Kayla suggested.

"I guess," Del said. "But it still doesn't explain the orange."

"Can you replace that . . . device?" Riki asked.

"Yes, though it will take some time," Harkawn replied. "The Scholars' Tower is the only source, and it is a long way from Zaradwin."

He took a deep breath, which triggered another coughing spell. When he recovered, he looked at Kayla. "I think it would be best to avoid further experimentation today. I'll find you some books to begin with. I'm afraid the library doesn't possess a copy of *The Lord Ungrex Compendium,* or I'd start you with that."

On Kayla's shoulder, Macavinchy shifted and twitched his wings. Kayla grinned. "I think I can scare up an audio version," she said. "Unless that's one of the books you couldn't get at, Macavinchy?"

"I have access to the entirety of that text, madam," Macavinchy said reassuringly. "It appears to be a collection of spells with a few passages on theory included." He paused, then added in a disapproving tone, "The spells are in no particular order, there is no index, and the theories appear to contradict each other. Furthermore, there are several versions, each of which contains a slightly different selection of spells."

Harkawn stared at Macavinchy for a moment, then slowly began to smile. "What a wonder! But what do you mean when you say you have access to the text?"

"What he said," Kayla replied. "Show us, please, Macavinchy."

" 'Section Two,' " Macavinchy said. " 'As to the Summoning or Dismissal of Insects. Raise up your energy, as suits your chosen insect's size and conditions. Fashion thence an image, the which you will call or discharge, and smite him in seven parts as you scald him through. Next—' "

Harkawn's mouth fell open. Waylan looked only slightly less startled. Archie's eyes went round as saucers and seemed to grow larger as Macavinchy went on.

Macavinchy continued his recitation uninterrupted for several paragraphs, then paused. "The section concludes with a description of the specific energies that allow the summoning of different insects. Is that a sufficient demonstration, or shall I continue, madam?"

"That's enough," Kayla said. She felt a little stunned by Macavinchy's performance herself, though probably not for the same reasons as Harkawn, Waylan, and Archie. Learning magic was going to be hard if all spells included directions like "smite him in seven parts as you scald him through."

Harkawn was now looking at Macavinchy with an expression of utter delight. "But this is marvelous! Can your familiar recite other books?"

"I expect he can repeat anything he can download," Kayla said. "We already know that some things are . . . restricted."

"Download?"

"Uh, anything he can get at," Kayla said. "Or anything in his memory. He can still play the music I loaded the night before we . . . left." She hesitated, then decided not to mention that they hadn't figured out yet how much he knew about this world, or how to get at it easily.

"Oh, excellent! I shall make up a list of volumes for you all to study, if that meets with your approval, my lady."

"Yes, please," Kayla said. From the corner of her eye, she saw Riki's forehead wrinkle, and she bit the inside of her lip to keep from saying anything. Riki's laser focus on getting home was starting to make Kayla uneasy. It was too much like the way Riki had behaved in the early days of Michael's illness, when she had been so certain that all they had to do was find the right doctor or the right treatment and everything would be fine. Reluctantly, Kayla added, "And after you get us started, could you make a list of everything you know of that talks about traveling between worlds?"

Riki's expression cleared, but now Harkawn looked uncertain. "There is nothing in this library on the subject, and it is not an area I know much about. And with all due respect, my lady, if you are as untutored as you say, there are far more important magics for you to learn."

"No, there aren't," Riki said, leaning forward. "We need to get home as soon as possible; the longer we're here, the harder it will be to straighten everything out when we get back."

Harkawn shook his head. "Traveling between worlds requires extremely rare and advanced magic."

"It can't be that rare," Riki said, her frown returning. "Those two women sent Kayla to our world, and *he*"—she glared at Waylan—"dragged us here."

"If there were any books here on travel between worlds, the Dark Lord removed them from the library after his daughter was stolen," Harkawn replied firmly. He broke off for a moment, coughing.

"He must have had *something*," Riki insisted.

Harkawn caught his breath and shrugged. "If he did, the Dark Lady will find it in her rooms, along with his notes."

"My rooms?" Kayla said, puzzled.

"The Dark Lord's—or Lady's—suite," Harkawn replied. "Surely Lady Detsini showed you?"

"We're going there this afternoon," Riki said.

Harkawn nodded. "Good. But even if you find the Dark Lord

Xavriel's notes, it would be most unwise to attempt to duplicate his work until you have had more experience, my lady."

"It figures," Riki grumbled. "Where does she start?"

They spent the rest of the morning bent over the scroll. It was handwritten in extravagantly curling letters, and maddeningly unspecific; Macavinchy was an enormous help in deciphering the words but was less useful when it came to explaining their meaning. Del and Archie joined in the ensuing discussion with enthusiasm. Archie's knowledge of Light magic proved to be of help in understanding the archaic phrasing, but their progress was still slow.

As the morning went on, Riki didn't say much, but Kayla could feel her intent stare. Finally, while Macavinchy was repeating a particularly convoluted sentence for Del's benefit, Kayla looked over and said, "Mom, watching me isn't going to make me get this any faster."

Riki shook herself. "No, I suppose not. I'm sorry. I just . . . This is going to take longer than I thought."

"If you do not wish to attempt magic yourself, Madam Jones, perhaps you should study something else," Waylan said from just behind her. Riki jumped; Waylan pretended not to notice and went on, "I know that during my travels there were many times when it would have been of great help to know more of the history and manners of the worlds I was visiting."

"That's . . . not a bad suggestion," Riki said. "Maybe there's something on time travel. I think we're going to need it." She wandered over and began examining the books, and Kayla gave a quiet sigh of relief.

By the time Detsini summoned them to lunch, Kayla was fed up with trying to make sense of the obscure phrasing in the scroll. "If this is what all these books are like, I'm not surprised that most Dark Lords have to learn magic somewhere else," she muttered as they headed back toward the center of the tower.

This time, at Riki's insistence, they bypassed the great hall and went straight to the kitchen. As they filed in behind Detsini, Kayla saw Yazmina talking to a tall, slim girl of about seventeen standing by the oven. The girl's black hair was tied back with a faded pink ribbon, and she wore an equally faded pink dress with wide, floaty sleeves and a full skirt completely covered in rows of ruffles. Kayla suppressed a shudder. She hoped no one expected her to dress like that.

The girl looked over as they entered, and her black eyes widened. "Oh dear," she said softly. She turned to face them, clasping her flour-covered hands in front of her, and sank into a deep, graceful curtsy. "My lady," she said to the stone floor.

"Geneviev," Detsini said in a disapproving tone. "What are you doing here?"

"Making the trenchers for supper." The girl gestured at several round, flattened pieces of dough resting on the clean end of the table. "I'm almost finished; there's only this last batch to bake."

Detsini sniffed. "It's no fit task for a member of the Dark Lord's family, but since you're almost done, you may as well finish." The words had no bite behind them, as if they had been worn smooth by much repetition.

"Family?" Kayla said. In her mind, she ran quickly over what she'd learned about her relatives since her arrival in Zaradwin. "Then you're my half sister?"

"She doesn't look like you," Del objected. "And she's tall."

"Del." Riki gave him a reproving look, and he subsided.

The girl raised her eyes and sent a quick, sharp look at Kayla and her family, then fixed her gaze on their boots once more. "If you are the Dark Lady Xavrielina, daughter to the Dark Lord Xavriel and his lady Athelina, then indeed we share the same mother." Geneviev's tone was soft and sweet. *Too sweet,* Kayla thought.

"I prefer to be called Kayla, but the rest is true." Kayla paused, uncertain what to say next. "I'm glad to meet you. I didn't know I had a sister before we got here."

"You are very kind," Geneviev said, still keeping her eyes down.

"The Dark Lady isn't kind!" Detsini snapped.

"Excuse me a moment," Geneviev said to Detsini, and reached around Yazmina to the side of the oven. She pulled out a long-handled wooden paddle and opened the oven door. The room filled with the strong scent of just-baked bread as she removed ten round, flat loaves from the oven. Kayla recognized them as the bread bowls they'd eaten from on the previous night. Geneviev spread the loaves out to cool, then inserted the last batch into the oven. Replacing the paddle, she turned and curtsied again. "There; if you'll take these out when they've finished baking, Lady Detsini, I'll take Mother her tray now." Her eyes flickered to Kayla again, so fast that no one else appeared to notice.

Stunned, Kayla watched as Detsini sniffed again and nodded.

Geneviev put one of the fresh trenchers on a large tray, along with a small pot, a wooden spoon, and a pitcher of water. As she picked it up, Kayla's brain kicked back in. "Wait! You're taking that to your—to our mother? She's still alive?"

"But of course she's alive, dear," Detsini said, sounding surprised. "Why wouldn't she be?"

Geneviev gave Detsini a wary, half-frightened look, then bit her lip and sank into a deep curtsy, her head bowed. "Forgive me, my lady," she began. "My—your—our mother is unwell."

"I thought— She's here? In this castle?"

Detsini made a sour face. "In this castle, though she hasn't left her room these ten years." Geneviev's mouth tightened and she shot Detsini an angry look that Detsini did not appear to notice.

Kayla shook her head, trying to clear it. "I— Why didn't anyone tell me she was here? Can I meet her?"

"I thought you were aware," Detsini said, shrugging. "It matters not. Lady Athelina sees no one but Geneviev." Her tone made her disapproval clear.

Kayla glanced at Geneviev just in time to catch the look of mingled fear and hatred that she gave Detsini before her face smoothed out into a too-sweet, too-innocent mask. She rose from her curtsy and picked up the tray she had prepared. "My—our—mother has been too ill for visitors," she said. "But I will tell her of your wish."

"Does she have a good doctor?" Suddenly, the shabbiness and disrepair in the castle felt less like laziness and neglect and more like Riki's long, futile struggle to pay off both the mortgage and the enormous medical bills they'd been left with after Michael's death.

"Athelina has all the care she desires," Detsini said dryly. "You don't need to concern yourself, Kayla dear."

"But—"

Detsini turned and made a shooing motion at Geneviev. "Off with you; there's no need to bother the Dark Lady now."

Geneviev dropped another curtsy and departed before Kayla could organize her scattered thoughts and object. Detsini turned and shook her head. "That girl has no sense of her proper position. Pink! I ask you, is that right, in the Dark Lord's castle? But that's young people for you; no sense of Tradition."

She's taking care of her sick mother, and all you worry about is what color her dress is? Detsini wasn't trying to help or pretending to care. Kayla felt a surge of sympathy for her half sister. If that was everyone's attitude, no wonder Geneviev didn't want Kayla barging in on their mother.

Some of Kayla's thoughts must have leaked into her expression, because Detsini glanced at her and paused. "Of course, I don't mean *you,* Kayla dear," she finished with an insincere smile. "Now, let me just see what lunch has been—"

"Sandwiches," Riki said firmly. She took a deep breath and rolled her shoulders, the way she did when they were tense from a bad day at the office. "We have the bread; all we need is cheese or a little cold meat, and a few fixings."

Yazmina brought out the necessary components and watched with evident interest as Riki, Kayla, and Del prepared sandwiches for everyone. Detsini grumbled, but she was perfectly happy to accept a sandwich in place of the usual midday meal, and lunch proceeded without incident.

CHAPTER 10

Choose Your Image Carefully

Intimidating your enemies begins with their first glimpse of you. You should therefore dress at all times in the way that best projects your chosen style of rule, whether that is suave, intelligent, desirable, unpredictable, manipulative, or authoritarian. Don't skimp on quality, however great your other needs.

—From *The Dark Traditions*

Just as they finished eating, one of the young guardsmen appeared and announced that the dressmaker had arrived. "Take her up to the Dark Lord's rooms," Detsini told Yazmina. "We'll meet you there."

As soon as Del had swallowed the last bite of his third sandwich, Detsini shooed them out of the kitchens and up the stairs. Three flights up, she opened a door onto a short, wide hallway with two plain doors on either side. At the far end was a large black door with a silver dragon's skull mounted on its center. Yazmina and a sharp-faced woman with her hair in a large gray bun were waiting in front of the nearest door.

"Welcome, my lady," Yazmina said. "This is Madam Lorna, chief dressmaker for Zaradwin."

"My lady." The sharp-faced woman curtsied. Her expression was studiously respectful, but her eyes swept up and down Kayla in a cool evaluation. "I understand you are in need of clothing suited to your high position. If you permit, I have brought some designs—"

"Yazmina dear, didn't you explain?" Detsini interrupted. "The new Dark Lady requires clothing immediately. You're to alter some of the previous Dark Ladies' wardrobes; new designs can come later."

Lorna's eyes narrowed. "As you wish," she said in a colorless tone.

"This is where you store old clothes?" Riki said.

"These are the personal rooms of the Dark Lords and Ladies of Zaradwin," Detsini told her. "The wardrobes of previous Dark Lords are stored in these first two, to be close at hand in case the current title holder has need of them." She gestured at the nearest two doors.

"Then let's—" Kayla opened the first door as she spoke, and the words died on her lips. The room was enormous, easily the size of the auditorium at her old school. Stacks of chests and trunks nearly filled the space, with narrow aisles left for walking. "Are all these full of clothes?"

"Of course," Detsini said smugly. "There have always been Dark Lords at Zaradwin Castle, for a thousand years at least."

"What's in there?" Del demanded, pointing down the hall toward the door with the silver skull.

"That is the entrance to the Dark Lord's private chambers," Detsini said. "Or the Dark Lady's, I should say; it's yours now, Kayla dear." She paused. "No one has entered those rooms since the last Dark Lord perished, but I'm sure that if you want to take a look—"

"Yes!" Del said, and started down the hall.

Riki grabbed his shoulder and hauled him back. "Not right now. We'll check it out when we're done arranging about the clothes."

"But that's boring!"

"Deal with it," Riki said. Madam Lorna's lips twitched.

"The dressing room is there," Detsini said, indicating the door to the right of the skull. "If you'll wait there, Kayla dear, I'll fetch you a few things to try on."

Kayla nodded uneasily and made her way down the hall. She opened the door and found herself staring into a room twice as large as her bedroom at home, lined with mirrors.

Through an archway next to a large fireplace, Kayla could see what looked like a bathroom tiled in silver-veined marble. Across from the archway was another black door with the carved dragon-skull motif; two silver chairs, a small mirrored table, and a black carpet completed the furnishings.

"Good grief," Riki said, peering in over her shoulder. "This is a dressing room?"

"Wow! Mom, are you sure we don't want to stay here?" Del said.

"Is *everything* in this castle black and silver?" Kayla's voice sounded plaintive even to her own ears.

"Of course not, dear," Detsini said from right behind them, and Kayla jumped. "Forgive me for startling you. Your father's theme was black and silver, and naturally no one has changed it since his death. It is entirely up to you whether you wish to honor his memory by keeping his colors, or choose your own." She pushed past Kayla and her mother and set a large pile of fabric on the nearest chair. "This should be plenty to start with."

"Thank you," Kayla said, eyeing the stack doubtfully. It looked as if her color choices were limited to poison green, blood red, and, of course, black.

Detsini started slowly for the door. "If you require assistance in dressing—"

"That's all right," Kayla said quickly. "I'll be fine."

"We'll wait outside while you change," Riki said, steering Del firmly out the door.

Kayla waited until the door had completely closed behind Detsini before lifting the first garment from the pile. She studied it doubtfully. It was a long dress made of bright red-and-pink-striped satin, hanging from a wide, thick collar of red and black feathers that looked like an enormous muff. The narrow sleeves had more giant puffs of feathers around the elbows and wrists, and the skirt had a muff of pink and red feathers circling it just above the knees and again at the hem.

Even if it weren't the tackiest dress Kayla had ever seen (and it was), Riki wouldn't allow her to be caught dead in a coal mine in it, much less be seen wearing it in public. "I don't think so," Kayla muttered. She tossed it aside and lifted the next one.

By the time she was halfway through the stack, she had

concluded that the previous Dark Ladies had a serious love of dressing up combined with an equally serious lack of taste. Everything was floor-length and spattered with fur, feathers, lace, or jewels. Several had all four. One of them looked a lot like a crimson bikini trimmed in green fur, with long strings of diamonds dangling at random.

Just for fun, Kayla tried on one of the more outrageous combinations, one that Riki would never have let her put on even in a dressing room. She quickly decided that she agreed with Riki's judgment about that, though she'd never admit it. She felt uncomfortable just wearing it in front of Macavinchy, though he politely turned his head when she changed. The fur itched, the lace and jewels were scratchy, the low neckline made her feel exposed, and between the thinness of the silk and the slits in the skirt, it was even colder than her T-shirt and shorts. To top it off, it was at least four inches too long.

She was just about to wiggle out of it and start hunting for something that her mother might actually approve of when the dragon skull on the inner door growled. Simultaneously, she heard a muffled shriek and a much louder roar from the hall. She hesitated, wanting to know what was going on but reluctant to leave the room in the overdone dress. Then Del's voice carried through the door, high-pitched with fear, and she hiked up the skirt and bolted for the hallway.

When she yanked the door open, the noise of the roaring tripled. The air in the corridor felt heavy and electric, as if a thunderstorm were moments away, and it smelled like coal smoke and hot metal. Automatically, Kayla looked toward the end of the hall, where the door with the dragon skull on it was located, and her stomach clenched as if she had just been sucker punched.

Del was crouched against the door, caught in a giant, bony dragon fist that had materialized out of the wood just below the skull. He looked terrified, but he was pulling and twisting in an attempt to get free. An instant later, the skull tilted slightly and flames shot from its mouth down the hall, filling the whole length with heat and bitter, acrid smoke.

As Kayla raised her hands to protect her face from the heat, the dragon's roar changed. Suddenly, she heard words under the sound: "Thief! Thief! Master, come; a thief has tried to enter your chamber!"

"Stop that!" Kayla shouted back without thinking. To her surprise—and relief—both the flames and the roaring ceased. She took a quick look up the hall. There was no sign of Riki, the seamstress, or the castle women, but the door to one of the storage rooms was open, so they had probably ducked in there. She hoped they were all right. "Del!" she called.

"Kayla!" Del tried to pull away from the claw, but it tightened. "Kayla, help!"

"Hold still and I'll try." Kayla took a deep breath, wondering what to do next. She was about to yell for Detsini and Yazmina when the dragon skull spoke again.

"Master?" The skull sounded uncertain.

"Mistress," Kayla corrected it. "Or madam, I guess. I'm the new Dark Lady." She hitched one shoulder, trying to keep the gown from sliding off, and hoped that the skull didn't judge on appearances. "I just got here yesterday."

She felt a pressure around her head, as if she were in a fast elevator that had taken her up too many floors too quickly. She stiffened, and something rose inside her and pushed back. The pressure vanished. An instant later, the dragon said, "Mistress."

Cautiously, Kayla stepped into the hall, barely managing not to trip on the dress. "Let go of my brother," she commanded.

The pressure returned for a moment, and then the skull said, "This is no brother of yours, but a thief who attempted to enter your chamber."

"He's my brother," Kayla insisted.

"Is not," the skull said.

"Kayla! Are you all right? What—" Her mother's voice broke off, and Kayla heard whispers from the open door at the end of the hall.

A wave of relief swept Kayla, but she didn't turn. She had to get Del free first. No wonder nobody had been into the rooms since the previous Dark Lord's death! At least the dragon was listening to her. "Let go of him," she repeated.

"Won't," said the skull.

"What are you, two years old?" Kayla snapped before she thought. "And aren't you supposed to do what I tell you? Let him go!"

"I have been here for nine hundred and fifty-four years," the skull said, sounding wounded. "And my job is to guard this door and dispose of would-be thieves."

"Kayla?" Del sounded desperate and scared and hopeful, all at the same time.

"Shush; I'm trying to get you out of this," Kayla told him. She looked back at the dragon. "He's not a thief, and you can dispose of him by handing him over to me."

"There is precedent for that," the skull said. Slowly, the dragon fist uncurled. Del scrambled away from the door, his eyes still wide with fear. He lunged for Kayla, wrapping his arms around her.

The dragon roared angrily. Kayla shoved Del behind her and said, "Hey! I told you to stop that!"

"He was attacking you!" the skull objected.

"He was not; he's just scared. And what kind of Dark Lady would I be if I couldn't handle a ten-year-old kid on my own?"

"I suppose." The dragon skull sighed and the bony hand pulled back into the door as if the surface were made of water instead of wood. "Can I eat the next thief that tries to get in?"

"No," Kayla said.

"I never get to do anything fun," it grumbled. The skull lowered its chin and pulled back until it was in the same position as it had been when they arrived. The electric tingle in the air faded. A moment later, Riki emerged from one of the doors at the far end of the hall, followed closely by Detsini and Yazmina. The seamstress brought up the rear. Riki made straight for Kayla and Del, and engulfed them in a hard hug before either of them could say anything.

"Mom," Kayla gasped after a moment, "could I maybe breathe a little?"

Riki gave them one last squeeze and let go. "What were you thinking?" she demanded, glaring at Del. "Detsini told you to keep away from that thing!"

"She did not! And I wasn't doing anything. I just wanted to see the skull up close. I didn't know it could move!"

"And you!" Riki rounded on Kayla. "You are so grounded. Coming out when that thing was breathing fire!"

"Somebody had to help Del!"

Riki took a deep breath. "And I'm glad it worked. But you could have been seriously hurt."

"No, I couldn't," Kayla said automatically.

"The Dark Lady speaks truly," Yazmina said. "She has claimed the castle for her own, and so long as it is hers, according to Tradition, no trap or guardian or protection within it may harm her. I tried to tell you."

Kayla glanced at Detsini, who nodded agreement. She didn't look as mussed as Riki or Yazmina, and Kayla wondered suddenly just how hard Detsini had tried to keep Riki from running out into the hall to rescue Del.

Thinking about it, Kayla had *known* that she was in no danger, though she had no idea why she'd been so certain. She hadn't been frightened of the dragon bones, only of what they might do to Del. And she'd *known* that she could control the dragon skull if she needed to. Some deep, dark part of her had actually been looking forward to making the skull bend to her will, and she could still taste a thread of disappointment that she hadn't forced the issue, even though Del could have been hurt in the process.

"Fire isn't particular about what it burns," Riki said angrily to Yazmina. "If she'd been caught in those flames—"

"She would not have been harmed," Yazmina said calmly. "She is the Dark Lady."

Riki snorted in disbelief and turned back toward Kayla. "I appreciate that you were trying to help your brother, but you can't just go running into things like that without thinking. Even if Yazmina is right, you didn't know about it when you came— What on earth are you wearing?"

Kayla looked down at the poison-green silk and hitched one of the gown's shoulders back into place. "Uh, one of the gowns? It doesn't really fit."

"The seamstress will tend to the fit." Yazmina sounded doubtful, but then her voice firmed. "If you like the dress—"

"No!" Kayla yelped at the same moment as Riki said, "Absolutely not. Whatever possessed you, Kayla?"

"They're all like this, Mom!"

"I'd better take a look for myself."

As Riki opened the dressing room door, a deep British voice floated out. "I take it that the excitement is over, madam?"

"Macavinchy!" Kayla said. A moment later, the familiar flew out, circled the hall once, and landed on Kayla's shoulder. "Where were you?"

"Inside, madam." He sounded vaguely embarrassed. "I appear to have retained more from my prior existence than I had realized. Extreme heat is particularly bad for computer circuits, and I fear my instincts took over."

"Computers have instincts?" Del asked with great interest.

"See?" Riki said to Kayla. "Even the flying monkey knows better than to rush out into a burning hallway."

"As I have reminded you before, I am not a monkey," Macavinchy said with offended dignity. "If you must refer to me by some appellation other than my name, you should call me a familiar."

"Fine." Riki shrugged. "Let's take a look at these dresses, then."

"The Dark Lady chooses her own style," Detsini said reprovingly. "Madam Lorna will be happy to alter the gown you've chosen, Kayla dear." Her tone said that Lorna had better do as she was told and nobody else had better object. Behind her, Madam Lorna's face emptied of expression, as if she was suppressing a reaction she knew would be unwelcome.

"I, er, haven't found anything," Kayla admitted.

"No?" Detsini's forehead wrinkled in puzzlement. "But surely the gown you're wearing—"

"I just . . ." Kayla stopped. She didn't want to say straight out that the Dark Lady gowns Detsini had chosen made her think of Halloween costumes.

"Bring them out and let me take a look," Riki commanded.

Kayla looked from Detsini's frown and Yazmina's worried face to the seamstress's confused expression, and ducked back into the dressing room. She took the opportunity to change back into her T-shirt and shorts before hauling the dresses out for Riki's inspection. As she had expected, Riki took one good look at the first few dresses and rejected all of them. After a brief but intense argument, Detsini took Kayla and Riki into the storeroom to look through the chests of clothes themselves.

Nothing in the storeroom was any better than the dresses Kayla had already looked at. Riki rejected one after another as "too old" for a fourteen-year-old. Kayla only half hoped that Detsini, Yazmina, and Madam Lorna couldn't hear the implied "and much too tacky" in Riki's tone. Finally, the seamstress cleared her throat.

"Perhaps I could design something more to my lady's taste?" she offered.

"It must be finished by tomorrow," Detsini said with a sniff.

"I'm sure I could complete a simple design, something plain, without trim—"

Detsini frowned and shook her head, even as Riki nodded cautiously. "Simple? Plain?" Detsini sniffed. "No self-respecting Dark Lady would wear such a thing, not even for relaxing around the castle. Dear Kayla needs something impressive, something that will reflect her position."

"Those things"—Riki waved at the pile of discarded silk, satin, and lace—"are not appropriate to a position of authority. Now, a nice business suit . . ."

"I don't think they have business suits here, Mom," Kayla said. She pulled the shoulder of her gown back up again. An idea was tickling at her brain . . .

"Well, she can't wear anything like *your* clothing!" Detsini said, sneering at Riki's T-shirt and shorts. "Traditional wear for Dark Lords and Ladies is elegant and formal."

"Formal wear is not appropriate for the State Fair," Riki shot back. "And I wouldn't call any of those . . . outfits elegant."

"They are all in keeping with the Traditions of Dark Ladies!" Detsini replied.

"Then bring me some Traditional Dark *Lord* clothes!" Kayla snapped. She was fed up to the eyebrows with Detsini's pronouncements about Tradition. "You can't object to those, surely!"

Detsini's mouth fell open. "I—but Dark Ladies—the Traditions—"

"Perhaps your book could provide some guidance, madam," Macavinchy put in.

"Good idea." Kayla dug the little black book out of her knapsack. Detsini's expression curdled at the sight of it, but Kayla ignored her. She flipped to the chapter titled "Choose Your Image Carefully" and skimmed it rapidly. "It doesn't say anything specific about styles," she informed everyone. "Just that I should wear things that reflect my authority and position."

Riki frowned slightly at the mention of her position. Kayla continued quickly, "So, Dark Lord clothes. Slacks and a jacket, in plain black, to start with." Several of the dresses had been black, so Detsini probably wouldn't object to it.

"Yes, my lady. I can make up a basic ensemble and deliver it in two days," Madam Lorna said briskly. Although her tone was respectful and her expression neutral, Kayla got the distinct impression that she was surprised by Kayla's choice, though not disapproving.

Detsini scowled. "That's not accept—"

"Two days will be fine," Kayla cut in. She looked at Detsini. "We decided at breakfast that the investiture is in five days, and it's not like I'm going anywhere before then."

Grudgingly, Detsini nodded. Madam Lorna stepped forward and took Kayla's measurements with rapid efficiency, then departed. By then, Detsini had recovered from her shock, though she kept glaring at Macavinchy. "Now that *that's* done, perhaps you'd like to look at the Dark Lord's private rooms," she suggested. "The guardian has settled down, so—"

"Absolutely not," Riki said angrily. "I'm not letting either of my children anywhere near that thing. If you want to get in there, do it yourself."

Detsini shot her a poisonous look, then glared down the hall at the skull, and Kayla's eyes widened in realization. *She does want to get in, but she can't! The dragon won't obey her.* Hard on the heels of that thought came another: *I wonder what she expects to find?* Kayla bit back a comment; she didn't want Detsini to realize she'd noticed. If only Del hadn't gotten on the wrong side of the skull guarding the door—it would take time and some serious persuasion before Riki would let them investigate.

"It would be best to outfit the rest of you now," Yazmina said, breaking the tension. Riki nodded, and they followed Yazmina away from the Dark Lord's rooms. As they left the floor, Kayla thought she heard the dragon rumble once, too softly for her to make out any words.

CHAPTER 11

Learning Your First Dark Spells

Begin your study of magic with spells that will quickly impress and intimidate the lesser forces that will oppose you early in your reign. If you wear fireproof garments, even the explosion of a botched spellcasting can frighten ignorant peasants and enhance your reputation without damaging your person.

—From *The Dark Traditions*

Outfitting Del and Riki took a while. The basic tunic and skirt Riki chose looked comfortable and far warmer than Kayla's fairgoing outfit, so Kayla overrode Detsini's objections and grabbed a set for herself. They spent the rest of the afternoon in the library.

As they made their way back to the kitchens for dinner, it occurred to Kayla that Detsini was becoming more and more unhappy with her. She shrugged it off. If her aunt had wanted a niece who understood and followed all her precious Traditions, she shouldn't have shipped Kayla off to a completely different world where she couldn't learn any of them.

When they reached the main kitchen, Riki shooed away the

hapless minion who had been assigned to produce dinner. With help from Geneviev and Kayla—and over Detsini's continued protests—she produced a much tastier and more edible one-pot meal than the one they'd been served the night before. Detsini's disapproval did not extend to refusing to eat Riki's cooking, Kayla noticed.

They camped in the guest rooms again that night. At breakfast next morning, while Archie and Del argued amicably over the last few pancakes, Ichikar cornered Kayla and gloomily requested that she inspect the treasury. "'Tis your duty as the new Dark Lady," he informed her.

"All right," Kayla said, after a wary glance at her mother. "Where is the treasury, anyway?"

On Kayla's shoulder, Macavinchy purred. "The primary treasury vault of the Dark Lords of Zaradwin Castle is located in the village of Ashwend near the first gatehouse on the road to the castle," the deep British voice answered.

Everyone except Kayla stared at Macavinchy. Kayla put up a hand protectively and said, "The main vault is in the village? You mean we passed it on the way here?"

"That is correct, madam," Macavinchy replied.

"Why put the vault down there?" Riki sounded simply puzzled, but Macavinchy answered anyway.

"The primary location was chosen for ease of access."

"Whose access?" Kayla muttered.

"Tax collectors, disbursement agents, and the armies of the Light, madam," Macavinchy said promptly.

"The armies of the Light?" Kayla frowned, puzzled. "Why do

the armies of the Light get easy access to the Dark Lord's treasury?"

"According to *The Rise and Fall of the One Hundredth Dark Empire,* every Dark Lord's treasury vault has been plundered by the armies of the Light during or immediately after the Final Battle," Macavinchy said. "I assume that is the case in this instance as well."

"So we don't have to walk down the mountain again?" Del said. "Great! We've hardly had a chance to explore the castle yet."

Waylan cleared his throat. "If the young lord wishes—"

"You're not going exploring, Del," Riki said firmly. "Not after what happened with that skull thing." She frowned at Waylan. "Don't encourage him."

"Skull thing?" Archie asked.

Del ignored him. "But, Mom—"

"No buts."

"It matters not," Ichikar put in. "The vault was indeed sacked by the armies of the Light after the Final Battle."

"What's the point of inspecting it if the armies of the Light took everything?" Kayla asked.

"They did not take quite everything," Ichikar replied. "The few coins that remained were brought to the castle and stored in the guardhouse, according to Tradition. Since that day, I have husbanded them and added what I could from the meager income provided by the village and lands, in hopes that when a new Dark Lord—or Lady—came to Zaradwin, there would be enough to begin rebuilding. 'Tis my duty."

Kayla shook her head. "If you know that the armies of the

Light *always* take everything in the treasury, why didn't you make it harder for them to get at?"

"Because it prevents them from sacking the castle," Macavinchy answered. "The Light expends great effort on breaking into the treasury and carrying off the Dark Lord's accumulated hoard in the belief that doing so will delay the rise of the next Dark Ruler. As a result, Zaradwin Castle has never been razed, allowing it to build its Dark power continuously for nine centuries until it has become the preeminent focus of Dark magic in the world."

He hesitated, then continued. "Furthermore, the known location of the main treasury vault has allowed the Dark Lords and Ladies of Zaradwin to safely leave a secret cache of money and supplies hidden within the castle itself, enabling their successors to expand their empire rapidly." He shifted uneasily on Kayla's shoulder as he finished, as if he was unsure whether he should have mentioned the secret cache or not.

"You mean the rulers of Zaradwin keep a secret vault where the Light can't get at it?" Archie sounded outraged. "That's *cheating*!"

"Of course it is," Detsini said with a sniff. "We're Dark Lords."

Archie looked as if he wanted to argue but couldn't think of anything to say. Riki just shook her head. "That makes about as much sense as anything else in this world."

"So where is this secret extra treasure?" Kayla asked.

"I regret to inform you, madam, that the Dark Lords and Ladies did not include directions to the secondary vault in any of the sources to which I have access," Macavinchy answered. "I presume that the discovery of the secret was intended as a test of the fitness of any new candidate for the position of Dark Lord of Zaradwin."

Ichikar nodded. "'Tis the first I have heard of such a hoard, but 'tis in keeping with the power and ingenuity of the Dark Lords of Zaradwin."

The rest of the castle folk murmured agreement. "So how do we find it?" Kayla asked.

"A treasure hunt!" Del said enthusiastically.

"Perhaps Xavriel left some clue in his private chambers," Detsini suggested.

Riki's eyes narrowed. "We are *not* going back there. Not—" She looked around the great hall, then down at the crumbs of pancakes that were left on her plate. She sighed. "Not unless there is absolutely no other choice." She looked at Ichikar. "You've managed on the income from the village for ten years; you can handle another couple of weeks, can't you?"

"Nay," Ichikar said, his expression turning even more sour than usual. "Not with the Dark Lady having new clothes sewn and planning her ceremony of investiture, let alone the recruiting that we must start. And 'tis Tradition for each new Dark Lord or Lady to inspect the treasury."

Kayla winced. She didn't want to hike down the mountain and back just to look at a nearly empty treasury. "Can't you do it?" she asked Riki, trying not to whine. "You're a bookkeeper; you know more about treasuries than I do."

To Kayla's mild surprise, Riki allowed herself to be persuaded, though she exacted promises from Del not to make trouble, from both Waylan and Archie to keep an eye on him, and from everyone to be back at the kitchens in time to make lunch.

As Riki left with Ichikar at last, Kayla heard her begin the Standard Lecture on Managing Money that she normally gave Del every couple of weeks. She wondered how Ichikar was going to react when her mom got to the part about not overspending his allowance. She suppressed a giggle, but she couldn't help being relieved. Having Riki hovering over her every minute had been getting more than a little wearing, and from the look on his face, Del felt the same way.

At the library, Macavinchy curled up like a cat on the mantelpiece and went to sleep. Harkawn brought out a stack of books and scrolls, then went off about some business of his own, leaving the rest of them to their studies. Del saw no point in deciphering the fragile handwritten scrolls, especially since he couldn't work any of the spells. After a few minutes, he persuaded Waylan to take him on a hunt for the Dark Lord's secret cache. Kayla would have liked to go with them, but she didn't want to let her mother down.

Kayla shifted uncomfortably on the hard library bench. She hadn't managed to work any of the spells she'd tried—not that she'd tried very many. Most of the ones in the books Harkawn suggested did things she didn't want to do, like summoning hordes of insects or creating huge fireballs. None of them seemed to do anything useful, like getting *rid* of hordes of insects or starting a campfire to cook things on.

Maybe that was the problem, she thought. When they'd done Harkawn's test, he'd asked them to think of a strong emotion.

When she'd stuck everyone to the walls of the castle, she'd wanted to protect Del. Maybe the Dark spells weren't working because they didn't do anything she *wanted.*

"Are you getting anywhere with these?" she asked Archie.

Archie shook his head. "I don't understand why. I'm supposed to be *good* at Dark magic. But everything is completely different from what I'm used to. . . ." His voice trailed off and he slumped over the book he'd been studying.

"Different?" Kayla sat back and rolled her stiff shoulders. "How? Maybe we can figure it out by comparison."

"Everything is so . . . random," Archie said, waving his hands. "Things that should be easy, like making a feather float, use long, complicated chants and six ingredients that are impossible to get, like a scale from a flameless dragon. Spells that should be hard, like raising a castle, take a lock of hair and a one-word command. As near as I can tell, anyway; half of these things seem to be written in code."

"It isn't just me, then," Kayla said, relieved. "I thought it was because I . . . don't know anything about all these Traditions they keep talking about."

"I don't know much about them, either," Archie pointed out.

"But you know Light magic," Kayla said. "Even if the Dark books aren't very well organized, there have to be some similarities."

Archie blinked, then frowned slightly. "Why?"

"It's all magic, isn't it?"

"Yes, but I don't see why that should make any difference,"

Archie said. "It's like saying that red and green are both colors, so they have to have other similarities."

It was Kayla's turn to stare. "But they do, sort of. I mean, they're both just different wavelengths of light."

Archie gave her a blank look. Kayla opened her mouth, then sighed. She didn't feel up to explaining light refraction and the spectrum, especially when she'd only gotten a B– on her science exam last year. "I'll get Macavinchy to tell you about it later."

"All right." Archie still looked dubious. "I don't think it will help with learning Dark magic, though."

"Probably not." Kayla sighed again. What she really wanted were some practical, everyday spells for things like keeping a room warm or . . . or finding lost socks. You couldn't get more ordinary than lost socks. "How did you learn Light magic, anyway?"

"I had a tutor. He came twice a week, one day to teach theory and assign me things to read and practice, and one day to put the theory and practice together into actual spellcasting."

"What kinds of spells did you learn?"

"I started with the easy things, like calling light and purifying water." Archie looked away. "I wasn't very good at it. It took me forever to move on to intermediate spells like healing, and I never got to the advanced spells at all."

Kayla perked up. Purifying water sounded practical. And if it was easy . . . "Have you tried any Light spells since you got here?"

"No, of course not!" Archie said. "Only a fully trained arch-mage can cast Light spells in the Dark lands."

"Really?" Kayla leaned back. "Try something easy."

Archie hesitated, then shrugged. "Calling light is pretty basic." He raised his right hand as if he were holding up an invisible baseball. Frowning in concentration, he made a complicated gesture with his left hand and muttered a word under his breath.

Light exploded from his upraised hand, bright and intense as a row of spotlights at a rock concert. Kayla flinched, automatically bringing up a hand to shield her eyes. "Ow! Turn it off!"

The brilliant light died. Kayla blinked, trying to clear the spots from her eyes. For a minute, it felt as if the afterimage was permanently burned onto the backs of her eyes, but finally it began to fade.

"If it would not be too much trouble, madam, a little advance warning in future would be much appreciated," Macavinchy said from the mantelpiece.

"I could have used a warning myself," Kayla told him. She looked up and saw Archie blinking in disbelief at his own hand. "That was a basic spell?" she asked cautiously.

"It should have been." Archie looked stunned; clearly he had not expected such dramatic results.

"Judging from the effects, it was an excellent example of a highly powered light-focusing spell," Macavinchy said at the same time.

"I— How can this be? I'm a Dark magician!" He raised a shaking hand to touch his two-tone hair.

"You said only an archmage can cast Light spells in the Dark lands," Kayla said slowly. "What if Light and Dark aren't so much about the spells as about where you are? If Light magicians get their power from something in the Light countries, it would be harder for them to do spells in the Dark countries. And Dark magicians—"

"—would have just as much trouble doing magic in Light lands," Archie said. His eyes widened. "Maybe all that training wasn't for nothing!"

"We'll have to test it," Kayla said. "Can you teach me that spell?"

"I can try."

Learning the spell was easy; Light magic was, as Archie had promised, much clearer and more logical than the Dark spells they'd been looking at. Actually casting the spell took Kayla the rest of the morning, but eventually she managed a soft golden glow in her upraised hand. She looked at it and grinned, feeling much better. She did belong here; she could do magic!

Still, it was a long way from creating a candle glow to teleporting people between worlds. She still had a lot of work to do. Kayla shut off the light-focusing spell just as Waylan and Del reappeared to take them to lunch. Del filled the walk to the kitchens with a blow-by-blow description of their unsuccessful search, so neither she nor Archie had to talk much. By unspoken agreement, neither mentioned their experiments with Light magic. Kayla had the feeling that the inhabitants of Zaradwin Castle wouldn't be happy if they found out the first spell their new Dark Lady cast was a Light one.

Riki was already busy when they arrived. She'd organized Yazmina, Geneviev, and Ichikar into a sandwich-making production line, while Detsini looked on with her usual disapproving frown. A large tray of sandwiches at one end of the table testified to the success of the system. As soon as she saw Waylan, Riki assigned him to take the tray into the great hall for the minions. Ichikar left with him, but everyone else stayed in the kitchen to eat.

Geneviev was dressed in another poufy pink confection of a dress that looked totally out of place in a Dark Lord's castle, let alone a kitchen. Kayla started uncertainly in her direction, but Geneviev immediately retreated to the far corner. Kayla wasn't sure whether to be relieved or not. She wanted to talk to her half sister, but she had no idea what to say. How did you start a conversation with a close relative you'd only just met?

Throughout the meal, Geneviev came no nearer, but every time Kayla looked toward the corner, Geneviev's eyes dropped, as if she didn't want to be caught watching Kayla. *Maybe she's as curious about me as I am about her.* Kayla found the thought heartening, but it didn't make it any easier to approach her.

As she finished her sandwich, Kayla heard a cough from behind her. It was Geneviev. "My lady, may I speak with you a moment? Privately?"

"I—"

"The Dark Lady has more important things to do this afternoon," Detsini interrupted her. "If you wish an audience, wait and schedule one."

Kayla frowned. Detsini had shooed Geneviev away the day before, too. Was she trying to keep Kayla from talking to Geneviev, or did Detsini just dislike the girl? Riki had noticed something off, too; she was giving Detsini her one-more-smart-remark-and-you're-grounded expression, even though Riki couldn't ground Detsini, and Detsini wasn't even looking at her.

Geneviev bit her lip. "A formal audience is far more than is needed for my paltry request. It is a matter of a few minutes, no more."

"Nevertheless—"

"I will always make time for my sister," Kayla said before Detsini could get any further. From the corner of her eye, she saw her mother glance at Geneviev, then give Kayla a narrow-eyed look. *She's probably worried about me going off by myself,* Kayla thought, and resolutely turned away. If Riki wanted to make a big deal out of it, she was going to have to say something, not just make Mom faces at her.

"Thank you, my lady!" Geneviev clasped her hands. "There is a room just down the hall where we can converse, by your leave."

"No," Yazmina said, more sharply than Kayla had ever heard her speak. "You should know better than to lure the Dark Lady off alone, especially before her investiture has taken place. Are you *trying* to get yourself executed?"

Geneviev's shoulders hunched. "I mean no harm."

"That's what they all say," Detsini muttered.

"Why don't the two of us go talk in the corner while the rest of you stay over there?" Kayla suggested, waving at the far door.

After some more unnecessary discussion, everyone reluctantly agreed to this proposal. Detsini and Riki took up positions by the doors, along with Archie. Del, oblivious to the undercurrents, stayed by the table to polish off the last of the sandwiches. Kayla and Geneviev walked back to the corner and stood there. All the awkwardness of the situation flooded back over Kayla. "You wanted to talk?" she said at last.

Geneviev's eyes flashed up in that penetrating look she'd given Kayla before, then dropped to the floor once more. "For most of my life, I've known this day would come," she said in a soft, trembling voice. "I wish to beg for clemency, my lady."

"Clemency?" The unexpected request unnerved Kayla. "What for?"

The other girl looked up, eyes wide and startled. "What for? I'm your half sister!"

"I don't understand."

A look of comprehension came over Geneviev's face. "I am not asking you to defy Tradition," she said earnestly. "But you have more choices than execution."

"Execution?" Kayla felt like a parakeet, repeating Geneviev's words in a high voice without grasping their meaning. "Does everyone here think killing people is a good way of solving problems?"

"Or exile, but everyone knows that exile is a foolish choice," Geneviev said as if acknowledging a point that Kayla didn't know she'd been making. "Exiled family members Traditionally return with an army at the most inconvenient time, or their children do. I am sure you are too smart to store up trouble for yourself that way."

"Okay . . ."

Geneviev looked down, but this time she seemed more embarrassed than shy or retiring. "I did think of requesting exile," she said in the tones of one confessing to something shameful.

"But I'm not strong enough magically to be a Dark Lady, and I'm not good with military strategy." She sighed. "I tried to learn, I really did, but even Mother—" She broke off, looking almost frightened. "Anyway, it's no use. And defeating an incompetent returning exile wouldn't make you look good, and I'd end up executed anyway after years of privation and misery. So it wouldn't be much of an improvement."

"I suppose not," Kayla said cautiously.

"But there's a third way in the Traditions." Geneviev leaned forward. "I found it in the archives a year ago, though if I'd thought about how the Dark Lord Xavriel dealt with his sisters, I'd have figured it out long before then. It's perfectly valid, and—"

"A third way of what?" Kayla interrupted her.

"Disposing of family members who could be a threat in the future, of course," Geneviev said impatiently. "I fit the profile perfectly: I'm two years older than you. I have more than the minimum amount of magic. I'm your half sister, with no actual blood claim to the throne, and I was raised in the Dark Lord's court in the absence of the true heir. You'd be crazy not to have me executed, if the only other option were exile."

"Uh—"

"But that's not the only other option," Geneviev went on in a rush. "You can marry me off instead! Either as a reward for one of your servants who performs especially well, like Aunt Yazmina and Uncle Jezzazar, or to cement an alliance, like Aunt Detsini and Uncle Mintrik."

"Aunt Detsini is married?"

"Was married." Geneviev shook her head. "Uncle Mintrik

was careless, and a Light assassin got him three months after the wedding. I think that's why Aunt Detsini acts the way she does sometimes."

Kayla nodded numbly. *The Light side uses assassins? Aren't they supposed to be the good guys?*

"Anyway, I would work very well for either purpose," Geneviev continued. "For a reward marriage, I'm your half sister and familiar with the court, which would be useful for an ambitious underling. For an alliance marriage, I'm young and reasonably pretty, noble-raised, close to you by blood but not too close." She hesitated, swallowed hard, and added in a more uncertain tone, "Of course, you must be careful to choose me a husband with little or no power of his own. Otherwise, my children might inherit enough magic to challenge you for the Dark throne."

"Wait a minute." Kayla rubbed her forehead. "You're asking me to . . . to give you away like some kind of medal? Like you're just a . . . a *thing*? And you're okay with that?"

"It's better than being executed," Geneviev pointed out.

"I'm not executing anybody."

Genevieve stared at her with a shocked expression for a moment, then gave a shaky laugh. "Of course not, my lady," she said in the tones of someone agreeing with a statement that both people knew was false.

Not feeling up to arguing with her, Kayla said, "Wouldn't you rather pick someone to marry yourself?"

"Well—" Geneviev looked down and her cheeks darkened. "If you will permit me to express an opinion—"

"Please."

"There's Florian. He's the heir to the Light family over to the west. They're not lords, but they're noble, and since they're Light, I wouldn't be able to raise an army even if I wanted to—their people wouldn't follow me. And there'd be much less likelihood of any children making trouble for you on their own. And—"

"And you like him?"

"We've met a few times. By accident. He's quite pleasant; I think we would manage well enough."

That didn't sound like a heartfelt declaration of love to Kayla, but maybe it was how they did things here. "I'll think about it, then," she told Geneviev.

"Thank you, my lady," Geneviev said fervently. "It is as much as I could have wished."

As Geneviev curtsied and turned to leave, Kayla burst out, "Did you speak with your—our mother? About me seeing her?"

Geneviev stiffened and her face smoothed into the expressionless mask she used with Detsini. "I have told her your wish, but as I said, she is not well. But you are the Dark Lady, and if you insist—"

"No," Kayla said hastily. No matter how much she wanted to meet her biological mother, shoving her way in on an invalid was not the way to go about it. "I do want to see her, but not until she feels well enough."

"Very well, my lady." As she left, Geneviev gave Kayla another of those quick, intense looks so at odds with her appearance and behavior.

Kayla watched her go, then said in a low voice, "Macavinchy, is she right?"

"Kindly phrase your query more specifically, madam," Macavinchy said.

"Am I going to have to execute people?"

"Mmmm." Macavinchy's purr went on longer than usual. "According to the histories I have been able to access, Dark Lords and Ladies frequently order executions, sometimes for the flimsiest of reasons. It is therefore expected that you will do the same. However—" The familiar stopped.

"Macavinchy?"

"However, despite the reverence with which your people speak of it, Tradition cannot *make* you do anything."

CHAPTER 12

Disposing of Your Family

The greatest threat to your new position will come from members of your family. If you have not disposed of your parents, stepparents, and siblings in the course of achieving your throne, do so immediately. You may delay removal of any aunts, uncles, and cousins, but be careful not to put it off too long. Ruthlessness is a quality essential to all Dark Lords and Ladies.

—From *The Dark Traditions*

As they were finishing lunch, Jezzazar entered the great hall with news that two of the ten remaining minions had vanished overnight. Detsini and Ichikar wanted to send out a press-gang to find the offenders and drag them back for punishment; Jezzazar proposed that they seal up the castle and prepare to defend it, while Waylan wanted to ignore the whole matter.

Waylan's comment led to another argument, this time over which of the three approaches was more Traditional. Kayla sidled over to Riki as the argument grew louder and muttered, "Mom, can we leave before they want me to settle this? I don't know anything about their Traditions and I'm sure to mess something up."

Riki frowned at the increasing volume and nodded. The Jones family slipped out the door, unnoticed. *Almost unnoticed,* Kayla corrected herself as Archie slid into the hall behind them. *That would be a useful spell to learn,* she thought, and added "spell for not being noticed" to her mental list, after "purifying water," "getting rid of mosquitoes," and "keeping a room warm." She had the feeling it was going to be a long list by the time she finished it, and resolved to see if Macavinchy still had something like the Notes app on the computer.

"Where are you off to?" Archie asked as he joined the three of them.

"Anywhere else," Kayla said. "They're going to start shouting any minute." They started down the hall toward the library, one of the two other places in the castle that Kayla thought she had a chance of finding.

"If you don't like them arguing, tell them to stop." Archie shrugged. "You're their Dark Lady, after all."

Kayla's head jerked sideways. She thought she'd gotten used to being referred to as "the Dark Lady." Waylan and the rest of the castle inhabitants did it all the time, but only, she thought, because she was the daughter of their previous Dark Lord. Archie, though, wasn't from Zaradwin and seemed to know almost as little about the place as Kayla and her family. Yet he called her Dark Lady as if he was serious. As if she ought to take it seriously.

While Kayla was fumbling with possible replies, Riki gave Archie a sidelong look and said, "No, she isn't."

"Yes, she is," Archie said, clearly exasperated. "And the sooner you admit it, the better off we'll all be."

"She's only the *Provisional* Dark Lady until that investiture ceremony," Riki shot back.

Archie rolled his eyes. "If she doesn't start acting more like a Dark Lady, there won't *be* an investiture. And if that happens, we're in trouble."

"She's a fourteen-year-old child," Riki snapped. "You people can't expect her to solve your problems."

"Mom!" Kayla said, shocked by Riki's intensity. "Nobody is trying to . . . Well, okay, maybe Geneviev, but—"

"And what exactly did she want?" Riki demanded.

Kayla hesitated. Geneviev hadn't actually asked her to keep her appeal a secret, apart from her initial request for a private interview, and Kayla could certainly use some advice. "It's these Traditions they all keep going on about," she said. "You all have to promise not to tell anybody else."

Del snorted. "Who'd I tell?"

"Anybody within earshot," Riki murmured, suddenly sounding far less cross and far more curious. "All right, Kayla. Now, what is this about?"

"She wants me to arrange a marriage for her so that she won't be executed or exiled."

"She *what*?"

"That's not a bad idea," Archie said at almost the same time.

Riki frowned at him. "She can't be more than sixteen or seventeen! And what's this about exile and execution?"

"She said those are the Traditional options." Kayla scowled. "I don't think she believed me when I said I wasn't executing anybody."

"I suppose you could come up with something else for her to do," Archie said, tapping his chin with one finger. "I don't know much about the Dark Traditions, but I'm pretty sure that one of them is doing whatever the Dark Lord tells you to."

"I need to learn more about all these Traditions," Kayla muttered.

"No, you don't," Riki snapped. "We're not going to be here long enough for—"

"Yes, we are, and you know it," Kayla interrupted. "Even if we'd already found the spell for crossing between worlds, it's not like I can learn to cast it in a week or two. That'd be like . . . like me designing a spaceship after studying engineering for a week! We're going to be here for months, Mom. Years, maybe."

"But—"

"And we can't keep mooching off these people," Kayla swept on. "Not for that long, not when they don't have much to start with."

"You're their Dark Lady," Archie said. "You can tell them to do whatever you want, and they'll do it. It's not . . . mooching."

"It is, too," Kayla told him. "And don't tell me it's a Tradition. I don't care." She shivered, thinking of Waylan, who'd expected to march off to his death because that was Traditional, and of Geneviev, begging to be sold into a loveless marriage in place of a miserable exile or an outright execution. At least Detsini and Yazmina and Jezzazar didn't expect her to kill them any minute . . . or did they just do a better job of hiding it? "It's not right, not when we can do something about it."

"Do something?" Riki's eyes narrowed as she considered it. "Like what?"

"Kayla can make them do stuff that's good for them," Del suggested. "Like eating broccoli for dinner."

"Or fixing the portcullis," Archie said, then added disapprovingly, "They've had ten years since the last Final Battle to make repairs, and they've hardly done anything."

"And we know how to do a lot of things they don't," Kayla said. "All the books in the library are written out by hand. That's what Harkawn's job is, copying books."

"No printing presses." Riki made a face, then sighed. "I admit, if I'd had another half hour this morning, I'd have started teaching Ichikar how to do double-entry bookkeeping. Those records are a mess. But we really shouldn't do anything that will disrupt their development."

"What development?" Kayla said, exasperated. "They're just doing the same things over and over! One hundred thirty-eight times, if Jezzazar was right about the number of Final Battles."

"One hundred forty-three," Archie corrected her.

"Whatever." Kayla waved her hands impatiently. "Don't you see, Mom?"

They had reached the library door. "I'll think about it," Riki said as Del pushed ahead of them.

As they followed Del into the library, Kayla blinked in the sudden light from the long expanse of windows. Harkawn rose from the desk, which was still piled with books and scrolls. "My lady, I have—"

"Del!" Riki's disapproving voice cut off whatever Harkawn had been about to say. "What have you done to your *hair*?"

"Nothing!" Del's answer was automatic, but he stopped and turned. Kayla felt her eyes widen. A vivid scarlet streak about an inch wide ran through Del's dark brown hair, from just above his left eyebrow up toward the crown of his head. It looked as if he'd run a paintbrush dipped in red paint across the top of his head.

"Has young Master Delmar begun coming into his magic?" Harkawn asked, moving forward. "I'm sure—" He stopped short, staring, as Del turned to face him.

"What?" Del pulled a brown curl down and crossed his eyes to look at it. "It's still the same. Why are you all staring?"

"Other side," Kayla said gesturing.

This time, Del got hold of the right hair. He peered up at it, then let go and gave Kayla a broad grin. "All right! I have magic after all! Like a hero in the comics. Abracadabra kaboom!" He waved his hands.

The top of the desk exploded, shattering two windows and sending flaming books and scrolls in all directions. Harkawn, who had been standing next to the desk, was knocked off his feet. Macavinchy screeched and took off toward the door. Kayla ducked automatically. Riki grabbed the open-mouthed Del and dodged behind one of the bookcases.

Archie raised one hand and shouted, "Halt!"

The flying glass and burning books froze in midair, then settled slowly to the floor. The small fires died out. Kayla straightened and ran toward Harkawn. As she reached him, the librarian sat up, coughing heavily. "Are you all right?" she asked.

"Bruised," Harkawn said between coughs. He looked past her at Archie. "Thanks."

Kayla turned, and Archie smiled ruefully at her. "I didn't expect it to work that well. It never has before."

"Good thing it did this time," she replied.

Riki and Del emerged from behind the bookshelf. "That settles the question of whether or not you have magic," Riki told Del a bit shakily. She hadn't let go of his shoulder.

"I'm sorry!" Del said. "I didn't mean to do that! You're not going to say I can't do it anymore, are you?"

"I sincerely hope you won't do anything like *this* again." Riki looked around the wreckage of the library, then back to Del. "You are not to try any more magic unless there is an adult around *and* someone like Archie who can protect you if things go wrong. Understand?"

Del nodded vigorously.

Harkawn stopped coughing at last. Climbing to his feet, he shook his head at the ruined desk and the charred, scattered books. "I believe we had best find somewhere besides the library for you to practice," he said mournfully.

Remembering his pride in the collection when he had first shown it to them, Kayla shot her mother a meaningful look. Riki studied the library a moment more, then nodded and said, "We can't fix all the damage, but once we're done cleaning up here"— she looked at Del sternly—"we can make it easier to replace your books in the long run."

"I could try a repair spell," Archie said, though he sounded doubtful.

"Me! Let me do it!" Del said. He glanced at Riki and added, "I blew it up, so I should fix it, right?"

"No," Harkawn said firmly. "No more experimental spells around the books; they're too fragile." He looked from Archie to Del until they both nodded, then focused on Del. "Why don't you make a list of things to try later, in a more suitable place? We do need to find out more about your . . . unusual magic."

Del agreed happily, and began muttering under his breath as they set about restoring order. Kayla had the feeling that a lot of his suggestions were going to involve blowing things up, but at least it was keeping him occupied.

Cleaning the library and setting up makeshift coverings for the broken windows took most of the afternoon. Waylan came looking for them eventually. He took in the charred desk and broken windows, listened closely to Riki's explanation, and nodded. "Keep a close eye on your brother," he said to Kayla. "There are those in the castle who may try to enforce the Traditions as soon as they realize he has manifested magic of his own, in hopes of earning favor with the new Dark Lady by removing a threat."

Kayla's eyes widened. "Like Geneviev! Exile or"—she swallowed hard—"execution."

"Nobody would execute a ten-year-old!" Riki said, but she looked alarmed.

"Unfortunately, they might," Waylan said. "Lady Geneviev has survived this long because there has been no Dark Lord in the castle and because her magic is not strong, so she is not a threat.

This . . ." He scanned the library and shook his head. "This will be seen as a threat."

"Not if we tell everybody else that I did it," Kayla said. She gave Del a stern look. "That means you can't go bragging about blowing up the library."

"That might work." Harkawn studied Del with bright black eyes. "There's still the problem of his hair changing color."

"Problem?" Riki said.

Harkawn cleared his throat, coughed, and cleared it again. "Magic is Light or Dark, and once it appears, it expands steadily until it reaches its full power. The change in a child's hair color is a token of this: the hair changes to lightest white or darkest black that grows slowly from the roots." He sounded as if he were reciting something. Then he looked at Del, shook his head, and went on in a more normal voice: "Yesterday, Master Delmar's hair was uniformly dark brown; today one streak, and only one, has changed completely."

"It was all brown at lunch," Riki said, nodding. "It must have changed on the walk here."

"And it is red. Magic doesn't *work* that way. At least, I have never heard or read of anything similar. Perhaps the Light mages . . ." He looked at Archie.

"No." Archie shook his head. "And believe me, I looked. There weren't any records of anyone's hair changing all at once, or into any colors but white for Light magic and black for Dark magic. Maybe it represents a talent?"

"Or it could be that my son's magic is different because we're not from this world," Riki said.

"Yes!" Del said, pumping his fist.

"Calm down," Riki told him. "It's just a theory."

Del wasn't paying attention. "I get my own kind of magic!"

"Perhaps; nevertheless, it would be best to hide your new abilities as long as possible," Waylan told Del. "At least until after the Dark Lady has been confirmed."

"Like a secret identity," Kayla put in.

The frown that had begun to grow on Del's face transformed to a delighted grin.

"We can dye your hair, the way I did," Archie suggested.

Del made a face. "Can't I just wear a hat?"

Archie looked hurt.

"You don't keep a hat on for more than ten minutes at a time even in the middle of winter, when you need one," Riki pointed out.

"We're blaming the damage on me," Kayla said. "Can't we blame Del's hair on me, too? We could tell people I was trying to make him magical, and it obviously didn't work."

Waylan and Harkawn looked from Kayla to Del with considering expressions. "That might help," Waylan said slowly, "but I don't think it will convince everyone."

As Waylan had predicted, Detsini noticed the change in Del's hair the moment they entered the great hall, where everyone had assembled for dinner. "What's this?" she demanded.

"Kayla did it!" Del shot back. "Right after she blew up the library!"

"Well, it's certainly *unusual*," Detsini said doubtfully. "It's not really useful, though, is it, dear? Or were you trying to blow your brother up, as well as the library?"

"It didn't work the way I expected," Kayla grumped. "And I'm still learning." Which was all perfectly true, though not in the way Detsini would assume.

"You should stick to small things until you have better control," Yazmina told her sternly. "It wouldn't do to blow up your brother by accident."

"It wouldn't have been an accident," Kayla couldn't help saying.

"Hey!" Del scowled up at her.

"Enough," Riki said. "Behave yourselves, or you'll be on cleanup duty as well as cooking."

After dinner, Riki insisted on an early night, claiming that after the day's events they all needed rest. Predictably, Del whined about it, but neither he nor Riki had any trouble falling asleep. Kayla lay listening to their regular breathing for what seemed like hours, her mind whirling in confusion.

Being a Dark Lady was nothing like what she'd have expected, not that she'd ever expected such a thing. She still didn't have any idea how to use the magic everyone said she had, or how to get herself, Riki, and Del home once she learned to use it. She didn't really understand why any of the castle folk acted the way they did. Nobody besides Kayla and her family had objected aloud to the meals or the dust or the other discomforts of the castle—certainly nobody had cared enough to do anything about them.

Yet despite the bad food, the uncomfortable sleeping quarters, and the strange noises, despite all the unclear expectations and the general unhappiness of the other inhabitants, some deep level of Kayla's mind felt at ease here. They'd been in this world for only four days—two on the road and two at the castle—but already she felt as if she fit into Zaradwin in ways she had never even realized she didn't fit at home.

But St. Paul wasn't really home, either, not since her adoptive father died and Riki had lost the struggle to pay both medical bills and the mortgage. Why had Detsini and Yazmina sent her there, anyway? If they wanted her gone, why were they helping her now that she was back? . . . And around the circle her mind went.

Finally, she couldn't stand it any longer. She rose and tiptoed out into the hall, pausing only to collect Macavinchy on her way. The sun had set, but someone had lit the torches along the corridor. They smoked terribly, and the yellow light they gave off flickered and wavered, making shadows dance across the walls, but it was enough to see by.

Kayla wandered down one hall and up another without meeting anyone. She found a circular stone stair with a rope fastened to the wall for a handrail, and went down it. At the bottom was a large, dark room with several doors on either side and a narrow bench along one wall. It felt as if it hadn't been used in a long time. She was about to go back upstairs when the door to her left opened. She squinted against the light; then a voice said, "Damn. I mean, what brings you here, my lady of Darkness?"

"You're Rache," Kayla said, remembering the voice from

breakfast the day before. "Where's 'here'? I thought Detsini said this was the guest wing."

Rache came fully into the room and shut the door. He wore a long dark cloak and carried a small lantern. Archie followed close behind him, looking uneasy.

"You're quite right, cousin," Rache said. "We're in the guest wing. Or rather, the servants' level of the guest wing, which is why finding the Dark Lady wandering through it is doubly unexpected."

"I couldn't sleep. Walking helps." Kayla eyed the cloaks and the lantern thoughtfully. "You look like you're going somewhere."

"Sharp as a carving knife, you are, cousin," Rache said.

"We're going down to Ashwend, to the tavern," Archie said. "Rache says there are some musicians playing tonight. He offered to show me the way."

Rache frowned at Archie. "You're not supposed to blurt everything out like that just because she asked, even if she is the Dark Lady!"

"Why not?" Archie sounded genuinely puzzled.

Kayla ignored him, focusing on Rache. "The village tavern? At this hour?" She looked at them skeptically. "It'll be midnight before you get there, and four in the morning by the time you get back! What are you up to, really?"

"It won't take that long," Rache said. "This is the servants' entrance. It's the quickest way down and back, but the rest of them are too full of themselves to use it. It wouldn't be proper for the Dark Lord's family, you see." He grinned mischievously, the first real smile Kayla had seen from him. "So of course I use it all the time. You won't give us away, will you?"

"No," Kayla said slowly. "But are you sure about this? Waylan said the town was dangerous."

"How would he know?" Rache shrugged. "He's been gone for ten years. Things have changed."

"Besides, Waylan's a commander in the Dark Hordes," Archie said. "You can't trust what he tells you."

"*Everybody* here is a Dark something-or-other," Kayla said, exasperated. "Even you. I have to trust somebody besides Mom and Del."

"Then trust us." Rache gave her a brilliant, not-quite-convincing smile. "Let us go, and keep our secrets."

"Or come with us," Archie suggested.

"Hey!" Rache said, scowling at Archie. "We can't take the new Dark Lady out on a lark, just like that."

"Why not?" Archie said.

"It wouldn't be . . ." Rache's voice trailed off and he stared into space for a minute. Then he looked at Kayla, his expression somewhere between terror and the wild recklessness of someone with nothing left to lose. "Will you come, then?"

"What? I—"

"It's perfectly safe, really, especially if you don't mention that you're the new Dark Lady. Nobody will figure it out, especially when you're dressed like that." He waved at her borrowed skirt and tunic, which Kayla had to admit looked nothing at all like the Dark Lady dresses she'd tried on earlier. Rache tilted his head, considering. "Well, Ivy might guess, but she won't tell anyone."

"I really—" Kayla broke off in mid-refusal, thinking. Several of her friends had bragged about older siblings who'd snuck out of the house to attend a concert. It hadn't appealed to her at the time, but suddenly it seemed like such a *normal* thing to do. A tiny voice in the back of her brain screamed that this was a terrible idea, that it wasn't safe, that she was just asking to be attacked by vampires or skeletal dragons or some other would-be Dark Lord, but the voice was rapidly swamped by curiosity and the desire to do something normal.

"All right," she said. "Let's go."

CHAPTER 13

Oppressing the Peasants

When oppressing your peasants, be careful to strike the right balance. On the one hand, randomly torturing and killing peasants will enhance your reputation as a Dark Lord to be feared; on the other, a dead peasant cannot work your fields or pay your exorbitant taxes.

—**From *The Dark Traditions***

Rache walked over to the far door and opened it. On the other side was a small, empty room. Two fat ropes ran through a hole in the floor the size of a coffee can, up around a double set of wooden pulleys, and out through a similar hole in the ceiling. Next to the ropes stood a large lever and a wheel. Unlike every other room she'd seen in the castle, the floor, walls, and ceiling were all made of wood. It looked more like a giant box than a room. In fact, it almost looked like—

"An elevator?" Kayla said in considerable surprise.

"Is that what you call it?" Rache motioned her inside. "We just call it a big dumbwaiter."

Kayla stepped forward, but Archie grabbed her arm. "Wait! We have to adjust the counterweights to work for three people. Don't your . . . elevators . . . need them?"

"We use a different method," Kayla said.

"So do we," Rache said, grinning. He set the lantern on the floor of the dumbwaiter and nodded at Archie. "Grab the wheel and hold it steady while I take the brake off."

"Are you sure about this?" Archie asked, but did as he was told. Rache pushed the lever over. The room lurched and dropped an inch, then stopped, swaying.

"Now we just crank our way down." Rache took hold of the wheel with one hand and nudged Archie out of the way. He turned the wheel, and the dumbwaiter started descending.

"How?" Archie demanded.

Rache shrugged. "It's something to do with the pulleys. My mother designed the system after the Dark Lord fell and the servants left, when we had to haul all the food and supplies up by ourselves. It took her two years to convince my father to let her install it. She finally told him that if he wanted to be that Traditional, he could assign two of his men to haul the old dumbwaiter up and down all day, or there wouldn't be any food at all."

"Yazmina designed an elevator?" Kayla shook her head, trying to picture her seemingly scatterbrained aunt as someone who invented elevators.

"No, just the pulleys. The big dumbwaiter is old. One of the first Dark Lords conquered a manor that had a regular dumbwaiter—you know, a little box that brings food from the kitchens up a level to the dining room—and he decided to build a big one to make it easier to get new servants up from the village. The idea spread; most castles have them now."

"I bet this is how the heroes get in to rescue people. It doesn't look like there's much security." Kayla frowned. She'd read enough books and seen enough movies to know that the hero or heroine always snuck into the castle either by impersonating a guard or by using the servants' entrance. If they had been captured and needed to escape, they got out through the sewers or the garbage disposal. She should make a note. . . . Oh. She'd gotten so used to her familiar's weight on her shoulder that she'd forgotten he was there. "Macavinchy."

"Yes, madam?"

"Start another list. We need to set up some security on the dumbwaiter and the sewers and garbage and all the other ways people sneak into castles."

"Of course, madam. Will that be all?"

"For now. No, wait. Keep an eye on things tonight, and warn me if you see anything suspicious." She should have thought of that earlier, too.

"Certainly, madam." Macavinchy purred quietly, then said, "Do you wish me to record events for your later review?"

"You can do that?" Kayla stopped to stare at him, shaking her head. "How does that even work?"

"I am not certain of the mechanism, particularly as regards video replay," Macavinchy said apologetically. "I can, however, assure you that my audio recording functions are in perfect working condition."

"Okay, record it." Even if nothing interesting happened, they could test out how everything worked before they needed it for something. *And it would be really cool if I had pictures to bring back home.*

Rache was staring at Macavinchy. "That is definitely the weirdest familiar I've ever seen."

"People keep saying that." Kayla frowned. "What's so weird about him?"

"I haven't ever heard one that's so . . . talkative. Or that sounds like that."

"I believe it is a consequence of the memory upgrade, madam, though it may also be related to your choice of voice files." Macavinchy's tail tightened around Kayla's neck. "If you wish, I can emulate a more typical familiar, either at all times or in public."

"Too late," Kayla said. "Besides, I like the way you sound."

"Very well, madam." Macavinchy seemed relieved. Rache just shook his head.

They reached the bottom, and Rache set the brake lever. They left the dumbwaiter and made their way down a short tunnel and into the village. The air was cool and smelled a little like the animal barns at the State Fair. No traffic noises drowned out the sound of footsteps; it would be hard for anyone to sneak up on them.

They were, Kayla guessed, on the far side of the mountain from where she'd arrived. Even in the dark, she could see that the houses here were sturdy, and the street was clear of rubble. Either the armies of the Light hadn't wrecked this side of the town, or someone had actually repaired the damage.

The tavern was only a short distance from the tunnel exit—about three blocks, Kayla estimated. Rache led them inside, to a large, fire-lit room. The ceiling was low and smoke-stained. Long tables and benches occupied much of the floor; about half of them were full. The buzz of conversation broke off as they entered, and someone called, "Rache! You made it!"

"So this is why you're late," another voice called. "Who're your friends?"

"New folk at the castle," Rache said. He swung his cape off and tossed it at a row of pegs on the wall, then blew out the lantern and set it with a row of others on a little table next to the door. "They're here to listen to the music. Kayla, Archie, everybody; everybody, Kayla and Archie." He waved vaguely at the villagers occupying the tables and made for the far corner of the room, where several people with instruments were pulling stools into a circle. "Can I borrow somebody's pitch pipe? Mine's gone missing."

Kayla looked around for a place to sit. Archie caught her eye and tipped his head toward the side wall, where a row of stools stood in front of a long bar. Kayla nodded, and they edged past the end of the tables and took seats. A pleasant-looking middle-aged lady behind the bar came bustling over immediately. "That Rache!" she said. " 'Everybody, Kayla and Archie' is not a proper introduction, even for castle folk. Really, he should know better. I'm Ivy; what'll you have?"

"I—" Kayla stopped. "I don't have any money." She looked down, embarrassed. "I ran into Rache and Archie as they were leaving and just came along; I didn't think to go back for anything."

"I have a little," Archie offered, but Ivy waved him off.

"Don't worry about it," she said cheerfully. "I'll put it on Rache's tab. He won't notice." She looked Kayla over with surprisingly sharp green eyes. "Not sure? Why don't you try the cider? I've got a bit of the early pressing from over the border. If you like it, you'll know what to order up to the castle in a few weeks when the rest arrives."

"All right."

A moment later, Ivy set two large mugs in front of them. Kayla sipped cautiously, then took a long drink. The cider was cold and the perfect blend of sweet and tart. "Oh, that's good," she said as she set the mug back on the bar.

"Isn't it?" Ivy smiled and leaned forward confidentially. "So tell me, what's the new Dark Lady like?"

Archie stiffened. Kayla poked him surreptitiously and said, "How do you know—"

"Everybody felt it when the castle was claimed, and then Lorna the seamstress said it was a Lady, not a Lord, just before she disappeared into her workroom," Ivy broke in, and winked. "Seems the Dark Lady wants to make an impression at her investiture, and needs a new gown."

"It wasn't my idea," Kayla said automatically. "Detsini insisted."

"Lady Detsini can be overly particular, it's true," Ivy said in a cool tone. Then she smiled. "But any Dark Lady with enough magic to claim Zaradwin Castle isn't likely to be taken in by the likes of her. Just stick with your mistress and you'll both be fine. For a while, anyway."

"Our mistress?" Archie gave the bartender a wary look, as if he wasn't sure how much she knew.

"The new Dark Lady." Misinterpreting Kayla's evident surprise, Ivy shook her head. "It's not hard to figure out. You're completely new in town, and you came down from the castle two days after the Dark Lady's arrival. Obviously, you're a pair of our new Dark Lady's attendants." She studied them briefly, then looked straight at Kayla. "You're her apprentices, right?"

Kayla let out a slow breath of relief. "Sort of."

"The familiar gives it away. If you live in the castle now, you came with the Dark Lady, and the only way a Dark Lady will tolerate another magician powerful enough to attach a familiar is if that magician is her apprentice." She turned to Archie, eyeing his two-tone hair. "You need to cut off the bleached part," she told him. "Some people will see the two colors and jump to conclusions without stopping to see that it's dyed. Somebody may have done so already," she added cryptically.

Archie's eyes widened. "I'll do that," he promised. "First thing tomorrow morning."

"I'm glad you came down tonight," Ivy went on. "It'll reassure people that our new Dark Lady is powerful enough to hold the castle and establish her empire quickly."

"Is that a problem?" Kayla asked uneasily.

Ivy shrugged. "Someone always shows up to test the new ruler when the castle changes hands. A strong Dark Lord means we only have to put up with a couple of them before most of them give up. I don't think we'll have much trouble this time, though. Not if your Dark Lady is as strong as she seems."

"I don't think—" Kayla started.

"Don't try to deny it," Ivy said. "As I said, we all felt it when the castle was claimed. And she has to be powerful, to have two apprentices like you." She leaned closer to Kayla and said in a low voice, "And once you've learned too much or gotten too pretty, and it's time to run, you send me word. I can usually work something out, as long as you don't want to take over as the next Dark Lady. If you get tangled up in the curse, though, I can't help you."

"Curse?" Kayla stared. "Wait, you mean that when everybody talks about 'this cursed castle,' they mean it literally?"

"Of course," Ivy said. "Everybody knows that. Well, everybody in Zaradwin; no reason you'd be aware of it, being from elsewhere as you are. It only affects people who live in the castle, and it takes a while to kick in."

"What does it do?" Kayla asked warily. *And how long will it be before it does it to us?*

"The castle folk don't exactly give out details, but it's probably something about losing what you need or want most."

"How do you know?"

Ivy gave Kayla a sidelong look, then shook her head. "Not up on curses, then? You've some catching up to do. A specific curse would have the same effect on everyone—whoever it affected would die of the rot, or go berserk and kill everyone in their way. The castle curse does different things to different people. Some lose their families; some lose their health; some get obsessed with a person or a thing or a secret. The only thing we know for sure is that they're all miserable in the end."

"Does the curse wear off if you stop living in the castle?" Kayla asked uneasily. She made a mental note to ask Macavinchy about this later, when they were in private.

"Maybe. Nobody's sure. It's why most people who work there live here in Ashwend, even if the walk up is a long one. You should see if the Dark Lady will let you do the same."

"Why hasn't anyone broken the curse?"

Ivy shrugged. "The curse has been working since the castle was built, so either it has impossible conditions for breaking it, or else it has advantages for the Dark Lords, so that they don't want to break it." A man at one of the tables yelled and waved an empty mug. Ivy clucked. "Back in a minute," she told them, and went off to get his order.

"What did she say to you?" Archie asked.

"Later," Kayla said. There was no time for explanations; the bartender was already on her way back.

"So," Ivy said with a smile as she rejoined them, "tell me about our new Dark Lady."

"What do you want to know?" Kayla asked cautiously. She liked the way Ivy referred to "our" Dark Lady, but she wasn't about to just answer her questions.

"Whatever you want to tell me," Ivy answered. "I realize you can't say much; I wouldn't want you to violate her trust. Still, every little bit helps. For instance, what does she look like?"

Archie's eyebrows drew together. Kayla stared. "What does she *look* like?"

Ivy nodded. "Lorna just said she was short, and that's not much to go on. I don't want any of my girls branded because they're fairer than the Dark Lady, so I'd like to have some idea who to send when the castle steward comes around asking for maids."

"Branded?" Kayla squeaked before she could stop herself.

Ivy frowned. "Where did you grow up? Dark Ladies don't want anyone around who's prettier than they are; everybody knows that. It's not so bad when they're young, but the older they get, the harder it is to please them. Some of them start executing every good-looking girl in the kingdom, just so they can stay the fairest in the land. It's actually a relief when the Light forces invade and put a stop to it."

"This Dark Lady doesn't care," Kayla said. "And I'm sure she won't be executing or branding people."

"It'd be nice," Ivy said wistfully. "But I'm not taking any chances with my girls."

"Your girls?" Archie leaned forward.

"I'm the head of the Maids' and Footmen's Guild," Ivy said. "I only tend bar between Dark Lords and Ladies, when the castle isn't fully staffed."

"Could you send some people up tomorrow?" Kayla asked without thinking. "It really needs cleaning."

Ivy gave her a sharp look. "I expect they'll summon me in a few days anyway, but it won't hurt to get a jump on things. So what does the Dark Lady look like?"

"Average," Kayla said uncomfortably. "Kind of like me."

Archie choked on his cider.

"Average like you. Right." Ivy's voice dripped disbelief. She set three mugs in a neat row at the back, ready to be filled for the next customers, and pursed her lips. "So, striking rather than beautiful? I can work with that, as long as she's not too capricious."

Striking? Kayla didn't quite dare ask what she meant. Instead she said, "Capricious?"

"Dark Ladies are always more unpredictable than Lords." Ivy shrugged. "It's a trade-off, I suppose. Dark Lords aren't hard to cope with on a day-to-day basis, but they start more wars and they're always experimenting on animals and monsters to make more fearsome war beasts. Sooner or later, the experiments escape and wreck most of Ashwend. Rebuilding the town takes forever And the battles between a Dark Lord and the Light-siders are always nasty.

"Dark Ladies, on the other hand, tend to be more into manipulation and making money than they are into wars, so business is better and we don't have to repair things all the time. And they're more practical than Dark Lords. Of course, I'm generalizing, but still, you don't see a Dark Lady throwing army after army at the toughest kingdom around for no results. Maybe one army, but if she loses that, she usually stops the direct attacks and gets sneaky instead. The best Dark Ladies are sneaky right from the start."

Kayla nodded. She could do sneaky.

"The downside is that, as I said, Dark Ladies are unpredictable," Ivy went on, "especially on a personal level. Meaning, the way they treat their servants. They'll give you a sack of gold one day and have you flogged nearly to death the next." Ivy sighed.

"Why do you put up with it? I mean, couldn't you move somewhere else?" Kayla asked.

"All the Dark kingdoms work the same way, and I'd rather live at one of the power centers. Zaradwin is more likely to become the center of the next Dark Empire than anywhere else, which means I won't have to move to keep running the guild."

"You could go to a Light kingdom," Archie suggested.

Ivy laughed. "I did, when I was younger. Spent two years in one of those places." She shuddered. "It took me less than a month to decide it wasn't for me, and twenty-three months more to get out. Terrible place, if you ask me."

"What's wrong with it?" Archie demanded.

"All those *rules*," Ivy said. "They have rules for everything. What you can do, how you do it, when you can do it, where you can live or work, what you can learn, where you can go, what you are allowed to wear and eat. *Everything.* And they enforce every last one of them."

"Rules aren't that different from Traditions," Archie objected.

"Different enough," Ivy told him. "You can ignore Traditions if you really want to, but there are penalties for breaking the rules. The Light castles are the worst. I have to pay people more to work in Light castles and manors, and it's still hard to find anyone willing. Even folks who've grown up Light don't want to serve in one of those places."

"But they don't have to worry about getting branded on a whim," Archie argued.

"Try it yourself and see," Ivy said. "At least in the Dark kingdoms, the Lords mostly let us do as we like." She turned away to fill a dented tin pitcher from a large keg.

Archie opened his mouth once more, and Kayla poked him again. Hard. He shook himself and took a long pull of his cider instead of saying whatever he'd intended. She raised her own mug and found that she had reached the bottom without realizing it.

"All finished? I'll get you another," Ivy said. "It's time I got back to work, in any case. The music's about to start." She whisked away Kayla's empty mug and replaced it a moment later, refilled. "Just let me know if you need anything," she said, and went off down the bar, leaving Kayla to ponder what she'd learned.

The music began a few minutes later. There were four people playing: a boy with a small flute, two girls, one with a lap drum and the other with a stringed instrument that looked like a banjo with an extra-long neck, and Rache, who had something that resembled a guitar, but shaped like half a giant hard-boiled egg with a short neck for the strings.

The first song was an instrumental piece. Kayla thought it was complicated and boring. The second was a humorous ballad, which at least had interesting words, something about a Dark Lord falling in love with a Light Lady and giving her all sorts of inappropriate gifts. The next couple of songs sounded like folk music. Kayla sipped at her cider and let her mind wander.

"Hey!" the girl with the lap drum called. Kayla glanced up, startled, realizing that the current song had ended. "You two at the bar! What kind of music does the new Dark Lady like?"

"Mostly rock," Kayla answered without thinking. "Not so much the heavy metal, but most of the other kinds."

The tavern fell silent. The musicians looked at her with blank expressions. "Rock?" the flute player said. "Is that a new style?"

Gathering her scattered wits, Kayla replied, "I suppose it would be, here. It's what they play where she comes from."

"How does it go?" Rache asked with a wicked grin.

"I don't think I can explain it," Kayla said. "You have to hear it."

"Can you sing us something, then?" Rache persisted.

"I can't," she snapped. "But if you really want, I'll show you. Macavinchy!"

Her familiar spread his wings, and the people at the nearest table flinched. The musicians looked terrified; one of the girls leaned forward to whisper urgently in Rache's ear. Kayla ignored them while she mentally reviewed her playlists. She didn't want lyrics that referred to cell phones or computers or anything else that would raise questions she didn't want to answer. "Play 'The Magic's Back,' " she said finally.

Macavinchy reared up, placing one hand on the top of her head. He flapped his wings once, and then the opening guitar riff filled the air. The song was one of Kayla's favorites, for all that it was from a local band that hardly anyone else had heard of.

A hypnotic drumbeat joined the guitar, and then the singer and the rest of the band joined in. All of the musicians' mouths fell open at once. No one but Kayla noticed; everyone else in the tavern was staring at Macavinchy. She saw several people tapping their feet to the beat, though there were others who looked as if they had swallowed something that disagreed with them. By the end of the first refrain, the drummer had recovered enough to start moving her fingers on the edge of her lap drum, imitating the rhythm in the song. Rache and the other string player were fingering the necks of their instruments and frowning.

Kayla glanced sideways. Archie was staring at Macavinchy,

just as dumbfounded as everyone else. Ivy, though, was watching Kayla with narrowed eyes and her mouth pressed into a thin line. Kayla smiled tentatively.

For another two bars, Ivy continued studying Kayla speculatively. Then she gave a slow nod, winked, and touched her finger to her lips in the universal gesture for silence. Kayla took a deep breath of relief. Rache had been right on both counts: Ivy had figured out who she was but wouldn't give her away.

When the song was finished, the room was utterly still. Then a creaky voice from the shadows at the rear said, "*That's* music?"

"I like it!" a young man said from up near the musicians. "Can you play another one?"

"No, do that one again!" the girl with the stretched-out banjo demanded. "I almost had the chords, and—" She stopped short, looked at Kayla, and swallowed hard. "That is, if you don't mind, milady."

"Macavinchy, can you find a couple of tracks that don't talk about cars or phones or anything they don't have here?" Kayla whispered.

"Of course, madam," Macavinchy said in his normal voice. Eyes widened all over the tavern.

"Do it," Kayla said, and turned back to the tables. "Two more," she told them. "I don't want to wear Macavinchy out." He'd had a pancake at breakfast and nibbled on the mystery stew, but she wasn't sure how long that would last him. It wasn't as if he still had a battery light.

There were eager nods all around, though the musicians looked torn. "Go for it," Kayla told Macavinchy.

The new songs received an even better reception than the first one. The musicians spent the next half hour trying to duplicate some of the sounds, until Ivy went over and informed them that her tavern wasn't the place to *practice* new songs; it was where they got to play them *after* they'd practiced enough. After a few sarcastic comments from Rache, the musicians reluctantly went back to their usual performance.

At the end of the set, Rache handed his instrument to the not-a-banjo player. She gave him a surprised look, and he said, "I have to get Kayla back up to the castle before someone notices she's missing."

The musicians and a lot of the patrons looked disappointed, but nobody argued further. "Can you get away tomorrow?" the drummer asked. "I want to try some of those new rhythms."

"Probably not," Rache said, "but it doesn't matter. You'll have to find another lute player anyway, after the Dark Lady's investiture. Might as well start now."

There were nods of comprehension at most of the tables, and the drummer pressed her lips together. "We will see you next week," she said, and it sound half like a command and half like a question.

Rache shrugged. He looked longingly at the lute, then pinned the other musicians with a look. "Take care of it for me." He turned away, and they ended up nodding at his back as he stalked over to Archie and Kayla. "Come on, then." Without pausing, he grabbed his cloak and continued stalking, right out of the tavern.

CHAPTER 14

Exploring Your Domain

Upon acquiring a new domain, the wise Dark Lord will familiarize himself with its people, customs, and terrain so as to exploit each of these to best effect. To avoid accidents, new territory should always be explored in the company of several strong and trustworthy guards.

—From *The Dark Traditions*

"So what was that about?" Archie said once they were well away from the tavern and any accidental eavesdroppers.

"Nothing," Rache snapped.

"Hey, I was just trying to be friendly!" Archie said.

"I don't need your friendship."

"Fine!" Archie scowled at Rache and moved so that Kayla was between them.

"Stop it," Kayla said. "If you want to argue, wait till we get back to the castle." She wanted to smack their heads together. *Is this how Mom feels when Del and I get into a fight? Probably.*

"I'm not the one arguing," Archie grumbled.

"You are now," Kayla pointed out. "Just hush. I had a good time and I don't want to ruin it."

They walked in silence for a minute. Rache kicked at a pebble. Without looking at Kayla, he said, "You had a good time?"

Kayla nodded. "I liked your music," she told him. "You're really good."

"Well, at least my last performance made the Dark Lady happy." He sounded as if he'd gone from sulking to gloomy. Kayla wasn't sure it was an improvement.

Archie frowned at Rache's tone and opened his mouth; Kayla shot him a glare and he closed it again. "Your last performance?" she said cautiously.

"I suppose I could come back tomorrow, but there's not much point, is there? Your investiture is in a few days, and after that . . ." He shrugged.

"After that, what? They put guards on the dumbwaiter?" Actually, she'd been planning to do that herself, hadn't she? "I can tell them to leave you alone. Or give you a pass."

"You would?" Rache raised his head, looking suddenly hopeful, but a moment later he dropped it again. "It doesn't matter. Once you start the new empire, I won't have a chance."

"Ivy said that people in the Dark kingdoms can mostly do as they like," Kayla ventured.

"Not if you're born into a Dark Lord's family," Rache said bitterly. "'Tis not *Tradition*," he added, mimicking Jezzazar's voice.

"Tradition can't *make* you do anything," Kayla objected halfheartedly. She hadn't believed that when Macavinchy said it to her—not when everyone here behaved as if Tradition in this world were somehow magically reinforced—but it was all she could think of.

"No?" Rache stopped and turned to look straight at her. "Look at what happened to you. They sent you all the way to another *world,* and you still ended up back here as the next Dark Lady."

"It wasn't Traditions that brought me back," Kayla said. "It was Waylan."

"It's always something. Or somebody. Always." He hunched his shoulders. "My mother, my father, Aunt Detsini—they have my whole life planned out, I think."

"You *think*?" Archie put in.

"They don't tell me, do they? Just do this, do that, learn the other, don't waste your time on music, it's not a proper pastime for—" He broke off.

"For what?" Kayla asked, feeling more sympathetic by the minute.

"For a Dark Lord," Rache said reluctantly. "I don't know for certain, but I've always suspected that that's why Mother helped Aunt Detsini send you off to . . . wherever you've been for the last fourteen years. Because she wanted me to be the Dark Lord's successor."

"But now I'm back."

Rache nodded. "You're back, and I don't know what they'll want me to do now. Either challenge you or romance you, I suppose; they're both Traditional."

"Romance?" Kayla said, revolted. "You're my cousin!"

"If I can't be the Dark Lord, being the Dark Lady's consort would be the next best thing." Rache kicked at another pebble. "Stupid parents. Consort, challenger—they're both high-turnover positions. I don't want to end up dead, even if there *have* always been Dark Lords and Ladies at Zaradwin Castle."

"You might win, if you challenged her," Archie pointed out. "Kayla doesn't know much magic yet."

"Hey!" Kayla scowled at Archie, feeling betrayed.

Rache didn't seem to notice. "The cursed castle is on her side," he told Archie. "I heard about what she did in the courtyard when she arrived. I can't match that. And they don't need me to uphold the family Traditions. She's part of the family; as soon as she's confirmed as the new Dark Lady, family Tradition will be taken care of."

"I'm right here," Kayla pointed out.

Both boys glanced at her, nodded, and went back to talking over her head.

"What do you want to do, if you don't want to be a Dark Lord?" Archie asked.

Rache took a deep breath. "I want to be a bard. You get to travel and see everything and play all over, and then when you've made a name, everyone comes to see you and the lords and ladies fight to be your patron. And you don't get killed, much," he added as an afterthought.

"A bard? You mean, playing music in the tavern, the way you did tonight?" Kayla asked. Rache nodded, and she shook her head. "It sounds better than your other options, I guess."

Especially if I get a say. Rache seemed pleasant enough, but she didn't really know him yet. She certainly wasn't in the market for a consort, let alone one who was her cousin!

Lukewarm reassurance apparently wasn't what Rache was looking for. "What do *you* think I should do?"

"You should start a band," Kayla told him. "You're good enough."

"A . . . what?"

"A rock band. A group that does songs like the ones Macavinchy played tonight."

Some of the life came back into Rache's face. "You think I could?"

"Why not?" Kayla said.

"My parents will never let me do something like that. It's not Traditional."

"It is where I come from," Kayla said. "All my friends' older brothers and sisters have started garage bands, or joined someone else's." It was only a small exaggeration, she told herself. Juana's brother had a guitar, and Sebastian's had actually been in a band for a couple of months.

"Garage band?" Archie asked.

"It's where they practice," Kayla explained.

"Maybe my parents would listen to you." Rache didn't sound like he believed it.

"I'll ask," Kayla told him. "It can't hurt."

They had reached the dumbwaiter. Rache and Archie took turns cranking the handle to raise it up the mountain; it was slow work, but it didn't look too hard, and it was a lot faster and easier than walking. When they reached the top at last, Rache set the brake and pushed open the door to the entry room. "Thanks for taking me along," Kayla said.

"Anything for the Dark Lady," Rache answered, bowing with his more usual flamboyance. Archie just smiled.

Kayla nodded her farewell and started up the stairs to the guest quarters. At the top she paused, uncertain of how to get back to their rooms through the maze of corridors. "Macavinchy—" she started, and then without warning, something unfolded in her mind and she knew exactly where she was, where she was going, and how to get there. Stunned, she stood motionless for a moment, then swallowed hard. *So I have internal GPS? How did that happen?*

Warily, Kayla followed the path her new ability indicated, hoping that it would take her where she wanted to go and not somewhere strange and potentially dangerous. The castle was quiet and spooky; it was later than she had realized. Her footsteps echoed in the hallways and stairwells. At last she came to a door that looked familiar. She pushed it open.

Sconces flared into light along the walls of a hallway as the door closed behind her, and she jumped. This was familiar, all right; it was the hallway that led to the Dark Lord's chambers.

"Beware!" a menacing voice hissed. "Beware, you who would— Oh, it's you." At the far end of the hall, the silver dragon skull sighed, then lifted with an air of hopefulness. "Come to chat?"

"Er, I hadn't meant to," Kayla said honestly, "but I suppose I could, for a minute."

"That's all right," the skull said with another sigh. "Head right on in. Nobody ever stops to talk to me. Nobody cares how bored I am."

Maybe I can get it to let Riki in, Kayla thought. *It might make her happier.* "Wouldn't you be less bored if more people came around?"

"Not for long. Most of my discussions tend to be quite short. I warn them, they ignore me, I roast them. Not what you'd call a lively conversation."

"Do you have to roast everyone? Is that part of the curse on the castle?"

"It's my *job.*" The dragon skull sounded indignant. "It's been my job for a bit over nine hundred years now."

"It doesn't sound like much fun," Kayla said cautiously. "Can't you complain to your boss?"

"I am." The skull faced her head-on. It would be staring straight at her if it had eyes.

"Oh." Kayla thought for a minute. "What's your actual job description?"

"My job is to roast people who threaten the current Dark Lord or Lady of Zaradwin, or who attempt to steal their secrets," the skull said proudly. "And not one thief has gotten by me in nine hundred years."

"How many have tried?" Kayla asked before she could stop herself.

The dragon skull snapped its teeth. "I've lost count," it confessed. "Nine hundred years is a long time, and one or two come along every couple of years."

"So somewhere between four hundred fifty and eight hundred?" Kayla said after a moment's calculation.

"About that. I'm quite good at my job, if I do say so myself," the skull confided.

"Can I change your job description?" Kayla asked, feeling slightly ill at the thought of all the people the dragon had killed.

"I suppose," the skull said slowly. "Just don't make it more boring."

"It's being stuck in this corridor by yourself that's boring," Kayla pointed out. "And I can't very well move you to the great hall if you're going to roast the guests."

"I'm not stuck!" the dragon skull protested indignantly. "This is my assigned post. I can move if you change it." It hesitated visibly, then added, "Somebody needs to guard this door, though. Especially now."

"Why now?"

"Transitions are always tricky," the dragon said. "And *some* people are always ready to make trouble."

Kayla frowned. "What do you mean by that?"

"Some people are trouble," the dragon skull repeated. "I know. But nobody ever asks what I think."

Questions cascaded through Kayla's mind—*Who does it mean? How does it know? What kind of trouble?* Finally, she said, "Okay, I'm asking. What do you think?"

The skull settled back against the door. "I think you should have let me roast that little thief who was here yesterday."

"Del isn't a thief! I told you, he's my brother."

"That doesn't mean anything when you're the Dark Lady," the

dragon countered. "And I could have gotten that other trouble-maker, too, the one who pushed him into trying to get into the Dark Lord's chambers. She's not as powerful, but she's been around for a long time, and she knows how to get other people to do her dirty work."

Detsini, Kayla thought. "Del wasn't trying to get inside," she insisted. "He just wanted a closer look at you."

The dragon skull tilted right, then left. "He's curious, and he's powerful. He might not have wanted to get inside this time, but he will eventually."

"Powerful?" Kayla said skeptically. All right, Del had blown up a desk in the library, but that didn't seem like enough to impress a dragon.

"Other than yourself, he's one of three people in this castle with enough magical power to become the next Dark Lord, and on top of that, he has old magic," the skull said with certainty.

"What's old magic? Is it bad?" Kayla was suddenly very worried about Del.

The skull snorted. "It isn't Light or Dark, so nobody understands it now. Once he gets a handle on his power, there'll be no stopping him."

"*You* understand his magic, though." How was she going to explain this to Riki?

"Well, yes," the dragon said modestly. "It's one of the benefits of being over a thousand years old."

Kayla opened her mouth to say that she thought he was nine hundred, then quickly closed it again. The skull said it had been *here* for nine hundred years, stopping thieves; the dragon had surely been alive for quite a while before that.

The skull didn't seem to notice her lack of response. It tilted to one side, as if studying her, and went on. "Your magic won't completely counter his, but you'll both be plenty of trouble for anyone else."

"Does that mean I have old magic, too?"

"No, yours is . . . a little of everything, mixed together. You'll want extra practice. Mixed magic is hard to control."

"Could you teach us?" she asked after a moment. "Both?"

"I've never tried teaching," the dragon said, considering. "It would certainly be different. You're sure you want both of you to learn? It will be a lot easier to defeat him if I just train you."

"If nobody shows him how his magic works, he'll blow something else up," Kayla said. "Probably himself. And then Mom will blame me, because I'm older." She had the feeling Riki wasn't going to be happy about having either of her children taught by the dragon skull that had nearly roasted one of them, but if they didn't get good tutoring from *someone,* it would take years for them to learn anything useful.

"It's your call," the dragon skull said.

"Then that can be your new job. I—" Kayla's brain caught up with her. "Wait. A minute ago, you said Del was one of three people in the castle who have enough power to be Dark Lords. Who are the other two?"

"The librarian and that new boy," the dragon said promptly. "The one who came with you and the thief."

227

"You mean Archie?"

"That's the one." The dragon stretched forward, and its two bony claws appeared on the surface of the door, as if it were bracing itself to lean out a window. "Either of the women could have been a Dark Lady once, but they don't have enough magic left now. The other three do, though. Archie, Del, and Harkawn. I'd keep a close eye on them if I were you."

Kayla nodded, disturbed. She liked Archie and Harkawn. And Del was her brother. She shoved the information to the back of her mind, to mull over when she had more time, and said, "It's been nice talking, but I should probably go now."

"All right. Let me know where you want me to drop you off when you come back out," the dragon skull said.

Before Kayla could respond, the dragon pulled itself back into the wood until only the skull showed, hanging against the door like a giant door knocker. A moment later, the door swung open and Kayla found herself peering into the darkness of the Dark Lord's rooms.

"Well?" said the skull after a moment. "How long do you expect me to hold this door open?"

Kayla hesitated. Riki didn't want her anywhere near these rooms. . . . But she'd already be in trouble if Riki realized she'd stayed out this late. And they'd belonged to her biological father. She took a deep breath and walked through the door.

Twelve three-candle sconces flared to life along the walls of the room, sending long ribbons of flame almost to the ceiling before they settled into clear, steady light. Kayla felt a wave of warmth and welcome that almost overwhelmed her for a moment.

"Have fun!" the dragon skull said, and the door to the hall closed. Kayla shook herself and looked around.

She stood in a large, five-sided room. There were no windows, and every wall had at least one door. Kayla would have called it an entryway if it had been smaller. A row of empty coat hooks decorated the wall next to her. An oversized armchair sat in front of the fireplace in one corner, large and comfy enough to curl up in; next to it, a small round table held an empty wineglass and a book with a battered leather cover. A bookcase and a writing desk were crammed on either side of one of the doors; there was a black marble bust on a pillar next to another. Several thick rugs in warm earth tones covered the floors. Nothing was dusty, and there wasn't a cobweb, snake, or skull to be seen. It looked . . . comfortable. And surprisingly normal.

All except for the last door on the right. It was a mottled greenish gray, the color of mold, with a straight handle that looked like old bone.

"If nobody can get in here, who's been keeping the place clean?" Kayla muttered.

"I would venture to guess that the castle itself manages these rooms," Macavinchy said.

"Right," Kayla said, feeling more cheerful. "What do you think we should do first?"

"A tour of the premises is indicated, madam." Macavinchy's tail twitched as she hesitated. "I suggest a systematic approach. Perhaps trying each door in order, clockwise?"

That seemed reasonable, and it left the unsettling gray door for last. Kayla turned to her left and opened the first door.

The investigation didn't take long. The first door led out to the bathroom, which contained a sunken tub large enough to swim in. There were no faucets, and she wondered whether it was filled by magic or by hordes of minions with buckets. The second door opened on a bedroom, as comfortably normal as the sitting area had been. Next came a small library, similar to the one Harkawn presided over, and the fourth room was an office-like room with a desk and a large window. Along the walls, where a normal office would have file drawers, stood seven large chests.

Kayla paused, studying the chests. They were made of dark, polished wood and bound with iron, like pirate chests in the movies. Except these were much larger; each came nearly as high as Kayla's waist, and they looked as long as a bathtub. She wondered what was inside, and almost without thinking, she reached out her hand to touch the first.

A tingle ran up her arm as her hand met the top of the chest. Slowly, the lid creaked open, and Kayla gasped. The chest was full to the brim with coins, mostly gold. "Pirate treasure doesn't begin to cover it," she muttered. "Are they all like this?"

"Not exactly," Macavinchy said.

Kayla glanced up. All of the chests were open. The first four held coins; the fifth was full of jewels; the sixth held carefully packed baskets of small bottles and a stack of packets that smelled faintly of herbs. The final chest held various objects; from where she stood, Kayla could make out a pale wand and a plain gold ring resting on a pile of silky fabric. The hilt of a sword was just visible in one corner, and a glittery pair of red shoes stuck up in another.

"I believe you have discovered the castle hoard, madam," Macavinchy said in tones of great satisfaction.

Del is going to be so disappointed that I found it first, Kayla thought. She started toward the last trunk, which looked the most interesting. Macavinchy cleared his throat.

Kayla stopped. "What?"

"You have not yet completed your inspection, madam," the familiar reminded her.

Right, she'd left the moldy gray door for last. Reluctantly, she went back out to the sitting room. The door didn't look any more appealing than it had before. "Maybe we should wait on this one."

"As you wish, madam," her familiar replied.

Curiously, his agreement made her pause. It wasn't as if waiting to open the door would make it easier to face whatever was on the other side. And everything else had been relatively normal. Except for the treasure chests. Kayla eyed the door warily. It did not look normal.

"I wish that dragon had stuck around," she muttered.

"What do you want?" the dragon skull's raspy voice said from behind her.

Kayla jumped and turned. The dragon skull was poking out of the door to the hallway. "Where does this go?" she asked, pointing at the gray door.

"The dungeon," the dragon replied. "The door won't open for just anyone, either. About a third of the Dark Lords never get inside." It clacked its teeth together. "They don't last long."

"That's not exactly reassuring," Kayla said without thinking.

The skull waggled from side to side. "Reassuring people is not my job. Try it and see what happens." It faded back into the door.

"Right," Kayla muttered. She stepped forward and took hold of the bone handle. It was smooth and cool, and she felt something click. A moment later, the door swung open. On the other side, a set of bone-white steps spiraled downward into complete darkness.

CHAPTER 15

Sources of Power

Remember that your personal magic is limited. You should therefore strive to increase the number of external power sources you possess. You may acquire new power sources by conquering other Dark Lords and absorbing their sources, or by finding and capturing new ones. Keep them contained and well protected, for they are fundamental to your ability to rule your people and expand your empire.

—From *The Dark Traditions*

Kayla peered into the gloom below. After a moment, she held her hand out and cupped it. "Light," she whispered, pushing at her magic the way Archie had shown her.

Light bloomed in her hand, not blindingly bright, but more than enough for her to see the next few steps. "At least I've learned something useful," she muttered. Had it only been that morning? She'd already thought of nearly a dozen spells she wanted to learn, if they existed. Judging from the books Harkawn had shown her, she'd probably have to invent some of them. Once she learned how to invent spells.

She set her mental grumbles aside and paused to think, then dragged the chair from the writing desk over to prop the door open. Taking a deep breath, she started down.

A torch flared to life half a turn below her, showing the next curve of the stairs. Kayla eyed it suspiciously and decided to keep her handful of light going anyway, just in case. She went on down the stairs.

As she reached the torch, a second one lit itself another half turn below her. Kayla looked back in time to see the light from the open door above her blink out. She stopped, fighting panic. She hadn't heard the door close, but . . .

Turning, she put a hand on the wall and started climbing. On the third step, the second torch below her went out with a fizzing noise, and the light reappeared in the doorway above. Kayla sighed in relief. She went up and down the section of stairs once more to make sure the motion-detecting torches worked, then continued on down the stairs.

The descent took forever. The stairwell never changed: a thin white ribbon of stairs curled from total darkness above to total darkness below. Without the torches lighting in front of her and fizzling out behind her, Kayla would have thought she was getting nowhere. *Like walking down an up escalator,* she thought.

The bottom of the staircase arrived without warning; Kayla stumbled from trying to take a step down on level ground. She shook herself and looked down. At first, she thought she was standing on a sheet of glass covering the rest of the stairs, but after a moment she realized it was only the reflection of the spiral in mirror-smooth black marble.

She took another step forward. The torches on the stairs went out, and two new ones burst into flame about ten feet in front of her. Between them was an arched black door covered by a faint silver shimmer.

Kayla hesitated. "Now what?" she muttered.

"I am afraid that specific predictions are not one of my specialties," Macavinchy said, snapping his wings nervously.

Hesitantly, Kayla took a step forward. The silver shimmer rippled, bulged, and formed into a dragon's skull. "Finally!" it said. "It took you long enough."

"I thought you were stuck on the door upstairs," Kayla said.

"No, that's my brother," the skull replied, sounding annoyed. "Can't you tell the difference?"

"I wasn't expecting two of you," Kayla said defensively. Her eyes narrowed. "Are there any more?"

"Not in this castle." The dragon skull sighed, making the torches flicker. "I'm guessing that you're the new Dark Lady and you want to get in, right?"

"That would be a brilliant guess, except that it's obvious," Kayla told it, feeling annoyed. "The only way to get this far is to get past the first skull that only lets Dark Lords or Dark Ladies down here. Why do you even need to be here, when there's already a guard skull to keep people out?"

"Oh, I'm not here to keep anyone out," the skull said, and Kayla got the distinct impression that if it were alive, it would be giving her a nasty, toothy grin.

"You're not?"

"I'm here to keep things in," it said, and dissolved back into the wood. An instant later, the door swung open and the torches on the other side lit with a loud *whoosh*.

The sudden light revealed a small room, made even smaller by the glowing bars that fenced off the back half. On the other side of the bars, barely visible through the blue glow, a figure hung from a pair of manacles fastened to the far wall.

Kayla took a step forward, then another, peering into the light in an attempt to see more clearly. As she crossed the threshold, the blue light dimmed to a faint glimmer. A moment later, the figure in the manacles raised its head.

It was a man of around twenty, dark haired and with eyes as flat and black as the polished marble. His black robe was dusty and worn, and his face was gaunt.

"Oh," he said. "You must be the new Dark Lord." He squinted in Kayla's direction. "Wait, no, that'd be Dark Lady. Not that there's much difference." His voice sounded as if it hadn't been used in a long time.

"Who are you?" Kayla said. "And why are you locked up down here?" *And who's been feeding him, if the only person who can get in here is the Dark Lord, and there hasn't been one in ten years?*

"You don't know?" The man shifted his shoulders. "Maybe you're not the Dark Lady after all. I know there's a new ruler, though; I felt it. Did she send you?"

"I'm—" Kayla hesitated, then said firmly, "I'm the Dark Lady. Or as much of one as there is at the moment."

"Really." The man studied her for a moment. "I suppose that explains why you're here."

"It doesn't explain why you are," Kayla said. "Or who you are. Will you please answer my questions?" She narrowed her eyes. "Or I can just leave, if you'd rather not."

The man flinched, then gave her a startled look. "How . . . You meant that."

"Of course I meant it," Kayla said. "You're still stalling."

"No, I— You said please. You were *asking*. You gave me a choice." The man took a deep breath. "I'm the spirit of Zaradwin Mountain."

"Spirit of the mountain?" Kayla repeated. That might explain how he'd survived without being fed for ten years. Mountains didn't need to eat; perhaps the spirit of the mountain didn't need to, either. "Like the spirit of the stones?"

"Like, and not like. You've met her?"

"Briefly. You look a lot older than she did."

"The mountain is a lot older than the stone circle. Also, the circle was put up by humans, so it took a while to . . . *become*."

"Does everything here develop a . . . a personality?" Kayla asked, intrigued.

The man shrugged, then shifted his shoulders again. "Everything that's been around for a few thousand years. Most human-made things don't last long enough."

"Why is the spirit of the mountain locked up in the Dark Lord's dungeon? Is it to keep the mountain from exploding?" Kayla asked cautiously. Her first impulse had been to let him out, if she could find the key, but there had to be a reason why he was chained up down here. Remembering the video on volcanoes Mr. Mobonyo had shown in science class, she thought that stopping an eruption was a reasonable guess.

The spirit gave her an incredulous look. "Why would I blow myself up?" His expression changed. "Though a few small explosions might be worth the pain, if I could get free."

"That doesn't exactly make me want to let you go," Kayla pointed out. "What is your name, anyway?"

The spirit glared at her. "Oh no. I won't be tricked again." The last few words were an angry growl, and Kayla felt a faint vibration in the stones under her feet. "Find out yourself, if you want a personal slave."

Kayla sighed. "If you don't want to tell me your real name, make something up. I just want to know what to call you. 'Spirit' sounds . . . generic."

"What kind of Dark Lady are you?" the spirit said, frowning. "I can feel your power; you must have a couple of us chained up somewhere. Although—" He pursed his lips and his eyes went out of focus.

A warm breeze swirled around Kayla, and the spirit's eyes widened. "You aren't drawing on anything!"

"What are you talking about?" Kayla had the uneasy feeling she wasn't going to like the answer.

"Don't pretend you don't know!" the spirit said angrily. "Every magician binds as many spirits as possible, to increase their own power. Like your familiar."

"Macavinchy? Is he right?"

Macavinchy hesitated. "I can find no documentation of the effect, madam," he said after a moment. "However, it is consistent with the degree of secrecy that surrounds the operation of Dark Lords. Possibly there is more information in that book that I cannot access." He snapped his wings in irritation.

The spirit gave Macavinchy the look of puzzlement that Kayla was getting used to seeing on the faces of the people of Zaradwin whenever her familiar said something. "I was referring to the binding between familiar and magician."

"I don't think we have one," Kayla said. "Computers don't work that way."

"Computers?"

"That's what Macavinchy was when I gave him his name, before we arrived here," Kayla explained. "We're not exactly from this world—at least, I was born here, but I've spent most of my life in St. Paul."

The spirit just stared. Kayla stared back. So far, she didn't like him much, but if she'd been chained up for more than ten years, she'd probably be just as grouchy. And not liking someone wasn't a good reason for leaving him stuck in a cage; not even Riki would object to letting him out, even if it was another one of those Traditions. She took a deep breath. "I'm going to call you Zar. 'Spirit of Zaradwin Mountain' is too long. If you don't like it, you can pick something else. Now, where are the keys?"

"Keys?" The spirit's—Zar's—face went blank.

"To that cell. And the chains," Kayla said. "So I can let you out after you promise not to take revenge on anybody."

Zar gave a harsh laugh that had an air of disbelief about it.

"I am a spirit," he said. "The bars and chains you see are not physical. They're a manifestation of the spells that have bound me here since the castle was built. There are no keys."

"Okay, how do I turn off the spells?"

"Theoretically, there is a way. But it takes time, and will." Zar snorted. "You aren't the first Dark Ruler who disliked the idea of keeping a prisoner in their private rooms, but their distaste never lasts past the first time they want to do something that needs more power than they have on their own. Once they draw on the binding, they get used to it. Especially when they realize how much more power they can accumulate by binding other spirits or absorbing another Dark Lord's power."

"Then we'd better get you out of there before I get used to it," Kayla retorted.

Zar gaped at her. Kayla sighed. You'd think that someone who'd been locked up for years would be happier at the prospect of being set free. She looked around the room, but it was frighteningly bare. There wasn't so much as a hook to hang a key ring on. "Macavinchy, do you have any suggestions?"

"As I myself have no information on the subject of binding and loosing spirits, I suggest you ask someone or something that does," the familiar replied.

"The librarian might know, or Archie," Kayla said. "The door dragon said they were the ones with enough power to hold the castle. Well, and Del, but he won't know any more about this than I do." Her eyes widened. "Or we could start with the dragon."

She turned back to the door and opened it. There was no sign of the dragon skull. Kayla studied the wood for a minute, then rapped it sharply. "Hey, dragon! Could you come out and talk to me for a minute?"

Slowly, the skull materialized. "That was different. Don't you know how to call one of us properly?"

"No," Kayla replied, feeling decidedly cross. "You can tell me about it later. Right now, I want to know how to let him out." She pointed at the spirit of the mountain, who was staring at her with a stunned look. "And anybody else who's chained up or tied up somewhere in this castle."

"You're going to set him free?" The skull practically squeaked.

"Probably. *Is* there anyone else chained up like this?"

"Not at the moment," the dragon skull answered. "There have been others now and then, but the spells holding them failed when the Dark Lords who captured them died. This one's the only permanent resident. Are you sure about this?"

"Oh, go ahead and tell her," Zar said. "It won't make any difference. They're always sure, until they change their minds."

"If you say so." The dragon sniffed. "Though really, it's obvious. If you want to let him out, you have to break the spells that hold him in."

Kayla rolled her eyes. "Fine. How do I do that?"

"Everything is woven together," the dragon said with a sigh. "Unravel the web, and the spell will come undone, too."

"You said the others were gone!"

"The other *captive spirits* are gone. Zaradwin Castle houses more than spirits of the land."

"Could you be any more cryptic?" Kayla grumbled. "Macavinchy, do you know what he is getting at?"

"I believe he is referring to the inhabitants of the castle, madam," Macavinchy replied. "That would be the guards and the family of the previous Dark Lord, at least. My references are unclear as to whether the two dragon skulls can be classed as spirits or not, so it would be wisest to include them."

"Hey! You can't— How could you just tell her that?" Zar demanded in disbelief. Macavinchy didn't answer.

"I asked him the right question," Kayla said. "That's how computers work."

"He's a familiar!" Zar said. "When you claimed the castle, the binding should have captured him the same as—" His teeth snapped together with an audible click, though it was plain he had intended to say more.

"He's an odd one," the dragon skull agreed. "No odder than she is, though."

"Macavinchy?" Kayla said. "Are you all right?"

"One moment, madam." Macavinchy shifted on her shoulder and purred briefly. "My diagnostics indicate that I am currently performing at normal efficiency. There have been several unsuccessful attempts to penetrate my firewall since our arrival at the castle. None have been serious enough to warrant a report."

"I guess it is a good thing we worked on your security program," Kayla said. She bit her lip as a problem occurred to her. "How long can your antivirus software keep up? I can't exactly download the latest upgrade from the internet."

"I do not have enough data as yet to make a projection." Macavinchy gave a small sniff. "My security spells are significantly more advanced than any of the attacks thus far, which lack sophistication and show no signs of evolving into a greater threat. I do not anticipate any difficulty in continuing to repel them, but I shall keep you apprised if that changes. In the meantime, perhaps we should return to the matter at hand."

Kayla nodded without speaking as she tried to collect her scattered thoughts. "So Zar is tied up by spells," she said slowly. "And those spells are tied to everyone who's been living in the castle. Where have I heard something like that before?"

"In the tavern, madam," Macavinchy answered promptly.

"The curse on the castle! Ivy said it latches on to everyone who lives here for a while." Kayla scowled. "That doesn't help me unravel—" She broke off, yawning. How late was it? She didn't need to fall asleep now, especially somewhere that no one could find her if Riki noticed she was missing. "How long will it take to get you out of there?"

Zar didn't answer. The skull waggled itself from side to side. "That depends," it said. "It took the first Dark Lord a couple of months to set up the binding, and the ones who came after reinforced it. It'll probably take at least as long to unwind it, unless one of the lords hid the secret upstairs somewhere."

"Months? That doesn't sound good."

"I've been stuck here for nearly nine hundred years," Zar pointed out. "Since shortly after the castle was built."

"All the more reason to get you out of there soon." Kayla yawned again. "Do you have any ideas, Macavinchy?"

"An investigation of spirit binding appears to be in order," Macavinchy replied. "Particularly since it appears to affect your position as Dark Lady, as well as Mr. Zar's situation."

"Harkawn might know something, but I can't wake him up to ask him now," Kayla said. "I'll have to work on this later."

"I believe that would be the wisest course of action," Macavinchy agreed.

Leaving Zar chained up in his cell made Kayla feel guilty, but her brain was going tired and fuzzy, and she couldn't think of anything else to do. The long climb up to the Dark Lord's rooms made her even tireder.

Kayla paused briefly in the entry room to catch her breath. She hesitated in front of the door to the office, but investigating the castle hoard would take a while, and she *was* awfully tired. And it was beyond late, and she still had to find her way back.

Wait, hadn't the door dragon said it could let her out wherever she wanted? She walked over to the main entrance and paused. "Er, dragon?"

The dragon skull poked out of the door at once. "Yes?"

"I need to get back to the guest room we're all staying in. Can you let me out in the hallway?" She didn't know whether a door appearing inside the guest room would wake Riki, but she wasn't going to take the chance.

"No problem," the skull said. "Go ahead."

Cautiously, Kayla opened the door. She was greatly relieved when she recognized the hallway just outside their rooms. "Thanks," she said to the dragon.

It nodded, then melted back into the door. A moment later, the door disappeared. Kayla took a breath and turned. She eased the door to the guest room open and slipped inside. As she started to close it, a hand reached over her shoulder and caught the edge.

Kayla jumped and turned to find Riki looking down at her. "Mom! You scared me."

"That's not all I'm going to do." Riki's voice was soft but cold. "Outside. I don't want to wake your brother."

"Mom, I didn't—"

"Outside," Riki hissed.

Kayla swallowed and stepped back into the hall. In the flickering torchlight, the anger on Riki's face was far scarier than it had ever looked in the light from their living room lamp. "Mom—"

"Where have you been?" Riki demanded. "Do you have any idea how late it is?"

"I just—"

"What possessed you to go wandering around this castle in the middle of the night? Are you *trying* to get yourself roasted by something?"

"Nothing would—"

"I was worried sick! And I couldn't leave your brother to go look for you." Riki crossed her arms and looked down at Kayla. "Well? What have you got to say for yourself?"

"I couldn't sleep, so I went for a walk." Kayla hated the defensive tone in her voice, but she knew that her mother was at least partly right. Knowing didn't make it any easier to be called on it, though. And Riki would go completely ballistic if she found out Kayla had left the castle with the boys. Not to mention visiting the dragon and going into the Dark Lord's private rooms and finding a spirit locked up in the basement. "I guess I got lost."

"Lost. You got lost. Anything could have happened to you!"

"No, it couldn't." Kayla knew as soon as she spoke that it was a mistake, but it was too late to take it back. "Remember, Yazmina said—"

"Yazmina said." Riki all but spat the words. "And what do you know about her? What do we know about any of these people? You're too trusting, Kayla. They kidnapped us; you have no idea what else they might do!"

"They've been fine since we got here! Kind of weird, but nice enough."

"That skeleton-thing almost killed your brother; didn't that teach you anything?"

"Yeah, to listen when somebody from here tells me to stay away from something!"

"Don't talk back to me! I'm your mother."

"They're my family, too, some of them! And they know more about Zaradwin than you do."

Riki's eyes went wide, then narrowed. "And I suppose one of them came to the door to show you around tonight? Kayla, this place is dangerous. You can't just wander off on your own whenever you feel like it."

A complicated mixture of frustration, anger, and fear swirled through Kayla. Part of her knew that Riki was overreacting because she'd been worried and scared, and that some of her points were good ones. Most of her, though, hated being lectured even if it was true. Besides, she was sick and tired of always having to adjust her behavior to keep Riki from getting upset. When was it going to be her turn to do things the way she wanted? "I went for a walk! It's not a big deal."

"Big enough to get you grounded for a week."

Kayla snorted. "Like that'll change anything. You already follow me around every minute. How is being grounded going to be any different?"

Riki took a deep breath and let it out slowly. "It's late. We'll talk about this more in the morning," she said carefully.

"Fine!" Kayla yanked at the door handle. "But I'm sleeping in the other room tonight!"

Without waiting for her mother's response, she marched back into the guest quarters. "Don't wake your brother," Riki commanded softly from behind her. Kayla glared at Riki over her shoulder, even though she knew the effect would be lost in the dark, and stormed into the second bedroom. It was some time before she slept.

CHAPTER 16

Principles of Delegation

Assign your largest, most difficult projects either to your most incompetent subordinates, or to the ones you dislike most. Their inevitable failure will give you the perfect excuse to have them executed, which will enhance your reputation for ruthlessness while allowing you to promote more competent followers without encouraging them to slack off.

—From *The Dark Traditions*

Kayla woke to the sound of low voices in the outer room. She shook her head to clear the sleep fog from her brain, then wrapped herself in the blanket and went to see what was going on.

Del and Riki were sitting on the bench beside the door. They broke off their conversation when Kayla appeared.

"It's about time you got up!" Del said. "Mom wouldn't let us go get breakfast until you came out, and I'm hungry."

"I was up late."

Riki sighed. "Kayla, I'm sorry I yelled at you last night. I was worried, and I overreacted. You're still grounded, though."

"You got grounded?" Del sat up straight, suddenly interested in more than breakfast. "What'd you do?"

"Never mind," Riki said.

"I just wanted to do some exploring." Kayla considered a moment. She didn't want to restart the argument, and she couldn't admit to visiting the Dark Lord's secret dungeon without riling her mother up again, but maybe she could ease into it. "I thought maybe I could find out something useful. If—"

"No exploring on your own," Riki said sternly. "Not either of you. This place is dangerous."

"Not to me," Kayla said without thinking.

"You don't know that," Riki said, and pressed her lips together as if to hold in some even angrier words.

"Yes, I do." Kayla sighed. "Mom, it's *magic*."

"Magic isn't automatically a good thing," Riki pointed out. "And this is the castle of a Dark Lord."

"And I'm the Dark Lady." Kayla shook her head, wondering how to explain. She didn't think saying *It's just like my internal GPS* would go over well. "It's like Yazmina said. Nothing in the castle will hurt me."

"Yazmina has a different idea of what's dangerous than we do."

"But she's right about this," Kayla insisted. "Mom, some things, I can . . . just tell. I don't know how. Like talking to the dragon skulls." Realizing that she might have given away her previous night's encounter, she added hastily, "When I was trying to get Del away from it," and hoped her mother wouldn't notice that she'd switched from talking about multiple skulls to just the one.

Riki's expression twisted, and for a moment Kayla thought that bringing up Del's first misadventure had been a mistake. Then Del frowned and asked, "Why can't I do that? I'm magic, too!" He tugged at the crimson streak in his hair as if it proved something.

"Your magic is different," Kayla told him, watching her mother warily out of the corner of her eye. "And it's not your castle." This was clearly not the best time to bring up the possibility of the skulls giving him magic lessons.

"It's not your castle, either," Riki said, but she didn't sound as if she believed it. Kayla just looked at her. After a moment, her mother sighed. "I hate this," she muttered, barely loud enough for Kayla to catch. She looked at Kayla and sighed again. "At least let *me* know when you know . . . things."

"There isn't always time," Kayla pointed out. "And I don't always notice. It's like stop signs; I see them, but they don't register. They're just there."

"Try anyway." Riki paused. "I hope you stop at stop signs! And no more exploring. You have to set a good example for your brother."

Kayla made a face. Being the oldest was a pain sometimes. "But—"

"No," Riki said sternly. "The way things have been going, you're lucky I didn't ground you until you're thirty."

"Fine." Kayla was relieved. When Riki started threatening to assign ridiculous punishments, she was done being mad. In a couple of days, Kayla could bring up the dragon skulls and the spirit in the dungeon; Riki would be cross again, but she probably wouldn't fly off the handle. And in the meantime, Kayla could look for a way to free the mountain spirit.

"Can we go eat now?" Del whined.

When they arrived in the great hall, most of the castle's inhabitants were already there. Kayla didn't see Rache, Archie, or Geneviev, but the guards occupied a table near the far door, and everyone else half filled one of the tables near the dais and the throne.

Del made a beeline for the nearest table and dove into the platter of pancakes before he even sat down. "These are good!" he said around a mouthful. "Who made them?"

" 'Twas Geneviev who cooked this morning," Jezzazar said with evident disapproval. " 'Twould be best if you did not partake, my lady. It may be poisoned."

"You think Geneviev would poison everyone?" Riki stopped short in the middle of serving herself.

" 'Twould be extreme," Jezzazar acknowledged. "But 'twould not be unprecedented. The seventy-eighth Dark Lord and his entire staff were poisoned by his elder brother in an attempt to seize the throne."

"Everyone else is eating, and nobody looks ill," Kayla pointed out. "You're eating yourself! And I'm hungry." She grabbed a pancake and took a bite.

"On your head be it," Jezzazar said. The far door opened, and Jezzazar scowled as Rache ambled in. "Rache, my son, 'tis long past time for you to join us."

"Good morning to you, too, Father." Rache yawned widely, cutting off the last word. Kayla had to tighten her jaw in order to suppress a sympathy yawn.

"Why so tired, my son?" Yazmina said.

"I was out late," Rache said. He sat down at the nearest table and began attacking a stack of pancakes.

Detsini gave him a hard look. "I suppose you were down at the tavern again, playing with your layabout friends."

At the next table, Waylan looked up from his meal, blinking in momentary confusion. Then his expression cleared. "Oh, Rache's musicians? One of the men said something about them yesterday. Told me they were pretty good."

Detsini turned to him and sniffed. "Performing in a tavern is not acceptable behavior for the cousin of the new Dark Lady." Behind her, Rache rolled his eyes. Plainly, he'd heard it many times before.

"You should have your familiar play some of your music for him," Waylan told Kayla. "He might like it." There was something about his eyes that made her think he disliked Detsini and her rigid notions almost as much as Kayla did.

"That's a good idea," Kayla said. And it would provide a good excuse if her mother ever went to the tavern and noticed the musicians imitating hip-hop guitar riffs.

"Ah, my child, you break my heart," Yazmina said to Rache. "And it will break yet again, should the Dark Lady take offense at your disrespect and have you executed."

"I'm not executing anybody just for coming late to breakfast!" Kayla said quickly.

"Not until after your investiture," Detsini put in.

"And how go the preparations?" Jezzazar asked in a blatant attempt to change the subject.

"I dispatched the last of the invitations yesterday," Detsini said proudly. "They had to go in several batches because there were so many."

"How many invitations were there?" Kayla said. "I thought it was going to be a small party."

"Your investiture is an extremely important ceremony, dear," Detsini said in a superior tone. "It serves as a notification to towns and villages—and any pretenders—that there is a new and powerful Dark Lady in residence at Zaradwin Castle. Of course I sent everyone invitations."

"Why?" Del asked. "Wouldn't it be better not to tell anyone we're here until you've at least fixed the front gate?"

"Portcullis," Yazmina murmured.

"An announcement is expected," Detsini said. "After all, there have always been Dark Lords at Zaradwin Castle. It's a pity that we couldn't give more notice, but I'm sure everyone will understand. I will order the entertainment and the food for the feast this afternoon."

At the end of the table, Ichikar's head came up. "And why have I not heard of this increase in the number of guests till now?" he demanded. "Or do you know of some secret fund with which to pay for such a gala?"

Detsini looked down her nose at him. "I will discuss it with you later, once the Dark Lady's dress arrives."

"Dress?" Kayla said uneasily, remembering the ridiculous costumes Detsini had insisted on. "I didn't order a dress." Across the table, Riki's eyes narrowed dangerously at Detsini.

"I know, dear," Detsini said gently. "I did. You can't attend your investiture or your first council meeting without an appropriate dress." She gave a disapproving look at Kayla's borrowed skirt and tunic.

"I was planning on wearing the Dark Lord outfit I asked for," Kayla said.

"Oh, I told the seamstress not to bring that." Detsini waved a hand as if to dismiss any objections before they were made.

"*You* told her?" Yazmina's voice was uncharacteristically harsh. "You do not have the authority to overrule the Dark Lady!"

"Provisional Dark Lady," Detsini corrected her. "And I merely wished to make sure she had something suitable to wear to the council meeting. And since she is obviously unfamiliar with the standards of dress in a civilized country, she'll need to practice wearing it for a few days beforehand, so there was no need for any other garments at this time."

"You have no right to make such decisions!" Ichikar said.

"Oh, but I do," Detsini replied sweetly. "The Dark Lord himself appointed me to handle all matters of ceremony and protocol, and the investiture of his heir plainly falls under both categories."

There was a moment of angry silence; then Kayla said firmly, "Well, I'm the Dark Lady, and I'm unappointing you." Detsini's idea of a suitable dress was unlikely to be anything Kayla would be willing to wear, let alone argue Riki into approving.

"*Provisional* Dark Lady!" Detsini snapped. "And you can't do that!"

"Funny how you only mention the provisional part when Kayla's doing something you don't like," Riki commented. "Besides, didn't somebody say that a Provisional Dark Lady has the same rights as a regular one?"

"That is correct, madam," Macavinchy said from Kayla's shoulder. "A Provisional Dark Lord or Lady has all the authority and all the ruling power of a fully invested Dark Lord or Lady." He flapped his wings once, then settled back on Kayla's shoulder. "It is Traditional," he finished in a dry tone.

Del snickered, and several of the adults at the table seemed to want to join him. For a moment, Detsini looked torn, but then her lips thinned. "I'm sure you'll appoint a new mistress of protocol eventually, but now is not the time. The investiture of a new Dark Lady is too important to risk . . . improvising."

"If this ceremony is so important, why hasn't anyone told me more about it?" Kayla said. "It's in only"—she did some rapid mental calculations—"three more days."

"It's quite all right, dear," Detsini said. "I'm handling everything. After all, you don't understand how things are done here."

"Whose fault is that?" Kayla shot back. "Besides—Macavinchy, what does an investiture need to have?"

"The investiture of a new Dark Lord or Lady represents an opportunity to show off their power and accomplishments," Macavinchy replied. "The ceremony itself is quite simple. The new ruler is presented to the assembled guests and makes a speech about the glories of their coming rule. An impressive feast and entertainment follow."

"What counts as impressive?" Kayla asked. "And why didn't anyone tell me I was going to need to give a speech?"

"As soon as your dress arrives, I will—"

"Kayla is not wearing anything that remotely resembles one of those dresses we looked at," Riki said.

"No way." Kayla shook her head, though she couldn't believe she was agreeing with her mother.

"Kayla dear, *you* are the Dark Lady," Detsini said with a sidelong look at Riki. "You don't have to wear what your adoptive mother tells you to."

"I know," Kayla told her. She took a deep breath. Politeness was all very well, but sometimes you had to hit people over the head with the verbal equivalent of a giant wet fish. "I'm not refusing to wear it because Mom says I can't. I'm refusing to wear it because everything you showed us was tacky."

Detsini looked outraged. "It is in the grand Tradition of the Dark Rulers of Zaradwin! I chose the colors particularly to honor both you and your father. Poison green and silver and black."

"With glitter and feathers, I bet," Kayla said. "No."

Detsini's face twisted. "You foolish child!" she spat. "You'll get us all killed with your insistence on having your own way."

"'Tis the nature of Dark Lords to have things as they will," Yazmina put in. "And there have always been Dark Lords—"

"—at Zaradwin Castle, yes, I know." Detsini leaned forward, shaking slightly with the force of her emotion. "There have always been Dark Lords here, but you keep forgetting that they haven't always been us!"

Silence fell. Kayla stared at Detsini. Something about her angry insistence felt both false and familiar. Across the table, Riki shifted and raised her chin. As the argument started up again, Kayla suddenly realized what she recognized in Detsini's posture. Riki had been just the same when the doctors told them Michael was dying. It had taken a long time for Kayla to realize that she was angry to keep from being afraid.

Detsini was afraid. The thought sent a chill down Kayla's back, as if someone had just dumped ice water over her head.

Voices replayed in her mind. Detsini: *You'll get us all killed.* Jezzazar, at their first meeting in the woods: *We are doomed to failure.* Waylan's offhand comment to Archie: *I am surprised they let you live.* The panicked minion: *Kill somebody and get it over with!* Geneviev: *You'd be crazy not to have me executed.* The sninks, naming their price for power: *One of the others. Any one.* Ivy, casually explaining the behavior of previous Dark Ladies: *Some of them start executing every good-looking girl in the kingdom.* The spirit in the dungeon: *They get used to it.*

"I am *not* getting used to it!" Kayla said aloud. "I refuse!"

Everyone stopped and stared at her. Kayla swallowed hard. How could she put this so they would understand? "You keep talking about killing and executing people, because I'm the Dark Lady and that's what you're used to Dark Ladies doing." She paused. No one said a word, but she saw Ichikar nod slowly.

"I get that you're worried because Mom wants us to go back," she went on, "but even if it turns out to be possible, it's going to take a while to work out how. Meanwhile . . ." Kayla took a deep breath. "Meanwhile, I'm here, and I'm the Dark Lady. You have all accepted that." She felt a pressure growing around her.

More nods. Riki looked as if she wanted to object, but she didn't interrupt.

"As long as I'm here, I'm going to be the best Dark Lady I can be," Kayla finished. "But I'm going to do it *my* way." The pressure eased, and she felt a flicker of warmth.

"The Traditions—" Jezzazar started.

"Are traditions, not hard-and-fast laws," Kayla said. "I'm not going to just dump them, but I'm not going to start executing people just because it's Traditional, either. And I'm not going to wear ridiculous dresses all the time just because some other Dark Ladies did."

"You have no idea what you are doing!" Detsini proclaimed.

Kayla shrugged. "Maybe; maybe not. But I know that throwing a party takes a lot more than a fancy dress and some invitations. Especially when there's only a few days to go."

"Fine!" Detsini snapped. "Do as you please. I resign!"

"Kayla already fired you," Del pointed out.

Detsini ignored him. "Ask Athelina to arrange your investiture, then, and much good may it do you!" She turned and marched out of the room.

As the far door closed behind her, Waylan shook his head. "My lady, are you sure— Your investiture is only a few days off. *Someone* must make arrangements."

"'Tis too late," Yazmina said, wringing her hands. "My sister will sulk for days after such an affront, no matter what apologies she receives."

"'Tis the end for us," Jezzazar agreed. "There is no escaping it."

"That's ridiculous," Riki said. "Detsini can't be the only person in this castle who can plan a—an investiture."

Jezzazar, Yazmina, and Ichikar looked at each other and shook their heads. "'Tis a massive undertaking," Ichikar said. "And everything must be perfect, for it reflects the power and abilities of the Dark Lady."

"But Detsini sent out invitations," Kayla said slowly. "Who do you think she invited?"

"She should have invited the guild masters, mayors, and chancellors of all the towns within a four-day ride," Ichikar said slowly.

"Should have," Riki said, her eyes narrowing. "Did anybody check to make sure she did?"

Nobody nodded.

"I bet she forgot somebody on purpose," Del said. "Somebody who'll make trouble, like the wicked fairy in *Sleeping Beauty.*"

Jezzazar looked ill. "'Twould be in keeping with the Traditions."

"Then that's the first thing to take care of," Kayla said. She looked around. "Is there still time, if she skipped somebody far away?"

Ichikar shook his head, but Waylan leaned forward and looked at Riki. "I still have your messenger mouse, and it is well fed and rested. If you are willing to loan it to us, I believe it can reach everyone."

"Go ahead," Riki said. "How likely is everyone to come? It's a bit last-minute."

"They will come." Jezzazar sounded even gloomier than usual. "Some out of fear, some out of curiosity, and some to judge the strength and character of the new Dark Lady, so as to better plan their first assault. They will find the castle in disrepair, no great feast, and neither a vast army nor a grand display of power. 'Twill be no more than a week thereafter before they march against us."

"We've only been in Zaradwin for four days!" Riki objected. "They can't expect us to repair the castle and recruit an army in four days."

"Kayla is the Dark Lady; her tenure matters not," Ichikar said unbendingly. "The castle and the feast reflect her status and her power."

"I guess that means they'd better be good." Kayla frowned, forcing her brain into gear. "At least the trash has been cleared out. What about fixing the portcullis? There must be someone in town who can do that."

Jezzazar shook his head. "There is no time. 'Twill take days just to dismount and mend the winch."

Kayla saw Yazmina make an awkward little motion, as if she wanted to object but didn't quite dare. "Yazmina, you built that gadget that makes it easy to hoist the supply closet up and down, didn't you?"

"How did you hear—"

"Rache told me," Kayla said quickly. "You did it, right? Can you fix the gates?"

Yazmina's eyes lit up. "Aye, 'tis something I have wanted to do these several years."

"'Tis not Traditional for such as you—" Jezzazar started.

"I don't care who takes care of it, as long as it gets done," Kayla interrupted. She looked at Yazmina. "Can you do it before people start arriving?"

"Yes, my lady," Yazmina said, and curtsied. "I'll need four of the men to help."

"Fine," Kayla told her. "Let us know if you need anything else."

Yazmina curtsied again, her eyes wide in a combination of excitement and fear. Jezzazar scowled unhappily, but all he said was, "I'll assign the guards at once." He and Yazmina started for the far door.

"Now, what about this feast?" Riki sounded resigned. "Where do we hold it?"

"'Twill be here, in the great hall," Ichikar said gloomily. "'Twas full to bursting when your father was invested."

Kayla looked around skeptically. "Really?"

"The Maids' and Footmen's Guild can handle everything, my lady," Waylan said.

"Can they fix the portcullis and the walls, too?" They needed proper fortifications even more than a clean and elegant dining room, in her opinion.

"I don't know," Waylan admitted. "But you can ask."

"And pay them," Ichikar snapped. "Which we have not funds for, since the Dark Lady forbade the hordes from raiding to replenish the treasury."

"I found something that I think will solve that problem, for now," Kayla said. "Go ahead and send for them."

Waylan nodded and reached into a small pouch at his waist. A moment later, his hand emerged holding a black gerbil-like creature that was a much sleeker, more streamlined version of the lavender messenger mouse that had been Riki's cell phone. He murmured to it for a moment, then set it down. It raced out of the room, and everyone looked at Kayla expectantly.

"What else do we need?" Kayla asked.

"Detsini mentioned food and entertainment," Riki said. "And

speeches. It sounds a lot like the corporate banquets I organize at work." She looked at Ichikar. "Is there a cooks' guild?"

"Nay," Ichikar replied. "The great cooks work alone and guard their secrets carefully. You will find none within a week's journey capable of providing the exotic foods a great feast requires."

"Exotic foods," Kayla repeated slowly. "Things nobody here has seen before?" She looked at Riki, who slowly began to smile.

"Pizza?" Riki suggested. "Or chili? Maybe tacos."

"Pizza," Kayla said, and started to grin. "Unless there's too many people, or we can't get the fixings. Do they have mozzarella cheese here?"

"We'll ask Geneviev," Riki said. "She's the only one here who seems to know her way around a kitchen."

"And she bakes good bread." Kayla nodded.

"So pizza and garlic breadsticks, and maybe chili if there's too many people," Riki said. "What else do we need to have?"

"Entertainment." Ichikar sounded halfway between fascinated and appalled.

"That's easy." Kayla's grin grew broader. "Rache has that group down in the village; we'll get them." She looked at Rache, who was staring at her, frozen in place with a bite of pancake raised halfway to his mouth. "That's all right, isn't it? You have a couple of days to practice."

"We'll make it, all right," Rache said. "If you'll allow me, my lady, I'll send word at once."

"Are you sure about this, my lady?" Ichikar said. "The Bards' Guild can probably find someone more Traditional, even at this short notice."

"I don't think there's any point in me trying to be too Traditional," Kayla said. She turned to find Riki giving her a disapproving look.

"You and Rache seem to have had quite a conversation," Riki said. "Was this last night?"

"Mostly. Can we discuss it later?"

Reluctantly, Riki nodded.

Kayla breathed a quiet sigh of relief. "Good. I'm done with breakfast; let's go see if Geneviev has the fixings for pizza."

CHAPTER 17

Project Management

It is beneath the dignity of a Dark Lord to involve himself with the mundane details of even the most vital operations. If your minions cannot correctly guess your requirements, a few torture sessions will set them straight.

—From *The Dark Traditions*

Less than an hour after Detsini swept out of the great hall, Ivy and her people began arriving with buckets and rakes and implements of dirt destruction. By then, Waylan had tracked down Geneviev, who went through a cycle of surprise and wariness before eventually agreeing to help out. Geneviev and Riki immediately went into a huddle with Ichikar, who had assembled a list of things to do and invitations they needed to check.

Detsini seemed to have vanished. On the one hand, this allowed everyone to get on with their work without interference; on the other hand, they had no idea what she might be up to. Kayla didn't have much time to worry about it; people kept coming to her with questions.

The first was Ivy, who approached as her crew of maids and

footmen were sorting themselves out. "If I may have a moment of instruction, my lady?" Her tone was perfectly polite, and so was her curtsy, but her eyes were bright and wary.

Kayla glanced back at her mother, who was waving her arms as she discussed supplies, quantities, and costs with Ichikar and Geneviev, and stepped away. "You're Mistress Ivy, the head of the Maids' and Footmen's Guild?" she said, hoping Ivy would take the hint and not mention her visit to the tavern where Riki could hear. "What do you need?"

Ivy cocked an eyebrow, nodded slightly, and said, "I wish to inquire about my lady's preferred style. Do you wish the spiders and cobwebs left as they are?"

"Left as they—" Kayla stopped short. "You mean some of this mess is here on purpose?"

"Probably not, since there hasn't been a Dark Lord in residence for ten years, and the last one preferred a more formal decor," Ivy said. "But this is your investiture, and if you want the spiders-and-bats look, it'll be faster to leave them than replace them."

Maybe that was why Detsini hadn't seemed concerned about the condition of the great hall; she'd seen it as suitably Traditional for a Dark Lady. Kayla shook her head. "Get rid of them all," she said firmly. "We're not throwing a Halloween party."

"A . . . what?"

"Never mind. Just clean everything."

"Of course, my lady." Ivy curtsied again. "Everything?"

"Kitchens first, so we don't get in each other's way when we start cooking," Riki called over her shoulder. "Then the great hall, and after that, the places people are most likely to see."

Ivy gave Riki a speculative look, so Kayla performed the introductions and left them to sort things out further. As she stepped away, Jezzazar entered the hall and marched up to her with a look of grim determination. "Dark Lady Kayla Xavrielina, I beg a mercy of you."

"What? And my name is just Kayla."

Jezzazar bowed stiffly from his waist. Without straightening, he said, "My lady, I beg that you allow my son to flee ere the investiture begins."

"Is this another one of those Traditions you like so much?" Kayla asked.

"'Tis in keeping with them," Jezzazar said cautiously.

Some of the things Geneviev and Rache had told her came together in her head, and she frowned. "Are you trying to set him up to challenge me?"

"I am trying to preserve his life!" Jezzazar burst out, then went gray. "Forgive me, my lady. Whatever punishment you deem suitable, I will accept, but please, spare my son."

"Spare . . ." Kayla paused. Now that she thought of it, Jezzazar knew a lot about his Traditions, but he didn't seem to like them much. He just didn't think there was any point in fighting them. And he and Yazmina had left before she asked Rache about the music, so he probably thought she intended to execute the whole family as soon as she was invested or crowned or whatever.

"I'm not going to execute *anyone,*" she said. "Besides, I need Rache. Ichikar said we should have entertainment at the feast, so I asked him and his band to play."

"My lady, please—" Jezzazar stopped, frowning. "His what?"

"His band. You know, the musicians down at the tavern." Kayla watched Jezzazar's expression shift from puzzled fear to angry parent, and realized that she'd just given away Rache's forays down the mountain.

"Fool boy!" Jezzazar sounded half-angry, half-despairing. "He will doom himself with this folly. He—"

"It isn't folly," Kayla said crossly. "He's good." *And he likes hip-hop,* she almost added, but thought better of it just in time. She had a feeling Jezzazar was going to react to her playlists the same way Waylan had. Some things stayed the same, even if you changed worlds.

"'Tis not Traditional," Jezzazar said, but he didn't sound as certain as he had a minute earlier. "Not the playing, nor the songs he . . . You really think he's good?"

"Yes." Kayla could see him weakening, but he clearly wasn't willing to give in just yet. "Also, Detsini won't expect it." *Especially if his group can learn a couple of things from Macavinchy before then.* "We can talk about it after the council meeting."

"My lady." Ichikar's voice interrupted their conversation. "Will you authorize five guards to requisition this list of foodstuffs from Ashwend?"

"I suppose I—" From the corner of her eye, Kayla saw Ivy stiffen. She paused and replayed Ichikar's request in her head. "Wait. What do you mean, 'requisition'? What would they actually do?"

Ichikar gave her a blank look. "They will locate the goods we need and seize them, as is Traditional."

"This is like starting a war to make money, isn't it?" Kayla said, and sighed. "Never mind. Just buy them. We have enough money for that, don't we?"

"For this, mayhap," Ichikar said slowly. "But there'll be little left to restock the castle."

"Then we'll eat leftover pizza for a week," Kayla said. "And oatmeal after that. There's plenty of oatmeal; I saw it yesterday." *And by then I'll be able to sneak into the Dark Lord's rooms and grab some of the money in those chests.*

Waylan joined them before Ichikar recovered from his shock. "My lady, if I may have a moment?"

Kayla sighed. "Sure. Now what?"

Waylan wanted to know what to do about the guards' uniforms, which still didn't have new helmets. Kayla added "spells to conjure helmets or the illusion of helmets" to her mental list of useful spells she needed to learn or make up soon, and told Waylan that she was sorry, but she wasn't going to give Detsini—or anyone else—the opportunity to slip a spy in behind the full masks that were part of their usual uniform. Del and Archie got involved in the argument, so she told them to help Waylan work something out and left them to it.

By then, one of the cleaners was back with another question, and so it went for the rest of the day. She finally fled to the kitchens, where she found Riki, Geneviev, and two of Ivy's people. Riki and Geneviev appeared to be taste-testing several different cheeses while keeping an eye on the oven shelves; the others were tending two large cauldrons hanging inside the walk-in fireplace.

On Kayla's shoulder, Macavinchy sniffed the air and began slowly flexing his wings. Kayla could see why. The scent of baking bread and the rich aroma from the cauldrons made her mouth water. "Is it almost dinner?"

Everyone looked at her. Geneviev and the two cooks curtsied. "We have new-made trenchers for everyone," Geneviev said tentatively. "And there will soon be— Oh!" She curtsied hastily, grabbed a large wooden paddle, and began removing several small, flat objects from the oven.

"You figured out the pizza!" Kayla said.

"Test run," Riki told her. She nodded neutrally at Geneviev, but there were tension lines around her mouth, a faint echo of the intense strain she'd been under in the months that followed Michael's death.

"We need to see how the ingredients work together," Geneviev said, looking doubtfully at the sample pizzas. "I did my best, but we just don't have everything, and I'm not sure about some of the substitutions."

Kayla shrugged. "Back home, some places make pizza with pineapple and artichokes on it. We can use anything we want. If you really want to see if it works, I'll get Del. He's fussy about pizza; if he likes it, it's fine."

One of the cooks immediately volunteered to find him. By the time Del arrived, Kayla had a classic pizza burn from not letting her first slice cool long enough, and pronounced the cheese too rubbery. Her second slice had a crumbly cheese that hadn't melted into the sauce, and some brown oval things that looked like olives but crunched like walnuts; her third had a gooey cheese over a white sauce, peas, mushrooms, and onions. Both of those slices were very good.

The fourth had cheese, tomato sauce, and round slices of some kind of spicy sausage that looked like pepperoni but wasn't. As she finished her slice, Kayla said, "This is better than pepperoni. And the one with the peas was weird but good."

Del nodded. "Really good," he mumbled around a large bite. "Can I have 'nother?"

"Don't talk with your mouth full," Riki said. "The peas were Geneviev's idea, and she did the seasoning on that one. And you're right; it is good."

"We'll have that one at the investiture for sure," Kayla decided. "The weird part won't matter. And the one that isn't pepperoni."

"The tomato sauce isn't right," Del objected.

"I believe the problem is with the seasoning," Macavinchy put in. "I cannot find any references to oregano, but basil or thyme may make adequate substitutions. I believe the addition of some garlic would also be beneficial."

"Thank you," Geneviev said. "I'll make up another batch after dinner and try your suggestions."

"Don't spend too much time trying to get it perfect enough for Del," Kayla said, ignoring Del's immediate objection. "These are good, and nobody here knows what pizza is supposed to taste like anyway."

"I am glad you find my efforts acceptable, my lady," Geneviev said.

Kayla swallowed another bite. "Acceptable? If you can make up food like this from just a description, you should be a chef."

Geneviev's eyes widened. Then she closed them and said sadly, "Would that I could."

"Why can't you? You like cooking, don't you?" Kayla said. Geneviev nodded tentatively, and Kayla went on, "And you're good at it. Wouldn't being a chef be better than marrying somebody you don't actually care for? Do you need a license to open a . . . restaurant or a pub here? Because if people like the food at this feast, I bet they'll want someplace to get it regularly."

Geneviev looked as if someone had hit her over the head with her wooden pizza paddle. "I . . . I will think on what you have said, my lady."

"You do that," Kayla said. "We're going to need somebody who's willing to learn to make pizza and tacos and hummus and stir-fry with noodles. Not that the stew isn't really tasty," she added quickly. "I just don't think I want to have it every single night for the next six months."

The line between Riki's eyebrows grew deeper, and she pressed her lips together. Geneviev began checking the stew cauldrons. She still looked half-stunned, but she studied the cauldrons with a new air of ownership that made Kayla think her suggestion was being considered seriously.

A flurry of activity followed as Geneviev and most of the kitchen helpers began dishing the stew into large wooden bowls and carrying them and the trenchers to the great hall for the cleaners and guards and other castle folk. Del grabbed one of the smaller trays and joined the procession; Kayla was fairly sure that he intended to grab a second dinner when he got to the hall.

They all fell into bed that night, totally exhausted. The next day was a repeat, but with everything farther along. The cleaners were almost finished with the great hall and started on the hallways and stairs leading to it. Ivy had assured Riki that every-thing that would be visible to visitors would be finished in good time.

Geneviev had started reinventing chili, with tacos to come next. Rache's group had arrived and immediately borrowed Macavinchy, after Kayla authorized him to answer any of their questions about music. The portcullis had come unstuck, which was progress of a sort. Yazmina had requested several chains and an iron rod, which she said she could jury-rig into something that would lift and lower it for a few weeks until they could get a blacksmith to make the actual parts they needed.

No one had seen Detsini since she stormed out of breakfast the day before. Kayla wasn't sure whether to be glad her aunt wasn't interfering or worried about what she was planning. She settled on glad; she didn't have time to worry, and she couldn't do anything about it anyway.

By evening on the second day, things were well in hand. "It won't be the kind of party they're used to," Riki fretted.

"I'm not the kind of Dark Lady they're used to," Kayla said. "So if the point is to show everybody what I'm like, it'll be fine."

"I suppose," Riki said with a sigh.

They camped again in the guest quarters—the cleaners hadn't gotten there yet, but Ivy said they should be far enough along with the public areas to work on those rooms next day. Riki was getting cross about everyone sharing a room, and Kayla hoped that once the rooms were all cleaned, they could move into sepa-rate quarters. That would make it easier for her to sneak out to the Dark Lord's chambers and collect enough of the hoard to pay everyone, and maybe visit the mountain spirit who was chained up in the dungeon. Kayla's last thought before she fell into sleep was that maybe tomorrow she'd have time to look for a way to free him.

Kayla was jerked awake by a yell from the outer room. She bolted upright, but all that followed was the muffled sound of Riki's scolding voice. Somewhat reassured, Kayla threw on her clothes and left to find out who'd messed up and how badly.

Del was sitting on the bench, kicking his heels, while Riki paced on the far side of the room. Kayla's copy of *The Dark Traditions* lay in the middle of the floor in front of Del. Kayla fixed her brother with her best glare and said, "Del, how many times have I told you not to snoop in my things!"

"I wasn't snooping!"

"Then how did that book get from my backpack to the middle of the floor?"

"Master Delmar removed the book from the backpack and then dropped it," Macavinchy said from the top of the water closet. He shook his wings out, flapped twice, and glided down to his usual perch on Kayla's shoulder.

Del shifted. "I just wanted to *see* it!"

"So you dropped it on the floor?"

"It tried to bite him," Riki said. "Does everything in this world eat children?"

"*Bite* him?"

"Yeah." Del grinned. "I was too fast for it, but Mom's mad."

"I noticed." Kayla crossed the floor and bent over the book.

"Don't touch that!" Riki snapped.

Kayla gave her a look, then deliberately picked the book up and tucked it into the crook of her arm. "What were you going to do, leave it in the middle of the floor and walk around it for weeks?" she said before Riki could comment on her actions. "It's my book; it won't bite me."

"This is one of those things you just know?" Riki said.

"Sort of," Kayla said. "It's that book I told you about, on how to be a Dark Lord for beginners. I haven't had a chance to read much of it yet, but nothing happened when I looked at the chapter titles before."

"Maybe it's mad because you haven't read it yet," Del suggested.

Kayla shrugged. "I meant to ask Harkawn about it, but I forgot."

"How could you forget a book that bites people?" Riki said.

"It doesn't bite *me*." Kayla waved the book at her, then flipped it open and riffled the pages. "See?"

"Kayla—" Riki shook her head. "Never mind. But right after breakfast, you're taking that thing to Harkawn. He's a librarian and a magician; he should know something useful about it."

"All right." Kayla shoved the book into her backpack and slung the pack over her shoulder. "Let's go eat."

Breakfast quickly turned into a meeting about the next day's ceremony. Between various reports and questions, the morning was more than half over before Kayla, Archie, and Del finally headed for the library.

They left Riki in the great hall to handle the ongoing decisions and instructions. Kayla couldn't help feeling relieved that she had someone with her who knew how to organize a giant party. *If Mom weren't here, I'd have to do it all myself. I don't think that would go very well.* Magic might help with the chores—she added "photocopying for invitations" and "amplification for speeches and music" to her mental list of spells to learn soon—but she doubted it would help her decide what food or music to have.

When they reached the library, Harkawn had a stack of books and scrolls waiting for them, presumably salvaged from the wreck Del had made of the library. Harkawn himself was sorting through a stack of half-charred papers at one end of the big table. Kayla sat down at the other end and dug *The Dark Traditions* out of her backpack.

"What is that?" Archie asked.

"A biting book," Del told him.

"It doesn't bite me," Kayla informed him as she opened it.

Archie squinted at the cover. "*The Dark Traditions*? Where did you find—"

At the sound of the book's title, Harkawn looked up sharply. "What's that? Where did you find that book?"

"On the bench in the guest room," Kayla said. "Why?"

The librarian sucked in his breath and started coughing.

"Are you all right?" Kayla asked.

Harkawn shrugged a shoulder and breathed carefully. "It's no matter." He stared at the book with a combination of desire and wariness. "*The Dark Traditions* is . . . unique, peculiar, and legendary. 'Tis said that only the truest and greatest of Dark Rulers ever possess a copy."

Which is just what a Dark Lord would say about something that nobody else has, Kayla thought. She glanced uneasily at the book in her hand. "It has my name on the cover. Is it dangerous?"

Harkawn's shoulders relaxed visibly. "Not to you, my lady."

"But to other people?" Kayla gave Del a worried look.

"It can't bite you if you're fast," Del said smugly.

"It can do far worse than bite," Harkawn corrected him. "It visits slow and horrifying death on anyone who touches it, other than its proper owner."

"It didn't do anything but try to bite me," Del insisted.

"How would you know?" Kayla turned back to Harkawn without waiting for an answer. "Is there a way to check and make sure Del is all right?"

"Not that I know of," Harkawn replied.

"Of course there is," Archie said at the same time. He and Harkawn looked at each other, and Archie went on, "Well, I don't know the spells that the healers use to find out exactly which curse someone has been hit with, because I wasn't training to be a healer, but I can do the basic curse-detection spell."

"Do it now, please," Kayla said. Remembering his first try at the light-making spell, she added, "Carefully."

"Right." Archie's eyes narrowed, and he muttered something and gestured.

The air around Archie began to ripple like the surface of a pond after someone dropped a stone into the water. The rippling grew stronger, then gathered together and surged outward from Archie's hand. *The Dark Traditions* pulsed purple in response, just once. As the ripple passed the bookshelves, one of the scrolls began to glow a dark purple. The walls of the room turned the color of dead lilac flowers; evidently Ivy had been right about the castle being cursed. Kayla turned her head. Del wasn't glowing at all. She sighed in relief and looked back.

The air around Harkawn had turned black.

Archie twisted his fingers and all the glows faded. He kept his hand raised, not quite pointing at Harkawn. "And who cursed you, librarian?"

"The Dark Lord that was," Harkawn replied, and had another coughing fit.

Kayla watched with much less sympathy than she'd had a few minutes ago. "My father cursed you? Why?" she asked when it seemed that Harkawn could talk again.

"I challenged him and lost," Harkawn replied.

There was a long, uncomfortable moment of silence while everyone absorbed that. Then Archie stepped smoothly between Kayla and the librarian. "So you're a Dark Lord," he said.

CHAPTER 18

International Politics

Bear in mind that until you have finished taking over the world, you will have to deal with other kingdoms and rulers. While it is tempting to simply attack them immediately, it is often better to negotiate first and betray them later.

—From *The Dark Traditions*

Harkawn shook his head. "No, I'm a *former* Dark Lord," he corrected Archie. He looked from Archie to Kayla and his forehead wrinkled. "I thought you knew."

"No one tells me anything," Kayla growled. "Macavinchy, is he telling the truth?"

"Yes, madam," Macavinchy replied. "That is to say, Mr. Harkawn was at one time the Dark Lord of Xennerarth. He was removed from that position when he challenged the Dark Lord of Zaradwin and lost. Insofar as I am able to determine from the records, he has been the librarian of Zaradwin Castle since then."

"Why didn't you say so?"

"You have not previously requested background information on any of the castle inhabitants, madam."

Kayla took a deep breath. "Ask the right questions," she muttered. She turned and glared at Harkawn. "Explain. In detail."

"The details aren't particularly informative," Harkawn said. "I'd built up a nice little kingdom off to the north, not large enough to attract attention from either the Dark Empire of Zaradwin or the Threefold Alliance of the Light. I'd been holding back, trying to keep it that way, but it was getting harder to maintain the balance." He glanced up. "When you're a Dark Lord, it's grow or die."

Kayla nodded, more to acknowledge that she'd heard him than because she agreed.

"Then we got word that the Dark Lord's sisters had banished his heir." Harkawn bowed his head in Kayla's direction. "He was distracted, and when a Dark Lord is distracted, things come apart. It starts at the edges, and the bigger the Dark Lord's territory, the worse it gets and the faster it goes. The Dark Lord of Zaradwin ruled the largest Dark Empire of the past five centuries, and I was out on the edge of it."

"You revolted," Archie guessed.

"He couldn't revolt," Del objected. "He just said he wasn't part of the empire. I bet he attacked."

"Not me," Harkawn said. "A couple of my neighbors. They started snapping up disaffected villages, which didn't leave me with a lot of choices. If I did nothing, they'd soon be strong enough to conquer my land and I'd be finished. If I joined them in annexing imperial villages, the Dark Empire would lose too much territory to ignore, and we'd all be facing the Dark Lord's armies in short order. Even working together, we couldn't have defeated them."

"So *then* you attacked!" Del said, bouncing in his chair.

"No," Harkawn repeated in a smug tone. "I sent a message to the Dark Lord's regional commander, pointing out what my neighbors were doing and suggesting that he put a stop to it."

So far, he sounded pretty reasonable for a Dark Lord. "How does this end up with you challenging my father and getting cursed?" Kayla asked.

Harkawn shrugged. "You wanted details."

"Fine. Go on."

"The Dark Lord's commanders were generally competent, and that one was no exception. He swept in with two legions and annexed my neighbors. Almost immediately, he and the legions were recalled to Zaradwin because the Alliance of Light was threatening to invade.

"Naturally, I took over both of my neighbors' kingdoms as soon as the imperial armies left, but that made it a certainty that the Dark Lord would come after me as soon as he'd finished dealing with the threat of the Light. My forces still were nowhere near strong enough to beat the Dark Lord's armies, but I thought I had a good chance of defeating him one-on-one."

"Why?"

"Xavriel hadn't faced a serious opponent in years. He was out of practice. And by then he had two things to distract him, the search for his heir and the threat from the Light. Also, as far as anyone knew, he hadn't punished his sisters for the kidnapping. He might have gone soft. Besides, it was confront him on my terms, or wait for him to show up with an army." Harkawn shrugged again. "If I challenged him and lost, my lands and people wouldn't face a war or penalties. They'd just be taken under the protection of the empire, so it seemed like the better choice. At least that part worked out."

"So you fought the Dark Lord and lost, and he cursed you," Archie finished for him. "Why didn't he just kill you?"

"He did. The curse is slowly destroying my lungs. The Dark Lord's passing lessened the speed of its progress, but as you have seen, it did not lift it."

"As we— That's why you cough so much!" Kayla said.

Harkawn nodded. "I've done what I could to find a counter, these past twelve years. But if there was ever a cure in this library, Xavriel removed it before he stuck me here. And I can't go looking elsewhere; the curse ties me to the castle."

"Ties you how?"

"As long as I'm here, the curse progresses slowly. If I leave Zaradwin Castle, I'll be dead in a week. It's an effective way of keeping me from raising a rebellion."

"That's—" Kayla shook her head, unable to find the right words. She'd known since their arrival that her biological father was a Dark Lord, but she hadn't thought much about what that meant. Despite Jezzazar's muttering about the various Dark Traditions, despite the ruined gates and the dragon skull that had almost hurt Del, despite the spirit chained up in the dungeon, she hadn't really believed that her father could have done anything *too* bad. Not when everyone here thought he was such a great ruler.

Such a great Dark Lord, she corrected herself. *What else did he do?* And Harkawn was a Dark Lord, too, or had been. She *liked* Harkawn. He'd helped them—hadn't he? *Can I really trust him?*

Archie seemed to be wondering the same thing; he still stood between Kayla and Harkawn, and he hadn't lowered his hands. "What were you planning?" he asked in a harsh tone.

"Planning?" Harkawn said. "Ah. I was planning to make myself useful enough that my lady here would lift the curse, once she comes into her full power."

"And then?"

"And then do my best to fulfill whatever orders she gives me," Harkawn replied. He sounded a little exasperated. "Really, are you expecting me to turn around and challenge her?" He shook his head. "You don't get a second chance at being a Dark Lord."

Kayla shivered at the bitterness in his tone. "Do you want a second chance?"

"I haven't thought much past surviving, to be honest." Abruptly, Harkawn grinned. "Though if I do and you're offering, I wouldn't say no to a duchy or a barony, or even a diplomatic post."

"I'll . . . think about it," Kayla said uneasily.

"Thank you, my lady," Harkawn said, bowing. "Now, if you'll excuse me, I should see about that cursed scroll your spell discovered. I thought I had put all of the cursed items in the secure room."

As Harkawn moved away, Archie relaxed at last. He sat down and leaned toward Kayla, frowning. "You didn't mean that, did you? About giving him a position? He was a Dark Lord; you can't trust them."

"You want to be a Dark Lord," Del pointed out. "So we shouldn't trust you when you say we shouldn't trust Harkawn. So that means we *should* trust him."

"Neither of them is a Dark Lord right now," Kayla said before Archie could react with more than an indignant expression. "So it's not a problem. But that thing is." She pointed at *The Dark Traditions,* which was still lying on the table. "Is it cursed or not?"

As she had hoped, the question distracted both Del and Archie from their budding argument. For a long minute, they both stared at the book; then Archie made a small, twisting movement with one hand.

Nothing happened. "It doesn't seem to be cursed," Archie said cautiously.

"If it's not cursed, why did it try to bite me?" Del objected.

"Maybe because you were poking into things that aren't yours?" Kayla suggested.

"No, that's not it." Archie was still frowning at the book. "It has a lot of magic attached to it, but—" He made another gesture, a little larger.

There was a soft popping noise and Archie flew out of his chair as if something had exploded in front of him. He struck the wall with considerable force and slid down it into a crumpled heap.

Kayla jumped up and ran over to Archie. As she bent to see if he was all right, Harkawn materialized from behind the shelves and pulled her back.

"What did he do?" the librarian demanded, then started coughing, as if the effort to stop Kayla had been almost too much for him.

"Let go of me!"

"Do as the Dark Lady commands," Waylan's voice said from

the doorway, "or I will slay you here and now, the old Dark Lord's will notwithstanding."

Kayla turned her head as Waylan drew his sword and stepped forward. Harkawn let go of Kayla instantly but stepped between her and Archie. "Touching him could be dangerous, even for you, my lady," he wheezed between coughs. "If he activated a curse . . ."

"He said it wasn't cursed," Del objected.

"Who said what wasn't cursed?" Waylan asked.

"Archie," Kayla replied. "And he said the book didn't *seem* to be cursed. He might have—"

At that moment, Archie groaned and sat up. "Ow," he said, rubbing the back of his head.

"Are you all right?" Kayla asked. "Macavinchy, is he—"

"Mr. Archibald appears to have sustained minor damage from his collision with the wall, madam," Macavinchy replied.

"Not from the book?"

"Only indirectly. The force that propelled him came from the book."

"So that book is cursed after all!" Del said triumphantly.

Archie looked up and winced. "No, it isn't. It just doesn't want anyone poking around in its magic." He rolled his head to one side and winced again. "Maybe it'd let Kayla."

"I would strongly suggest limiting further investigation to simply reading the volume in question," Macavinchy said, settling his wings in place.

"What have you been doing?" Waylan said, sounding as if he wasn't sure he actually wanted to know.

"Seeing if anybody is cursed," Kayla said. "Did you know that Harkawn used to be a Dark Lord?"

Waylan looked slightly surprised by the question. "Of course. Everyone knows that."

"I didn't," Kayla growled. "Just like I didn't know my mother is still alive, or that I have a half sister, or aunts and a cousin." Her voice rose as she spoke. Vaguely, she noticed that the bookshelves were shivering and Harkawn was backing away from her. "You all go on as if I should know everything, including what's important and what's not, just because my father was a Dark Lord. How am I supposed to get anything right if nobody tells me anything?" By the time she finished, she was shaking in anger and frustration.

"By drawing on the knowledge of the castle," Harkawn said in a matter-of-fact tone.

"I don't know anything about the castle!" Kayla snarled. Archie and Waylan flinched away from her, but Harkawn seemed unruffled.

"Of course you do," Harkawn said. "You claimed it. Even if the castle had rejected you, you'd know something about it. Since it accepted your claim, you should know whatever you need to know about it, whenever you need to know it."

That must be where that internal GPS came from, Kayla thought. *It's probably why I'm so sure that things like the dragon skull won't hurt me.* She frowned. She wasn't doing any of that on purpose, but was she using the magic that bound the spirit of the mountain to do it? Would it make matters worse for him?

Del cocked his head to one side. "Can you know anything you want? Ask it something—ask it what I can do with my magic!"

"Create chaos," Kayla said promptly. "I don't need a magic castle to tell me that."

Archie snickered, and Del scowled at him. Before they could start another argument, Waylan cleared his throat. "Your lady mother awaits your presence at lunch," he said. "Perhaps you should postpone this discussion until later."

The promise of food distracted both Del and Archie from their squabbling, and they started for the door. Kayla stuffed *The Dark Traditions* into her backpack and followed them out.

While Del and Archie traded off explaining to Waylan what had happened, Kayla had a chance to think, and she didn't like where her thoughts were heading. She didn't want Harkawn to die, even if he was a former Dark Lord. But did she have enough power to stop the curse that was killing him? If the only way to save Harkawn's life was to draw on the power of the spirit imprisoned in the dungeon, could she do it, knowing she was condemning him to more years of imprisonment? But she couldn't just let Harkawn die!

I need to talk to Mom about this. The thought floated up as she entered the great hall, and it nearly gave her mental whiplash. She wanted to discuss the problem with Riki, but she wasn't ready to confess the details of last night's excursion just yet. Besides, she didn't want Riki using the ex–Dark Lordness of the librarian as another excuse to go home as fast as possible. Going back to Earth would leave both the spirit and Harkawn in their current bad situations, the one chained up in the dungeon, the other cursed and dying.

Maybe she could talk to somebody else. Kayla ran over the possibilities. There weren't many. Most of the castle folk were so steeped in their Dark Traditions that they probably wouldn't understand why she wanted to free the spirit and uncurse Harkawn. The only real candidates were Waylan and Archie, and neither one was entirely satisfactory. Waylan might not be quite as Traditional as Jezzazar or Ichikar, but he still took it for granted that Dark Lords would torture and execute anyone who was inconvenient. Archie didn't approve of torture and executions, but his distrust of Harkawn had been apparent from the moment they'd learned that the librarian had been a Dark Lord himself.

Kayla sighed, then pulled her attention back to the great hall. Riki and Ichikar sat near the entrance, deep in conversation over a platter of sandwiches. Riki looked up as they approached.

"Did Harkawn have anything to say about that book?" she asked.

"Lots," Kayla said. "It's not cursed, though, and neither is Del."

"Harkawn is," Del said, grabbing a sandwich. He took a bite and added something unintelligible.

"For the umpteenth time, swallow before you try to talk," Riki said. "And what do you mean, Harkawn is?"

"He's cursed," Archie told her.

Del finished his first bite and started telling the whole story, with much excited hand-waving. When he stopped to take another bite, Archie filled in and provided corrections. Kayla snagged a sandwich and settled on the bench, listening with half an ear while she tried to decide what to do about Harkawn.

She was on her second sandwich and still hadn't come to a conclusion, when she felt a hand on her arm. She looked up into her mother's worried face. "Honey, are you all right?" Riki asked.

"I'm fine," Kayla said automatically, and smiled slightly. Having her mom worry about her made her feel almost normal. If curses and biting books were normal.

"If you want to talk . . ." Riki's voice trailed off, leaving the choice up to Kayla.

She really wanted to say yes, but talking to Riki would mean explaining about the spirit in the dungeon, which in turn would mean admitting to her visit to the Dark Lord's chambers. She'd end up grounded until she was thirty. "Maybe later," she mumbled.

Riki nodded, but she still looked worried. Kayla hunted for something else to say. "At least the hall looks better now," she said. Ivy's people had done wonders; the walls and floor gleamed, and the trestle tables and benches were clean and polished. "Are the cleaners coming back after dinner?"

"They haven't left," Riki said absently. "They've moved on to the rest of the castle."

"It's kind of bare, though," Kayla went on. "Maybe we should look for some decorations? Tapestries or something?"

"I don't think there's time," Riki said.

"You should get that dragon," Del put in. "You could put him right over the throne."

"I don't think that would be a good—" Riki started, and the wall over the throne rippled like a puddle of oil. A moment later, the dragon skull broke through the surface and shook itself, like a wet dog shaking off droplets of water.

Riki made a half-startled, half-frightened noise, and most of the people in the hall backed away from the throne.

"You called?" the skull said.

"No!" Kayla said. "I didn't say anything!"

"Not you." The dragon tilted in Del's direction. "Him."

"Me?" Del sounded as if he couldn't decide whether to be horrified, terrified, or delighted. Then he grinned; delighted had won. "I can call dragons!"

"No," Riki said shakily. "No more dragons. And get rid of this one, right now!"

"But, Mom!"

"He can't get rid of me," the skull said in a smug tone. "I don't answer to him."

"Then why did you come?" Del asked.

"You're my new job," the skull informed him. "I'm going to teach you about your magic."

"Cool!" Del said.

Kayla dropped her head to the table, wondering how long it would be before Riki realized that Kayla was the one who had suggested that the dragon skull teach Del.

"You're not teaching him anything!" Riki said.

"I don't answer to you, either," the skull told her.

Riki's eyes narrowed. "Who do you answer to, then?"

"And what makes you think Del has magic?" Archie put in. "He melted the test globe."

"Oh, please! You think he could have done that without magic? I'm surprised he hasn't accidentally turned someone into a chicken already."

"I can turn people into chickens?" Del looked speculatively at Archie. The few guards and cleaners who hadn't already left the hall edged closer to the doors.

"No," Riki said. "I told you, you're not allowed to do magic without proper supervision."

"Archie's right here! You said he could supervise me."

"He can't supervise you if he's a chicken," Riki pointed out.

"Then *he* can supervise me," Del said, pointing at the skull. "He said he was going to teach me."

Riki looked at the skull in outrage. "I didn't agree to that. Who thought that would be a good idea, anyway?"

"She did," the skull said, tilting in Kayla's direction.

Busted. Kayla sighed and raised her head. Next time she came up with an idea like this, she was going to swear everyone within earshot to secrecy.

"When did— *That's* where you went the other night, when you were out so late?" Riki turned and gave Kayla a look of disappointed betrayal that made her want to crawl under the table. "I told you to stay away from that thing! It almost killed your brother!"

"He was just doing his job!" Kayla said. "And I told him not to do that anymore. And he's the only one who knows anything about Del's kind of magic."

"Why would he listen—"

"Because she's the Dark Lady." The skull sounded almost respectful. "We answer to her."

"*We?*"

Kayla sighed again. She might as well get everything out of the way at once. "There are two of them. The other one is guarding the room under the Dark Lord's chambers. I didn't tell him he could leave, so he's probably still guarding the prisoner down there."

Riki stared at Kayla for a long moment. Then she took a deep breath and said, in a voice that was dangerously calm, "Tell me exactly what you did that night. All of it, in detail."

"Fine, but not in front of everyone."

"I don't think that's a concern," Waylan's voice put in from behind them. "Unless you would prefer that Master Archibald and I leave? Everyone else is gone."

Kayla looked over her shoulder, startled, and Waylan nodded toward the main part of the hall. When she turned, she saw that the five of them were the only people left in the room. Everyone else had slipped out the doors during their conversation with the dragon skull.

"Stay," Kayla decided. She felt the way she had just before her father's funeral, when Riki had had a meltdown and somebody had to make sure things got done. Only now she was fourteen instead of ten, and the Dark Lady, and people *had* to listen to her. "And sit down, please. I need some advice, and I wasn't sure which one of you I should talk to. So I'll talk to all of you at once."

Riki's eyes narrowed, but she didn't say anything as Waylan

took a seat farther down the bench. Kayla nodded and gave her mother a wary look. "Please don't freak out until I'm done, all right, Mom? Or we'll be here the rest of the day and all night afterward." With that, she plunged into a description of her adventures.

CHAPTER 19

Your Dark Council

Membership on your Dark Council should be reserved for those sensible minions who will enter into your ideas and plans with enthusiasm and energy instead of making tiresome objections.

—From *The Dark Traditions*

Going through everything that had happened three nights before took some time. At first, Riki kept her promise not to comment, but Del interrupted several times to ask why Kayla hadn't taken him with her, and whether Archie would take him down to the tavern next time he went. Finally, Riki told him in no uncertain terms to settle down. Del subsided reluctantly, and Riki turned to Kayla.

"So the three of you came back to the castle, and you started toward our rooms," she prompted.

Kayla nodded. "I wasn't sure where they were, and I got distracted. And then—" She explained about the unexpected sense of direction that had led her to the door guarded by the dragon skull.

"If you were trying to get to our rooms, why did you end up somewhere else?" Riki asked suspiciously.

"I don't know."

"The castle called her," the dragon skull said. "It was getting impatient. It's very rare for a new Dark Lady to avoid the center of her magic and the heart of the castle's power. Practically unheard of."

"The castle is alive?" Riki wrinkled her forehead skeptically.

"Not exactly, madam," Macavinchy said before the dragon skull could answer. "It has not existed in its present form long enough to develop an independent spirit of its own. However, it does have a certain degree of awareness."

The dragon skull nodded. "It'll be fully awake in another couple of hundred years, I expect, and it won't take more than another thousand after that for it to manifest as a spirit. The process speeds up when there's a lot of magic thrown around a particular place, and this castle certainly qualifies."

"You mean there'll be another spirit locked up down there?" Kayla said, horrified.

"Not unless someone binds it, madam," Macavinchy replied. "Imprisonment in the dungeon is not automatic."

"Dungeon?" Riki and Del said together.

"I hadn't gotten to that part yet." Quickly, Kayla summarized her exploration of the Dark Lord's chambers. She skipped over her discovery of the secret castle hoard, which would only distract everyone, and focused instead on climbing down the long staircase and finding the spirit of the mountain chained in the dungeon.

"Spirit binding," Archie said in awe. "No wonder Dark Lords are so powerful."

"Keeping a spirit chained up in the dungeon is wrong," Kayla snapped.

"I don't disagree," Archie said quickly.

"Then—" Riki started.

"I don't know how to let him go!" Kayla burst out. "And I might need to use his power to break the curse on Harkawn, but if I do that, I don't think I'll be *able* to let him go! But if I don't break the curse, Harkawn will die."

This led to another round of explanations, at the end of which Riki sat back, frowning. "I don't like this."

"You don't like *anything* about Zaradwin, Mom," Del observed.

"That's not the point," Kayla put in hastily. They didn't need Del starting an argument with Riki right now. "How can I fix Harkawn without using Zar's power and locking him in that dungeon for another couple of hundred years?"

"You could try that stuff Mom used on Archie," Del suggested.

"Heal-all only works on injuries and illness," Archie said. "It won't break a curse."

"No, but it might buy some time," Waylan put in thoughtfully. "If the heal-all repairs the damage the curse has already done, we'd have several more years to find a permanent solution that doesn't involve the mountain spirit." He looked directly at Kayla. "That is, if you are certain of this path, my lady."

"Harkawn is a former Dark Lord," Archie added. "You don't know what he'll do once he's free and back in good health."

Waylan nodded. "Just so. And if the spirit—Zar?—is the source of Zaradwin's power, letting it go may have a negative effect on your ability to rule."

"I can't leave Zar stuck down there," Kayla said. "But Harkawn"—she shivered and finished in a whisper—"Harkawn looks like Dad did, right before he went into the hospital."

Archie, who had opened his mouth to say something, closed it without speaking. Riki reached across the table and took Kayla's hand. "We will figure this out," she said, and even though Kayla knew there was no certainty of that, she felt better.

"What we really need is more information about Harkawn and the curse, from somebody who isn't Harkawn," Archie said after a moment. He looked at Waylan. "You were here then, weren't you?"

"I was in the castle, but I was not in the Dark Lord's confidence," Waylan replied. "Even if I had been, I am no magician. I knew that the would-be Dark Lord Harkawn had been defeated, and that he was compelled to stay in the castle and watch the true Dark Lord's triumph for the remainder of his life, but more than that I cannot tell you."

"Then—"

"Ask her mother," the dragon skull said in a bored tone.

"Mom doesn't know any more about Harkawn than I do," Kayla objected.

"Not this mother," the skull said. "The one that's been hiding in her rooms for the last ten years."

"Lady Athelina would know more, if anyone does," Waylan said, nodding again.

Kayla bit her lip and looked down. "She doesn't want to see me."

"What?" Riki switched from looking as if she wanted to object to following the skull's advice, no matter how logical it was, to looking as if she wanted to strangle someone.

"I asked Geneviev right after I found out our mother was still here. She said Athelina wasn't feeling well enough, but—but I don't think she was telling the truth," Kayla whispered.

"So?" the skull said. "Summon her for questioning."

"I can't do that!" Kayla objected. "She's my *mother.*"

"Then go to her," Waylan said. "Lord Archibald is right; you must know more if you wish to make a decision based on more than custom, and Lady Athelina is the only one in the castle who can provide the information you need."

"But if she doesn't want to see me—"

"It's not as if she can keep you out," the skull said, sounding exasperated. "You're the Dark Lady of Zaradwin. The castle answers to you."

Kayla ducked her head. Ever since their arrival at the castle, she'd wanted to meet her biological mother, but to just barge in on her . . . especially if she wasn't well? And what if her biological mother was as Traditional as Detsini? What if she expected Kayla to execute her, the way Geneviev had? What if she was disappointed by the way her daughter had turned out? *What if she just doesn't want to see me? What if she's glad I disappeared?*

"There's no need to start off by barging in," Waylan said, as if he could sense her thoughts. "I'll speak with Geneviev."

"All right," Kayla said reluctantly. *Best get it over with.*

Waylan bowed and left. Once he was out of the great hall, Archie turned to Kayla. "Are you sure about this?"

"About what?" Kayla said. "Talking to my mother? Freeing Zar? Healing Harkawn?"

"All of it." Archie waved his arms comprehensively.

Kayla shrugged, swallowing her misgivings. "I have to do something. It's my responsibility."

"No, it isn't," Riki said.

"Of course it is," the dragon skull said. "She's the Dark Lady."

"And a Dark Lady is supposed to watch out for her people," Kayla added, thinking of what Harkawn had said. He'd challenged Xavriel at least partly to protect his people, to prevent a war that could have destroyed them.

"*This* Dark Lady is supposed to learn enough magic to get us home," Riki said. "*That* is your responsibility: to get your family back where we belong."

I belong here, Kayla thought, but she wasn't ready to say that out loud. "That could take months," she told Riki instead. "Until then, I'm the Dark Lady, and I'm supposed to take care of things here."

Archie and the skull nodded in tandem.

Riki opened her mouth, then closed it again. She sighed. "You've always taken more responsibility than a child your age should. You don't need to feel that way, honey."

"But I do."

Del cocked his head. "And if we go back, Kayla and I won't have magic anymore."

"Nope," said the dragon skull.

"I *like* having magic," Del announced. "I want to stay and use it for things."

"I like having magic, too," Kayla said quickly. "But no more explosions."

"What if I need to explode things? Somebody might attack the castle," Del pointed out. "So I need to know how."

"I—" Riki's mouth worked unhappily, as if she didn't know which of sixteen objections to make first.

"I was born here," Kayla pointed out, trying hard to keep hold of her temper. "My birth father left me this castle. Shouldn't I try to fix some of the things that are wrong with it?"

"It's not your job!" Riki almost wailed.

Del frowned. "It is, sort of." Everyone looked at him. "Dark Lords always try to conquer the world, but there's no way Kayla can even start when the castle isn't repaired and there's no money or supplies. The first thing you do in a war game is build up your resources."

"This isn't a computer game," Riki said. "This is real."

"Which means we can't stop playing," Kayla pointed out. "And we have to get it right the first time. If we mess anything up, we can't just reload."

Behind her, someone coughed. Kayla twisted in her seat to find Waylan and Geneviev standing behind her. It looked as if Waylan had caught up with Geneviev just before she left to take Athelina's lunch up to her; she carried a wooden tray that held a small pitcher and a covered bowl.

"I apologize for interrupting, my lady," Waylan said, "but Lady Geneviev is ready to escort you to your mother."

Geneviev nodded, her face blank. Kayla wondered how hard Waylan had to twist her arm to get her to agree. All her misgivings roared up another notch, and she was about to suggest putting off the visit when Riki leaned forward and said, "I'm coming with you."

"As my lady commands," Geneviev said. Her eyes never left Kayla, and her voice as expressionless as her face. "No others, though, if it pleases you."

Both Riki and Waylan looked as if they wanted to argue, but Kayla was already nervous enough. She didn't want a big audience for her first meeting with her biological mother. "Fine," she said, rising. "Let's go."

Geneviev led Kayla and Riki through the castle warily, as though she expected someone to stop them if they were seen. They did not encounter anyone. They climbed the spiral stairs, passed the floor where the skeletal dragon had guarded the Dark Lord's rooms, and stopped in a short hall on the floor above. Geneviev knocked softly on a plain wooden door.

For a moment, there was no response; then Kayla heard a murmur on the other side. Geneviev leaned forward, balancing the tray on one arm, and opened the door a crack. She held a brief, low-voiced conversation with someone inside, then pushed the door fully open and went in. Kayla and Riki glanced at each other, then followed.

They entered a sitting room that had an air of shabby comfort. Firelight cast warm shadows across the walls. A worn rug, a tapestry-draped bench, and a wooden chair without arms occupied the center of the room; a narrow table stood against the far wall, holding a brace of lit candles, a large book, and some writing materials.

Just in front of the table was a stool, slightly off-center, as if someone had stood up hastily and shoved it aside. Beside it, a pale, tired-looking woman with a halo of shadowy gray hair leaned against the table as if she needed its support just to look at Kayla and Riki. "So," she said in a whispery voice.

There was a long silence while they all looked at each other. Finally, Kayla cleared her throat. "I'm Kayla. The, um, Dark Lady. You must be . . . Are you . . ."

"I'm your mother," the woman said. "Athelina. Or rather, I was."

"Was?" Riki said sharply.

Geneviev made a choking sound. Athelina nodded and came toward them. As she crossed the room, the candles behind her flickered, and Kayla realized that she could see the flames clearly.

In spite of the fact that Athelina—her mother—was standing directly in front of them.

"Wait," Kayla choked, and Athelina stopped moving. "You're, you're . . ." She couldn't finish.

"Dead? A spirit?" Athelina sounded quite calm. "Yes."

"Mother!" Geneviev sounded desperate.

"Hush, Daughter," Athelina said. "We have come to the end of this deception. You have always known it could not last forever."

"She was going to let me marry Florian!" Geneviev cried. "I could have brought you with me! You would have been safe!"

"Safe?" Kayla repeated while her stomach sank even further.

Athelina shook her head. "Geneviev, my dear, the magicians of the Light are no safer than those of the Dark for such as I. The time we have had is more than I ever expected."

Geneviev bit her lip and looked away. Athelina looked at Riki with a faint smile. "You will be Madam Jones," she said. "Geneviev has told me of you."

Riki raised her chin. "I am Rikita Jones."

"Thank you," Athelina said, barely above a whisper. "Thank you for raising my daughter."

Riki took a half step backward, then gave a sharp nod. "You're welcome."

"How long— What—?" Kayla's brain felt fuzzy and slow. "I don't understand."

"Come and sit down, and I will explain," Athelina said, waving toward the bench and the chair.

Kayla hesitated, then sat on one end of the bench. Macavinchy flew up to perch on the mantel above the fireplace. Riki took the chair. Geneviev hesitated, then retreated into a corner, surreptitiously wiping at her eyes.

"Well?" Riki said.

"It is difficult to begin," Athelina replied, shaking her head. "Xavriel—your father—had too much faith in the strength of his power and his magic. He never understood the power in sheer meanness and spite, not even after you were lost to us."

"What does that mean?" Riki said crossly.

"Detsini," Kayla said. "You're talking about Aunt Detsini."

Athelina nodded. "In their family, she was next in magic after Xavriel. She always planned to take his place one day, though I could not say whether she meant to be heiress or usurper. Either way, she saw us as a threat from the day Xavriel married me."

"Us?" Riki said.

The spirit nodded again. "Me, because I might bear Xavriel's heir; Geneviev, because she is a magician and might become a rival."

"You must have known that from the start. Why did you marry him?" Riki's voice was a little too neutral.

"One does not refuse a Dark Lord," Athelina said. "And Xavriel was not unkind. Also, he promised that my daughter would be as safe as he could make her, so long as she made no attempt to seize the throne. At the time, it was enough."

"And when he died, you stayed because . . ."

Athelina hesitated. Geneviev made an angry gesture. "Because she was ill."

"And because you were only six," Athelina said gently. "I was not yet so sick that I could not have taken you away, if we had had somewhere safe to go. But the Dark Lord's widow and her daughter would have been a target for the armies of the Light . . . and for any magician looking to take Xavriel's place. Here in the castle, Xavriel's spells still protected us."

"But then why—" Kayla stopped short. She wanted to know why and how Athelina had died in spite of the protections, but asking straight out felt horribly awkward.

"Spells can do only as much as they are made to do," Athelina replied as if she knew what Kayla had been thinking. "And even then, there are limits. Xavriel's enchantments guard us from malicious spells and from the people he felt were most dangerous.

Accidents or natural illness . . ." She shrugged. "Magicians both Dark and Light have tried to ward against them, but none has ever truly succeeded."

"I was eleven when Mother . . . died, and became as she is now," Geneviev said. "She'd been bedridden for two years by then, and everyone in the castle knew that she never left these rooms, and that I brought her meals to her. It wasn't hard to keep up the pretense that she was still here."

"Especially since I am," added Athelina.

"Xavriel saw to that." Geneviev sounded angry.

"Hush, Geneviev," Athelina said. "It is not Xavriel's fault."

"Xavriel's spells held your spirit here, prey for any Dark magician who discovers you," Geneviev snapped. "And his sisters can still work Dark magic! If he had stripped them of all their power, instead of taking only part of it—"

"Detsini and Yazmina were all that remained of his family," Athelina said. "Even though they betrayed him, he would not have taken all their magic. It would have destroyed them."

"So instead he left them with enough power to bind a spirit to their will, if they should find one," Geneviev said bitterly. "And look! Here is a spirit, held in place where finding should be easy."

Athelina shook her head. "I do not think he meant for that to happen. Not even he could have predicted the wasting disease that took my life."

A chill ran down Kayla's spine, bitter as the midwinter wind off a frozen lake. "He did it to Harkawn," she whispered.

"What?" Athelina and Geneviev said together.

"Harkawn. The librarian." Kayla swallowed. "He's dying of a

curse on his lungs. He said that . . . that Xavriel did it and tied him to the castle after Harkawn challenged Xavriel and lost."

"I remember." Athelina nodded slowly. "Harkawn was one of the last Dark Lords to challenge Xavriel before the armies of the Light invaded. I was surprised; from what I knew of him, Harkawn was not one to seek to endlessly increase his power, the way most challengers wished."

"So Harkawn wasn't so bad," Kayla mumbled. A distant part of her remembered coming here to find that out. She hadn't reckoned on all this new information.

"Not for a Dark Lord." Athelina smiled slightly.

"Why?" Kayla burst out. "Why would he . . . Why would Xavriel do this to you? To anyone?"

"He was a Dark Lord," Geneviev snarled.

On the mantelpiece, Macavinchy coughed. "I cannot speak for the Dark Lord's motives, madam," he said. "However, the timing is suggestive. As your aunts had sufficient magic to send you to Earth, the reduction in their power must necessarily have happened between then and the time the Dark Lord died in battle. Master Harkawn's challenge also occurred during that time, by his own testimony."

Athelina turned almost transparent. "I felt the beginnings of my illness barely a week before the Final Battle. But . . . no. Xavriel would not have done this"—she gestured at herself—"for his sisters. Not when he spent so much time creating their punishment for stealing away his daughter."

"Punishment?" Riki raised her eyebrows.

"Just so." Athelina recovered slightly, becoming more visible.

"Xavriel felt that draining power from Detsini and Yazmina was appropriate after such a misuse of it. Also, it prevented them from further mischief and forced them to make some small amends."

Kayla shook herself. "Amends?"

Athelina hesitated again, then nodded. "Xavriel used the magic he took from his sisters to power the talisman he gave to Second Commander Waylan, to let him search other worlds to find you. It was especially potent for that purpose because they were the ones who'd cast the original spell to send you away." She looked at Geneviev. "So you see, he would not have trapped my spirit here as a gift for his sisters. He would more likely have cursed them."

Another chill breeze brushed Kayla's neck. *Ivy said the castle was cursed. Harkawn's tied to the castle. And the first dragon skull said something about Detsini being tied here, didn't it? Zar is chained to the castle, and the second skull said the only way to set him free was to unravel the spells. If it's all tied together . . .* "I think Xavriel did more than that. I think he cursed everybody in the castle."

"No," Athelina said, but she didn't sound as if she believed it. "His sisters did it themselves. No one helped them. He wouldn't have—"

But he did, Kayla thought. Aloud she said, "Geneviev was right. He was a Dark Lord, and not just a little one like Harkawn. He was the most powerful Dark Lord in centuries. Everybody says so."

"He was powerful but not capricious," Athelina objected. "He did not do things out of petty revenge, without reason."

"He had a reason," Kayla said. The pieces fit together, no matter how much she hated the shape they made. "Everyone here knows about all the Final Battles; he must have known, too."

"Of course he knew," Athelina said. "But he also knew that he could not avoid it. Cursing everyone in the castle would have made no difference in the outcome."

"He didn't do it for himself," Kayla said, forcing the words out through lips that felt frozen. "He did it for his daughter. For me."

CHAPTER 20

Major Spellcasting

Every new spell should be rigorously tested in your private underground lab or dungeon before being unveiled publicly. You do not wish a premature failure to damage your reputation.

—From *The Dark Traditions*

For a moment, everyone stared at Kayla. Then Riki shook her head. "Kayla, you can't know—"

"Yes, I can," Kayla interrupted. She felt sick. *Dark Lord. My father was a Dark Lord.* She'd been told that, over and over, ever since they arrived. She'd been told, over and over, how Dark Lords behaved, how everyone expected *her* to behave now that she was a Dark Lady. Yet she hadn't taken it seriously. Time and again, she had refused to believe that her biological father had really been that bad. But this . . .

She couldn't deny this. She could feel in her bones that it was true. "It's the only thing that makes sense," she said to Riki's bewildered expression. "He wanted his daughter to be the next Dark Lady. He knew he wouldn't be around, so he set things up to make it easy for her to take over." It was easier to talk about it as if

308

Xavriel had set up the whole horrible scenario for someone else's benefit. For his daughter Xavrielina, not for Kayla Jones.

"I'm not following you," Riki said.

"I am," Geneviev said grimly. "We're all tied to the castle, aren't we? And if we die here, we'll become spirits—easy for you to bind."

"A starter set." Kayla swallowed hard. "A way to boost my magic fast, so that I could catch up on whatever I missed by growing up in another world. It's like the chests of gold that are stored in the castle so that new Dark Lords don't have to waste time getting funding for their first army, only instead of storing gold, he arranged for a bunch of spirits for me to bind."

Athelina nodded slowly. "By the time you have bound the last of those who live in the castle, you will have enough power to subjugate even ancient spirits like the dragons, or the spirit of the mountain. You will burst onto the world as the greatest Dark Lady who ever lived."

A cold wave swept through Kayla, and for a moment she felt as if she were alone on a mountaintop, looking down on a world of ants. She could do anything she wanted. No one would stop her; no one *could* stop her. All she had to do was follow the path her father had laid down for her. Her father, the Dark Lord Xavriel, the greatest Dark Lord ever.

No. Kayla squared her shoulders and pushed back against the cold. *People aren't ants.* "No," she said aloud. "I may have to be a Dark Lady, but I'm not going to be that kind of Dark Lady. I am not binding *anybody.* It's just wrong."

The cold pushed at her again, this time with images of a stern, dark-haired man with power flowing from his hands. Kayla lifted her chin. She didn't want to think about her father . . . her biological father, and what he'd done. She wanted her Dad.

The Dark magician vanished, replaced by the memory of a thin, tired man making jokes about being bald from chemotherapy. Kayla shook her head, and that image, too, vanished.

"I doubt you have a choice," Athelina was saying. "Xavriel will have done his best to leave you none, not if you want the throne."

"Kayla doesn't want the throne," Riki said firmly. "It's a horrible job."

Geneviev and Athelina looked at her without comprehension.

Riki shrugged. "From what everyone says, the first thing that happens when you become a Dark Lord is that all the Dark Lord wannabes come and try to kill you. If you beat them, you get to rule for a few years, and then there's another 'Final Battle' and you die. The bragging rights aren't worth it." She looked at Kayla expectantly.

"I—" Kayla stopped. She certainly didn't want to be killed in one of those stupid "final" battles, but . . . "What happens to everybody here if I just leave?"

"Curses are not so easily defeated," Athelina said slowly. "Most probably, the binding would not allow you to depart, or would kill you if you tried. If you die or never claim the throne, I expect the focus of the spell will move to young Rache. Xavriel would have wanted such power to remain with his blood kin, if his daughter never returned."

"Rache wants to be a musician," Kayla said absently. Something was nagging at the back of her mind, something important.

Riki shook her head. "Why would this thing suddenly go off when it's been sitting here for ten years without doing anything? It doesn't make sense."

Kayla rolled her eyes. "I'm the trigger, Mom. Weren't you listening?"

"If you were the trigger, everyone would have died the minute you walked through the gates." Riki's voice wobbled, then firmed. "There has to be more to it than just you arriving here."

"The spell is tied to the castle, and ties us to the castle," Athelina said slowly. She looked at Kayla. "When you first arrived, you claimed the castle, and perforce the spell with it. But claiming the castle is but the first step. You are not yet truly the Dark Lady."

"*Provisional* Dark Lady," Riki whispered. "That's why Detsini keeps making such a point of it. The enchantment won't go off—"

"—until the investiture," Kayla finished. "But would my— my father really want everybody to drop dead in the middle of the ceremony?"

"He had a flair for the dramatic," Athelina said distantly. "And you can't deny that it would be dramatic."

Kayla made the rudest noise she could think up on the spur of the moment. "Right. Can we postpone my investiture?"

Riki looked thoughtful, but before she could speak, Macavinchy broke in unexpectedly. "I believe that a postponement is inadvisable, madam."

"Why?" Riki demanded. "It would buy us some time."

"Everything that is known about the late Dark Lord Xavriel indicates that he was highly intelligent as well as exceedingly determined," Macavinchy said. "It would be entirely in character for him to have arranged a way to prevent his chosen successor from being denied the throne—and the potential power boost he arranged. Postponing madam's investiture would almost certainly set off such a failsafe, with catastrophic results for everyone."

"How can you know that?" Geneviev objected. "If there's a chance—"

"Also," Macavinchy continued, "the ongoing attempts to breach my firewall increased by a factor of ten when you mentioned postponing the investiture, madam."

"The attacks on your what?"

"We won't postpone the investiture," Kayla said quickly. "Did that help?"

"There was never a danger from a mere increase in quantity, madam," Macavinchy said with a dismissive sniff. "However, the attacks are now returning to their normal frequency."

"I am *so* glad your firewall transferred," Kayla said. She noticed the bewildered expressions that Athelina and Geneviev were wearing and sighed. "Firewalls and virus-protection programs are standard security features on computers back where we come from. I don't know what you'd call them here."

"You brought your own enchantments with you?" Athelina said tentatively.

"It's not—" Kayla paused. Coming to Zaradwin had changed her computer to a living familiar, and the security programs to something that zapped owlhead vultures with lightning. *Enchantment* was probably as good a word for that as any. "I suppose."

"If this spell of yours is strong enough to defeat the enchantments that the Dark Lord left on this castle, why haven't you just cast it on everyone?" said Geneviev skeptically.

"It's not a spell," Riki said. "It's a computer program."

The niggling was back. Kayla shook her head. Something Zar said—

Not Zar. The second dragon skull. *Unravel the web, and the spell will come undone, too.* But spells weren't something she could grab and tear apart with her fingers, and she didn't really know how to use magic yet.

Wait. She might not know how to use magic, but she knew a fair bit about getting computers to do what she wanted, even if she wasn't actually a programmer.

"Computer apps from back home turn into spells and enchantments when they're in Zaradwin," she said slowly, feeling her way. "Macavinchy, if we could take the spell on the castle back home, what kind of program would it turn into?"

Macavinchy shifted until he was pressed against her left ear. "I am not certain, madam. The spell behaves like malware or viruses in the way it attempts to infect individuals in the castle, but it also links everyone who has been affected with everyone else, rather like a local network."

"If we could install a firewall—" Riki started, but Kayla shook her head before she'd even finished the sentence.

"Not the firewall, Mom. That just keeps viruses out, and the spell is already here. We need an antivirus program that can scan and clean everything in memory. Something that will automatically scan anything that gets plugged in to the network, so it will cover everyone in the castle." She looked at Macavinchy, ignoring Geneviev's expression of utter bewilderment and Athe-lina's uncomprehending stare. "Desktop apps do that, but you started off as a tablet. Can you quarantine and delete the spells from everybody?"

"My security systems are far more advanced than anything I have encountered here," Macavinchy said with a sniff. "Remov-ing any malicious spells from the castle and its inhabitants is well within my capacity. The difficulty lies in the time constraints."

"Time constraints?"

"Based on my current power and processing capacity, as well as the size of the castle, the complexity of the enchantment to be removed, and the number of persons involved, I estimate that it would take between two days and a week to perform a complete scan," Macavinchy said apologetically. "As we presume that your investiture tomorrow will set off the full effect of the curse—"

"A full scan will take too long." Kayla wanted to bang her head against something. If only she could go home for long enough to grab a more powerful computer. *Make that a supercomputer, as long as I'm wishing for impossible things. I wonder what a super-computer would turn into on the trip between worlds. . . .*

"Best get started, then," Riki said, giving Macavinchy a pointed look.

"I cannot begin without a connection to the castle," Ma-cavinchy said, unperturbed. "In addition, authorization from an administrator will be required."

"Oh, great. It's not like the castle has Wi-Fi or cable or—" Kayla broke off. *Wait. We don't need Wi-Fi or a supercomputer. We need what they would have turned into if we'd brought them here.*

If Mom's cell phone turned into a messenger mouse and my tablet turned into a familiar . . . "Macavinchy, could you . . . upload and install your security programs to something larger and faster?"

"That is well within my capabilities, madam," Macavinchy said.

Riki shook her head. "Kayla, we don't have anything bigger and faster."

Kayla grinned. "We didn't bring a faster computer with us, but what about what's already here?" She took a step sideways and knocked on the wall. "Hey, dragon! I need to talk to you."

"Kayla!" Riki's cry was too late; the stone wall was already rippling and pulling back, like water sheeting from the sides of a submarine rising from the depths of an ocean.

"What now?" the skull said.

"You're connected to the castle, aren't you? Magically, I mean."

"What gave it away? The moving-through-walls part?" Kayla got the feeling that the skull would have rolled its eyes, if it had still had any.

"Can you guard more than just the Dark Lord's chambers or dungeons? Like, the whole castle?" Kayla went on.

The skull drew back, as if mildly offended. "Easily. What is this about?"

"We need your help," Kayla said.

It took longer than Kayla expected to explain everything. She had to keep stopping to translate from computer terms to magical ones—or rather, to her best guess at what the magical terms would be. Riki understood Kayla's terminology, but she knew less about magic than Kayla did, so that wasn't much help.

Geneviev was the one who put it all together. "Your familiar bears powerful protective enchantments that you brought from your other world," she said. "You believe they can remove the spells that the Dark Lord left behind. But your familiar does not have the power to affect the entire castle quickly enough to prevent the spell from activating during your investiture. The dragon guardian has the magical power, and it is already part of the castle, so you wish to transfer the protective enchantments to it, and then have it remove the Dark Lord's spells."

"Close enough," Kayla said. "Except I don't want to erase anything from Macavinchy, just upload a copy. I don't want to"—*accidentally wipe his operating system or corrupt part of his memory*—"damage him by accident."

"What about damaging me?" the dragon skull said indignantly. "Aren't you worried about that?"

"You're from here," Kayla said. "And you've got nine hundred and some years of experience dealing with the castle and Dark Lords and spells. I don't think you'll have any problem."

"I *am* good at my job," the skull said, sounding pleased.

"Are you sure this is going to work?" Riki asked doubtfully.

"Certainty is not possible in this case," Macavinchy replied. "I would be remiss if I did not acknowledge that there may be unexpected consequences, but the approach is a valid one."

"What kind of unexpected consequences?" Kayla asked.

"If I could determine their nature, madam, they would not be unexpected," Macavinchy replied. "Even if there is a one-to-one correspondence between magic spells and computer programs, we do not yet have enough information to determine what it is. Consequently, I can make only general predictions."

"It's not going to hurt you, though? Or the dragon?"

"It is highly unlikely that an exchange of information will damage either of us, madam."

Kayla took a deep breath. "Okay. How do we do this, then?"

With a snap of his wings, Macavinchy launched himself into the air, circled the top of the dragon skull, then came to rest on Kayla's shoulder. "The three of us need to be in contact to initiate the transfer," Macavinchy said. "I will then ask you for authorization. At that point, I can begin without any further involvement on your part." He paused. "I do not know precisely how long the process will take, but everything should be complete in time for your investiture tomorrow morning."

"You're not going to touch that . . ." Riki waved at the dragon skull.

"Mom! It's not a big deal. It's . . . like recharging your phone," Kayla said. "You have to plug it in to the charger yourself, but you don't get fried by electricity when you do it." At least, she hoped that was what it would be like. Swallowing her own misgivings, she moved closer to the skull and put one hand on its silver jawbone.

At first, the bone felt cool and smooth under her fingers; then it warmed, and a tingle ran across her palm like an electric current. Macavinchy climbed down her arm and set a paw against the jawbone next to her hand. The tingle grew stronger.

"Request authorization for program upload and installation," Macavinchy said. His voice was still the deep, British-accented one she had picked the first night she'd had the tablet, but it echoed slightly, as if he were speaking from the bottom of a well.

"Upload and install the security programs, and then scan and remove any . . . all viruses, malware, or their magical equivalent, Macavinchy," Kayla said.

"Voice recognition successful. Authorization accepted. Initiating data transfer."

The tingle in Kayla's hand spiked unpleasantly, then stopped. The silver dragon skull brightened, as if someone had polished it. Macavinchy shivered and pulled himself up from Kayla's arm to cling to the bones. He shifted as if to find a comfortable position, then settled between two of the skull's giant teeth and went still.

Kayla let her hand fall and stepped back. Riki grabbed her shoulders in a hard hug. "I'm fine, Mom," Kayla said.

"It's my job to worry," Riki whispered. "It's in the handbook."

"Nothing is happening," Geneviev said, frowning.

"It will . . ." Kayla hesitated, wondering how to explain about program sizes and upload speeds and rebooting after an upgrade. "It'll probably take a while."

"We should have asked the flying monkey for a time estimate," Riki muttered.

"He doesn't like being called—"

"What's that?" Athelina interrupted Kayla. "Something feels . . . different."

Everyone turned back to the dragon skull. At first, Kayla didn't notice a difference; then she realized that the shine on the skull's surface was more than the candlelight reflecting from highly polished silver. The skull was glowing.

The glow brightened. Neither the skull nor Macavinchy moved. Kayla started to reach out, but Riki held her back. The glow became painfully bright, then popped like a giant strobe light flashing, leaving utter darkness behind. The air felt unnaturally still.

"Mom? Geneviev?" Kayla's voice dropped into the silence, and for a moment she thought she was alone.

"Is that what usually happens?" Geneviev sounded shaken.

"Not unless something shorts out," Riki's voice replied.

Kayla blinked and shook her head, trying to clear her vision. "Macavinchy?" she said cautiously, not wanting to distract him.

Something flickered off to one side. She turned her head and found herself looking at the dimly lit room. Her head whipped back to stare at the dark, blank wall in front of her.

Macavinchy and the dragon skull had disappeared.

CHAPTER 21

Avoiding Unpleasant Consequences

Spells that are truly world changing inevitably have unanticipated repercussions, which can be fatal to both the Dark Lord's ambitions and to the Dark Lord himself. In fact, many of the most powerful and respected Dark Lords never cast any major spells at all, preferring to stick to dramatic but reliable and well-tested spells such as firestorms, tornadoes, lightning blasts, and so on.

—From *The Dark Traditions*

Neither the dragon nor the familiar responded to Kayla's cry. The wall remained blank and flat. The air around Kayla felt unnaturally still and silent, as if even the small sounds and little drafts had stopped.

"Something is changing. I can feel it." Athelina's voice sounded muffled and far away.

"That's probably a good sign," Riki said uncertainly.

Kayla ignored them both. She stepped forward and knocked on the wall, the way she had when she summoned the dragon before. "Dragon! Macavinchy!"

Nothing happened. Kayla chewed on her lower lip, then squared her shoulders and looked at her mothers. "I'm going to see if Zar knows anything. I shouldn't be more than half an hour."

"I'm not sure—" Riki paused, studying Kayla's expression. After a moment, she sighed. "All right. Just . . . be extra careful."

"Zar is still chained to the wall, Mom. He can't do anything to me except talk me to death." As she left Athelina's rooms, Kayla wondered briefly if that comment was as reassuring as she had meant it to be. At least Riki hadn't made any serious attempt to keep her from leaving. Maybe she was finally getting used to the castle.

The corridors and stairs were as empty and silent as if there were no one else in the castle. Kayla had to remind herself that she'd just left Riki and Geneviev, that Ivy and her crew were still hard at work, and that Del was off somewhere with Waylan and Archie. The creepy silence continued, and her feet moved faster and faster until she was running. Her sense of where she was faded, as if the batteries on her "internal GPS" were dying, but she remembered the route well enough.

The Dark Lord's chambers appeared to be shut tight when she reached the final hallway. No dragon appeared as she approached, but the door swung wide at her touch. So did the doorway to the dungeon stair. The torches lit and put themselves out with less enthusiasm than they had on her first trip down the spiral stairs, and they shed less light than she remembered, but at least she wasn't trying to race down the steps in the dark.

As she rounded the last turn, Kayla saw the door to the dungeon room standing open. With a sinking heart, she realized that the second dragon skull had also vanished. She slowed, panting, and entered the dungeon.

The room on the far side of the door had changed. It resembled a tiny cave, less than half the size it had been, with walls that dripped and an uneven floor. There was no sign of Zar or his cell. Where the bars had been was only the rough rear wall of the cave. The mountain had taken everything else back.

"He'll be all right, won't he?" Kayla whispered. "He's the spirit of the mountain." But the words were not reassuring. She didn't know how spirits worked. Zar could have dissolved back into the mountain along with his cell and chains, for all she knew. Or just dissolved. Or . . .

She tried to stop imagining things, but her mind kept presenting more and more horrible alternatives. Finally, she began to yell. "Zar! Are you okay? Dragon! Macavinchy!"

The words dropped into silence. The cave was too small for echoes. Kayla yelled again, and a third time. Nothing.

Kayla wrapped her arms around herself. "I guess there's no point in staying," she said to the empty cave.

Turning, she began the long climb back. Riki and Geneviev were waiting in the hallway outside the Dark Lord's chambers. When she saw Kayla's expression, Riki stepped forward and opened her arms. Kayla walked into them and leaned against her mother.

"They're gone," she whispered. "Zar and the second dragon and half the dungeon. And it feels different."

Beside them, Geneviev nodded. "Everything is suspended. I

think we could all walk unprotected into the Dark Lord's chambers now without fear."

Kayla raised her head at that, just in time to see Geneviev's speculative look at the half-open doorway behind them.

"No," Riki said firmly. "We are not taking chances just to satisfy your curiosity. Especially when we don't actually know whether or not going in would cause problems."

"They're not very interesting," Kayla offered. "But if you really want, I'll see if I can give you a tour later. When this is over."

"If we're here to see," Geneviev said.

Riki stiffened. "What?"

"Your counterspell has done *something*, but we don't know what. We may all be spirits by this time tomorrow."

She sounds like Jezzazar, Kayla thought. Still, Geneviev had a point. "Maybe we should evacuate the castle, just in case."

Riki nodded, but Geneviev shook her head. "I doubt the Dark Lord's spells could be defeated so easily."

"We can still try," Kayla said. "Come on."

The creepy silence affected all of the hallways they traversed on their way back to the great hall. They met two of Ivy's cleaners along the way, both of whom seemed relieved to be told to get everyone out to the courtyard.

When they reached the great hall, Kayla stopped in the doorway. The floor and tables were clean, and the cobwebs hadn't returned, but something felt . . . off.

Archie and several of the men-at-arms were still in the hall. Kayla sent one of the men to find Waylan, Del, and anyone else who was still in the castle, and told everyone else to get to the courtyard. They obeyed with an air of relief that told her that they, too, felt something wrong.

As Kayla turned toward the far door, the castle shuddered. The enormous hearth opposite the throne shrank to half its size. The dais rippled and melted into the floor, leaving the marble throne on the same level as everything else. An instant later, the throne itself became a wooden chair with wide arms.

"Everybody out!" Riki shouted. "Right now!"

Kayla was already running for the door. She heard Riki and Geneviev stumbling along behind her and almost stopped to see if they were all right. Then it occurred to her that the best thing she could do was get out of the way, and she ran faster.

She skidded out of the great hall and past the arrow loops to the outer door. The wooden stairs along the outside of the tower hadn't changed. As she ran down them, she saw Del and Archie waiting in the courtyard, which was half-full of confused guards, footmen, maids, and castle inhabitants.

Waylan lunged out of the crowd and grabbed her arm as she reached the bottom of the stairs. "What is happening? My lady," he added belatedly.

"Doom, that's what," Jezzazar snarled from behind him. "Doom and destruction." He waved at the castle walls, which had shrunk to half their original height and turned an uneven gray. As Kayla watched, a large piece of stone broke off of the upper walkway. It vanished before it hit the ground, but that explained why everyone was clumped together in the middle of the courtyard, away from the walls.

"Is everybody here?" Kayla asked urgently. "Archie? Rache? Ichikar? Hark—" She broke off as she spotted the librarian. He was bent over, coughing so hard that he had trouble breathing.

The curse! Kayla thought. "Mom! Harkawn needs that healing stuff right now." She pointed.

Riki took one look and hurried off, digging in her tote bag with one hand as she went. Kayla wanted to follow, but Jezzazar caught her arm. "My lady, what should we do?"

"Find out if anyone else is hurt or missing," Kayla said. Wasn't that obvious?

There were a few moments of confusion while Jezzazar and Ivy counted heads. As they finished, Riki came over. "Harkawn is doing a bit better, but I wish there were somewhere he could lie down. We might have to get him down to the village."

"It's a curse, and taking him away from the castle will make it worse," Kayla told her.

"So will sitting on cold flagstones," Riki grumbled. "Did everyone get out of the castle?"

"Everyone's here except Detsini, my lady," Waylan reported, coming up behind her.

It figures, Kayla thought. "Nobody's seen her for days. Are we sure she's still here? Because if she is, somebody should get her out and tell her what's going on."

"I know what's going on." Detsini's voice rang out from above them.

Kayla looked up. Detsini stood in the open doorway at the top of the wooden stairs. Her hair was piled on top of her head in a series of curls that emphasized the two white streaks and must have taken hours to get right. She wore a too-tight black-and-silver-and-poison-green-striped dress positively buried in lace, feathers, and sequins. Her right hand was raised as if to throw something down into the courtyard, and her chin was lifted imperiously.

"Drama queen," Kayla muttered, then called back, "So explain."

Detsini's chin went up another half inch. "The Dark Lord Xavriel was the greatest Dark Lord Zaradwin has ever seen," she proclaimed. "Knowing the customs and Traditions of Zaradwin, he was aware that his glorious reign would soon end, and he conceived a plan to make his name and reputation grow even after his inevitable death, so that he would be unquestionably known as the greatest Dark Lord, founder of the greatest line of Dark Lords ever to walk the world.

"It was a plan worthy of so powerful a magician, yet even one as great as he can err."

The people in the courtyard had gone silent. Kayla frowned. Something about this was familiar, but she couldn't quite place the feeling.

"His daughter, his Xavrielina, was to be the second of his line, for she was strong in power, with the potential to one day surpass the Dark Lord himself, and she was marked for Dark magic," Detsini went on.

A few feet away, Archie shook his head. "Do all Dark ceremonies require people to go on and on about history?"

Kayla stiffened as memory hit her. Waylan had used the same words about her, *marked for Dark magic,* during his speech when they first arrived at the castle. This must be another formal ceremony.

"To protect his heir, his Xavrielina, the Dark Lord arranged for her to be raised apart and in secret until she returned to claim the glory he had prepared for her. And so she was, for ten long years, until last week she returned to Zaradwin at last."

"What does that have to do with the castle falling down?" Kayla said loudly.

"You have returned, Xavrielina—"

"My *name* is *Kayla,*" she snapped without thinking.

Detsini's smile was nasty. "You have returned, and you have rejected your name, *Kayla,* and with it, your heritage, and so the castle has rejected you."

"Lady Kayla claimed her birthright when she arrived," Waylan pointed out. "And the castle accepted it." He pushed his way out of the crowd to stand at Kayla's right.

"The castle had lain unclaimed for ten long years," Detsini replied confidently. "It is no surprise that it would accept the Dark Lord's designated heir. But since her arrival, she has repeatedly shown herself unworthy of succeeding the Dark Lord Xavriel."

Jezzazar stepped forward to stand on Kayla's left. "A serious charge," he said to Detsini. "What proof have you of what you say?"

"First, she rescued a powerful and potentially dangerous Dark rival, one who has proclaimed himself already a Dark Lord under several names." Detsini's eyes sought out Archie. "Next, she refused the gift of the sninks, which no true Dark Lady would ever do. She has publicly stated that she wants no assassinations, kidnapping, or raids to increase the treasury. And all of you saw her once again reject her very name, as she has done from the beginning."

"Xavrielina is a dumb name," Kayla and Del said together.

"She clings to her other-world family," Detsini went on with another nasty smile. "She stays with them in the guest wing and refuses to acknowledge those of us who are her blood. She wears peasant clothing, rejecting the grandeur of Dark Ladies past. Even her familiar has abandoned her."

"Macavinchy is busy doing a job for me," Kayla said, hoping it was true.

Detsini sniffed. "No familiar can work independent of its master. Of course, since you were raised elsewhere, you do not know that . . . nor anything else about being a true Dark Lady!"

Kayla stared up at Detsini for a minute. Then she laughed. "You think I don't know anything about Dark Lords because I grew up on Earth?"

"Of course," Detsini said, but she did not sound quite as sure of herself as she had a moment before. "Earth has no magic, so it cannot have true Dark Lords."

"It doesn't have your kind of Dark Lord," Kayla retorted. "But ours are much nastier than any of the ones I've heard of here. They have to be smarter and sneakier than your Dark Lords, because they don't have magic."

"Nonsense," Detsini said. "I tested that world before I sent you there, and saw no mention of Dark Lords or Ladies."

Kayla rolled her eyes. "They don't call themselves Dark Lords. That would let everyone know what they were up to."

"Really." Detsini's voice dripped with disbelief. "And who are these evil non–Dark Lords of yours?"

"Politicians," Kayla said. "Lawyers. Giant corporations."

"Insurance companies," Riki muttered. "Mortgage brokers."

"Dentists!" Del chimed in.

Riki scowled at him. "Dentists are not evil pseudo–Dark Lords."

"They are so," Del insisted. "They drill your teeth!"

"Those . . . people, whatever they are, are not the Dark Lords of our Traditions!" Detsini cried.

"Well, of course not," Kayla said. "Yours keep *losing*."

"You are not—"

First Commander Jezzazar raised his fist, and Detsini broke off. Jezzazar let the silence deepen for a moment, then said heavily, "'Tis well stated on both sides. Yet by our *Traditions*, a formal challenge to her as Dark Lady must wait for her investiture."

"That will be too—" Detsini's mouth snapped shut, as if she had said more than she intended.

She knows about the curse, Kayla thought. *At least, she knows that it will take effect when the investiture is done. But she doesn't know about Macavinchy's antivirus program.* She opened her mouth to explain, but Detsini cut her off.

"She is worthy of neither investiture nor challenge," Detsini said, pointing at Kayla. "I claim the throne of Zaradwin in her place."

"The Dark Lady Kayla has already made formal claim of this castle, and it has accepted her," Jezzazar pointed out.

"She is no Dark Lady! The castle has rejected her!" Detsini

all but shrieked. "Enough! Here, in the foremost citadel of the Dark, I, Detsini, sister of the late Dark Lord Xavriel, lay claim to the position of Dark Lady of Zaradwin, left vacant by my brother and rejected by his heir. I make this claim in accordance with the Dark Traditions and by virtue of my own power demonstrated in times past."

As Detsini finished speaking, the courtyard was enveloped in the same unnatural silence that had shrouded the castle since the disappearance of Macavinchy and the dragon skull. No one moved; Kayla was not sure anyone even breathed. Then, just when it seemed that nothing else would happen, a familiar chime echoed through the courtyard. A moment later, a mechanical voice sounded from every direction, as if the walls themselves were speaking.

"Password?"

CHAPTER 22

Public Challenges

A public challenge is not the time for subtle magic. Fireballs, ice storms, lightning strikes, and other visible and highly damaging spells will demonstrate your power and skill to the trembling spectators, as well as damaging and demoralizing your opponent. Also, should you lose the battle, your reputation as a worthy Dark Lord will be preserved, as it will be clear that only an even greater Dark Lord could have defeated you.

—From *The Dark Traditions*

On the landing at the top of the tower stairs, Detsini looked around wildly, as if she expected something else to happen. Nothing did. The courtyard remained unnaturally still until one of the cleaners whispered, "What was that?"

"Password," the mechanical voice repeated.

"Macavinchy?" Kayla said hopefully, even though the voice sounded female.

"Password incorrect," the voice said. "Password?"

"I have claimed this castle in accordance with the Dark Traditions!" Detsini cried.

"Password incorrect," the mechanical voice repeated implacably. "Answer the first security question: Who was the first president of the United States?"

"That's—" Riki started.

Kayla couldn't help grinning. "That's on the list I gave Macavinchy. He must have uploaded the whole suite of security programs, not just the antivirus."

"I am Detsini, sister to the Dark Lord Xavriel!" Detsini shouted, and Kayla could hear the desperation in her voice. "This is my castle now!"

"Answer incorrect," the voice said. Kayla thought it sounded less mechanical than it had. "Access denied."

A relieved sigh rippled through the crowd in the courtyard. Detsini fell back against the castle wall, spluttering. A bit of the castle above the door crumbled, showering her with rock dust. Behind Kayla, Del snickered.

"Looks like it's my turn," Kayla said.

"The castle has rejected you," Detsini shouted. "It has to have rejected you! You don't understand. We'll all die if . . . You have to . . ."

"I have to make sure the antivirus program has finished running and quarantined anything it found," Kayla said sternly. "Which I could have done a lot sooner if I'd known about this curse."

"Curse?" Del said.

"In a minute," Kayla said. "I have to claim the castle."

"You have claimed the castle already," Jezzazar objected. "Upon your first arrival, as is Tradition."

"Yes, but Macavinchy probably had to reboot the whole system after he installed the security programs," Kayla said. "If he did, I have to log in again." *Assuming the castle spells work as much like computer programs as they have so far.*

Jezzazar and most of the rest of the people in the courtyard looked completely bewildered. Only Waylan, Del, and Riki showed any signs of comprehension.

Riki's expression went suddenly thoughtful. "You think that's what this is about?" She waved at the deterioration around them.

I sure hope so. Kayla nodded, hoping her doubts didn't show. She turned back toward Detsini and raised her voice. "I, Kayla Jones, claim this castle. Log me in."

"User name confirmed." The voice definitely sounded less mechanical now. "Voice recognition confirmed. Password?"

"Mississippi-zero-nine," Kayla said, making a note to change it as soon as she was somewhere private.

"Password correct," the voice said. "Access granted."

The air shivered and distorted like a heat mirage rising from a highway in high summer. Kayla heard a sound like glass breaking, and the unnatural stillness vanished. She could hear people coughing, the creak of the portcullis shifting, and the crunch of pebbles underfoot as people shuffled back and forth, trying to find either a safer position or a better view.

"You are a fool," Detsini said in a voice that was suddenly calm, and much scarier than her earlier shrieking. "You don't want the castle, and you don't want to be the Dark Lady. If you had let me claim the castle, I could have let you live. Now there is only one way left. Traditions or no, I challenge you, magic against magic." She gestured, and a dark purple lightning bolt cracked into the ground a few feet in front of Kayla.

Kayla jumped. She could feel her heart pounding. "I don't want to fight you," she told Detsini. "And I don't think the castle will accept you, even if you win."

"No? But I have the . . . password now." Detsini raised her hands. "I, Detsini, sister of the late Dark Lord Xavriel, lay claim to this castle. Mississippi-zero-nine."

"That user name is incorrect." The voice sounded mildly annoyed. "Access denied."

"I claim this castle! Mississippi-zero-nine!"

"Absolutely not," the voice said with considerable irritation, and the castle shuddered. Half of the people in the courtyard stumbled or fell into each other. The walls of the keep rippled. The ripples shifted and swirled, forming two dark whirlpools, one on either side of the keep doorway. They reminded Kayla of water circling the bathtub drain. Everyone in the courtyard took a step backward, away from the keep, and Detsini smiled triumphantly.

The whorls moved faster, and then Macavinchy shot out of the left-hand one. He circled the courtyard once and then landed in his accustomed perch on Kayla's shoulder.

"Macavinchy! Are you all right?"

"I am quite well, madam," the familiar replied. "I regret that the removal of the various curses and traps took so long. There were more of them than expected."

"So your familiar has returned," Detsini said, ignoring the

black vortexes on either side of her. "It doesn't matter. The castle is mine now."

"'Absolutely not' was too hard for you?" the voice said, and it didn't sound mechanical at all. "Let me make it easy. No."

"Obey me!" shrieked Detsini.

The two whirlpools made a popping noise, and a silver dragon skull emerged from each of them. "Oh, now, that was a mistake," said the one on the left.

"Annoying the castle is always a bad idea," the skull on the right said, nodding. He looked across Detsini's head at the other skull. "Do you want to eat her, or shall I?"

"You can have her," the left-side skull said as Detsini whirled to face them. "It's your turn."

"The castle is mine," Detsini repeated shakily. "You will do as I command!"

"I don't think so," the right-hand skull said, and snapped at her. Detsini barely dodged in time. She tried to retreat down to the courtyard, but the left-hand skull stretched itself out to block the stairs.

"Hey! Stop that," Kayla called.

"You don't want her eaten?" The right-hand skull sounded puzzled.

"She didn't want the little thief roasted, either," the left-hand skull said. "Come to think of it, she told me not to eat anybody."

"She didn't tell me." The right-hand skull leaned toward Detsini.

"Well, I'm telling you now," Kayla said quickly. "No eating people, either one of you."

"If you insist." The right-hand skull shifted to block the door, leaving Detsini trapped on the landing. "What do you want to do with her?"

"Just keep her out of trouble for now," Kayla told him. "We have more important things to worry about."

"No, we don't," Riki objected. "She threw lightning at you, Kayla!"

"The dragons can keep her from doing that again." Kayla looked back at the dragons. "Can't you?"

The dragons nodded.

"So we need to figure out what to do about the investiture ceremony tomorrow," Kayla went on. "I'm not sure the castle is stable, and—"

"Oh, the castle won't be a problem," a cheerful voice said. Kayla turned to see a man with shoulder-length black hair, flat black eyes, and skin the mottled color of granite standing next to the crumbled remains of the barracks that had been along the outer wall. He looked much more dangerous than he had chained up in the dungeon under the castle, but Kayla still couldn't stop smiling in relief.

"Zar! You're okay! I was afraid that the mountain swallowed you." Kayla stopped without adding *chains and all.* She didn't want to think too hard about that part, especially since it obviously hadn't happened.

"I'm the spirit of the mountain," Zar pointed out, as if he knew exactly what she was thinking. "Getting swallowed up by it is good for me." He straightened, stretching his arms. "I haven't felt this well in centuries."

"The spirit of . . ." Jezzazar's awed whisper trailed off.

The rest of the people in the courtyard stared in shock—except for Detsini. Ignoring the dragon skulls, she lurched forward to lean over the railing and cried, "Spirit, I bind you to my service, in the name of the Dark Lords of Zaradwin, from Szarimex to Xavriel, by the power of—"

Zar snorted and raised a finger. The tower shook violently, sending more rock dust down on Detsini and nearly throwing her off the landing. She broke off her spell, coughing and clutching at the railing.

"A little warning would have been nice," one of the skulls grumbled.

"Did you really think I would allow myself to be enslaved again?" Zar's tone was cold and mocking. "Besides, you have the wording all wrong. It wouldn't have worked, even if you had the power."

"Yazmina! Xavrielina! Help me bind him, or all is lost!"

Yazmina took a hesitant step forward, her eyes darting from Detsini to Zar. "I— No."

"Sister, you must!"

"No," Yazmina said, more strongly. "Once before, I followed your lead, and no good came of it. Never again."

"Xavrielina, assist me!"

"Not a chance," Kayla said, folding her arms. "Especially if you're going to call me that dumb name."

"Don't you understand? We must bind him before he vanishes." Detsini sounded frantic.

Kayla turned her head. Zar was leaning against the

crumbling outer wall, examining his nails with an air of boredom. She looked back at Detsini. "You've tried to get rid of me twice now, once when I was just a baby. I don't trust you. And I'm sure not helping you chain anybody up, spirit or not."

"You will destroy everything that has made Zaradwin great!"

"If keeping Zar locked in a dungeon for hundreds of years is all that made Zaradwin 'great,' it deserves to be destroyed," Kayla retorted.

"Can I help blow things up?" Del's voice said hopefully.

"No," Riki, Archie, Waylan, and Harkawn all said at the same time.

"You can't be the Dark Lady of Zaradwin without him!" Detisini insisted frantically.

"Watch me," Kayla snapped.

"Kayla—" Riki's tone usually meant the don't-get-smart-with-adults lecture was coming next, but she stopped short. Kayla turned to see her studying Detsini with a thoughtful expression on her face. "You know, I don't think this is the right time for a bland and deadly courtesy. Carry on."

Kayla looked up. A thick gray coating of rock dust covered Detsini's hair and streaked her face and gown. She looked pathetic. Kayla sighed. "What am I going to do about her? The dragons can't keep her there forever, and she's in the way. I ought to arrest her, but I don't have a dungeon anymore."

"I can fix that, too," Zar said, and glanced at the tower. Kayla felt a warm breeze swirl around her. The flagstones directly under the stairs bulged upward. A glistening gray bubble broke through the surface of the courtyard. It rose rapidly to form a half dome against the tower wall. Where it touched the wooden stairs, they vanished, leaving sooty streaks on the wall. An instant later, Detsini shrieked as the landing dissolved underneath her. She fell into the dome and vanished.

"Zar!" Kayla said, horrified.

"She's perfectly safe," Zar said with a cold smile that belied his words. The shine faded from the bubble, leaving a granite half dome pushed up against the tower wall. "You asked for imprisonment, not punishment. I even left a door on the other side of her nice new cell." He paused. "Mostly new. I reused the chains; I hope you don't mind."

"It's fine, as long as I can take them off her when I want to." Kayla couldn't blame Zar for his attitude, but she certainly didn't want Detsini chained up in a dungeon for centuries. She didn't deserve that much. Probably.

"She would have enslaved me once more," Zar snarled. Kayla just looked at him. Finally, he sighed. "Yes, all right. She intended much toward me, but she did not succeed. Her greatest crimes were against you. Do as you wish with her."

"My lady," Jezzazar said hesitantly. "Would you wish to add her execution to tomorrow's festivities?"

"No," Kayla and Riki said together. Kayla looked around the courtyard and shook her head. "Can we get everything fixed before people start showing up for the investiture tomorrow?"

"Don't worry about the cleanup," Zar said. "I'll take care of it. It's the least I can do for my lady here. Though I'm not putting the spells back."

"Spells?"

Zar snorted. "Don't look so surprised. Why do you think everything changed so much when your familiar and the guardians cleared out all the malicious magic? This castle has been the home of Dark Lords for ten centuries, and every one of them added some kind of spell to it."

"I don't understand," Ichikar said hesitantly. Several other people nodded.

"I suppose you wouldn't." Zar leaned back against the wall once more; Kayla got the impression that he was enjoying the attention. Then she shook her head. If the only people he'd seen for the past ten centuries were the Dark Lords and Ladies who'd kept him chained up, of course he'd be glad of a bigger—and friendlier—audience.

"Your new Dark Lady here decided to do some long-overdue maintenance," Zar went on. "Unfortunately, your previous Dark Lords were idiots; hence the current damage."

"The rulers of Zaradwin have been the most powerful and skilled Dark Lords in the world, feared by the Light more than any other," Jezzazar objected.

"Power and skill don't keep someone from being an idiot. The first few were too lazy or too cheap to build better walls and expansions to the castle. They used magic instead of stone and mortar. After a few centuries, the Dark Lords started booby-trapping their spells so the armies of the Light couldn't take down all the defenses just by canceling the wall spells. *Then* they started leaving traps for their successors to make them prove they deserved the castle. They never bothered to find out in advance whether their new spells would interfere with one of the older ones; whenever something went wrong, they just slapped on another spell to patch up the problem instead of fixing it properly."

"And if they were setting traps for their successors, they wouldn't have left any record of what they did, in case someone figured out how to get around it." Kayla shook her head. "So after a while, there was no way of figuring out what would work even if somebody wanted to."

Zar nodded. "Exactly. Instead of things getting better with every new Dark Lord, they got worse."

Kayla took a deep breath and blew it out. "There should be some spells, though, shouldn't there? To keep out magical attacks."

"You'll have to do that part," Zar said. "As well as making any design changes you want. The original fortress was rather small and unimpressive, compared to ten centuries of magical additions."

"Can you add a shower?" Del put in.

"Del!" Riki said.

"What? I was just asking!"

I can do without impressive, but Del's right about the shower, Kayla thought. "It wouldn't hurt to have more rooms," she said aloud. Maybe something more like Edinburgh Castle—the pictures she remembered made it look pretty large. "You'll have to show me how to add the spells and change the design, though."

"The spells will come later," Zar said. "If I'm rebuilding this castle, I'm going to do it right. Solid stone, not rickety spellwork."

That seemed like a reasonable position for a mountain to take, Kayla thought. "Would adding showers be all right with the castle?"

"All right with the castle?" Riki said before Zar could reply.

Kayla waved at the two dragon skulls, which were leaning over the edge of the landing, observing the crowd in the courtyard with an air of curiosity. "The castle is sort of awake. I don't want to annoy it. Or Zar."

"Good point," Riki said, following her gesture.

Zar looked surprised and gratified, and Kayla remembered that he was used to people who kept him chained up as a sort of magical battery. "What is a shower?"

Explaining showers took a while, and they had to get Macavinchy to provide the details of the plumbing and drainage. At last Zar nodded his understanding, and agreed to add shower rooms, but he warned them that he wouldn't provide the spells to pump the water or heat it. "The repairs shouldn't take long," he said. "The . . . plumbing for the showers will be a little tricky, but since you're going to handle all the magic, everything should be done by midnight."

"Plumbing is always tricky," Riki muttered.

"So is the castle okay with all this?" Kayla asked again. "I thought you said it would be a couple of centuries before it woke up."

"I wasn't counting on someone dumping nine centuries of unraveled spells into her," Zar said dryly. "She's definitely come to consciousness well ahead of time, though I don't think she can manifest a spirit yet."

Kayla frowned. "Will fixing it up force it to go back to sleep? I don't think I want that."

"If you did the plumbing yourself, you'd have to draw on the power that woke the castle, which would put her back to sleep,"

Zar said. "If I do it, that won't happen." He hesitated, frowning thoughtfully, then shrugged. "It will tie us together, of course, but she's already sitting on top of me, and neither of us is going anywhere. It'll be fine."

"Great!"

"We'd best get started, then," Zar said. "Picture what you want, and give me your hand."

A little uncertainly, Kayla reached out, trying to remember as much as she could about every castle she'd ever liked from movies and real-life pictures. As she touched Zar, she felt a tug, and a wave of weakness.

"This'll be fun," Zar said, letting go of her hand. "I'll do the walls first; I'll come back for you when it's time for the spells." He leaned back against the wall and melted into it. A moment later, a line of dark stone appeared at the base of the outer walls. The line crept slowly upward, marking the change from the deteriorating blocks above to smooth, solid granite below.

"Wow," Del said. "Can he teach me how to do that?"

"I don't think it's something you can learn," Kayla said, watching the line of new stone creep upward. "It's part of being the spirit of the mountain."

"I don't mean *that*." Del waved at the slowly changing stone. "I mean the walking into walls."

"I'll see if I can work it into your lessons," the left-hand dragon skull said to Del. "But it'll be a while before we get to it. It's advanced magic for a human."

"Make it a long while," Riki grumbled. "He's already impossible to keep track of."

"What else do I get to learn?" Del asked. He and the skull began an intense discussion of possible alternatives.

A hand touched Kayla's elbow lightly. She turned to find Ichikar looking wary but determined. "My lady, if I may?" he said hesitantly. "There will be nothing for Mistress Ivy's people to do until the castle is restored. We should release them now, and summon them back when their services are required." His voice dropped to a whisper. "To avoid unnecessary expense."

"I suppose we have to, if Zar won't be finished until midnight."

"Make sure they can come back early tomorrow morning," Riki advised him. "There are always last-minute preparations, and we'll need help with cooking and serving everything."

Ichikar waved Ivy over, and he and Riki started explaining their plans. Within minutes, they had Geneviev and Yazmina involved. Kayla backed away from the discussion, which had quickly become alarmingly technical, and bumped into Harkawn.

"My lady?" The ex–Dark Lord had more color, and he wasn't coughing.

"Harkawn! Mom's healing stuff worked."

"The heal-all helped, but it didn't make this much difference," Harkawn said. "I feel like a new man. What did you *do*?"

Kayla shrugged. "Is your curse gone, then?"

"All of the curses, hexes, and malicious spells have been eliminated, madam," Macavinchy answered from Kayla's shoulder. "Mister Harkawn's difficulty was especially stubborn, as it was linked both to the castle and to his life energy. It took some time to determine how to remove it without damaging him. I do hope the process was not excessively uncomfortable."

"The results are worth it," Harkawn assured him. "But how did you do it? I've never seen or heard of anything powerful enough to unravel even one major curse, much less do all this." He waved at the walls and the keep.

Kayla sighed, and began attempting to explain about computers and antivirus programs and uploading everything to the castle. Archie and Rache came over while she was talking, but they didn't interrupt. Archie looked almost as interested as Harkawn, who was practically bouncing in excitement by the time Kayla finished.

"This is astounding!" Harkawn said. "Once we determine how your . . . apps? . . . overlap with spells and enchantments, we will revolutionize magic."

"Maybe." Kayla wasn't sure revolutionizing magic was a good idea, if all they used it for was fighting wars with the Light. She thought of her mental list of practical, everyday spells. Ordinary people would care a lot more about those than about calling up swarms of insects or striking other people with lightning. Most people weren't all Light or all Dark. They were in the middle somewhere.

Maybe revolutionizing magic wouldn't be so bad if she could get everyone to focus on things like showers and antibiotics and printing presses. She didn't want to think about it right now, though. After everything that had happened in the last couple of hours, she felt wrung out. She hoped Riki wouldn't assign her any of the work. She just wanted to sit down for a while.

The dragon skulls finished their talk with Del and withdrew into the walls of the keep. Del bounced over to Kayla and announced, "I'm going to learn magic from a dragon!"

"I know." Kayla wasn't sure, in the cold light of day, that it had been a good idea. Oh well. Too late now.

Del grinned. "You're the best sister ever." He paused. "So what happened after you and Mom left the lunchroom?"

"It's the great hall, not a lunchroom," Kayla said. She looked around and spotted some benches in front of the barracks that still seemed to be in good shape. "Come and sit down, and I'll tell you."

CHAPTER 23

Formal Occasions

Celebrations are an excellent way of enhancing your reputation. A military parade instills fear of your mighty armies in the populace; the execution of prisoners, incompetents, and traitors demonstrates your ruthlessness; a feast displays your wealth and power. Combining two or more such events is particularly useful if one has visitors, as they will spread tales of your greatness everywhere they pass as they return to their homes.

—From *The Dark Traditions*

Kayla spent most of the next hour sitting with Del, Archie, and Rache, telling them about her ghost-mother and watching the castle rebuild itself. It looked as if the mountain was growing a crown of walls.

The crowd of cleaners and guards and castle folk milled around in the center of the courtyard, unwilling to get too close to anything that might suddenly crumble and fall on them. Periodically, someone came over to Kayla to ask a question. Kayla answered as best she could and sent them back.

After about an hour, the cleaners and most of the guards began trickling out of the castle to spend the night in the village. Ivy stayed to consult with Riki, Ichikar, and Geneviev regarding the plans for the investiture next day, and the musicians stayed to practice.

Around midafternoon, a string of wagons arrived with the last of the supplies ordered for the ceremony. The wide-eyed drivers reported that the road up the mountain had repaired itself under their wheels, and the derelict guard towers stood tall and imposing once more. On hearing this, Waylan and Jezzazar exchanged glances and delegated several of the remaining guards to accompany the wagons down the mountain and man the towers once they reached them.

By evening, the outer walls were smooth and shining, taller and wider and solider than they had been. The courtyard inside them was much larger as well, and the crumbled buildings around the edges had been replaced. New buildings were growing out of the flagstones, all of them made of dark granite as Zar had promised.

The central keep was changing, too, but slowly. Kayla thought it looked bigger around than it had been. It seemed to be growing taller as well, but until the stairs up to the door were replaced, there was no way to get inside and see what, if anything, had really changed.

Dinner was sandwiches and fruit swiped from the supply delivery, since they couldn't get into the kitchen. The outer buildings seemed to be finished, but no one wanted to take the chance of going inside while Zar was still working. As the sun set and the air cooled, Waylan and Jezzazar had the guards build several small fires near the new barracks. Everyone huddled around them, occasionally peering toward the keep even though it was too dark to see what was still changing.

For several hours, nothing more happened. Kayla suspected that Zar was busy with the castle's interior, but since it was just a guess, she didn't say so aloud. Del fell asleep leaning on Riki. Rache and his friends had long since stopped officially rehearsing and switched to slower, quieter songs. Everyone waited, though no one was quite sure what they were waiting for.

Finally, the half moon rose over the castle walls, providing enough light to show the last of the ruined barracks sinking into the ground. A moment later, the flagstones bulged upward and a dark bubble rose from below, very like the one that had imprisoned Detsini. As the edges of the bubble reached the spot where the barracks wall had been, they flattened as if the bubble were filling an invisible box. A few moments later, the dome-shaped top collapsed into a roof, and openings appeared in the stone for windows and doors.

"Is that everything?" someone asked, just as a broad stairway began rising in front of the keep. It curled up toward the door, covering Detsini's prison, narrowing a little at the edges as it went. The top step clunked slightly against the tower wall as it locked itself into place in front of the doorway, and a waist-high stone banister popped up along the edges.

There was a pause, and then the world seemed to sigh and

relax. Kayla felt as if a weight had been lifted, one she hadn't even noticed until it was gone. At the foot of the stairs, a shadow moved.

"All done," Zar said from out of the gloom. Half of the people seated around the fires jumped. "You'll want to start enchanting it again sometime in the next few days, but at least now you have something solid to start with."

"Thanks," Kayla said. "Will you come to the investiture tomorrow?"

"Maybe." Zar tilted his head, considering. "It's too late to keep everyone from finding out that I'm free, so I might as well. I doubt that anyone would try a binding in the middle of your investiture."

"Wouldn't the antivirus spell stop that?"

"Possibly. I am still connected to the castle, but I don't know if that will be enough to extend its protection over me. I shall have to do some investigating."

"Tomorrow," Riki said firmly. "You may not need sleep, but we do, and tomorrow is a big day."

The guards were already putting out the fires and moving toward their new barracks. Ichikar and the other castle folk looked at Kayla. She shrugged, then yawned. Riki was right; everything else could wait on a good night's sleep.

Kayla led the way up the stairs and into the keep, where everyone scattered to their rooms. The guest quarters were larger, and Zar had added a shower, though it probably wouldn't work until someone got around to enchanting the plumbing to provide water. *Tomorrow,* she thought, and fell asleep.

Morning arrived much earlier than Kayla wanted. Riki grumbled about coffee as they dressed. Del was the only one who was awake and eager to explore. On their way to the keep, they passed several maids and footmen, who had arrived early and were already busy whisking away nonexistent dust and running mysterious errands.

They had a hasty breakfast in the great hall, where the trestle tables and wooden benches had been replaced with polished marble tables and chairs that looked like granite but were much lighter and more comfortable than solid stone would ever be. The dais was back, but the massive marble throne had been replaced with an elegant silver chair. Behind it, a large mosaic broke up the black marble wall, depicting Detsini falling into her granite prison. *I guess Zar wanted to make a statement,* Kayla thought, and grinned.

The morning was a blur of last-minute preparations, many of which were in the kitchens. Kayla saw Del laying out the not-pepperoni slices in a smiley face on one of the pizzas, but decided not to say anything. If Riki caught him and banished him from the pizza-bakers' kitchen, fine, but Kayla wasn't going to help him get out of working.

Shortly after noon, Ivy approached. "You and your family had best get ready, my lady. I've word from town that the first guests are on their way up the mountain, and they're the ones you'll need to impress the most."

"Just because they got here early?" Kayla grumbled, but pushed away from the table.

"No, because it's Lady Amaryllis and Lord Governor Niktrax,"

Ivy replied. "She had to be invited because she's your nearest neighbor, but she's Light-side, which means she'll be sending a report to the archmage as soon as she gets home. Niktrax is an even bigger problem—he's ambitious and intelligent, and he's been trying to get his hands on Zaradwin for the last five years, at least. If he thinks you're weak, it's a toss-up whether he'll demand a high-level position in your court or go straight to a challenge."

"Great," Kayla sighed. "I haven't even figured out what to do about Detsini yet."

By the time Kayla dashed back to their rooms, changed into her Dark Lord clothes, and dashed back, the early arrivals were at the gates. The guards and castle folk stood in two long lines from the gates to the foot of the stairs, making a corridor to lead everyone to Kayla. Kayla was glad to have Riki and Del behind her, but even happier to have Ichikar beside her to announce each arrival.

The first person through the gates was a fragile-looking blond lady, followed by an equally blond young man who strongly resembled her. Both of them wore pastel colors, and Kayla was unsurprised when Jezzazar announced them as the Light Lady Amaryllis and her son Florian. As they started up the line, a dark-haired man in a maroon robe entered. Jezzazar stiffened, then in a stifled voice announced, "Lord Governor Niktrax."

"Macavinchy, what's bothering Jezzazar?" Kayla whispered.

"Lord Governor Niktrax and First Commander Jezzazar were both members of the Dark Lord Xavriel's council, madam," Macavinchy replied in an equally low tone. "I believe they did not get along."

"Remind me to ask Ivy later if she knows more about him."

"Of course, madam."

Lady Amaryllis's approach put an end to the whispered conversation. She greeted Kayla with a sweet vagueness that was belied by the way her sharp eyes took in every detail of her surroundings. Her son's eyes widened and he hesitated when his turn came; then he bowed and kissed Kayla's hand. *Maybe the Dark Lord clothes were a bad idea,* Kayla thought, then shook herself. It was too late to second-guess herself, and anyway, unless there were two Light-side Florians in the neighborhood, this was the person Geneviev wanted to marry. Kayla stuck to the greeting that Yazmina had drilled into her, then handed the pair off to the footmen Ivy had provided, to be escorted to seats in the great hall.

Lord Governor Niktrax came next. His bow was smoothly formal, giving away none of his thoughts or reactions. "My lady Xavrielina," he said as he straightened. "I was one of your father's closest allies. Allow me to express my pleasure at your return to Zaradwin."

"I prefer to be called Kayla, but thank you for your kind words." Something about him rubbed her the wrong way, and Kayla had to force herself not to snap at him. Yelling at one of the guests would not be a good way to start the ceremony.

"I see you have already begun to make your mark." His eyes flickered from the castle walls to the new staircase, brushed over Riki and Del dismissively, and finished with a considering look at Macavinchy. "I look forward to seeing the rest of your reign."

"Thank you, Lord Niktrax."

His eyes narrowed as she signaled the next footman to escort him inside. Kayla wondered if he had expected a stronger reaction to his words, or just a different one. Was he plotting something, or just checking to see if the new fourteen-year-old Dark Lady was up to the job? Well, whatever he was thinking would have to wait; the next visitor was already stepping up to meet her.

For the next hour, a steady stream of people flowed through the gates and up the stairs. Some had traveled for several days to get there; others were important people from the village below. Kayla began to worry that they wouldn't have enough pizza. *It's too late to do anything about it now,* she told herself.

Finally, Jezzazar signaled to the guard at the top of the wall. A trumpet blew twice, and the new portcullis lowered effortlessly into place. The line of guards saluted, then swung into formation, marching two by two up the stairs and into the keep. The castle inhabitants followed. Kayla and her family came last.

They could hear the murmur of voices as they approached the great hall. As the first pair of guards walked through the door, silence fell. In eerie quiet, the procession entered the hall. The guards took up positions around the dais; the rest of the castle's inhabitants broke off to find their seats at the front row of tables.

As planned, Waylan escorted Kayla up the stairs to stand in front of the throne. As she turned to face the audience, he stepped back and froze in a defensive position. A tingle ran up Kayla's spine, and all around the edge of the room, tall braziers flared into light. The visitors shifted uneasily, and she could feel the tension in the air.

Jezzazar stepped forward and began a more elaborate version of the speech Waylan had made when they first arrived at the castle. He described her background and the spell that sent her to Earth (he called it exile), then summarized the trip to the castle and the week that followed. Several times, he shifted uncomfortably, and Kayla realized that he was skimming lightly over every incident where she'd refused to execute or exile anyone according to the Dark Traditions.

Exile . . . Kayla's eyes widened, and she had to stop herself from grinning. The problem with exiling people was that they always came back, usually with a large grudge and an army. Even Kayla had come back, when Detsini and Yazmina sent her to another world. But it would be nearly impossible for Detsini to come back from the Scholars' Tower if the oaths were as powerful as Harkawn had described. Detsini might even be willing to stay there without making more trouble; she liked knowing obscure things and giving people advice.

Jezzazar finished his speech with a dramatic rendition of Detsini's ill-fated attempt to claim the castle for herself, and the Dark Lady's rebuilding of the crumbling structure into the new, impregnable fortress they now occupied. He ended with, "These things I know and have seen with my own eyes, as have many others here today. This is the Dark Lady Kayla."

The musicians in the corner did a quick drumroll-and-fanfare, and Kayla stepped forward, right to the edge of the dais. According to the Traditions, she was now supposed to make a speech. From what Macavinchy had told her, past Dark Lord speeches were long and dull, except for occasional pauses to cut the head off anyone who coughed or looked bored or didn't pay attention. Kayla had had teachers like that.

Begin as you mean to go on. She couldn't remember where she'd seen that, but it sounded like good advice.

"Thank you all for coming," she said. The audience shivered in surprise. "I didn't expect to become a Dark Lady, but I will do my best. It probably won't be what you're used to, though. Does anyone have any questions before we start eating?"

Most of the guests looked at her warily. After a moment, someone at the back of the room whispered, "That's *it*? That's all she has to say?"

Kayla shrugged. "First Commander Jezzazar told you I didn't grow up here. I'm not used to making speeches." She paused. "Any other questions?"

"What grim fate awaits your rebellious aunt?" a large woman at the back asked.

"I'm going to banish her to the Scholars' Tower," Kayla replied. There was a startled stirring among the guests, and Kayla raised her eyebrows. "I believe exile is a Traditional punishment for disloyal family members." And if she remembered her history class right, medieval rulers frequently sent inconvenient female relatives to a convent, so Kayla could claim it was a Tradition in her world if anybody objected.

"Did you really turn down the sninks?" someone else demanded.

"Yes."

"It doesn't sound like anything Xavriel's daughter would do."

"It is certainly something *my* daughter would do," said a new voice, and Athelina floated out of the back wall.

Kayla smiled. She hadn't seen Athelina since the castle started crumbling the preceding day, and she'd been half-afraid that her mother had been caught in the deteriorating magic. Hiding her relief, she said, "Hello, Mother. I wasn't sure you would come."

"Since you have broken the curse and attained your throne, I no longer need to hide in my rooms."

"Broken the curse?" Niktrax sounded as if he were only mildly interested, but his eyes were sharp. "What curse was that, and how was it done?"

"Providing specifics at this time would be a very bad idea, madam," Macavinchy said.

"I figured as much," Kayla told him, while the visitors stared. She looked back at Niktrax. "Most of the Dark Lords who lived here left curses behind. We got rid of all of them."

"*We?*" Niktrax relaxed his shoulders and gave Harkawn a sideways speculative look. "You had assistance?"

Kayla felt something ripple behind her. She glanced back just in time to see the two dragon skulls emerge from the wall, one on either side of the mosaic. "That would be us," the first skull said.

The second skull nodded, tilting its head so that the light from the braziers glinted from its teeth. "Are you sure you don't want us to roast someone?"

"Quit pestering me about it! If I want someone roasted, I'll tell you," Kayla said.

Most of the audience appeared terrified, and even Niktrax's eyes widened at the sight of the skulls. He made a little half bow. "I am well answered, my lady." His tone was much more respectful than it had been.

"Anyone else?" Kayla scanned the room, but no one moved. She looked at Jezzazar. He nodded and stepped forward.

"The forms and Traditions have been satisfied," he declared. "Today, the Dark Lady Kayla begins her reign."

Kayla took her place on the silver throne and everyone applauded politely. The doors around the hall swung open, admitting lines of footmen carrying pizzas. Kayla got one all to herself. Eating all alone at the front of the hall felt extremely odd and uncomfortable. She resolved to change that before the next formal occasion. The dais was big enough for a table, even if it would only seat six or seven people, and then she'd have someone to talk to besides Macavinchy. Kayla sighed quietly. At least the pizza was good.

"You did very well," a soft voice said in Kayla's ear. "I am glad that I could be here to see my daughter on the throne of Zaradwin at last."

Kayla jerked, almost dropping her pizza. Athelina was floating next to the throne. *Well, I wanted someone to talk to.* "Thanks. Are you . . . Now that the curse is gone . . ."

"I will stay for a time," Athelina said. "I wish to know my second daughter better. Also, I have a great curiosity to see what you will make of Zaradwin, now that it is truly yours."

"I have some ideas," Kayla admitted.

"I look forward to seeing them."

They talked for the rest of the feast, while the crowd in the great hall slowly relaxed a little. The music helped. Kayla didn't recognize the first few tunes Rache and his group played, but the visitors obviously did. She thought she saw Zar once, lurking in the shadows behind them, but she didn't wave. He'd hinted that he didn't want to attract attention from other would-be Dark Lords, and after Detsini's try at binding him, Kayla totally understood.

As soon as she finished eating, Kayla got up and joined the table just below the dais, where her family was sitting. A nervous ripple ran over the room, but it quieted when nothing else happened.

The music shifted and took up a beat Kayla recognized. *Needs electric guitar and a drum set, but it's not bad.*

Riki sighed. "You let them listen to your playlist, didn't you?"

"They wanted to know what I liked."

"Still, we probably shouldn't contaminate this world with too much—"

"Mom, we just introduced a room full of people to pizza, and you've been teaching Ichikar how to do double-entry book-keeping. Letting Rache learn a couple of hip-hop tunes isn't going to make things any worse."

"Every Dark Lord and Lady brings change," Jezzazar said, and paused. "If you bring more than most, 'tis but a sign of your greatness."

"There's a lot to do," Kayla said as the reality of her position began to sink in. The castle was in good shape now, but she didn't think Zar had done anything about the ruined parts of Ashwend, or the dry fields that surrounded it. She needed to learn more magic, in case another would-be Dark Lord showed up when Zar and the dragon skulls weren't around to help. She had to find a way to generate income so Jezzazar and Ichikar wouldn't want to attack other towns to replenish the treasury—the secret stash in the Dark Lord's chambers wouldn't last long if there was nothing coming in. She should really see if she could do something about people trapping and binding spirits; that just wasn't right. And—

"I'll help!" Del put in. "Soon as I learn how to blow things up properly."

"Blowing things up is not always a good solution," Riki told him.

"There's a lot to do, but not today." Waylan slid into the seat beside Riki. "Today is a celebration of our new Dark Lady."

"To Dark Lady Kayla," Ichikar agreed. The whole table raised their cups to her.

As the rest of the hall followed their example, Kayla smiled. Waylan was right. They'd get back to work tomorrow. Today was for celebrating.

Acknowledgments

I'd like to thank my editors, Mallory Loehr and Tricia Lin, for their infinite patience; my friends Beth Friedman and Lois Bujold for much useful plot-noodling and encouragement; and Stella Gibbons and Nicolo Machiavelli for inspiring very different aspects of this book.